Because They
THINK
They Can

Because They
THINK
They Can

STEVEN SWERDFEGER

Star Cloud Press
Scottsdale, Arizona

Because They **THINK** *They Can*

Copyright © 2005
by Steven Swerdfeger
All rights reserved

cover art © 2005
by Lucy Swerdfeger
All rights reserved

Cover design by Trisha Hadley

Published by

~ STAR CLOUD PRESS ~

6137 East Mescal Street
Scottsdale, Arizona 85254-5418

www.StarCloudPress.com

ISBN: 1-932842-11-X — cloth — $ 29.95
ISBN: 1-932842-12-8 — paperback — $ 21.95

Library of Congress Control Number: 2005909468

Printed in the United States of America

Omnibus quibus discere
placet discendi causa

Page	*Chapters*
1	Anticipation of the Unknown
20	A Gathering of Forces
37	A Refusal, A Chat, and Two Dreams
59	Mentors and the Need to be in the Know
100	Organizing for Learning
121	The Need for Critical Thinking
135	A Flock of Fallacies Found Wanting
154	The Giant's Son Speaks of Learning
177	Strength in Diversity
192	A Psychologist Comes to Speak
211	The Swami's Booth of Ten Thousand Screams
242	Hypnosis Really Works
266	A Journey into Guided Imagery
286	They Can Because They *THINK* They Can
305	Assembling the Parts
333	Play Preparations
367	A Play is Presented
393	Awards and Plans for an Awards Dinner
423	A Special Call is Made to Mr. Vasiloff

Chapter One
Anticipation of the Unknown

"**Y**A SHOULD'VE BEEN THERE, DAVID," grinned Bobby, "so solemn a scene, everybody so still-like and payin' such real close attention to old Ferlinghausen."

David was pouring a glass of milk for himself, preparing for their daily tide-me-over ritual of enjoying a small snack after school. Taking two large chocolate chip cookies, courtesy of Aunt Lillian, from the ancient tin in the cupboard next to the oven, David motioned for Bobby to join him at the kitchen table, whispering, "Now calm down, and tell me what happened again, but more slowly this time and in more detail."

"Okay, okay," Bobby reported, "Ferlinghausen comes to the door of our English class about half an hour after class begins and gives the old nod to Mrs. Martin, who turns to us and says, 'I've got to go talk with your new teacher. He will come to class tomorrow. I'm pleased that everyone managed to pass this class last semester. Today, January 29th, marks not only the beginnin' of a new semester, but also a new way of doin' things. As you know, I've been very patient with your dislike for English, probably more than most teachers would be, so try to get off on the right foot with Mr. Gregory. Thank you all and good luck.' And out she flies like one of them hummin'birds."

"So it's a Mr. Gregory," mulled David.

"But that ain't the *half* of it. Yeah, it was the first time we had even heard the new dude's name, but get this: after Mrs. Martin flies out, old

1

Ferlinghausen goes to the door and says, 'Okay', and in walks guess *who*?"

"I don't know. Maybe Mr. Dandy?" David guessed.

"There ain't no reason on earth or in heaven that any soul would want a ne'er-do-well like *that* walkin' into a decent run classroom. I say let 'im rot in his little stinkin' hole of a guidance office, and not allow him to be out preachin' to everybody. No. You just won't believe who makes his grand entrance, David."

"I give up," said David, wide-eyed.

"I'm clewin' you in, David, the best I know. *Grand.* Think grand! I mean, think the *grandest* of grands."

"The Giant?" David puzzled.

"*Yes*! The *real* doctor of education who talked to us at the special assembly we pulled off a couple of weeks ago."

"Dr. William Gregory," David reflected to himself. "I *really* liked him and what he said."

"Remember how he went on and on about what he didn't like in education, and how sick to death he was of the traditional gradin' system, not to mention his payin' out a certain little ne'er-do-well guidance counselor who once put on airs about bein' an *almost* doctor of education? Talk about hooey."

"Mr. Dandy's embarrassment was the direct result of a certain individual's very rude question, namely *yours*," laughed David.

"As honest as the day is long," said Bobby. "I ain't to blame for how red that little ne'er-do-well's face got, or how he started coughin' when the Giant talked about not puttin' on airs you ain't deserved. Guess the Giant made it real clear that somebody's either a real doctor of education or not a doctor of education, and that nobody ever ain't an 'almost' doctor of education."

David smiled as he remembered the spectacle, adding, "Anyway, what did Dr. Gregory say to the class?"

Bobby smirked and folded his arms.

"Well?" David prompted, taking a huge bite of cookie.

"I ain't tellin' 'cause all *you* do is sneak outa our class to suck up that nasty little independent readin' and writin' contract in old Lowery's library," said Bobby triumphantly.

"That's not fair," argued David. "Mrs. Martin and I have a special arrangement, and we've had it from when I was first transferred into your class."

"Ain't right when you can get away with murder like that and never have to come to class," Bobby asserted.

"You're just jealous," grinned David, breaking one of the chocolate chip cookies and dunking it in milk before eating it.

"Damn straight I am. But it ain't gonna help me, and it ain't gonna help you neither, 'cause you ain't privileged to know what went on today, 'cause you ain't a proper member of the class," Bobby chided.

"Bobby, you *know* how bored I'd be if I had to sit through English 9," David remonstrated. "That's why Mrs. Martin made the independent study contract with me in the first place. And it's worked out beautifully. Why should I waste my time sitting through something I already know."

"It ain't right to be that smart," observed Bobby.

"Look, we're all smart in different ways. My way just happens to be with language and words."

"Yeah. I'm good with my hands, but English is my bugeroo."

"You mean Waterloo."

"No, bugeroo. What's Waterloo?"

"It's a village in Belgium where Napoleon Bonaparte suffered his great defeat in 1815. I think it was in June of that year."

3

"Sean could cite chapter and verse on how many died and what time of day it happened," said Bobby. "Betcha ten to one."

"It helps to have a photographic memory, doesn't it?" sighed David. "I envy Sean that ability."

"Hey. What's a battle in Belgium got to do with my failin' English skills?" asked Bobby suddenly.

"Oh. To meet one's Waterloo means to suffer a decisive defeat," explained David.

"I don't need a defeat, David. So please pray for me, and don't jinx me with this Waterloo jive, 'cause I'm nothin' but marginal in English. I'm hopin' to squeak through. Mrs. Martin would've let us all squeak through. There's a kind, decent lady."

"You just mean she's a soft touch," David teased.

"I mean the woman's got a real heart of gold and knows when some poor soul can't get somethin'," Bobby replied.

"Where were we?" asked David.

Bobby slipped his hand over to take part of the chocolate chip cookie on David's plate.

"Hey, get your own. There are plenty in the tin."

"But the tin ain't on the table," Bobby objected, as he chewed the portion of cookie he had won for his effort.

David closed his eyes and then laughed.

"What's so funny?" asked Bobby.

"We were talking about Waterloo after you said bugeroo. But now I know what you meant: you meant to say 'bugaboo'."

"I did?" asked Bobby.

"Yeah. You were in the right church but in the wrong pew of pronunciation," explained David.

"We ain't in no church. This is a kitchen," said Bobby.

David laughed again. "Don't take everything so literally. I only used a metaphor to suggest that you had the right word, but didn't pronounce it correctly."

"Tell me one thing," Bobby dead-panned.

"Yes?" prompted David.

"What the hell's a bugeroo? Or bugaboo? Or whatever it is?"

"A bugaboo is something that's upsetting, at least, I think that's what it is. Let's look it up," announced David, springing from his seat and going to fetch a dictionary.

Bobby finished David's second cookie.

"Hey," scolded David when he returned, "I demand another cookie, buster. It's the least you can do for my going to the trouble to look up this word for you."

"Ain't you lookin' it up for the *both* of us?" Bobby coyly observed, leaving the table and returning with the entire cookie tin.

David pawed through the B's.

"Here it is," he announced, "bugaboo means: bugbear."

"Well, if that ain't just enough to complete my day. *Now* I understand," said Bobby sarcastically.

"You don't stop there," scolded David. "You look up the new word they give. Here it is: 'bugbear: an imaginary hobgoblin or terror described in order to frighten children into good conduct; anything causing seemingly needless or excessive fear or anxiety'."

"Well, the first part's right, the second wrong," concluded Bobby.

"How so?" asked David.

"Well, the hobgoblin part is ever so serious 'cause it represents my terror at maybe not passin' English 9 this year. The second part ain't right, at least for me, 'cause my fear ain't needless."

David studied Bobby's face as he spoke, nodding in agreement.

"Well, you've passed *so* far," David said, cheerfully.

"Yeah," agreed Bobby. "But that was with kind ol' Mrs. Martin. If a little bird fell out of its nest during class, she'd run outside and pick it up. This cat Gregory is a whole new outfit, what I once heard someone call an *unknown quantity*."

"You mean like Mr. Dandy, an enigma?" asked David.

"Don't go startin' with me on all those fancy fifty cent words," warned Bobby, "'specially when you mention that little no good Rumpelstiltskin."

"Anyway," teased David, "Tell me what the Giant said."

"If you ain't around to hear, words come pretty dear. That's sort of a poem."

"BOBBY, tell me what the Giant said, or I'll paste you a good one," warned David, clenching his fist.

"Now that ain't no way for a good Quaker son to talk," Bobby grinned. David started to throw a playful punch as Bobby leaned back, inadvertently knocking David's book bag onto the floor.

Bobby smiled in triumph, "I'll tell you what the real doctor said. He said his son's a-comin' to take over *our* class. Guess his son is a real famous-like poet."

"Not like Coachman, I hope," David groaned.

"No way," Bobby hastened to explain. "I asked about that, and the Giant said that his son's gotten a couple of real books published and has even had his poems in some major literary magazines. He said just trot down to the public library and look up Nathan Gregory."

"Nathan Gregory," repeated David, musing over the name.

"Sort of a namby-pamby name, ain't it?" asked Bobby. "Ain't gonna help him to get order."

"He might be tougher than you think," warned David.

"With a name like that, we'll have our way," yawned Bobby. "Anyway, Tammy Young remembered how death the Giant was on the gradin' system and asked him what his son thought about grades."

"And?" asked David.

"That's when the miracle struck. The Giant gives this real big smile and pulls out this contract for all of us to fill out and to get our parents to sign. I've got it here in my folder. See?"

David examined the contract.

"Hmm. Maybe we should talk about this at dinner."

A car horn tooted cheerfully.

"Aunt Lillian," said Bobby as he and David raced to the garage to help retrieve groceries. One of the new house protocols since Bobby had moved in before Christmas was that Aunt Lillian would go to the market on Mondays and plan to arrive home shortly after the boys returned from school. They, in turn, would carry the week's groceries into the kitchen and put them away.

"Wow!" said David, when he saw the number of bags. "This sure is more than usual. Are we going to feed an army this week?"

He noticed a twinkle in his great aunt's eyes as she took off her winter coat.

"I was thinking today how long it's been since we threw that marvelous Advent party in December. It gets a little depressing in Midville in the deep of January, especially with no winter thaw this year. I thought it might be fun if we threw a mid-winter blues party a week from this coming Friday."

"That's not giving people much notice," David worried.

"What else are people doing in this weather except sit home and stare at each other?" rejoined Aunt Lillian.

"Some folks go skiin'," offered Bobby.

7

Aunt Lillian laughed and scolded herself, "Now, Lillian, don't go getting depressed by the mid-winter blues. You know you should have moved to a warm, sunny climate years ago. It might have helped your arthritis. Never mind. You've become a fixture here in Midville, and fixtures don't travel, and they certainly don't throw parties."

"We're going on a special vacation this summer out to Arizona," cheered David.

"Ain't never seen the Grand Canyon," said Bobby, ruminating on his own comment. His eyes grew slightly wider as he added, "Ain't never been much of anywhere, come to think of it."

"Do you think we'll have another blizzard?" asked David, fondly remembering their famous Advent party.

"If they could come through that, they'll come through anything," Aunt Lillian smiled. "But boys, this time I thought we might do it a little differently."

"How so?" asked David.

"I would like us to invite a smaller group of friends for an intimate dinner party, say a dozen including us. We have an extra table we can brace up against the long dining room table."

"What will we have to eat?" asked Bobby.

"That is what you're unpacking," announced Lillian. "There was a special on pork loins today, so I bought three large ones. I still have some rosemary from last summer's garden in the cold cellar, and I bought a lot of garlic for the pork as well."

"Only if you make your marvelous gravy," David insisted, "or no party. Your gravy is so good."

"Perhaps I'll teach you and Bobby how to make it, that is, if you'd like to learn."

"Why not?" said Bobby.

"Count me in," added David.

After the groceries were put away, Aunt Lillian made preparations for dinner and the boys began their homework.

* * * * *

The delectable aroma of cheeseburgers wafted upstairs.

"Boys, dinner's ready," called Aunt Lillian.

David and Bobby scrambled downstairs to the kitchen table.

As usual, Aunt Lillian had set their places. She liked to lay out the cloth napkins and place mats. The boys were responsible for clearing the table and doing the dishes. It had proven itself to be an equitable arrangement, although there had been talk here and there about the boys learning how to cook. David had, in fact, mastered a credible lemon chicken dish. Bobby had yet to unfurl his culinary sails.

Sitting down in their usual places, with Aunt Lillian at the head of the table and each boy sitting next to her, they shared a silent blessing, and began to enjoy the cheeseburgers and salad.

"Hmm. Please pass the blue cheese dressing," requested David.

Bobby shoved it toward David as he reached for a cheeseburger.

"No salad, Bobby?" asked Aunt Lillian.

"Ain't gonna rob these scrumptious cheeseburgers blind. They are just perfect for the eatin', so I'll have salad later," Bobby winked at Aunt Lillian, as he proudly added, "European style."

"Good idea," she agreed. "I think I will follow suit."

"What does a suit have to do with it?" asked Bobby.

"Just an expression which comes from playing cards. If I follow the suit of card you put down, it means I copy you."

"Oh. Never felt as ignorant as when I'm with the two of you."

"Yeah, yeah, yeah," teased David. "You just want a third cheeseburger."

"You been countin', too?" grinned Bobby.

"It's all yours. Two will be more than enough for me," said David.

"Bobby," announced Aunt Lillian, "when I went to set the table, I found an interesting contract for some major changes that appear to be in store for your English class. Could you tell me more?"

Bobby's eyes popped wide, not only because he had forgotten all about the day's amazing events, but also because his mouth was now completely full. Chewing quickly and gulping down what had been in his mouth, he proceeded to describe the class session, finally asking Aunt Lillian, "Ain't it cool?"

"Well, as best I understand it, you are going to become part of an experimental program where grades will no longer be used to assess your school work. The new distinctions will be merely pass, fail, or incomplete," said Aunt Lillian.

"Ain't that just the cat's meow?" exulted Bobby.

"Pajamas," corrected David.

"Whatever," said Bobby.

"The contract is also very specific in stating that, since grades are no longer going to be a factor in a student's passing or not passing, a personal letter from your new teacher will become part of your personal record," continued Aunt Lillian.

"That don't mean nothin'," Bobby observed. "What could a letter say 'cept I'm the most sterling person in class, with the possible exception of somebody who hides away in the library?"

"The contract also states, and quite clearly," continued Aunt Lillian, "that all work is to be completed in a timely manner, and absolutely no later than the date it is due."

"Uh-huh. So what if we miss a little work here and there? Mrs. Martin always gave us chances galore. We knew she would, too, so we counted on it."

"Sounds to me as if you haven't had to do very much work," observed David.

"A little busy work," agreed Bobby. "I mean, Mrs. Martin knew we all hated English. Why try to push a dead horse? Most of the kids put in their time and keep their mouths shut, just like in the prisons. Ain't that the real part of it, havin' to sit through all that tripe?"

"Maybe it isn't all tripe," said David.

"Maybe," mused Bobby. "Maybe not. So much dang repetition. Grammar stinks to the high heaven. I know I ain't good at English, but I don't see any need to get better. I can talk with folks just fine."

"Think of what you'd become, Bobby, if you could speak the King's English," teased David. "They would be dusting off a seat for you in Congress."

"Yeah, 'til they found out I ain't a no-good-lyin' weasel bent on makin' a million clams under the table. Then they'd sure as heck throw me out," Bobby rejoined.

"Cynical, cynical," said David, shaking his head.

"You run, then," suggested Bobby. "I'll vote for ya."

"You're both too young to vote," Aunt Lillian reminded the boys.

"You're right. But isn't it a sad thing to think of Congress as being so corrupt?" asked David.

"Boys, please do not judge an entire Congress on the foibles, misfortunes, and dishonesties of some of its members. Don't they call that making a hasty generalization?" implored Aunt Lillian.

The boys looked at each other, pondering her words.

"Bobby, tell me more about your new teacher," asked Aunt Lillian.

"Well, he ain't gonna be there 'til tomorrow. But he's the son of the Giant."

Aunt Lillian smiled, for she had heard many repeated stories about the Giant, the professor of education who had captivated the hearts and minds of so many of the students at Midville's Middle School.

"He's gonna have two big problems, though," predicted Bobby solemnly, "or, at least, two big ones in our class."

"And what are they?" inquired Aunt Lillian.

"His first name," Bobby reminded his listeners, "is *Nathan*, and he's a bloomin' *poet*. That ain't gonna help him to keep any sort of order. At least not in our class."

"Maybe he's as tall as his father," suggested David.

"Naw. Nobody is that tall 'cept the Giant his own self. His little midget son's probably five foot two, eyes of blue, or somethin' like that. Wouldn't that be funny?" said Bobby, adding, "I predict that if he's less than six feet tall, he's gonna have fearsome, *serious* trouble."

"Do you think the class would be rude?" asked Aunt Lillian.

"Not rude, really," explained Bobby, "We ain't smart enough to be rude. We just ain't the types who care a dang about school."

"That's a shame," rejoined Aunt Lillian. "Why not?"

"Well, for starters, we all hate English, 'cause it stinks. An' we only want to do what *we* want to do, not what some dude forces on us. Why waste time doin' somethin' you hate?"

"To get better at it," suggested David.

"Ain't gonna *get* better. Don't *want* to get better."

"Surely your class knows that they hamper their own chances for success when they work against themselves in that way," objected Aunt Lillian.

"Ain't nobody cares. School ain't compellin' the way the movies are, or goin' out with friends, or hikin', or fishin', or the like," Bobby explained.

"Don't your classmates worry about failing, Bobby?" asked Aunt Lillian.

"Sure. So do I. But, honest to Pete, I do just enough to get by. A lot of 'em don't give a darn, even if they do fail. Mrs. Martin was good about that. She hated to fail anybody, and everybody knew it."

"It isn't really about failing or passing," David chimed in, "or, at least, it shouldn't be. It should be about *learning*."

"Ain't nothin' valuable to learn," Bobby argued with conviction.

"Are you sure? I liked the part in Mr. Gregory's letter where he promised to give you all his best for *your best*. That's a pretty good deal, if you ask me," said David.

"I ain't never gonna need the words of some Philadelphia lawyer. I *know* my place. Education ain't for everybody, 'specially me. Give me a simple job and, then, maybe a family," Bobby replied.

"But you could do better than that," David urged.

"Why bother? The cards are dead against me. Always have been."

Aunt Lillian wiped her lips with her napkin, considering Bobby's words. Her eyes looked sad, and David wondered what she was thinking, but he knew it would be intrusive to ask.

* * * * *

The next night at dinner Bobby was full of news and excitement, and Aunt Lillian and David were held in rapt attention as they sliced their meatloaf. Bobby was all astir in trying to describe Nathan Gregory.

"Did you see 'im?" Bobby asked David.

"How could I miss him? He was looming over everybody in the office before school when I went in to make an appointment with Mr. Ferlinghausen," said David.

"And?" urged Bobby.

"And what?" asked David. "I mean, I saw him, so what?"

"The Giant's son's a livin' human wall, that's what he is, and all you can say is 'and what?'" reproved Bobby.

"He's not as tall as his dad," observed David, adding, "I would estimate he's only about six foot four."

"It don't matter how tall you are if you're built like a tank," said Bobby. "I mean, the dude has *no* neck. The short hair ain't flatterin', neither, 'cause it makes him look like one of them college football brutes."

"He *was* one of the top defensive linebackers on his university's football team," reported David.

"What?" exclaimed Bobby. "Don't scare me like that!"

"It's true. After I saw Mr. Ferlinghausen, I introduced myself to Mr. Gregory and asked him if he would grant an interview for our *Bare Fax* newspaper. I met with him during the lunch hour in his room."

"Why you ... you slyboots. You been holdin' back on us," Bobby sputtered.

"No way. After all, journalists have to protect the integrity of their lead stories. You can read about it in the paper tomorrow," answered David.

"And you can read about this in the paper tonight," threatened Bobby, extending his clenched fist.

"Now boys, before you start scuffling, we need to finish our dinners and clean up, as usual. But David, I must say that I'm intrigued by this new teacher. Please tell us more."

Grinning, for he had been bursting to share all he had learned, David nodded as he began. "He's really amazing. Not what you'd expect at first. He's a real poet who was also a star football player as well as a star wrestler. He majored in creative writing and world literature, graduating with top honors. After college, he traveled around Europe for two years writing articles about his adventures. He also has two books of poetry to his credit, the second one having won a prestigious literary award from a southern university. He's been working on his Master of Fine Arts degree in poetry at Cornell, and he hopes to teach in a college some day."

"What's he doin' slummin' around a hole like Midville Middle School, then?" snorted Bobby.

"Taking a semester off to earn a little money. Mr. Ferlinghausen told me that Dr. Gregory had recommended his son as a possible one semester replacement for Mrs. Coachman. That will give the school more time to shuffle staff members around as well as to decide on the teacher it will hire for this coming fall. The Giant also warned Mr. Ferlinghausen that his son tends to be quite unconventional."

"I knew it," said Bobby, "I just knew it. You even dare say you hate poetry and he'll paste you into tomorrow and back again."

David smiled. "Do you still think Mr. Gregory is going to have any trouble getting control of your English class?"

Bobby gave David and Aunt Lillian a sheepish look, knowing in exasperation that he would have to eat his words from yesterday.

"No way, José. I never would've guessed a poet named Nathan could be so ... so ..." Bobby began.

"Intimidating?" prompted David.

"If that means he gives ya the willies, you're damn straight he does. Oh, I know," continued Bobby, "He's nice enough when you meet 'im. That's when they wrap everythin' in sweet nothin's; but just you cross him, and hell will pay for it. These poets ain't your normal folk, you know. They ride along on their own little jitney, but don't dare cross 'em or step in their way, or you'll be part of the pavement."

"Bobby," laughed Aunt Lillian, "what are you saying?"

"I'm sayin' that everythin's hunky-dory as long as ya don't let on that ya think poetry stinks to the high heaven. These poet types ain't rational if somebody nixes their poetry; they're strictly emotional."

"I wonder if you'll be doing a lot of poetry this semester?" David speculated gleefully, meeting Bobby's eyes and receiving a rueful look.

"It ain't gonna be business as usual," predicted Bobby.

"Why not?"

"'Cause he ain't the conventional type," explained Bobby.

"How so? Sounds like a normal jock to me," grinned David.

Bobby glared at David, "How many jocks write poetry?"

"I think I'm beginning to see your point," replied David. "The real difference is that you've now got to deal with a brain who also has a lot of brawn. Nobody will dare cross him for fear of being throttled."

"It ain't just that," explained Bobby. "Today he's just sittin' at his desk when we all waltz in. Mind you, nobody dared to be late, and I betcha nobody'll ever be late again. The bell rings, and he stands up, and the difference is quite imposin' on our minds. Then he says, 'Good morning, my name is Mr. Gregory, and I'll be your teacher 'til the end of this semester.'"

"What's wrong with that?" asked David.

"Nothin' really, but it's just the way he's there peerin' atcha, like he's got X-ray vision and is lookin' right through ya. Then he says, 'Do any of ya have any questions regardin' our contract for this semester?' And there ain't a peep outta nobody, so he asks us to pass in the contracts, checkin' to make sure all the parents signed 'em, too."

"Sounds pretty smart to me, especially if there's going to be any trouble down the road," said David.

"Well, ain't we the Jolly Roger and all," said Bobby, looking with worry at David. "Somehow I get the feelin' we all just signed our worthless lives away in that contract. Somehow it's gonna come back to haunt us, and I mean big time."

"Be positive. Now that there aren't any grades, you don't have to worry as much about failing," suggested David.

"Yeah, but what does a P mean for passin'. That's the *big* question now," asked Bobby.

"Guess you'll find out,' David said, shrugging.

"But, then," Bobby continued, "the Giant's son looks straight at the class and says, 'I know you students got a union, and I want to know who the leaders are, so that they can bring all the problems to me, and I can deal with them *di*-rectly."

"Any takers?" asked David.

"You kiddin' me?" replied Bobby. "There ain't nobody in that class who wants to be dealt with *di*-rectly. Hey. Ain't we the ones who just get by? Just leave us alone and let us coast. *That's* what we're really good at. Doin' absolutely nothin'."

"So, what happened?" asked a fascinated Aunt Lillian, pouring a little more gravy on her meatloaf.

"We had one of them elections. Guess who won," said Bobby.

"No," David smiled. "Really?"

"Yep. Yours truly is now the class president. And Zeke is the vice-president, which means if there's any trouble, we take *our* precious little ol' necks up to the choppin' block, and get dealt with *di*-rectly, right in the neck, for what somebody else did or didn't do," Bobby lamented.

"It can't mean *that*," laughed David. "When he said 'deal with them directly' — he was only talking about the problems, not you two. You are the new class leaders, so you get to help him work out any problems. Sounds like a good idea to me."

Bobby dubiously considered David's interpretation.

"Then what happened?" asked Aunt Lillian.

"He sits down at his desk and says, 'I want to get to know each one of you today, so why don't we go 'round and you tell me a little bit about yourselves. Why don't we start with our new president?'

"God in heaven, I just about went through the frickin' floor. Everythin' started to sway a bit, and I almost blacked out, 'cept Zeke elbows me real hard like to bring me out of it. So the Giant's son looks at me, and says, 'Bobby, tell me a little 'bout yourself.' So I start yattering on and on, and before I knows it, I tells him half my life history, and he's up there takin' notes for all he's worth. And just like that for the rest, too."

"Did he ask any particular questions?" Aunt Lillian inquired.

"No," said Bobby, shaking his head. "That would've been a heckuva lot easier. He just let us start and ramble on. Now why would anyone do that, 'cept maybe for torture? The time flew along, although we did get through the whole class. Funny how everyone told him so much personal stuff."

"That is a commendation to Mr. Gregory and to his ability to listen to others," observed Aunt Lillian.

"Did you get any homework?" asked David.

"Yeah. A stinkin', little fairytale from the Grimm brothers. That ain't English. We should be doin' the same stuff we always do, like grammar and spellin' and vocabulary," Bobby complained.

"What was the fairytale about?" asked Aunt Lillian.

"Ain't got a clue," said Bobby, "except that it's some silly story 'bout four animals who run away to become musicians."

"Oh, it's called 'The Bremen-Town Musicians'," said Aunt Lillian, adding, "That's a *wonderful* story."

"Well, I ain't gonna read it," said Bobby. "Not a fairytale, at any rate."

Aunt Lillian's right eyebrow lifted.

"That's not so wise," warned David, "especially if you want to get off on the right foot."

"Hey. Nobody all year has read a lick of stuff Mrs. Martin dished out. Why bother to start now? It'll be the same old game. We go in, we sit down, he asks a few questions, we look at him blankly, and then he yatters out all the answers at us," Bobby predicted.

"You may be opening yourselves to trouble," David warned.

"No way," Bobby protested. "Worst thing that'll happen to us this semester is that we'll probably be made to swallow some really long unit on poetry. And that will be pretty awful, but what can we do or say, if it means we live to see the tenth grade?"

"Don't you think you should set an example as class president?" asked David.

"Yeah, I do. So I'm definitely NOT readin' any fairytale," insisted Bobby. "If Gregory puts up a fuss about no one doin' the work, we'll just let him know that we ain't a class inclined to readin', and he can lump it."

"Those are brave words when Mr. Gregory is not here," said Aunt Lillian.

Caught in his bravado, Bobby pondered her words, looked at her and replied, "You're right, as usual, Ma'am. I ain't so brave as to say them words to the Giant's son, and do you know why?"

"No, why?" asked Aunt Lillian.

"'Cause I ain't got no hankerin' to die in my tracks and I would really miss your delicious meatloaf," said Bobby.

"I'll do dishes for both of us," offered David, "so you can read the story."

"Thanks a bunch, brother of mine," replied Bobby. "You know how much I hate to read, and I ain't gonna do it. Let's stack the plates and get started."

Chapter Two
A Gathering of Forces

M R. NATHAN GREGORY WAS WRITING FURIOUSLY on the chalk board when Bobby entered English class. Taking his seat, Bobby looked at the board and felt his feet go cold amid the twirling of some butterflies in his stomach, for he read the following:

The Bremen Town Musicians

Story plot: recounting of story line by class members
beginning/common traits/mutual support
subsequent actions/discoveries/
goals/discoveries/importance of food/satisfaction
story development/plot/symbolism/
common elements/significant changes

The bell rang and the teacher, wiping chalk dust off his hands, turned to the class, surveying his new students. Likewise, they studied their new teacher, sitting in collective and guilty anticipation of soon being revealed for the academic backsliders that they were.

"We will begin today by reviewing the plot of the Grimm brothers' story, which is a simple recounting of what happened. I will call on you at random until everyone has had a chance to share. Let's begin with Sheila Morrison," announced Mr. Gregory.

Sheila sat stiffly, her eyes widening in disbelief. Her immobile expression would have left one to wonder whether or not she had fallen into a catatonic state, except that immediately before class she had been sharing the latest gossip with two of her friends in the most animated manner. This stark contrast in observable behavior now rose up to haunt this normally loquacious girl.

An eerie and uncomfortable silence followed. The actual duration was slightly less than a full minute, but it seemed *much* longer, especially to Sheila. The other fourteen members of the class fidgeted in their seats and stared down at their desks.

Mr. Gregory's eyes studied Sheila intently, as if he were intuiting something from the heavy silence that now hung over the class, perhaps the confirmation of an emerging conclusion. Since the instructor had called on her, the onus of breaking the silence rested on Sheila, but she was literally paralyzed by so keen a scrutiny.

"Do I take your silence to mean that you failed to read the assigned story?" asked Mr. Gregory.

Sheila nodded slightly.

"Then you have voided our contract, Sheila," announced Mr. Gregory. "No longer should you expect *my* best, because you have failed to give me *your* best. Your work is incomplete, and will remain that way until you can convince me that you actually are interested in learning, and I hasten to specify: *loving learning for its own sake.* Is that clear?"

Sheila gave a weak smile and a partial nod and stared down at her desk in embarrassment.

"Well, let's see who'll pick up the ball and run with it," continued Mr. Gregory. "Why don't we go to Mickey Drexel. Mickey?"

"Didn't get a chance to read it," was all Mickey could say, looking down in shame at his desk.

"The same goes for you, then, Mickey, as goes for Sheila."

Before Mr. Gregory could continue, Tammy Young, known to be both opinionated and aggressive in the face of attack, raised her hand and announced, "I didn't understand the story."

Her stratagem was familiar to her classmates. On many past occasions such similar ploys had impelled Mrs. Martin, after surrendering a heavy sigh, to explain the story in exacting detail, *ad nauseam*. It was Tammy's obvious hope this same ploy would also work on Mr. Gregory.

"What part or parts of the story did you have trouble with, Tammy?" asked Mr. Gregory.

"The whole story," Tammy persisted.

"Well, do this, then: tell me what confused you," offered the teacher.

"Everything," scowled Tammy, not used to having her self-professed ignorance being probed or questioned.

"How about the part near the end where one of the animals is boiled to death?" asked Mr. Gregory.

"That was gross," said Tammy. "I hated that part. It was really *gross*."

"It's strange that you can hate a part that *wasn't even in the story*, Tammy," challenged the teacher. "No animals are boiled to death. Did you even bother reading it?"

His intent focus on Tammy was too much for her to withstand, now that her ruse had been clearly unmasked.

"Oh, screw it. Who cares about a stupid old story about animals anyway?" huffed Tammy.

Mr. Gregory stood unflappable in the face of her ire, and restated their new relationship. The basic message was 'if you're not going to work for me, I'm not going to work for you: your work is *incomplete*.'

Six additional class members endured the same scrutiny until Mr. Gregory finally asked, "Did *anyone* read the story?"

No hands were raised, as class members averted their eyes from their teacher's perceptive and disarming gaze.

The instructor paused and closed his eyes. The gesture was both dramatic and sad, for it was clear that in this, only their second day together, the entire class had scuttled its contract. At this point all the students in the class, even the most reluctant readers, now wished that they *had* read the story.

Mr. Gregory resumed his seat at his desk. The class began to wonder if they had actually bested him until he looked up, his eyes both smoldering and furious, as he sternly announced: "Until you, as an entire class, convince me that you are interested in learning, and that means that you must show me you *love learning for learning's sake* and not just to fulfill some course requirements, we have very little to say to each other. I will be here, reading and writing, and I do not wish to be disturbed. Each day, you will arrive and sit at your desks. Until further notice, on Mondays, you will read; on Tuesdays you will each take the entire class period to write a letter to me about what you read the day before; on Wednesdays you will read again; on Thursdays you will write. Fridays will be reserved for silent readings or discussions, *if* we decide to have any discussions. I will read your letters and write replies. There will be absolutely *no* talking during class, except if you need to ask me a question or if there is assigned group work."

Class members nodded in unison, grimly contemplating their fate.

"You may read whatever you choose to read," continued Mr. Gregory. "You will write in pen about what you read in whatever way you choose. Whatever you write will not be for any grade. It is merely a letter to me, which will be kept confidential. In other words, I will not read any of your letters in class. With any luck, your writing might bring you personal clarity, the better to enable you to find a way out of this mess into which you have gotten yourselves."

Some of the wittier members were trying to calculate in their heads what a minimally passing semester grade would become when averaged with an F. But before further speculation could continue, Mr. Gregory addressed their unspoken concern.

"As for your status in this class, I will assign an "I" for each of you, which stands for INCOMPLETE. It's not so much that you will fail this class as you will be sitting here until you fulfill all course requirements as well as all of my expectations for what it means to receive a 'P' for passing. It might take one year, two years, perhaps even three. But we'll make it. I will change my personal academic goals and plan to return here to work with you until you have all earned the privilege of proceeding on to English 10 at the regional high school. There are not many students who have the opportunity to spend one, two, or even three extra years in ninth grade English. We are going to enjoy an intense and productive relationship that spans several years."

This future scenario had never occurred to anyone, least of all Bobby. As newly-elected president of the class, he felt compelled to speak up for his peers.

"Sir," he began, standing up next to his desk.

"Yes, Bobby?" Mr. Gregory replied.

"Sir, what can we do to make this work up?"

"Nothing. I'm only interested in working with students who have a little pluck. You failed to do your part, the part *you* promised to do, so you all have voided our contract, and your status and work will remain as incomplete. I am now convinced that this class does not want to learn and, therefore, I have lost all interest in teaching you. We will remain at that impasse until you, as a group, convince me that you are genuinely interested in learning, and I mean that you show me that you *love learning for its own sake.*"

"So are we just supposed to sit here?" asked Bobby.

"You may either read or write, and that doesn't mean passing notes to friends. Until you convince me that you are truly interested in learning, reading and writing will remain our standard, daily protocol, and none of you will be promoted to English 10. Perhaps if you have a semester to think about why you are sitting here in this school building, you will decide to become more engaged with the learning process. Too many teachers and parents today do not expect enough from their students and children, and if one has low expectations, one gets very little in return. I expect nothing less than your best. It's true that I don't believe in grades, but I *do* believe in hard work."

The class sat thunderstruck. There seemed absolutely no way out. They were now condemned to sit and rot until June, and then they would have to repeat ninth grade again, all because of English 9. What had been a merry little ride down the stream of Mrs. Martin's expectations, had suddenly become a dangerous and threatening waterfall in the face of Mr. Gregory's new demands. Many ships were going to founder as they were washed over this rocky precipice.

Bobby sat in silence, feeling very guilty and foolish. David's and Aunt Lillian's words of admonition haunted him. He now wondered if even one member of the class had read the story if that would have been sufficient to save the entire group from their new status. Previous teachers had simply implored the class to work harder, which had resulted in the same scenario repeating itself *ad infinitum*. This, however, was a new rub that no one, least of all Bobby, had expected. Briefly he wondered if Mr. Gregory had anticipated that the entire class would not keep their part of the bargain. The contract they had all signed now bore cruel testimony to their collective laziness and inaction. And there appeared to be no way out.

—David will think of a way, Bobby thought, brightening. But David's admonition the night before caused him to wonder if there were any alternate solution.

—Ferlinghausen, thought Bobby. —Me and Zeke will go appeal to old Ferlinghausen just as soon as class is over.

* * * * *

"Mr. Ferlinghausen, Bobby Perkins and Zeke Minturn are here to see you. All right. Thank you. Gentlemen, please go right in."

As the boys entered the office, they saw their principal's prominent bald head bent over an expansive table, studying a long row of sheets. Looking toward them as they entered, Mr. Ferlinghausen smiled and said, "Excuse me. This is the master schedule of classes that I am going to propose for next year. I need to line them all up like this in order to make sure it all works. Please take seats over by my desk."

Assuming his accustomed position in his black-leather chair, the principal continued, "Now, what can I do for you?"

Bobby looked over at the long table where the tentative master schedule was fully arrayed, and answered, "Ain't tryin' to tell you your business, but you might think of addin' another section of English 9 for our class, 'cause we ain't gonna make it this year."

The principal's eyebrows lifted in interest, "I'm not sure that I fully understand."

"The whole kit and caboodle of us. We're as good as doomed," answered Bobby looking at Zeke, who nodded in agreement. "And we come to you as the class president, which is me, and vice-president, which is Zeke."

"I take it that you're not exactly hitting it off with Mr. Gregory? Is he not doing a good job?" asked the principal.

"Ain't his fault. Maybe he's doin' too good a job, if you know what I mean. Maybe he takes teachin' a little too serious-like. This dude comes on real strong, if you know what I mean, and out comes this contract, which turns into a damn noose, but we put our own heads into it willingly-like, so it ain't no one's fault but our own. You just think he could maybe cut us a little slack," explained Bobby.

"I still don't understand," responded the principal, giving a slight frown.

"Do you know about the contract?" asked Bobby.

"Yes. I approved that two weeks ago. Did everyone sign it?"

"Yes. And parents, too," lamented Bobby.

"Has there been a breach of contract?" asked the principal.

"You might say that," said Bobby. "More like the sinkin' of the whole ship, if you want the plain truth."

Mr. Ferlinghausen sat in silence, listening intently.

"We was given a story to read about some nutsy animals and a journey they make but *nobody* had the gumption to read it, includin' me. We assumed we could just coast through the way we always did with Mrs. Martin, nothin' against that grand lady, neither, 'cause she knew we ain't gonna do no more English than necessary. Anyway, when Mr. Gregory discovered this mornin' that not a frickin' one of us had even read the story, he gets on his high horse and says he's only interested in workin' with students who have pluck, whatever that is, and tells us straight out that our work is incomplete and will be incomplete until we convince him that we love learnin', and if he means learnin' English, he's gonna have to wait until the comin' of the Lord, and that means we're just gonna have to repeat the class, like it or not."

Mr. Ferlinghausen nodded in sympathetic understanding, and responded, "To have pluck means to have courage or spirit. Did Mr. Gregory say exactly what it would take to change your status?"

"We gotta convince him that we love learnin', and learnin', mind you, for *its own sake*," explained Bobby.

"Any idea on how you might do that?" asked the principal, looking directly Bobby.

"No sir. Not a one," sighed Bobby.

"Zeke?"

"No, sir," answered Zeke.

"Well, all that I can say is that I'm afraid that we're at an impasse. Unfortunately, unless things change, all of you will be repeating, or perhaps I should say continuing, your English 9 studies next year. If it would help, I think that I could probably add two or three excellent electives in the area of improving study skills and time management and give you all a study hall," suggested the principal.

"Can't you do something to save us this year, sir?" asked Zeke.

"I'm reluctant to become involved in any issue where a contract freely agreed to by participating parties has been called into question. It seems to me that the various parties must work out their own problems. Now, if any need for negotiation arises, I would be more than happy to serve as an arbiter."

"What's an arbiter?" asked Bobby.

"Someone who tries to bring the parties together," explained the principal. "As it stands now, I believe that there has been a rather serious breach of contract, and that until your entire class satisfies Mr. Gregory, you will remain at an impasse."

"Sir, what if he don't come back, Mr. Gregory?"

"Oh, I know that he's only planning to be here this semester, but I think if any of his classes had to continue their studies, he would offer to stay and, if so, I would certainly accept his offer. I don't like loose ends. A contract is a contract, and we all have to learn to live up to our part of any bargain. Please let me know if I can be of further assistance. I'll build in those extra courses into next year's master schedule so we'll be prepared should worse come to worse," concluded the principal.

The boys left in shocked silence, forgetting even to offer thanks for their meeting with the principal, who resumed his scrutiny of the tentative master schedule with new purpose.

Gloomily the boys walked to the cafeteria to join the end of the lunch line.

"Ain't gonna be no picnic no more," Bobby confessed to Zeke.

"What really stinks will be if we have to sit around here do nothing until June, and then come back next year," Zeke observed.

"We cooked our own goose, sure as shootin'," Bobby added.

"Do you think there's a way to convince the Giant's son that we are really serious about learning?" asked Zeke.

"Not after the way he raked Tammy over the coals when she tried to snow him," replied Bobby.

"I mean: is there any way we can make it believable?" asked Zeke.

"Ain't no way to pull the wool over the eyes of the Giant or the Giant's son," concluded Bobby.

"I mean: can we maybe learn to like learning?" asked Zeke.

"Not sincere-like, if you ask me," said Bobby.

"Why not?"

"We hate it. That's why," said Bobby.

"But if we don't want our lives to rot away in this school, we'd better learn to like it," suggested Zeke.

"Well, then" sighed Bobby, "You tell *me* how."

Zeke scratched his head as the boys joined the end of the line, finally saying, "Darned if I know. Maybe we need to ask for help."

"We are the president and vice-president. We should know," chided Bobby, with growing impatience.

"But we *don't* know, so maybe we should ask," said Zeke. "How about David?"

Bobby had dreaded this embarrassing possibility, for now he would have to eat the words he had so proudly served up at dinner the night before.

"Okay. I'll ask him tonight," Bobby agreed.

* * * * *

Dinner chez Lillian Biggs & Company was a treasured favorite, namely sweet and sour meatballs, with pineapple, together with a side dish of boiled peas.

"Bobby, you've been very quiet ever since you got home," Aunt Lillian observed.

David nodded in agreement.

"Ain't been lookin' forward to what I need to say to both of you," Bobby began. He then recounted the day's misadventures, as Aunt Lillian and David listened with growing concern.

"So," Bobby concluded, "we're at a standstill, with no way out. And here I sit, president of the class, and the class is gonna go down, and I can't think of any darn way to save us. Can you?"

"There must be a way out, perhaps several ways out, Bobby. There are always options," said Aunt Lillian.

"And if nothing you can think of helps," announced David, "we'll still be able to walk to school together next year."

Bobby glared at David in exasperation, unamused by the latter's attempt at humor.

"I'm sure we can help you and your class to find a way out," said Aunt Lillian confidently. "But that will take some time and planning.

30

It would also seem to me important to gather the class for a meeting to discuss strategy."

"But when?" asked Bobby. "We ain't got no time like that at school, and the Giant's son allows nothin' but readin' or writin' and absolutely no talkin', and nobody has taken the notion yet to cross 'im 'cause nobody wants to collide with them rocks up there on Mars. And even one day of doin' nothin' but sittin' there readin' is wearin' thin 'cause we ain't exactly been a class famous for our literary pursuits, if you know what I mean."

"Sounds as if you're beginning to change a little," observed David.

Bobby nodded grimly.

"It also sounds to me as if you're going to have to change a lot more than that just to get to first base," added Aunt Lillian.

"But here's the real humdinger," said Bobby, recollecting his conversation with Zeke at lunchtime. "If it ain't genuine, the Giant's son is gonna see straight through it in a minute and sink it dead in the water. He ain't to be toyed with, that one."

"I wonder if he could be removed for some reason," David speculated.

"No crane big enough in this hick town," replied Bobby.

"There must be some way," David plotted.

Bobby slyly whispered, "Maybe we could frame the little hoodlum and get the Giant's son to deep six 'im. Two birds with one stone, ain't that the expression?"

"Sean could never be framed. He's too quick," said David.

"Maybe we could get 'im to trash the Giant's son's poetry in the hallway just outside the door. There'd be murder and mayhem galore, and we'd get front row seats," suggested Bobby.

"Well, be that as it may," interceded Aunt Lillian, "it still doesn't bring poor Bobby and his class any closer to a solution. David, you're always good at thinking of alternatives, maverick that you are. What would you do if you were in Bobby's shoes?"

David looked at the candles on the table, watching them flicker and glow, as he contemplated Aunt Lillian's question. Suddenly brightening, he announced, "I'd form a Learning Club."

"A what?" asked Bobby.

"A Learning Club. I'd call it just that. I'd make sure that everybody in class attended, and I would plan on each meeting lasting two hours, and I'd schedule each meeting for right *after* school, maybe twice a week, say on Tuesdays and Thursdays," said David.

"That would fly like a lead balloon. A lot of the kids've got jobs after school," said Bobby.

"Do they want their jobs or do they want to pass ninth grade English?" asked David bluntly. "Sometimes people have to make choices."

"We ain't never gonna get everybody," lamented Bobby. "And the Giant's son says he won't bend an inch 'til he has evidence that the whole class's comin' around to likin' learnin' for its own sake."

"And just *why* wouldn't you get everybody? Doesn't everybody want to pass?" asked David.

"Well, maybe, since everybody's beginnin' to see the writin' on the wall. But it ain't right to take honest-earned money outa the mouths of kids," Bobby returned.

"The kids who have jobs could always get their jobs back this summer," suggested David, "or work different hours."

"It will be important to get parental permission for all who attend," said David.

"Why?" asked Aunt Lillian.

"For their support. The parents need to be ready to help this whole attempt to save Bobby's class. And we're talking about their kids, too.

The topics to be discussed and learned will be chosen by the kids themselves. That will help to take the curse off of it."

"Yeah," agreed Bobby, "it might even be a little interestin'."

"I'd also open it to the entire school, because it will only be a feather in your cap if you can get even more kids involved," David added. "That would look really impressive to the Giant's son."

"There's no way he'd approve of our methods," said Bobby.

"Methods?" asked David.

"At gettin' some poor devils to go sit in some frickin' classroom for two hours after the school is over," lamented Bobby. "Probably have to threaten murder and torture."

"Just try to get some more kids to come," David urged.

"It ain't right to make others suffer with us," said Bobby.

"They wouldn't be suffering. They'd only come because they were interested in the topics, something like racing cars or muffler repair or making a dress," said David.

"I can just see Zeke sittin' through a lecture about makin' a dress," laughed Bobby. "He rather be shot. Maybe he'd even shoot 'imself."

"Fair is fair. The girls in your class have their own interests that you would need to open yourselves to learning about," David admonished his Bobby.

"But why not just skip that meetin'?" asked Bobby.

"Because the whole point of the club is to prove that you are all interested in learning *for its own sake*, no matter the topic."

"Ain't that just the lousiest whammy you ever heard of?" asked Bobby.

"I'm sure club members will be able to vote on topics," suggested Aunt Lillian. "You might even consider inviting guest speakers."

"Great idea," David agreed. "There's no way any class could keep bi-weekly meetings going solely on what members could present, at least not for the rest of the year."

"The rest of the year!" moaned Bobby.

"In for a penny, in for a pound," said David. "If you're sincere about starting a Learning Club, you've got to see it through, even if the Giant's son relents and gives you all another chance. I would also be sure to invite him to come to *every* session and I would make sure that it was apparent that everyone attending was absolutely riveted by the subject being discussed."

"That ain't natural," protested Bobby.

"Then pretend," David answered.

"Ain't right not to be sincere," opined Bobby.

"But who's to know?" David questioned. "Who can ever really know the heart of another? Maybe in the process you might actually *become* interested in some of the stuff being discussed, especially since you'll all be picking the topics."

"Public speakin' scares us silly. I mean, I'd just as soon go through the floor as give a talk, and everybody else would, too."

"Then go heavy on getting speakers. You could invite faculty, parents, members of the community, and even other students," urged David. "It would be easy to set up a calendar."

"Easy for you," snorted Bobby. "You're Mr. Talk, Talk, Talk."

"No. Sean is Mr. Talk, Talk, Talk. With his photographic memory, he could give talks on all kinds of things," said David.

"Ain't many girls who'd be interested in guns, shootin', medieval torture, wars, or the rack," said Bobby.

"Well, on those days they'd have to take their fair turns for when the guys listen to presentations about dressmaking," David added.

"Ain't gonna be easy sellin' any of this to the class," said Bobby dejectedly.

"Look. You're the president. They respect you. They'll listen. They may not like it, but they'll listen."

"Perhaps we should invite your classmates here for our special dinner party so that you can plan strategy, and include any parents who would like to lend their support," suggested Aunt Lillian.

"Do you think any parents are going to complain to Mr. Ferlinghausen?" asked David.

"How can they?" asked Bobby. "They signed the contract, too. If they go in, all old Ferlinghausen will say is 'a contract's a contract' and then give 'em a glimpse of that dang master schedule that's probably already showin' our special classes for next year. It ain't normal. I'm tellin' you. School ain't never been like this."

"It's certainly going to be different," said David.

Bobby nodded.

"Oh, Bobby, you'll need to get a faculty advisor for the Learning Club. It also needs to be someone who'll agree to be there for every single meeting, or else who'll get a replacement for those two hours after school," suggested David.

"Two hours!" lamented Bobby. "I still say that's *murder*."

"Look. You've got to make a statement to the Giant's son that this club idea is real, and anything *less* than a two hour meeting is going to seem pretty thin," David cautioned. "And remember, since your class will be picking the topics, the meetings should be interesting."

"How 'bout the advisor?"

"I'd ask the Giant's son. Since he's partially responsible for all of you being in this pickle, let him share in helping you find a way out. If he's not willing to be the advisor, then you'd have some real leverage to negotiate different terms, since he is not supporting what he's requiring you all to do," David explained.

"Hey. That's right, David. Great idea. Strap it onto *his* back and see how he likes it," Bobby said cheerfully.

"Don't be surprised if he accepts right away," said David. "He apparently walks his talk."

"I'll call Zeke after dishes and explain what you've just come up with and see what he thinks. Then we'll ask the Giant's son tomorrow if he'll be the club advisor and also ask the class about everyone comin' here next Friday," said Bobby.

"Remember that *everyone* has to come," David reminded Bobby. "This is going to work only if everyone stays committed."

"Do you think everyone is worried about not being promoted to the tenth grade?" asked Aunt Lillian.

"You bet. The class has got a major case of the willies, and the Giant's son's got us just where he wants us: right in the palm of his hand."

Chapter Three
A Refusal, A Chat, and Two Dreams

AVID WAS STANDING IN LUNCH LINE, trying to decide whether he would have a rubber hot dog or a dry hamburger. The Midville Middle School cafeteria had made an art form out of serving up inedible food. Suddenly David felt two arms surround him and pick him up and heard Bobby's unmistakable whoop.

Turning to see Bobby and Zeke standing before him, both grinning at him, he managed to asked, "What was that for?"

"For helpin' us to find a way to get the Giant's son to see that our class likes learnin'," said Bobby triumphantly.

"I take it he agreed to be the Learning Club advisor," David concluded.

"Even asked if he could make some presentations," said Zeke.

"Congratulations," said David, mockingly hitting each of their shoulders, "and good luck with your club."

"Your club?" repeated Bobby. "You mean 'our' club."

"Naw. I'm too busy to stay after school for two hours twice a week. If I had more time, it'd be fun, but I'm really busy on some projects which are taking most of my time," said David.

Bobby's face had fallen and Zeke was looking displeased.

"You can't just launch us out and let us float adrift with no further direction," implored Bobby. "*You* thought of the club. Now *you've* got to help us get it launched."

"It's your club now," said David, nonchalantly, "I'm giving it to you: lock, stock, and barrel. It's all yours. Good luck."

"You're gonna help us get on the right track, ain'tcha?" asked Bobby, panic rising in his eyes.

"No way!" David asserted loudly. "I'm just too busy."

Looking as if they had lost their best friend, Bobby and Zeke shook their heads, turned, and walked into the cafeteria.

David thought about his blunt refusal. It now seemed a little cold, but the essay he had been working on was taking all of his spare time, and what he did with his own time was his *own* business. Why should he become the nursemaid for a bunch of lazy students who didn't know enough to do their work on time? They could sink if they didn't have the gumption to learn how to swim. Why mince words? They were lazy, and they needed to pay the price for their laziness. All the convolutions that would be necessary to help Bobby's class come to a clearer focus about themselves and their work were too staggering to consider. Isn't everyone entitled to some free time, time that can be spent any way one wishes to spend it? The essay deadline was only a month away, and a lot of revision would be necessary in the interim. Revision took time. Time was precious. Time was too precious to waste on a bunch of dolts who had boxed themselves into a corner. Let them find their own way out. Maybe life's experience could be their teacher, if people like Mr. Gregory had failed.

Reaching the table of his lunch partners, David glared at Sean, Mary, and Lisa as he slammed his tray on the table.

"There he is," observed Sean Potter, lending a gangster tone to his voice. "The *dirty rat*." Sean was much taken with anything having to do with violence and guns and blood and gore. His brown hair was cut in a short, military fashion under which a pair of stealthy amber green eyes observed almost everything and forgot next to nothing. A small scar under his right eye served as an appropriate insignia to cast Sean in the formidable role as a member of the warrior elite, a fellowship to which Sean ardently aspired to belong.

"Oh, shut up!" growled David.

"Bobby and Zeke stopped to ask us to help them form some sort of learning club," Lisa explained, "and they made a huge point about your not wanting to help them."

"I hate triangular conversation," David grumped.

"What do you mean?" asked Mary, Sean's fraternal twin, her long-curly-brown hair accentuating a soft and gentle face, her intense eyes, like her brother's, revealing an uncommonly keen intellect.

"I mean sending a message to one person through another. I know Bobby's upset, but I just don't have the time to help them. I'm sure they're up to it."

"Yeah, and up to repeating ninth grade next year," quipped Sean.

"Bobby went on about students being a union" Lisa explained, "and how he's president of his English 9 class, and how all students had better stick together in times of trouble. He's afraid of letting them down."

David looked at Lisa, admiring once again her lovely smile, now that her braces had been removed. What first drew David to Lisa was not her lovely brown pony-tail, nor her penetrating crystal blue eyes, but rather their shared love for reading. She had become a good and faithful friend, one whose advice he could trust. He worried about the furrow he occasionally noticed on her brow, for he knew that she was under pressure to earn good grades. Neither of her parents had gone to college, and their expectation that she should was a constant worry to her. The irony was that, although Lisa had more than enough ability to go to a good college and do well, the pressure and worry at home interrupted the natural rhythm of her learning and brought needless frustration and constraints. Still peeved at Bobby's slight, David grumped to himself, and then snorted, "Well, if they had *read* the short assignment given to them, we wouldn't be having this conversation, would we?"

"What a brother you are," scolded Sean. "Bobby needs your help and all you do is spin a couple of ideas and expect them to do the rest. Why not help him and his class out?"

"For three reasons," bristled David. "One: I've sat in that class and I know how much they all hate school. It's like pulling teeth. I'd rather wade ten miles through a river of molasses. Two: It's not my fault that they're in the pickle they're in. They brought it on themselves. Let them figure their own way out. Third: I'm just too busy. I don't want to be bothered with all the minutia a Learning Club would bring and I don't want to become responsible for whether or not they like learning, because *somebody* is going to sink that ship. I guarantee you that: it's all going to end up in ashes."

"Bobby's going to have to repeat next year then," said Lisa.

"Well, better he learn the price of passing now rather than when he's a senior in high school," David snapped.

An awkward silence fell over the four friends.

Finally, Lisa looked at David, saying, "David, is there something you're not telling us? This doesn't sound like you. Something isn't right. What's going on?"

David looked exhausted. Lisa, perceptive as always, had struck to his quick. He closed his eyes, choosing his words carefully. Sighing, he opened his eyes, looking at his friends. "I'm sorry. I'm really sorry. I'm planning to enter an essay contest. It's a national contest and the first prize is five thousand dollars."

"Wow!" said Sean. "Where can we apply?"

"There's a poster in the guidance office that gives all of the details," said David.

"Forget it. It wouldn't be worth the risk of running into Dandy-Pandy," said Sean. "Maybe I'll send my slave Mary in."

"Get real," said Mary.

"Why don't you want to see Mr. Dandy?" asked David.

Mary laughed and looked at Sean, waiting for him to explain.

"Shut up," Sean growled at Mary.

"Well?" asked David.

"You first," said Sean. "You owe us an explanation."

"Okay," agreed David. "I want to win this prize money as a surprise for Aunt Lillian."

"Cool," said Lisa. Sean and Mary nodded in agreement.

"She'd really be surprised, wouldn't she?" said Sean.

"She's given me and Bobby so much, and all the money from my parents' estate goes directly into a trust fund. She also set up another trust fund for Bobby, in case he can get into college or decides to start a business."

"We should be so lucky," quipped Sean.

"What would you do?" jabbed Mary, "Maybe become an arms dealer?"

"And I'd get very rich, too," said Sean, taking a huge bite out of his sandwich.

"Let David finish," urged Lisa.

"Well, two weeks ago I heard Aunt Lillian talking with her broker. From what I could gather, she's lost a bundle of money in stocks. I don't know how serious it is. Two days after that I asked her if she still wanted Bobby and me to go with her to Arizona this summer to visit her old college friend and to see the Grand Canyon. She smiled and said, 'Absolutely.' Never even mentioned the call from her broker."

"How do you know she lost anything?" asked Lisa.

"It was just the tone of the conversation. She looked kind of worried, too. Anyway, I thought if I could win this essay contest, I could give her the prize money to help with our trip."

"You're *so* lucky," said Mary. "Going to see the Grand Canyon."

"Wish the three of you could come, too," said David. "Now do you understand why I don't have any extra time? And I won't have any, at least not until I send this essay in. I've only got a month before the deadline, and I'm already feeling pressed to the wall."

"Does Bobby know why you're refusing to help?" asked Lisa.

"No. I don't want Bobby or Aunt Lillian to know about the contest unless I win something," said David. "It would totally ruin any kind of surprise."

"Maybe you should talk to your aunt about it," said Lisa. "Maybe it's not as bad as you think."

"She wouldn't let on even if anything were wrong," said David. "She's very strong, you know."

"We know," said each of the twins simultaneously, looking at each other and laughing.

"Okay. Your turn," David reminded Sean.

"My turn what?" said Sean blankly.

A muffled thump could be heard under the table.

"Missed," Sean grinned, looking at Mary.

"You know what I mean. Why don't you want to go to the Guidance Office?"

"It's Mr. Dandy's profile," Mary laughed.

"What profile?" asked David with interest.

"Should I tell it, little brother?" asked Mary.

"You yap all the time anyway, so you might as well," sighed Sean, folding his hands in his arms and frowning.

"Each October," Mary began, "Mr. Dandy visits all the seventh grade English classes and asks students to complete a questionnaire about their interests. He then reviews what they've written and tries to create a profile that will help to show them where their strengths and weaknesses lie. The whole thing is meant to help kids know what jobs they might enjoy after high school or college."

"Yeah, the counselor at my old school did the same thing last year," said David. "Her conclusion was that I would be a good social worker, teacher, librarian, journalist, or writer."

"Those are pretty boring jobs," Sean determined. "No action."

"Better safe than sorry," kidded David.

"Better dead than bored to death," quipped Sean.

"*Anyway*," continued Mary, "Dandy has to meet with each of the seventh graders to discuss these profiles. Guess which seventh grader drove him up the royal wall?"

David looked quickly at Sean, and said, "I don't have a clue."

"Get on with it," said Sean, impatiently.

"Sean suspected something was wrong from the beginning," continued Mary. "With all the other students, Mr. Dandy makes a big production out of not being interrupted. He closes the door, orders his secretary not to put any calls through. It almost seems as if he thinks the interview will be *the* special moment where every student will choose a career."

"But not with Sean?" David asked.

"No. With Sean he leaves his door wide open and even invites his secretary in to take shorthand."

"That's unusual," David observed. "Did he ask your permission to get a written record of the meeting?"

"Yeah," sighed Sean. "He gives me all this jive about what a poor memory he has. So I told him okay. It didn't matter to me."

"So, what happened?" asked David, looking at Sean.

Smiling to himself, Sean recollected his encounter with the counselor. Looking back at David, he confessed, "I led him on."

"Led him on?" David asked.

"Yeah. I was bored and I wanted to see if he would swallow what I was telling him," Sean explained.

"You were just being yourself," corrected Mary.

"Whatever. Anyway, he showed me this silly little profile. It even had five different colors. He tells me that I'm aggressive, but that I like to work with people. So I corrected him and said, 'Yeah, I'm aggressive. But I don't want to work with people. I'd rather shoot them.' 'Shoot them?' he said, all sick and nervous, nodding to his secretary to make sure she was writing it all down, but she had been going like a .30-06 slug ever since we sat down," Sean explained.

"Wow!" said David. "What happened after that?"

"He asked me to tell him more about my wanting to shoot people, so I did. He started mopping his brow and coughing. I asked him if I could get him a glass of water and he said 'No thanks.' So I just sat there and told him that I wanted to become one of two things: either a CIA agent, with a license to kill and torture people, or a Mafia hitman. Then Dandy-Pandy sputtered a lot and asked 'Have you ever thought of the Special Forces units of our Armed Forces? You'd get some action there.' So I said maybe I'd consider those jobs, too," Sean continued.

"That's not the half of it. How about the phone call home," Mary reminded Sean.

"Oh, yeah. Almost forgot. Dandy called up the next day to ask permission to have the school psychologist test me. Mom was working at the ER and Dad was at the university, so POTS takes the phone and tells him who she is and tells him that she has the legal right to approve the testing, because she is authorized to serve *in loco parentis*, which means that she has the power to act in the place of my parents. She also tells him that she thinks I am crazy as a loon, and have been for years—"

"POTS has her lucid moments," quipped Mary. POTS was the acronym the twins had many years before given to their nanny, meaning Poor Old Thing, Shame!

"Shut up," scolded Sean.

"I wonder if the pantry had anything to do with her opinion?" asked Mary coyly.

"That was years ago," protested Sean.

"You were all of ten, weren't you," said Mary.

"What of it?" challenged Sean.

"The pantry?" asked David.

"Mom and Dad were renting this great big, old Victorian house not far from Harvard, and it had an absolutely huge pantry. POTS would go into the pantry once a week to take inventory and shut the door after her to keep the cats out," explained Mary.

"Makes sense," said David.

"Yeah," agreed Sean, "but POTS is afraid of closed in spaces. She hated taking inventory. Isn't that what they call claustrophobia?"

"Taking inventory?" teased Lisa.

"No," corrected Sean, "being afraid of— " Sean stopped as he caught Lisa's grin.

"Baited and hooked again," Sean acknowledged.

"Tell them, little brother, what you did," said Mary.

"Did you ever hear of implosive therapy?" asked Sean.

"No," said David.

"Never," said Lisa.

"I remember reading one of the psychological books in my mom's medical library and it talked about different kinds of therapy. One kind is called 'implosive therapy' and it's designed to help people face their fears."

"Sounds a little dangerous," said David. "I mean, just the name."

"It works this way," continued Sean. "If somebody's afraid of swimming, you push the poor devil into a swimming pool. If somebody's afraid of spiders, you throw a bucket of spiders on the person," and here Sean's gaze moved toward Mary, as if he were considering some particular future course of action.

"So help me," she said, intuiting his thoughts, "I'd kill you."

"It'd be hard to get a whole bucket of spiders anyway," admitted Sean. "No worry. You're safe."

"But POTS," said David, "What did you do to POTS?"

"I decided that I would help her get rid of her fear of the pantry, and maybe even get rid of her claustrophobia. So I waited one day until she had gone in, and then I wedge three door stops in place so she couldn't get out when she tried to open the door."

"That was mean," scolded David.

"Look," said Sean, "I was only trying to help her."

"What happened?" asked Lisa.

"I waited and waited," Sean continued. "Finally, she tries the door, and it doesn't budge an inch. Then panic sets in and she starts pounding on the door and yelling for help. I wait exactly three minutes, because I don't want her to have a heart attack, and I finally go to the door and say, 'What's wrong?' And she says, 'Child, I'm locked in. Let me out.' And I say to her, 'I think the door is stuck. Let me try it.' So I try it and, of course, I can't budge it on purpose, but it sounds as if I'm tearing the house down to get her out. Then I turn the light switch off so she's suddenly in the dark. I shout to her, 'Sorry! In trying to get you out; I hit the light switch by mistake. Now, don't *panic*, but I think a little mouse just ran under the pantry door. Did you feel anything scamper over your feet?'"

"You are *so* wicked, Sean," said David. "You're really going to pay for that some day."

"Look," corrected Sean. "I was only trying to *help* POTS. This implosive therapy stuff seemed pretty cool, so I ran a long feather under the door so she could feel something tickling."

"What happened?" asked Lisa.

"Well, when I mentioned the mouse scampering over her feet, she went nova—I mean, absolutely *berserk*, a ten plus on any Olympic score card, even worse than those elephants that go mad in India and have to be shot. She started screaming to the high heaven, thumping and banging against the door, and I could hear lots of glass breaking in the pantry," continued Sean.

"You're so lucky to be alive to tell about it," said David. "What did you do next?"

"I got worried that POTS might be trashing all my mom's jars of strawberry jam, which I really like. So I removed the doorstops and hid them in a nearby cupboard," said Sean.

"Did POTS strangle you when she walked out?" asked Lisa.

"She was still thrashing around in the pantry. How could she know that I had removed the doorstops, or had even used doorstops? She was sounding more and more like a crazed elephant, so I put the crowbar in between the pantry door and the door frame and heaved really hard, so it forced the door open just a tad, just enough to let a little light in," Sean explained.

"I can't believe you're still alive," said Lisa. "What happened after that?"

"POTS yelled, 'Mercy! I'm saved.' She gives a final thump on the door, which I had quietly unlatched, just enough to make it give way, and she stumbles out and falls on the kitchen floor next to the stone hearth. She looks at me, saying, 'Child, child, fetch me the smelling salts.' When I brought them back to her, she *really* breathed them in, and then she looked at me, and at the crowbar, and at the pantry door, and bursts into tears, saying, 'Child, you saved me. Saved me, you did.'"

David and Lisa could only shake their heads in marvel at Sean's ruse as well as his uncanny luck at not getting caught.

"I was hoping she was healed of her claustrophobia, but I never got to find out. Any time she ever went into the pantry after that, she'd wedge a huge chair against the door, so nothing would cause it to shut. Never seemed to mind any of the cats trying to get in after that, either."

"It's a wonder POTS hasn't killed you yet," quipped Mary.

David and Lisa nodded their heads vigorously in agreement.

"Wait!" exclaimed Lisa. "We were talking about Mr. Dandy."

"Mary keeps interrupting and we go off on tangents. I'm telling this, so let me. Anyway, going back to Dandy-Pandy. Dandy got all flustered to hear the little Latin that POTS spieled to him over the phone and he scheduled me to see the psychologist pronto. So the shrink comes in and he seemed nice enough. We went into the library workroom and he asked me all kinds of questions and showed me all sorts of pictures and asked me what I saw. Then he asked me about my interview with Dandy," Sean continued.

"And," prompted David.

"And what? That was it," Sean answered.

"David wants to know if the psychologist decided you were a homicidal maniac," said Mary.

"Naw. The only thing he told Dandy-Pandy was that I was merely a normal, healthy, robust seventh-grade male," Sean laughed.

"I bet that really frosted old Dandy," said Lisa, "especially since he had put his prestige on the line by calling in a psychologist. Made him look like quite the fool."

"He didn't need anything extra to look quite the fool," Sean observed dryly, considering the counselor. "That was in early January. Since then he sort of glares at me whenever he sees me, trying to give me the evil eye. Then, one day last week, out of the blue, when I was opening my locker one morning, he pushes up behind me and whispers into my right ear, 'Don't think you have *me* fooled, you little reprobate. I know exactly who and what you are and, just remember, I'm going to be watching you. Just don't you dare try anything, or you'll be in the chair before they can say Jack Lightning,'" Sean grinned.

"What chair?" asked Lisa.

"The electric chair," sighed Sean. "Don't you girls know anything about what they do to killers in this state?"

"But you're not a killer," laughed Lisa.

"No," said Sean slowly, looking directly at Mary, "at least, not yet."

"Oh, bug off," said Mary.

"Well, at least now I know I'm immortal," beamed Sean.

"And how's that?" asked David.

"I survived old Dandy whispering in my ear. God in heaven, none of you could ever have faced old-lobster breath at that distance. It was a matter of inches! His breath could kill a skunk at a thousand paces. If he had whispered any longer, I would have been gagging for air. That's the *only* reason I didn't turn around and argue with him: I didn't dare take a full blast right in my face. It would have been curtains."

"So, has Dandy been on your case ever since?" asked David.

"Every so often I see him peering at me from around some little corner. Probably thinks I'm going to whip out a mini Uzi and spray a lot of lead into some students," sighed Sean.

"Good thing he doesn't know about the little toy derringer you pulled on Bobby," David kidded.

"He'd go bonkers, if he did," Sean concluded. "Let's *tell* him."

The passing bell rang and the Gang of Four look at each other in astonishment, for no one had guessed the time had passed so quickly.

* * * * *

Dinner at home that night was unusual owing to the strained civility with which Bobby treated David. Its icy chill on the evening's mood fully discouraged any kind of amicable discourse.

Bobby and David did dishes in silence. After Bobby repaired to his and David's room, Aunt Lillian motioned David to the seat next to her in the library and whispered, "What on earth is going on?"

"It's a long story. I don't have time to help Bobby and his class prove to Mr. Gregory that they like learning for learning's sake. I just don't have time. He doesn't understand that, and he thinks I've betrayed him."

"He looks up to you so. I think that your idea of the Learning Club inspired his confidence that the class would succeed. Now, with you not being able to guide the process, I think he must believe he is going to fail," Aunt Lillian speculated.

"But he won't, if he just opens himself to knowing that," said David. "I wish I could help, but I can't, and I won't."

The door bell rang and Bobby yelled from upstairs, "I'll get it. I'm expectin' Zeke."

Aunt Lillian heard him running down the stairwell and opening the front door.

"Hi, Zeke. Thanks. I'll show 'im as soon as possible. Come on in."

Bobby and Zeke entered the library.

Zeke took his wool ski cap off, bowed and said, "Ma'am," to Aunt Lillian.

"Hello, Zeke. How are you?"

"Just fine, Ma'am, thank you."

"David," began Bobby, trying to sound very formal, "Zeke here, as Vice-President of our ninth grade English class and me as President have a petition to give to you."

David accepted a rolled scroll held together by a large red ribbon. Untying the ribbon, he unrolled the document and read aloud: "Let it be known that the students of English 9 now ask David Andrews to become their mentor, to help guide them through the tests and trials they face into the passing days in June. To that end, we each promise to do whatever David Andrews requests or requires, without objection and without question. Let is also be it known that David Andrews will hold our thanks and gratitude forever for his help. Signed..." and here David looked at Aunt Lillian, announcing, "Everyone signed it."

The scroll was crudely constructed, but great care and attention had been given to the lettering. David was touched by the promise of the class to do anything necessary to pass. It was clear they did not look to him to do their work, but only to help them know what to do and when to do it. Their signatures must have been secured, one by one, after school. The length to which they had gone in order to present so dramatic a request for help reflected a high degree of panic, but promised commitment. Nevertheless, David still wasn't sure he wanted to devote the many hours of time required, even though he would be largely in an advisory capacity. It would still mean attending most meetings of the Learning Club.

David studied Zeke and Bobby, their eyes hopeful and expectant, their bodies taut with tension, not knowing what his decision would be. Searching himself, he found that even he didn't know.

"Gentlemen," announced David, deciding that he, too, should be formal, "Thank you for your kind offer. I am not prepared to say tonight whether I am able to honor your request. I only ask that you give me a night to sleep on it; in fact, I will try to dream about it. I sometimes get important answers in my dreams. I will give you my answer in the morning."

"If it helps, David, Bobby and I went to old Pennythorpe. He said that we wouldn't be able to get a better club mentor than you. After school I asked the Giant's son if that would be okay, and he said, 'Absolutely yes,' as long as *we* do all of the work by ourselves. You can help us think of things to do, but can't do the work for us."

David pondered Zeke's words, nodding as he answered, "That sounds fair enough. Anyway, I'm going to sleep on it. I hope I'll have at least a couple of dreams that will help me to decide what I need to do. So, until tomorrow, good night."

"Good night," said Bobby.

"Night," said Zeke, replacing his ski hat and turning toward the door.

David went upstairs, brushed his teeth, put his pajamas on, climbed into bed and meditated for half an hour, hoping his conscious thoughts would help him to incubate a dream or two that might help him make his decision. Bobby visited with Aunt Lillian for over an hour after Zeke left and when he retired he found David fast asleep. Before Bobby turned the light out, he looked intently at his step-brother's face. In repose, David looked almost angelic. Bobby hoped that angels would come to help David see that he was needed. Please say 'yes' Bobby prayed as he slipped into sleep. The room was cold with winter's chill and light snoring could soon be heard from both beds.

* * * * *

The next morning David lumbered out of bed, brushed his teeth, showered for ten minutes longer than usual, dressed, and then joined Aunt Lillian and Bobby in the kitchen. Bobby was having his usual milk and cereal. David opted for his traditional white toast with strawberry jam. On weekends, Aunt Lillian would cook the boys a fabulous breakfast, which often served to tide them over until supper.

Aunt Lillian was taking a sip of tea when David entered the kitchen. Lifting her teacup in a salute, she said, "Welcome sleepy head."

Looking at the clock, David remonstrated, "It's still twenty minutes earlier than usual."

"You're absolutely right, dear. I am duly reproved. How did you sleep?"

David inserted two pieces of bread into the toaster and took the strawberry jam out of the refrigerator. Stretching and yawning as he stood waiting for the bread to toast, he answered, "Pretty well, I guess."

"Have any dreams?" Bobby asked in wide-eyed expectation.

"Yep," answered David, a twinkle stirring in his eye.

The toast popped up. David quickly smoothed jam over both slices and brought them to the table on a separate plate.

"Well," asked Bobby.

"Well what?" asked David.

"Tell us about your dream," implored Bobby.

"Can't talk without some orange juice," David announced as he began to wolf down the first slice of toast. He had looked at Bobby and nodded at the refrigerator, and the meaning had been clear. Bobby rose to go fetch some orange juice.

"David, I think you're being perfectly mean about this," scolded Aunt Lillian. "You're keeping us on tenterhooks. If I were Bobby, I would certainly not get any orange juice for you."

"This is what's called the pregnant pause, or maybe it's called the dramatic moment," David shot back.

"I'll give you a dramatic moment," threatened Bobby as he placed a full glass of orange juice in front of David.

"Okay, okay. So this is what happened," announced David, taking two huge gulps of juice. "I didn't have one dream. I had two. But I don't understand either of them, or how they relate to each other. I plan to see if Mr. Pennythorpe can meet with me during lunch hour. He might have some insights."

"Don't we get to hear your dreams?" asked Aunt Lillian.

"Sure. I was hoping you could both help me, too. Sorry to be such a pill about it. I wrote my dreams down as soon as I woke up. Let me run upstairs and get my notes. I want to read them to you verbatim so I don't leave anything out."

David bolted upstairs as Aunt Lillian rose to take her breakfast dishes over to the sink, although Bobby stood and took them for her. When David returned, he found Aunt Lillian and Bobby waiting patiently for him.

"See what you think of this," announced David, "I made some notes so I wouldn't forget anything. This is what happened: I find myself entering school but nobody is around. The halls are empty, and I start to get scared because I know it is a school day, but nobody is there. I go from classroom to classroom, but it's like everyone has just disappeared for some reason. The books, papers, and book bags are where they usually are, but not a soul to be seen. I try all of the offices, even Mr. Dandy's, but nobody's there."

"You got the last one right," Bobby chimed in.

"Then I hear a horn honking," continued David, ignoring Bobby's jab on the guidance counselor, "so I follow it outside. A bus is sitting there with Bobby and his class, and the funny thing is that nobody is sitting in the driver's seat, and the horn seems to be honking by itself. I get on the bus and everyone is just sitting there, giving vacant stares. The class doesn't even seem to know that I'm there, but the horn keeps honking until I sit down in the driver's seat. Then the horn stops and the bus starts itself automatically. So I take the wheel and decide to drive out of the school parking lot. The funny thing is every time I come near the exit, the wheel won't turn, and I keep going around in circles. This happens for a couple of times, so I decide to stop the bus, but it won't stop. So there we are, just going around in circles. It's so weird. Finally, the Giant's son comes out and stands in front of the bus and I try to brake to keep from hitting him and he simply puts his hands out and stops it, and he lifts it up and throws it really hard and we all go flying right over the school, and the bus crashes on to its side right in the middle of the sports field, but thank goodness nobody's hurt. It's also a lucky thing that nobody was playing in the field at the time. The flight of the bus wakes everybody up, and we all scramble out the back door. I'm the last one out, and when I get out, I notice that the class has formed itself into two teams and is expecting to play a game. I also get the feeling that I'm supposed to decide, so I pick red rover. But the funny thing is that nobody can break through either team's line except for me. And one kid, I think his name is Joey Harris, sits down and refuses to play. I go over and try to get him interested, but he keeps staring at the grass, saying how it's growing really fast."

"Sounds like Joey," Bobby concluded, "he's usually chillin' out on something."

"But then, the grass really *does* start growing, and pretty soon we're all trapped by it, it's so tall, and I can hear the class yelling, but can't see anybody. The grass has cut us off from each other and we can't even walk through it. It's like a prison. No way to go. Then I hear thunder, but it's really a giant lawnmower coming, and somehow I know it's the

Giant's son whose driving it. I try to warn everyone to run, but I can only hear crying and then screaming as it gets closer."

"And?" asked Bobby.

"That was it. My first dream. It stopped at that point," said David.

"Bummer," said Bobby. "It ain't no good not knowin' what happens."

"I'd like to know, too," said Aunt Lillian.

"Here's the second dream," continued David, studying his notes. "I'm suddenly back in school again, and its empty like before, except I can hear the voices of students somewhere. I go into the closest classroom and the lights are off and all the shades are drawn and nobody's there. For some reason I feel the urge to pull the shades up, so I go over to them and pull them down and let each one fly up. As I do this, more and more light enters the room. It's like the late afternoon light, giving off long shadows. When I turn around, I find your class, Bobby, all of you, sitting there like statues, just like in a wax museum. It really spooked me out. So I go and turn the lights on, and it turns out that the lights give off every color of the rainbow, and as the light showers down, the whole class comes alive and starts talking, I mean really talking and excited about something on the chalkboard. So I look at the chalk board, and all I can remember was seeing a pyramid inside of a sphere which was inside a square cube; it was sort of three dimensional and it was rotating. And somehow I got the impression that this was really important, and I saw some sentences on the board that were in a language I had never seen. So I turned to all of you and asked what it meant, but none of you seemed to know that I was even there. I looked at the clock and it read four-thirty p.m.. It seemed funny that anyone would still be in school. Then I looked at the chalkboard again and saw a picture of the class playing red rover, but then a stage curtain closes over the scene and opens again, and there is some sort of play going on. Then the Giant's son enters and watches, applauding when it's over, and then in comes the Giant himself, accompanied by Ferlinghausen. They applaud, too, and then I see a huge banquet of food out the window and everybody looking out at it and everyone begins to leave for this feast. For some reason, I can't leave the room. So I look out the window, and I see everyone down there, including a lot of townspeople. The funny thing is that everyone's having a merry time, but whenever they pick up the food, it disappears. But they seem to eat it anyway. Then it gets really dark outside, as if a bad storm is rolling in. I begin to sense that something is terribly wrong, and I try to get out of the room, but can't. I even try to open one of the windows, hoping to jump, but it's locked tight. That's it."

Bobby eyes were wide with wonder, "Wow, that's *really* long."

"And complex," added Aunt Lillian. "What do you make of it?"

"Darned if I know," answered David. "I was hoping you could both help me out. Obviously, it gives me two pictures of maybe what might happen if I were to accept this job of mentor."

"One good, one bad," Bobby suggested.

"Or maybe both are not so good," said David.

"Why?" asked Bobby, furrowing his brow.

"I just couldn't understand what the disappearing food at the banquet was all about in the second dream," said David. "But I bet Mr. Pennythorpe will be able to help me out. He's such a great listener. Besides Aunt Lillian, he's one of the wisest people I know."

"Exceptin', of course, your wise, old step-brother," Bobby reprimanded.

"My brother who doesn't do his school work and who may fail the ninth grade," David scolded.

"Not if you come on board to show us all the way," said Bobby.

"We'll see," said David in a tone of studied non-commitment. "I don't want to make any mistakes with this, for your sake as well as for mine."

Chapter Four
Mentors and the Need to be in the Know

THATCHER PENNYTHORPE HAD TAUGHT at Midville Middle School for only two years, yet his reputation and popularity were enormous. His ability to remember every student's name at first hearing, as well as to bring humor to almost any situation, had quickly endeared him to students and staff alike.

Short of stature, almost gnome-like in appearance, his shiny bald head resting on a brow of wrinkles below which danced two penetrating eyes, eyes that were kind but also truthful, Thatcher Pennythorpe had also become the subject of popular conjecture by a host of middle school youth who had little sense of age. Some had maintained that Pennythorpe had fought in World War I, while others argued that it had been the Spanish-American War, and still others affirmed it must have been in the Civil War. The general understanding that Pennythorpe had heard Lincoln deliver the Gettysburg Address soon gave way to the firm belief that Pennythorpe had even walked with Lincoln, which soon gave way to Pennythorpe having known Franklin, Washington and Jefferson. Several students firmly believed that they could point out this singular Mr. Pennythorpe in a famous painting depicting the signers of the Constitution. In short, Thatcher Pennythorpe did more than teach history at Midville Middle School; he had become, rather, a living icon for history itself.

Motioning for David to sit across from him at his desk, Mr. Pennythorpe smiled as he opened their conversation, "David, how good of you to join me for a bite of lunch. I see you brought yours, too, but please help yourself to some of this excellent potato salad the Missus made last night."

"Thank you, sir," said David, helping himself.

"I've missed our weekly conversations ever since you started working on that essay. How's it going?"

"So so," said David. "I think I will be able to make the deadline, but something has come up and I need your advice."

David proceeded to explain the plight of Bobby and his class and their insistence that he become their mentor.

"Yes," agreed the history teacher. "Zeke Minturn was in just yesterday to ask me what I thought about you as their potential mentor, and I said that they couldn't do better. I still believe that, but I wonder if you could please tell me about your dreams once more, and a little more slowly this time. I want to take some notes."

David obliged, while Mr. Pennythorpe sat and listened and scribbled some notes as they both partook of the delicious potato salad that Mrs. Pennythorpe had prepared, which was one of the best potato salads David had ever tasted. After David had finished recounting his dreams, Mr. Pennythorpe closed his eyes, contemplating the many images had they evoked. Finally, he looked at David and asked, "Well, what do you think they mean?"

David's mouth dropped open as he exclaimed, "That's why I came to you. You tell me."

"Oh, I'm afraid it's never quite as easy as all that. Even if I did tell you what I thought your dreams were about, it would do you very little good. And your first task is not necessarily to figure them out, but rather to decide whether or not you will help a group of students who have made an urgent appeal."

Suddenly, David felt ashamed. Put that way, it made his refusal to help seem pretty heartless. Swallowing hard, he began, "I don't really want—"

"Oh, I well understand," interrupted Thatcher Pennythorpe. "You have your own project, and you need real time for it if your essay is going to have a chance of winning that contest."

"But no one seems to understand that," David complained.

"Well, they probably don't see it from quite the same perspective. After all, they risk real failure and you don't. Here, try a little lemon pepper on the salad. Better than salt, I think."

"Thanks. Um. Sure is. Hmm. Where were we?"

"I had just suggested that Bobby's class is fearful of failure, and they are looking for a way out," said Mr. Pennythorpe.

David nodded grimly, confiding, "I know they're up against it. I can sympathize with their situation."

"Can you really?" asked Mr. Pennythorpe.

"Sure. It's frustrating not to be able to succeed at something," said David. "I mean, we all have our Achilles' heel."

"Where's yours?"

David thought a moment.

"My impatience. I become impatient with others who don't learn as quickly as I do. I think that's one reason I'm reluctant to help. I think the whole thing will drive me up a wall," David explained.

"Something, certainly, to consider. Just now you mentioned that it's frustrating not to be able to succeed at something. Were you referring to Bobby and his class?" asked the history teacher.

"Yes," said David.

"I wonder why they can't succeed," Mr. Pennythorpe mused.

"I don't know," said David. "Maybe they're just rotten with language."

61

"I wonder if they work very hard," Mr. Pennythorpe ruminated.

David thought of Bobby and considered several others in the class whom he knew, and none of them had ever impressed him as having been very persistent or reliable workers. He looked directly at Pennythorpe confiding, "I doubt it. What do you think?"

"I think people learn what they *choose* to learn, which is not necessarily what they *need* to learn or *ought* to learn, if we can even speak of 'oughts' any more in our modern education. What do you think about that?"

"Bobby said that none of his class even bothered to read the homework assignment that got them all into trouble," said David.

"Ah, yes. I've heard about that. I wonder if Mr. Gregory's approach might not be a more direct way of addressing this perennial problem after all."

"What problem?"

"That at least one-third of the students in school are not engaged in their academic work. It's probably something you never thought much about, because you're one of those rare individuals who is interested in almost everything," explained the teacher.

David considered Mr. Pennythorpe's words.

"But why would kids buck learning?" asked David.

"I'm sure there are many reasons and factors to weigh into the equation: some probably believe that the subject has no relevance to them or to their lives. Others probably have learning disabilities that cause them real frustration, as well as having cultivated the habit of avoiding doing their work. Others are probably used to doing just the minimum to get by so that they can watch TV or go out with their friends. A few might even suffer the kind of chronic boredom that comes from constant depression. Those are just a few possible reasons. How about you? What do you think?"

"I'm still trying to absorb all you said," David replied. "I think there are some kids who are afraid to do their best in most schools because it's just not a cool thing to excel academically."

"So much more the pity for those who have talent but who refuse to let it shine. How sad," Mr. Pennythorpe lamented.

"I wonder," began David. "If very many of those factors are at work in Bobby and his class, just think of how hard it would be to work with them. If kids don't want to pass, they won't."

"I suspect most, if not all, *want* to pass; they just don't want to do the necessary work," Mr. Pennythorpe observed. "But it seems that this new teacher, this remarkably tall and fit Mr. Gregory, has turned the tables on them. How would you assess the current mood of the class?"

"Very gloomy. In fact, it's one of panic and fear, an abject terror at the prospect of repeating the ninth grade," David reported.

"Yes. Perhaps a necessary first step, but that won't carry the day if their ultimate task is to love learning for its own sake."

"Why not?" asked David.

"Because fear is an enemy to real learning and to real love," explained Mr. Pennythorpe. "I also stand by what Ralph Waldo Emerson said in his American Scholar essay: 'All fear springs from ignorance.'"

"So what did Mr. Gregory really do?" asked David.

"He upset the status quo. Bobby and Zeke's class has been accustomed to going through the motions, doing just the minimum to get by. In comes the new teacher who will not take second or third best, and he gives them an ultimatum: learn to love learning or forget moving on to the tenth grade. He also wisely threw out grades."

"Why do you say that?"

"Well," continued Mr. Pennythorpe, "if I remember correctly, research would suggest that many students believe in the value of a diploma, but *not* the learning that such a diploma would represent. It's ironic, in a way. But who likes to struggle through material that seems too difficult or too remote to prove of any lasting value?"

"Kind of bleak, isn't it?" suggested David.

"Yes. And if you choose to help Bobby and Zeke and the rest of the class, you're going to have to know who you are dealing with and exactly what they expect from you. It'll probably be the only way to figure out what your dreams meant," Mr. Pennythorpe suggested.

"No way," said David. "That's not fair."

"Fair or not, it seems to me that your dreams are predicting your involvement in the fortunes of your friends."

"Well, if I become a mentor for them, I will probably need to talk with you about their progress and what we are doing," said David.

"I'd be honored to listen and to help in any way," volunteered Mr. Pennythorpe, as he refit the plastic top on to the salad container.

"I guess I would describe you more as a mentor's mentor," said David, rising to leave.

"Thank you for such high praise, David, which I certainly don't deserve. I merely like to listen and to help. I hope I have."

"Thank you, sir," said David as he opened the door to leave.

* * * * *

As he returned to his locker to get his books for his sixth period class, David thought about all that Mr. Pennythorpe had said during their lunch. Much had been said that deserved further thought. David felt a fleeting disappointment, however, for he had hoped that he would emerge from their meeting with a definitive answer as to whether he would lend his help and support to Bobby and his class.

"Hey, partner," came Bobby's voice, as footsteps pounded against the hallway floor. "How did it go?"

"It was helpful, but I'm still not sure, Bobby," David answered, turning to face his step-brother. Zeke stood beside Bobby, and both boys looked like forlorn canines, searching for a new home.

"Look," said David, "I need to know more about each member of the class, so we can plan a strategy, that is, if I decide to help. Maybe Bobby and I could sort of review everything tonight, Zeke, going over strengths and weaknesses and all of that. It would sure help me to know what I might be dealing with, and it would help you, too. How was class today?"

"Just the same as yesterday," lamented Bobby.

"Tomorrow the Giant's son is gonna talk to us after he gives our letters back," said Zeke. "Maybe he'll loosen up a bit."

Bobby gave Zeke the 'Are you out of your mind?' look. Zeke sputtered defensively, saying, "Well, he could, couldn't he? Anything's possible."

"Yeah, and the moon could tumble down on my head tonight," said Bobby sarcastically.

"Hey, give the guy a break," scolded Zeke.

"Yeah. How about the clock?" challenged Bobby.

"The clock?" asked David.

"Today we were just sittin' in class, readin' and writin' and mindin' our own beeswax, and suddenly—bam, bam, bam, the Giant's son goes nailin' a wooden sign up on the wall, right next to the clock. And guess what the frickin' sign says, I mean, talk about being *really* rude?"

"You should've seen Bobby's eyes bulge out," laughed Zeke.

"What did the sign say?" asked David.

"*Time* will pass; will *you?*" Bobby scowled.

"It's a pun. It's supposed to be funny," said David.

Bobby and Zeke stared icily at David, to which Zeke responded, "Yeah, yeah, yeah."

"You've got to keep a sense of humor, guys," encouraged David.

"What time do you want me to come tonight?" asked Zeke, looking at his watch.

"How about seven o'clock?" said David.

"Okay," said Zeke, turning to go to his next class.

David looked at Bobby.

"Well," he said.

"We really needja," said Bobby, "really bad. You don't know the half of it. The Giant's son is not to be trifled with. We ain't got a prayer unless we have you, David. I just know you ain't gonna let us down. We'll even guarantee the entire class'll make good on those promises to do anythin' you say, so long as you help us."

"We'll see, Bobby," said David. "I'd like to, but I just don't know yet. Please give me a little more time. Okay?"

"Got it, brother," said Bobby, turning to go to his next class as the warning bell sounded.

* * * *

"So old Pennythorpe didn't help much after all," Bobby concluded, taking a newly washed pot from the drainer, his towel wiping away the fleeting water with a deftness that comes only from experience.

"Well, he did and he didn't," David explained, washing the wok in which Aunt Lillian had made a sumptuous chicken and veggie stir fry. "I went in wanting a definitive answer, but I walked out with the old questions still unanswered and many new ones to consider."

"Just forget it," said Bobby, as he put the pot which had held the rice away in a lower cupboard. "It's not worth all this fuss and bother. Me and the class will get along somehow."

"Now wait," said David. "I don't want to let you down if I can see my way clear to helping. I think we need some pretty basic ground rules, both for my sake as well as for the class. What I really need to know is the kind of student I'll be dealing with. Does Zeke have one of those cameras that develops pictures in a few seconds?"

"Ain't never seen him with one. But maybe his sister does. In fact, I think I seen her with one. Why?"

"Remember the old *Mission Impossible* series? The one where they would pick their team from a series of dossiers that had photographs of each person considered?" asked David.

"Ain't never seen it, I don't think," said Bobby. "Pop and I never had enough money for cable."

"Well, this is what I want you and Zeke to do. Tonight you should get somebody to take you around to get a photograph of every single member of your class, including yourselves. That would be how many?"

"Fifteen," said Bobby, counting with his eyes closed.

"I bet Zeke's mom can drive us," said Bobby. "Between me and Zeke, we know where everyone hangs out on weekends."

"Then tomorrow, after you've gotten all the photographs, I want you both to attach each photograph to a cardboard folder, which I'll give to you tonight. Write down each student's strengths, weaknesses, special skills, interests, and so on. That will help me to get a feel for the students. We can review the dossiers together on Sunday. That will give me time to prepare a strategy for the big dinner party we're hosting here for the class a week from tonight. That way we'll be able to get organized. I also want a signed statement from each student that promises that he or she will do all the work required and will attend all our meetings. How does that sound? I don't want any backsliders."

Bobby shook his head in doubt, answering, "Ain't never thought about tryin' to get the whole class to cooperate in that way."

"Why do you say that?"

"Hey, you know me and my gang. We're stubborn mavericks, always swimmin' against the stream. We ain't used to takin' orders or doin' what's expected of us."

"Does the class want to pass?" David asked sternly.

"Most of them, I think," answered Bobby.

"Well, just tell them that I'm their ticket into the tenth grade. They'll believe you. After all, they elected you as their president. It's just a matter of getting their attention."

"The Giant's son 'as *got* our attention," Bobby observed.

"Good. Now all we have to do is to focus that attention so that everybody will end up loving learning for learning's sake."

"Ain't much hope for that, not if you expect to get 'em all," said Bobby. "We got a few who don't care whether they pass or fail."

"You and Zeke will have to find a way to address that," said David. "That's not going to be my problem. I predict that we'll actually get a good response about loving learning for learning's sake."

"How so?" asked Bobby.

"Remember, we'll be picking the subjects. After all, it's going to be *our* Learning Club, and that means *we* set the agenda," explained David.

"What if everybody wants somethin' different?" asked Bobby.

"There'll be time for all of it and, if not, I'll decide," said David.

"The class ain't gonna cotton to no dictator," warned Bobby.

"The class may not have a choice, that is, if anybody really wants to see the light of the tenth grade next year," David responded. "One of the problems is that most, if not all, of your class lacks real discipline. That is something that I can help you to get, but if I do, I've got to be tough. You and Zeke plan to present those folders to me on Sunday morning. No excuses, either. Or I'm out of here. You'll be on your own."

"Yes, your highness," said Bobby.

David gave him a reproving glance, saying, "It's your neck, not mine, that's on the chopping block. Think it over."

After David had retired, Bobby knocked on Aunt Lillian's bedroom door.

"Come in," came her soft and gentle voice.

"Ain't too late to talk, is it?" Bobby asked as he entered. Aunt Lillian was in bed reading.

"Never too late. Wake me, if you ever need to talk," she said, smiling and pointing to a place for Bobby to sit on the bed.

Bobby sat down and looked at the royal blue and white bed sheets, the stately patterns of Doric columns accentuated by various depictions of the Parthenon.

'Yes, Bobby, what is it?" prompted Aunt Lillian.

"It's David," Bobby began. "Ain't like his normal self."

"I know what you mean. He seems awfully on edge these days. He's short of temper, and that's not like him. He must be putting a lot of stress on himself. Maybe I should have a talk with him. Has he decided whether or not to help you and your class?" asked Aunt Lillian.

"His Highness is still considerin' it," grumped Bobby. "Ain't no one in the class is gonna like him puttin' on his holier than thou airs. We ain't very smart, but we're still human beings with feelin's."

"David probably has good intentions, but good intentions are sometimes misdirected," Aunt Lillian pondered. "I wonder what's going on."

"Darned if I know," said Bobby.

"Well, let's sleep on it and see where it goes," suggested Aunt Lillian.

"Okay, good night," said Bobby.

"Good night, dear. Sleep well," answered Aunt Lillian.

* * * * *

Bobby and Zeke had successfully secured most of the necessary photographs by late Friday night, but needed to finish their work on Saturday morning. Following David's suggestion, they arrived a little before noon to begin assembling the required folders on each member of their class.

As Bobby and Zeke worked at the dining room table, David took a break from his own writing project. He sat pensively at the kitchen table, finishing a blueberry muffin, as he visited with Aunt Lillian.

"It seems to me, David, that you might be taking this opportunity to help Bobby and his class a little too much to heart," Aunt Lillian observed.

"How so?"

"You seem more on edge than I've ever seen you. Is anything wrong?" she asked.

"No. I'm just a little stressed out. I need a lot of time for a big project and this stuff is cutting into it. I know Bobby and his friends need my help, but I also know that most of them hate school. The only way that *I'll* succeed is by taking a firm hand at the very beginning."

"Don't they say one can catch more flies with honey than vinegar?" Aunt Lillian asked softly.

"Yeah, they do. But don't forget: this class has already tasted vinegar. In fact, they taste it every day. For them, the vinegar is school itself, coupled with the very real prospect of not passing. I'm going to help them find some discipline," answered David.

"I hope you're not making a mistake," said Aunt Lillian pensively.

"Why do you say that?"

"Bobby and most of his classmates suffer from a long history of failure. They've been receiving negative feedback for years," Aunt Lillian explained.

"Oh, I'm not going to be negative. I'm just going to say, 'Hey, folks, this is the way it's going to be …'" announced David.

"And what makes you think they'll even listen to you?"

"Because they're scared. The Giant's son has got them terrified that they're going to rot away in ninth grade," said David confidently.

"So you think they're in need of a good dose of discipline?"

"Aunt Lillian, you know how little Bobby works at his homework. It's always just the minimum, if that. I work to get my grades. Maybe the main difference is that I happen to like most of the subjects that I'm taking and I find them interesting."

"I can't help but feel that something is lost in your grand equation, David," Aunt Lillian sighed. "I don't know what it is, but I feel that you're not taking something very important into account."

"Well, please let me know if you latch onto it. Okay?"

"Deal."

"Zeke and Bobby are working pretty hard in the dining room right now putting those folders together on their class. They've got this afternoon and this evening to do it. The information is going to help me to plan a master strategy," David explained.

"Will Zeke be staying for dinner?"

"Probably. I suspect it will take them three or four hours," David predicted. "Maybe longer if they're not organized."

"Aren't you going to help them?" Aunt Lillian inquired.

"No way. It's their class, not mine. I'm going to be working on an essay. They've got to take *some* responsibility."

"I had better add a little more filler and spice to the hamburger," said Aunt Lillian.

"I hope you're making meatloaf," David brightened.

"Yes, my dear. Just for you. I know it's your favorite."

* * * * *

Rarely noticing that Bobby and Zeke were hard at work preparing the dossiers on their classmates, David continued to work on his essay throughout most of Saturday afternoon. That evening, during dinner, he acknowledged their presence and what they had done, but his interest seemed far removed from the issue that most concerned them, namely whether or not they and their classmates would pass into tenth grade.

On Sunday morning, Zeke arrived shortly before ten. Bobby greeted him at the door and together they went to the old music cabinet in the den where they had been working in order to fetch the dossiers so they could review them with David.

David had agreed to meet them in the family library at ten. Bobby and Zeke took their places at the coffee table, waiting for David to come downstairs. They began to wonder if he had overslept.

At ten past ten Zeke asked Bobby, "Do you think David forgot?"

"Dunno," answered Bobby. "Maybe I'll go see what's keepin' him."

Just as Bobby stood up, David's footsteps could be heard on the stairwell.

Walking into the room, David curtly acknowledged both boys and took his place at the table. Bobby handed him the first folder, and David groaned inside as he noticed part of the cover, which proclaimed in large red letters: DAS HE, Eh? Part of David wanted to cry out in rage, for how obtuse could anyone be to letter a folder in that way? Another part of him urged compassion on the not inconsiderable efforts of the two peers who now sat in front of him. Deciding that he would abandon them to their fate if the work inside their folders matched the carelessness on the outside, David gave a huge sigh and said, "Okay. Let's begin."

"Ask any questions you'd like. Here's a pen in case you want to make notes. We had to go to Joey Harris's house to get his picture yesterday morning. He was little spaced out, but he got the message after Zeke grabbed him by the collar."

"Sounds pretty violent," said David.

"Naw. I just had to get his attention. I grabbed him by the front of his pajamas and pulled him up a little and said, 'Hey, Joey, this is the Earth callin'. We need your picture, so comb your hair and get ready.' So he went in and combed his hair and came back out and we took the picture," Zeke explained.

"He won't even remember we were there," snorted Bobby. "He's off in space more than he's here on Earth."

"That may be a problem for the whole class if Joey doesn't fall in line and work," David worried.

"Don't worry," said Zeke. "Joey and I are beginnin' to understand each other. He'll fall in line, or else he'll fall in a different way."

"I don't like the method," said David. "He needs to learn to love learning for learning's sake."

"He will. He will," promised Zeke. "But maybe first he'll need to learn that he likes learnin' more than he likes fallin' down."

"Well, we might as well get started. As we review each member of the class, I want to take some notes. It will help us when we make plans for our Learning Club," said David.

"You're holding the first folder," said Zeke. "We're giving them to you alphabetical, including our own. Nicknames follow the real ones, in most cases."

David looked again at the folder which read: DAS HE, Eh? GLORIA ADAMS. Opening the folder, David saw the photograph of a determined looking girl with piercing gray eyes and short black hair that sat over a prominent jaw that seemed to jut.

"She looks a little hostile," said David. "Please tell me about her."

"You got it," said Bobby. "She's a chronic complainer with a short fuse. Nothin' is ever right, no matter what happens."

"Bet she's having a field day complaining about the Giant's son," said David.

"In her glory," said Zeke. "Even got her old man to make an appointment with Ferlinghausen. But all her dad did was to come back and tell her that a contract is a contract and that was the end of it. So now Gloria is really stressed out big time."

"What kind of student is she?"

"C to B, on time, and sometimes even early on her work," said Zeke. "She's not that bad when things are going her way."

"Aren't we all?" retorted David as he scribbled a few notes before reaching for the next folder, which read: RYAN BAXTER, "The Weasel". David studied the strong, rugged face, bestrewn with freckles, that lay beneath a thick shock of wavy brown hair. Ryan's alert brown eyes seemed to be stalking something very far away.

"Why do they call him 'The Weasel'?" asked David.

"'Cause all he cares about is huntin', fishin', and trappin'," explained Zeke. "He must have missed two weeks of school last fall."

"What kind of student is he?"

"Does enough to get by, meaning solid C work, but mostly he just keeps lookin' out the window," said Bobby.

David wrote more notes and took the next folder, which read: THOMAS GORDON CHASE, "Gordie". The photograph showed a retiring youth with black hair combed straight back, sensitive blue eyes shadowed by circles, and a weak chin. He looked as if he were hiding from the camera.

"Tell me about Gordie," David requested.

"He's all right, but you'd hardly ever know he was around. He never says 'boo' and if anyone asked him to give a speech, he'd go right through the floor. Very quiet, if you know what I mean," said Zeke.

"What kind of student?" asked David.

"B or better. Keeps his nose to the grindstone. Kind of a loner, though. Nobody really knows him very well."

When David took the next folder, he needed no introduction to the dossier he picked up. It read: MICHAEL DREXEL, "Mickey". Mickey was a member of Bobby's circle of friends; he was also, without dispute, the class clown. David looked at the photograph, noting Mickey's engaging smile, his huge dimples more pronounced than ever. There was a twinkle of confidence in his eyes that transformed the photograph. Here was a person who most people couldn't help but like. Mickey's shaggy brown hair even lent the appearance of a clown's wig.

"Say no more," said David. "What kind of student is Mickey?"

"B to A if he feels like it," said Bobby.

"You should've heard him going on at lunch today," exulted Zeke, looking at Bobby. "Giving perfect imitations of Bobby and the Giant's son. He even threw old Ferlinghausen in."

"Never mind," said Bobby.

"What happened?" asked David.

"The Giant's son threw us a few curves today," explained Zeke. "He announced at the beginning of class that we were sitting to *our* advantage and *not* to the advantage of learning. Then he handed out a new seating chart, and everyone went berserk, until he shouted, 'Pipe down, or you'll all be staying after to learn some manners.'"

"Here," said Bobby, "Just look at it."

David examined the chart Bobby handed to him.

Joey Harris	Maureen Grant	Lawrence Jones	Sheila Morrison	Ryan Baxter
Mickey Drexel	Jennifer Lawler	Gordie Chase	Gloria Adams	Jiggs Stevenson
Zeke Minturn	Dana (Beth) Foley	Bobby Perkins	Tammy Young	Danny Taylor

Door   Teacher's Desk   *Windows*

"So what?" asked David.

"*Look* at it," said Bobby.

"Oh, you mean the boy-girl, boy-girl seating," said David.

"Yeah, I mean the boy-girl, boy-girl seating," sighed Bobby.

"Bet it eliminates any temptation to engage in small talk," David teased. "Probably a pretty smart move on the part of the Giant's son."

"A frickin' dictatorship. It ain't right," Bobby protested.

"He seems to be really clamping down," Zeke added. "At the end of class, when the bell rang, everybody stood up to go. Then the Giant's son jumps up and says, 'The *bell* does not excuse you. *I* excuse you.' Then he waits ten seconds and says, 'Class dismissed.'"

"It's war," said Bobby. "Just like in the old war movies, and this here is one of them special situation rooms, 'cept we ain't got no funny maps or pointers."

"That's 'cause the Giant's son is holding all the cards," Zeke lamented. "No matter what we do, we're gonna fail."

"Now stop it," ordered David. "I don't want any negative thinking. The Giant's son does *not* hold all the cards. *No one* holds all the cards."

76

"Well, maybe we should give *no one* a buzz and ask him to deal us in," suggested Zeke.

"We just haven't figured out which cards we're holding," David explained, "but once we do, we're going to play one heck of hand with them. And we're *not* going to lose."

"You're helping me to get my confidence back," said Zeke. "The class is gonna need it more. Everyone's really depressed."

"With David we'll win," proclaimed Bobby. "You'll see."

"Let's get back to our dossier review," David requested.

David picked up the next folder which read: DANA ELIZABETH FOLEY, goes by Dana. Immediately David liked what he saw, which was an attractive fifteen year old girl with long blonde hair styled in a pony tail. Her blue eyes conveyed an unmistakable impish quality, revealing a desire to participate in fun and games, and her smile radiated genuine warmth.

"Wow," said David. "Please tell me about Dana."

"Probably the sharpest kid in the whole class," said Zeke, "and with looks that would kill you."

"She's real spunky," said Bobby. "She's not too bad in readin' or writin', and she can sure cut to the center of any argument and make her case. It's no use tryin' to say no to her once she has her mind made up. She always gets what she wants, in a good way, if you know what I mean. A real live wire."

"Excellent," said David. "Bobby, your first official act as President of the class is to appoint Dana Secretary-Treasurer. The same officers will also preside over the Learning Club."

"We ain't got no money," said Bobby.

"But we might," said David. "One never knows. Anyway, if she's hard to refuse, we want her in our corner, ready to bend the ear of the

Giant's son right and left until he caves in. You know, feminine wiles and all that. It might help to throw him off balance."

"If feminine wiles means that women can get what they want through crying, I know the truth of it only too well," said Zeke. "I've got three little brat sisters at home who pull that number all the time."

"Hey. Dana ain't like that," Bobby protested. "She jollies you into whatever she wants, and she's *so* good she makes you think it's your idea."

"She's perfect. After our review, please call her and ask her if she would be willing to serve as Secretary-Treasurer, both for the class *and* the Learning Club."

"Heaven help us," exclaimed David, as he opened the next folder. He looked at the cover again, which read: MAUREEN GRANT. He looked at the boys for explanation.

"She's as sour as Dana is cheerful," said Zeke. David looked at the photograph, which showed an unattractive, slightly overweight, teenager with a bad case of acne. But something much more negative was conveyed by the picture and David recoiled under its weight.

"She seems really depressed or something," was all he could say.

"Doom and gloom," continued Zeke. "If you're feeling glad when you say hello to her, you're feeling rotten a few seconds later."

"What kind of student is she?" asked David.

"D minus to C minus, tops," said Zeke. "She could make a sunny day turn into a thunderstorm."

"There's trouble there," David predicted. "Any suggestions?"

"Tell her to get *over* it, whatever it be," said Bobby.

"I'm afraid that kind of advice usually proves counterproductive," lamented David.

David reached for the next folder, which read: JOEY HARRIS.

The photograph revealed a pale, sickly looking kid who looked very unhappy. His eyes seemed unfocused and his brown hair was only partially combed.

"I see you straightened Joey's pajama tops before you took the photograph," David announced to Zeke.

"We should've combed his hair for him, too," Zeke answered.

"What kind of student?" asked David.

"Undependable. Misses a lot of days and doesn't turn in more than half of his work. Mrs. Martin passed him out of simple charity," said Zeke. "He'll never make it under the Giant's son."

"He ain't got no prayer if he ain't gonna stop takin' drugs," predicted Bobby.

David shook his head.

"Maybe Bobby and I can convince him," said Zeke, pounding his clenched fist against his left hand.

Looking reprovingly at Zeke, David reached for the next folder.

"Not a bad picture of Larry," said David. The folder read: DAS HE, Eh? for LAWRENCE JONES, "Larry Hairy". David knew Larry because he was one of Bobby's old friends. His modest attempt to raise a beard the previous year had earned him his nickname, which at first he resented but then tolerated. He was a tall kid for his age and his sparse beard lent the impression that he was more eighteen than fifteen. His bushy black eyebrows were among his most prominent features, and his black hair was cut in a stylish, British look. His green eyes conveyed an alertness and street savvy that David knew only too well, for he no longer took bets from Larry.

"How's Larry in school?" asked David.

"Can't read or write worth a darn, but only Dana can match him when it comes to arguing a point. He's mostly into his music. It's a wonder he doesn't come to school wearing headphones," said Zeke.

"'Cause the Giant's son would make 'em a permanent part of his brains," explained Bobby.

"Let's dare him to do it," Zeke suggested.

"Bobby's gang would be conducting a funeral," predicted David.

"Better than sittin' in the Giant's son's class," Bobby rejoined. "Maybe I'll wear headphones my own self. Ain't we got some?"

David sighed, saying, "Let's keep going. We're half way there."

David looked at the next folder, which read: JENNIFER LAWLER. Jennifer had sandy hair that fell over her ears but not as far as her shoulders. Her eyes were quick and alert and her smile pleasant. A small mole marked her lower right cheek.

"Please tell me about Jennifer," requested David.

"She's dependable and works hard," said Zeke.

"But don't ever get her angry," said Bobby. "She's a pistol when she's mad. She stomps her foot really hard. One day it was right on top of my right foot. I limped for a week."

"What did you say to her?" asked David.

"We was havin' an argument about whether men are smarter than women, and I took the wrong side," explained Bobby.

"She looks as if she could be plucky," David observed, reaching for the next folder, at which he gave a hearty laugh, for the new name read: EZRA EZEKIEL MINTURN, "Zeke" or "The Zeke".

"Has anyone ever called you Ezra or Ezekiel?" asked David.

"No one now living," answered Zeke. "I was named for my great-great-grandfather. He was famous for inventing a gadget that they used in processing milk. Made a fortune, but my grandfather lost most of it in the Crash of '29."

"Too bad," lamented Bobby. "We could all be sittin' pretty on easy street."

"*I* could be on easy street," corrected Zeke.

"I don't think there are any easy streets," said David. "Some just seem easier than others, but we never get to walk in other people's shoes. If we did, we'd probably think a lot differently."

"Couldn't walk in Bobby's," Zeke retorted. "They'd fall off."

"The larger the foot, the more painful the kick," warned Bobby.

"Zeke, what kind of student are you?" asked David.

"C to B, mostly, with an occasional D or A," said Zeke. "I have trouble reading, just like most of the others in class, and I also have trouble concentrating. My mind just wants to go in too many directions at once."

David continued to scribble notes, asking, "So reading and certainly writing are really hard for most of the class?"

"You've got it," said Zeke.

Taking the next folder, David read the name: SHEILA MORRISON. Her photograph revealed a strong, self-assured chin as well as the fact that she was a good looker, as Bobby had once described her. Her blonde hair was cut in a bowl shape, hanging over a pug nose and teasing eyes.

"What's Sheila like?" asked David.

"Talk, talk, talk," said Zeke. "She's a real social butterfly."

"She's interested in anything social, but nothing relating to school," Zeke observed.

"Probably not an especially good student?" asked David.

"C minus at best, and often D or D plus," said Zeke. "She can't seem to concentrate on anything except the most recent gossip."

David reached for the next folder and threw it quickly into the pile he had already reviewed. It had read: ROBERT EVANS PERKINS, "Bobby".

"Wat dja do that for?" asked Bobby.

"I know you," said David. "You're an open book. No need for any additional information."

"The price of being a step-brother, eh?" asked Bobby.

"Right on," said David, taking the next folder and examining the name: JONATHAN MAPLETHORPE STEVENSON, "Jiggs".

"Why Jiggs?" asked David.

"Look at him," said Zeke. "Notice that stocky build. He's also on the short side, but he's pretty dignified, too, and can even be abrupt. He's also a real dresser, but with stuff like you'd see in the old movies. Mickey saw a butler in an old movie that looked just like him and the butler's name was Jiggs, so we carried it over."

"Does he know the name connection?" asked David.

"Certainly. At first he was real mad, and then he ignored it, and now he just accepts it," explained Zeke.

David looked at Jiggs Stevenson's photograph. He had long straight brown hair that was impeccably combed and his shirt looked as if it had just come off an ironing board. David could see Jiggs as a butler, someone who was almost pathologically formal and fastidious.

"We may need to loosen Jiggs up a bit," said David.

Zeke began to slam his clenched right fist into the palm of his left hand, announcing, "Hey, boss. We can loosen up anybody you say."

David rolled his eyes at Zeke and shook his head.

"Not that way," he answered. "There's got to be a better way."

The name on the next folder read: DANNY TAYLOR, who was a longtime member of Bobby's gang. Danny's sleek build and narrow face made the blond hair that draped to his shoulders seem stringy. His eyes were alert, however, and he seemed to be looking at something beyond the camera.

"How's Danny as a student?" asked David.

"Generally C plus to B minus," said Zeke. "He and Ryan do a lot of outdoors things together, although Danny isn't allowed to miss as much school."

David took the next folder which read: TAMMY YOUNG. David was a little taken aback when he saw the prominent jaw and sharp-featured girl in the photograph, with closely cropped black hair and pronounced eyebrows. The vaguest cloud of paranoia could be seen in her eyes, which seemed to gaze outward with the smouldering anger of a caged animal glaring at the camera. Her rounded face did nothing to soften her other features, and a definite air of hostility imbued the photograph.

"Tammy looks like trouble," said David. "Tell me about her."

"Always fights for her rights," said Zeke. "A real fighter."

"Always thinks she's bein' cheated or rooked," said Bobby. "Never happy 'bout nothin'. Kind of depressin' to be around."

"I wonder if there's trouble at home?" asked David.

"Father left the family years ago," said Zeke. "Tammy has to watch out for her four little sisters. Her mother works herself to death. I guess I'd look that way, too, under those conditions."

"What kind of student?" asked David.

"Solid B average," said Zeke, adding, "but she has to work for it."

"Well, I guess that's it," said David.

"Not quite," said Bobby. "Zeke and me have a surprise for you."

"A surprise?" asked David.

Zeke pulled out one last folder and handed it to David. It read in bold letters: DAS HE, Eh? NATHAN GREGORY, "The Giant's Son".

"Wow!" exclaimed David. "You two *are* thorough."

"We thought it might be good to get whatever we could on the enemy," explained Zeke. "Bobby and I went to the district office, the newspaper, and the library. The dude's really got two books of poetry to his name and one of them took a big award. He really was a defensive linebacker on his college football team."

"What's even more interesting is that he graduated *summa cum laude*," said David.

"What's that mean?" asked Bobby. "It sounds like Italian."

"It's Latin and literally means: 'With the greatest praise," David explained. "Aunt Lillian did the same thing in her music studies."

"Bet she wasn't a *defensive linebacker*," observed Zeke.

"Gosh," said Bobby. "This dude's both strong *and* smart."

"Either the Giant's son is real smart, like you say Bobby, or the Giant took him by his ear and made him work really hard," said Zeke.

"I bet he's really smart," said David. "That makes our work even harder. I don't think we'll be able to outwit him."

"We'd better go tell old Ferlinghausen to book those special courses for the next two years," Bobby lamented.

"Hey," said David reprovingly, "We're not giving up without a fight. The next thing to do is to have a meeting with the entire class. This coming Friday we'll meet here for dinner. By then I'll have a plan for our first couple of weeks. Any questions?"

"Does that mean you're gonna help us?" asked Bobby.

"Yes and no," said David.

Bobby looked puzzled.

"I'll help you to help yourselves, and no more," said David.

Both boys nodded, grateful for David's offer, but not quite understanding what he meant.

"Any questions?" asked David.

"Yeah," said Bobby. "What will this here Learnin' Club learn about anyway?"

"Anything we're interested in learning about, although I think we'd be pretty clever to tie topics into something that the Giant's son thinks is important. That would only be good politics," said David.

"This is war," protested Bobby, "and it ain't no time for no politics or fraternizin' with the enemy."

"Well, what would you suggest?" asked David.

Bobby thought a minute and then announced, "Let's ask that there little hoodlum Sean to come in and show us how to make a whopper of a bomb. Knowing him, he'd probably set the damn thing off and blow us all to smithereens, includin' the Giant's son. That would be just dandy with me. Better than sittin' there day after day, readin' and writin' 'til our eyes fall outa our achin' heads or our hands turn white and numb. It's war, I'm tellin' you, and it's hell for sure."

"Let's save that idea for an emergency," said David, as he studied the seating chart.

"Anything wrong?" asked Bobby, noticing David's interest in the seating chart.

"Not really. But I think that there's a mistake on this seating chart."

"It's the Giant's son's chart," said Bobby.

"Oh, I know. But the Giant's son doesn't know he made a mistake," explained David.

"Where?" asked Zeke, as he and Bobby bent forward to see.

"Here," said David. "Zeke, you and Jiggs Stevenson should trade places. That way Jiggs can answer the door, just like any other butler."

Bobby and Zeke broke into laughter.

"Do you have any questions for us?" asked Zeke.

David thought a moment and said, "Yes, I do. I don't understand what you've written on these folders in red above the names. What does 'DAS HE, Eh?" mean?"

"That's what you told us to bring," said Bobby.

"We couldn't find out how to spell it," explained Zeke. "But we knew that it was a folder telling about somebody. So we figured it out on our own. I found out that in German DAS means 'that'. We figured then that the person in the folder would be 'he'. Then Bobby suggested that the last part was what Canadians often say, when they ask, 'Eh?' So the folder says: 'That's he, right?'"

David sat spellbound, his mouth hanging open.

"You invented a pun on the word *dossier,*" was all he could say.

"What's a pun?" asked Bobby.

"Das he, eh?" David said to himself, letting the words sink in. Suddenly he began to laugh so hard that tears streamed out of his eyes. Bobby and Zeke looked confused, and the more confused they looked, the harder David laughed.

"He's lost it, for sure," Zeke said to Bobby.

"Now we'll need to get a new mentor," said Bobby. "Maybe Aunt Lillian will do it."

This, of course, made David laugh even harder, and he fell to the floor and began pounding it. Aunt Lillian appeared, mildly interested in the laughter, and looked quizzically at Bobby and Zeke.

"Stress was too much for him," explained Zeke.

"Apparently so," Aunt Lillian smiled. "I've made some hot cocoa for you boys. It should go well with the ginger cookies."

Bobby and Zeke bolted into the kitchen.

David suddenly found himself alone, and soon followed the others, shaking his head and muttering to himself, "Das he, eh?"

* * * * *

Conversation at dinner focused on making plans for the gathering of Bobby's classmates the following Friday.

"*Everyone* has to come," insisted David, "or else none of this will work. We've got to establish a common bond as soon as possible."

"Zeke and I'll make sure everybody's here," promised Bobby.

"Aunt Lillian, should any of the kids bring food or beverages?" asked David. "I mean, twenty people is kind of a mob."

"Twenty," asked Bobby, "There ain't gonna be twenty."

"Sean and Mary and Lisa are coming," David announced. "Will twenty be too many, Aunt Lillian?"

"Nonsense. I'm already planning the menu, which will be both delicious and simple," Aunt Lillian explained.

"Cheeseburgers?" asked Bobby hopefully.

"Not quite, but close," said Aunt Lillian. "I'm going to prepare a couple of large pans of Hedges' Casserole, which is a combination of hamburger, rice, and onions. It's easy to make and I've never had a complaint in over forty years."

"Funny name for it," said David.

"It was a recipe of the uncle of my dear friend and college roommate Louise Cummings, who now lives in Arizona. We're going to go visit Louise this summer. I'm sure you boys will love Arizona. I did the first day I visited, which is nearly thirty-five years ago. I haven't seen Louise, poor dear, in over three years. I'm a little concerned about her health."

"You know, that's going to be an expensive trip," said David. "Maybe you should just go out there by yourself. Bobby and I could batch it here."

"Batch it?" inquired Bobby, looking at David.

"You know, bachelors making it on their own," David explained.

"I won't hear of it. I want you boys to see the Grand Canyon and Sedona. Louise lives just outside of Sedona in a little village called Oak Creek. It's one of the loveliest spots I've ever known, with all those gorgeous and majestic red rocks towering in every direction."

"We all won't be able to sit down for dinner next week," said Zeke, looking around the kitchen and into the dining room.

"We'll do buffet style, the way we always do at parties," said Aunt Lillian. "People will select whatever they want from the buffet and then find empty chairs which will be stationed all over the house. We have plenty of chairs, which I bought many years ago for the recitals of my piano students."

"Sounds good to me," said Zeke, "especially the part about the casserole. Can't wait."

"I promise you won't be disappointed," Aunt Lillian smiled.

"David," asked Bobby, "how are you going to run the meetin'?"

"Not sure yet," said David. "I've asked Sean, Mary, and Lisa for help. I think I'm going to have to establish my authority as mentor as soon as possible. So we'll have to come up with some sort of gimmick that will make it clear that I'm in charge."

"Just ride in on a frickin' elephant," suggested Bobby.

"Not a bad idea, if we had one," said David.

"How about my German shepherd?" asked Zeke.

"I don't think our furry resident feline, Her Majesty, would approve any canine presence in her castle," said Aunt Lillian. "And after all, she *does* have seniority."

"The photographs and information on class members really helps," said David. "I'm going to memorize all of that material and go right for the jugular next Friday. I want everyone in the class to know that this is going to be a real commitment, or else I'm out of here."

"Some of the class can be pretty stubborn," said Zeke. "Maybe a quieter approach would work better."

"Hasn't seemed to yet, has it? Remember, we've got them where we want them," said David. "They're in abject terror about not making it into the tenth grade, and I am the one they believe can help them get there. They will also have signed new pledges committing to any work that I require. That'll put me in the driver's seat."

"Just don't be too harsh," said Zeke.

"I agree, David," said Aunt Lillian.

David sat back from the table as if he had been wrongly understood, saying, "I'm not going to be harsh; I'm going to be clever."

* * * * *

The next Friday brought bitter cold temperatures but a glorious heaven, for the stars were spangled brightly across the night sky. Bobby, Sean, and David made sure that a roaring fire was going in the fireplace before anyone arrived. Ample wood lay in wait of the flames. Mary and Lisa had set the dining room table, which looked inviting, and the delectable smell of the Hedges' casserole perfumed the entire house.

Zeke Minturn and Mickey Drexel were the first to arrive.

"My mom wanted us to bring you these rolls," said Zeke to Aunt Lillian. "She bakes bread a lot and these rolls are her trademark."

"Homemade Parker House rolls. That's great," said Aunt Lillian. "We'll warm them in the oven and set them out just after the blessing. Here Lisa, please put these on the kitchen table."

"Hey, who invited the seventh grade rug rats?" teased Mickey, looking at Sean and Mary.

"Rats have teeth," said Sean, assuming a karate posture.

"Hey, man, keep it cool," said Zeke. "Mickey gets on everyone's case. He's our class clown. Just laugh it off."

"Ha, ha," said Sean.

"Ha, ha, ha," responded Mickey.

Sean broke into a huge grin and shook Mickey's hand.

As other members of the class arrived, small clusters of friends stood around talking. The last to arrive was Joey Harris, whose mother accompanied him to the door in order to ask when he should be picked up. She had deep worry circles under her eyes and spoke softly. Her hair was steel gray and she looked very tired.

"Better let him call you," Aunt Lillian said. "I don't think we have any way of knowing just how long the meeting will be."

"All right. Be on your best behavior, Joey," said Mrs. Harris as she left. After she left, Joey turned to the group in the room, looking for a place to hide in the corner.

"I'm David Andrews," announced David, extending his hand to Joey, "glad you could come. I'm really counting on your support."

Joey gave a noncommital grunt as he avoided eye contact. David did not like the fish-like handshake he had received, and made a mental note to do some special problem solving over what he stylized, in his mind, as the 'Joey' issue. He looked directly into Joey's eyes and was grateful that they were not dilated.

"Friends of Bobby and David, thank you for coming," announced Aunt Lillian. "We will have dinner buffet style. Just help yourselves to a plate and join the line after we have grace. The beverages are on this table next to the door leading into the kitchen. If you need anything, please ask. There are plenty of chairs for everyone. David?"

"Let us pray," intoned David. Only a few of the youth bowed their heads as David continued, "We give you thanks, Lord, for this food and fellowship and the time you have given us to know each other better. We pray that our efforts in all that we do will be rewarded with success. Amen."

One or two 'Amens' rustled through the group.

Sean was the first to pick up his plate and go through the buffet line, commandeering heaping portions of everything, although he had to return for one of the rolls Zeke's mother had sent.

Dinner proceeded as small groups clustered to chat privately among themselves. The mood was subdued and cautious, but everyone ate lustily. As dinner plates were being taken to the kitchen and the buffet table cleared off, David and his Gang of Four excused themselves to make preparations for the meeting. Zeke and Dana organized and managed the clean-up while Bobby set up five rows of three chairs each in the music room in preparation for the meeting. When dishes were done, Bobby asked class members to take their seats and to sit in the corresponding positions assigned in English class.

When all were seated, Bobby took his place and shouted toward the stairwell, "Okay."

A pause of no more than a minute followed, but the silence and anticipation made it seem much longer. Suddenly a horrendous horn blare was heard. Several of the class started in their chairs. The horn blast repeated itself twice, followed by Sean's solemn intonation, "Make way for the mentor. Make way for the mentor."

Lisa descended the stairwell, carrying a primitive brass horn, which she sounded again. Sean, carrying a wooden sword, followed her, intoning again, "Make way for the mentor."

David walked behind Sean, dressed in what had been Aunt Lillian's organist's gown at Midville's Episcopal Church, and was followed by Mary, who held a fan like feather over his head.

The four entered the room as David assumed his seat at the corresponding place of the Giant's son. Cuing his three comrades, the four sat down in unison.

The class looked uncomfortably at their mentor, and he intently studied each of them in turn. David's gaze also noticed Aunt Lillian, who was sitting next to the dining room table. She looked very sad and, as he tried to puzzle out her mood, he began to feel the warmth of embarrassment rise from the base of his spine, finally bringing prickles to his backbone and neck. Suddenly he felt very foolish and, in an instant, he knew why, which also brought him fresh clarity about Aunt Lillian's reserve.

—Idiot, he thought to himself, scolding further: —All these charades and machinations are okay for kids who are passing, like Sean, Mary, and Lisa, but this is totally inappropriate for Bobby and his classmates. They're not here for fun and games. They're facing failure, and here you dress up like an idiot to parade your expertise in front of them.

A new flush of embarrassment rose to David's face, and he began to look beet red, his freckles disappearing as the new hue colored his face. He felt himself perspiring and knots growing his stomach. The awkward stares of the class members confirmed what he was feeling.

Searching himself to know what to do, he intuitively realized that all would be lost if he did not immediately drop this posturing. Originally he had planned to crack the proverbial whip, to lam into them all for their lack of skills, their persistent avoidance of school work. David wondered what it would be like not being able to read fluently, as he was so used to doing, how it would feel to struggle over words and phrases. He had planned to chastise each of them, bringing each up short under the advantage of his recent knowledge of their skills and habits and interests. That plan now seemed both ignominious and cruel. The fire crackled softly in the fireplace, soon to die out. David quickly considered his options, which were fast receding.

In a few short minutes, the class would tune him out, the way it had tuned out countless others for so many years. The Giant's son had only been able to call the question, to refuse to accept them for anything less than their best, whatever that best might be, both individually and collectively. Surely the sum of the parts would prove greater than whole, just as each individual sitting here would shine in some special way.

David now understood that the opportunity to shine in school had never been a genuine option for these kids, owing to their various difficulties in mastering the language from the very beginning. Language, something so basic, something taken for granted by so many, yet both confuting and elusive for those who now sat before him. They had come to him in good faith, urgently requesting his help, and he was merely going to mirror to them their own deficiencies and failures, demanding change but offering no real way out.

Closing his eyes and taking a deep breath, he prayed that the right words would come to him so that he wouldn't betray their loyalty and trust. When he opened his eyes, he felt an inner voice prompting him to take action before uttering any words. Without thinking about it, he stood up and removed the choir robe, tossing it aside.

Resuming his seat, he looked at the floor in front of him, searching for words. Sighing to himself, he found words were stirring to come out, so he opened his mouth, beginning, "I'm sorry. I owe you all an apology."

Looking up at them in frank confession, he continued, "I have been very foolish. In fact, I am an absolute idiot. Here I come to you, you who have asked for my help, all trumped up as something or someone called a mentor, willing and eager to lord it over you. No real mentor would do that, I assure you. And I am so sorry that I did not realize that truth until just now.

"The word mentor comes from the Greek, and means: 'advisor'. A person named Mentor was the advisor to Ulysses. The word has come to describe someone who is a loyal and wise advisor. I have no right yet to claim that title, least of all from you. I can only promise to give my total allegiance and talents toward helping each of you, so that some day, perhaps when we celebrate our common victory, I may, by then, have come a little closer to being a mentor to each of you.

"We are all foolish, each of us in different ways. I have had the benefit of a real mentor since last October. His name is Pennythorpe. Unfortunately, I have not appreciated him until this very moment.

"No matter. If anything, he has taught me to learn from my mistakes, and I can assure you that I have made many, many mistakes, including this whopper that you have just witnessed."

The class members sat spellbound, listening intently to every word, for in the shower of David's honesty and intimate confession a new focus of attention could be felt. Bobby wiped a tear from his left eye.

Looking first at Zeke, David began to address each student in turn. "Zeke, I'm sorry I didn't listen to your caution to go gently. My ego obviously got in the way. I had fancied myself the expert, the straight A student coming in, like the cavalry, to save the day. All that was needed was to whip everybody into shape. It seems to me there's been enough whipping, and I suspect that everyone in this room continues to punish himself or herself about stuff that should have been let go of years ago. We all carry baggage, whether it's an inferiority complex, or a grudge, or a fear, and we're going to have to try to discover and get rid of any obstacles that may prevent us from achieving our goals.

"Mickey, thank God we have a clown among us. We'll need your humor and antics to keep us laughing, both at ourselves and at our mistakes, for we will make mistakes. That's one price we pay for trying to do anything, and it is almost a sure-fire guarantee: we will make mistakes. But if we never fail, we'll never grow.

"Joey, I don't know you very well yet. I hope that you will come to feel yourself a part of this class. Like it or not, we're all in this together now, and each of us has got to pull his or her own weight, at different times and in different ways. I hope you will let me know how I can be of assistance to you.

"Dana, I look forward to getting to know you, too. Congratulations on your new job as Secretary-Treasurer. Thanks for accepting it. I sense that you're going to be able to help us secure an advantage that we could not normally have attained otherwise.

"Jennifer, I know you're a hard worker, and that you don't take any guff. I'm surprised you didn't jump up and let me have it just now when I made my so-called grand entrance."

A ripple of genuine laughter bubbled around the room.

"Bobby, brother of mine, I will do all that I can to help you and your class, now that I've gotten off my high horse. Thanks for not knocking me off it earlier. I think I needed to learn this lesson on my own.

"Gordie, I know you don't like to speak in front of others. But I am afraid that I can't promise you that you won't have to do that. Maybe it would be a good thing if you did. We all have to face our fears, and someone once said that walking into them is one of the best ways. If you ever have to speak, please know that I will have worked with you so that you will be confident in whatever you are talking about.

"Larry, I respect your love for music. Maybe we can tap into that interest in some way as we travel this journey together. I happen to like classical music, but I would like to know more about the current stuff that's out there.

"Tammy, I've been told that you're a fighter for your rights, and I admire that. This world would be a more honest place if people had the courage to speak out for themselves when they felt they were slighted or cheated. I also hope that you will come to trust my intentions to be of help to you and the others.

"Gloria, I get so frustrated when I believe people aren't listening to me. I promise to listen to you, so let's make a deal that you will let me know what's bugging you, especially if I do anything that you believe isn't helpful.

"Sheila, you are very outgoing, and I know we will need that special ability to engage others as we go along. I will look to you for your support and help.

"Danny, I know you, because you are a good friend of Bobby's. I also recognize and know that school is not your first interest, but maybe we can work together to make it more interesting as we chart our collective journey together.

"Jiggs, how they tease you, but only because you tend to be a bit of a stuffed shirt. I'm the same way, you know. We have a lot in common. I've had to loosen up this last year, thanks to these two twins and to Lisa, as well as to Aunt Lillian and brother Bobby.

"Ryan, I'm told that if this were the fall, we'd rarely see you. I'm glad that it's not the fall, because we need you. We need every single member of the class. We don't know quite yet what we're facing with the Giant's son, except that it's no longer 'business as usual' and that your progress toward the tenth grade is on hold until we can convince him that you, all of you, no, correction, that all of *us*, love learning for learning's sake. That's a tall order any day, but I bet we can do it."

The class members sat in solemn consideration of David's words.

David looked at Aunt Lillian, who was smiling at him and who gave him a silent 'thumbs up.'

"Well, do you want me, or don't you?" asked David.

The class members looked at each other, not realizing they had been expected to discuss the issue of David's continuance.

Raising his hand, Bobby coughed, saying, "We ain't just *want* you. We *need* you."

"Well, then," David smiled as he continued, "I have some ideas which might help to get us there. The first is that we will begin to organize and create a Learning Club, which will meet Tuesdays and Thursdays after school for two hours. We're not ready to invite speakers yet, but we should start meeting during those times to make plans. Mr. Pennythorpe has offered his room and has promised to stay after with us on those days until the Learning Club is up and running. Remember: it's very important to commit to those days. I know that some of you have jobs, so please see what you can do to free up your schedules so that we can all share together in this cause. The Learning Club will help us to demonstrate our curiosity as a group; as for individual indicators, that may have to be left up to each of you, although we can probably assist in finding ways to satisfy Mr. Gregory.

"I know that I've talked a lot, so before I open it to questions or to suggestions, why don't we all take a ten minute break."

As David rose, a slight pause ensued before the class, as one person, began to applaud its appreciation and thanks. David bowed in acknowledgment, pointing to the dining room, saying, "Cookies coming. Please help yourselves."

"Guess you got your big foot out of your huge mouth," said Sean, brushing by David in search of the aforementioned cookies. Others followed, noticing that Lisa and Mary were bringing out a huge tray of goodies.

David could only reply, "You got *that* one right."

Turning, he saw Aunt Lillian standing in front of him.

"Thank you, dear one, for doing the right thing," she said. "I was very worried at the beginning, for obvious reasons—"

"I know. I felt it," said David. "I feel like such a fool."

"I don't think that you could have won their trust or loyalty in any other way, at least not as quickly as you did by merely telling the truth. And you could never have planned something so honest and direct. There is a great value, sometimes, in spontaneity."

"I'm sorry I've been such a pill," said David.

"That's okay. We all take our turns at that. Has anything been bothering you?" asked Aunt Lillian.

David sighed and decided to seize the bull by the horns and blurted out, "I've been worried about your finances. I overheard you talking to Mr. Simpson last week, your broker, and kept hearing you say 'Oh dear, oh my,' so I thought you must be taking a bath with your stocks."

Aunt Lillian hugged David and laughed.

Perplexed, David asked, "It can't be funny, can it?

"David, what big ears you have. I wasn't talking with Mr. Simpson about *my* stocks, but rather about Louise's financial situation, which isn't good. You see, Mr. Simpson, Louise, and I knew each other in college. He's been our broker for years. But Louise's investments have not done as well as mine. I try to help her out here and there as I can, in a quiet, anonymous way, that is, through Mr. Simpson. He's a little worried about her overall health, particularly how rational she is. That's one reason we're going out West this summer. Louise lives alone, and it's hard to know what's really going on. In any case, *my* financial situation is very healthy. You and Bobby need not worry about your futures, or mine. We're sitting pretty."

David was so relieved, he felt fifty pounds lighter. —No need to mention the essay contest, he thought, —I still might win.

"What is your next step after your group reconvenes?" asked Aunt Lillian.

"We need to plan a way to open, or to repair, communication with the Giant's son. I believe it is essential that we all start talking to each other. Where there's no communication, there can be no growth."

"Well said," Aunt Lillian approved.

"I'm going to request, by formal letter, that Mr. Gregory meet with Bobby, Zeke, Dana, and me this coming Monday after school. That way, we can begin to try to get things back to normal."

'What will your reason be for meeting with Mr. Gregory?" asked Aunt Lillian.

David reflected for a moment, and then announced, "We want him, of course, to be the first speaker at our new Learning Club. And we will ask him to talk about learning."

"Isn't that what they call scouting out the enemy camp?" asked Aunt Lillian.

"Where did you learn that?"

"From Sean. Who else?"

"Good point," David rejoined. "I'd better call everyone back together so we can announce our plans and take any questions."

"Shouldn't you confer with Bobby, Zeke, and Dana?" asked Aunt Lillian.

"Yes," answered David, calling, "Bobby, please ask Zeke and Dana to come over here for a very short conference."

The youths arrived, and David announced, "I'm really sorry for the pill I've been, especially when I said I didn't want to help all of you get out of this jam. I was worried about Aunt Lillian; I thought her finances were going bust. She just explained to me that her broker was talking about a friend of hers out west. So, I don't need to try to win an essay contest that I was hoping would bring in a little money for the family. Anyway, I've been pretty rude, and I'm sorry."

"Hey, brother-pal, don't sweat it. We knew you'd come around eventually," grinned Bobby, as the others nodded in agreement. David heaved a sigh of relief and proceeded to explain his strategy for Monday, and all present agreed it was as good a plan as anyone could conceive.

Chapter Five
Organizing for Learning

BOBBY AND ZEKE CONSULTED WITH THE GIANT'S SON after their English class to see if he could meet with David, Dana and them after school to plan for the Learning Club's meetings. The initial plan had been to scout out the enemy camp, but such plans go astray when careful surveillance has not been conducted.

The group was cordially welcomed by Nathan Gregory, who invited everyone to sit in a circle of five desks he had assembled for the meeting. David was amazed at how someone of Mr. Gregory's height and breadth could look so comfortable sitting at a student desk, but then wondered if it was merely that Mr. Gregory was comfortable no matter where he was.

"Who's running the meeting?" he asked, as the students sat down. This first question, of course, threw everyone for a loop, for if David offered to chair the meeting, it might appear as if he were horning in on Bobby's prerogative as the duly-elected president of the class and club.

Noticing the panic in Bobby's eyes, David announced, "Sir, we hadn't even considered who would do that, although it would probably be Bobby, if we had planned a formal meeting." Bobby's eyes no longer reflected panic, but rather terror. He had never 'run' a meeting before, not even having the slightest idea of what that concept meant, but he was sure of one thing, and that was that he never wanted to 'run' one.

"But Bobby has asked me," David continued, "to report to you on behalf of the class and club some of the preliminary ideas that we have come up with so far and to solicit your input and opinion."

The Giant's son nodded as Bobby exhaled a deep sigh of relief, stretching in his chair so as to relax his body from its previous coiled terror. The knots in his stomach were also uncoiling.

"First, we thought we would have our meetings after school, until five o'clock. Attendance at the club would be mandatory for class members, and only illness would be accepted as a valid excuse for missing. Guests would always be welcome at our meetings. We are beginning to brainstorm for topics of interest as well as for potential guest speakers, and we wonder if you would do us the honor of being our first speaker?"

"I'd be delighted," replied Mr. Gregory.

A silence followed during which David had expected that the Giant's son would begin to talk about things they should further consider for their club. But he didn't; he merely sat there, looking at David and smiling, which made David feel awkward.

To fill the silence, David continued, "Perhaps you would consider offering us some insights on learning and its importance?"

Mr. Gregory answered, "I'd be glad to take that as my topic. When do you want me to speak?"

Once again, confusion ran its chaotic course beneath the subdued trappings of this informal gathering, for no one had actually contemplated when the club should begin its meetings. David decided, however, to take an aggressive lead and said, "How about next Tuesday, a week from tomorrow?"

"I'd be very happy to come," agreed Mr. Gregory. "What will your meeting be about on Thursday?"

Here David and the others felt stymied again. It now was very clear how very unprepared they were, and David felt his embarrassment as he shook his head, confessing, "We just haven't gotten that far, sir. Maybe we could discuss what you talked about on Tuesday."

"Let me suggest," said Mr. Gregory, "that if you plan to have any sort of deliberations, that you apprize yourselves with what it means to think and speak critically. Such clarity of thought is absolutely necessary to any genuine discourse; otherwise, discussion can be lost in a swirl of emotion and opinion."

"I don't think any of us have learned much about critical thinking," said David, his peers nodding.

"No matter. I will take it up with the class, beginning tomorrow, and we'll spend about four or five days on it. By next week, you should all be ready for more focused discussions. I will look forward to making my presentation to the Learning Club one week from tomorrow."

"The club could start meeting this Thursday, so as to discuss what it has been learning in class."

"I'm afraid that I can't be there this Thursday, but I will be able to stay every Tuesday and Thursday, beginning next Tuesday, from now on. Perhaps Mr. Pennythorpe could stay with you?"

"I'll ask him tomorrow," said David.

"Is there anything else?" asked Mr. Gregory.

Everyone looked blankly at each other.

"Guess not," said David. "Thanks for your time."

"Glad to have been a part of it," said Mr. Gregory.

* * * * *

As David and Bobby walked home, snow crunched under their feet.

"Guess we made fools out of ourselves," said Bobby.

"No, we didn't," said David. "But it was obvious that we weren't very well prepared. That's sort of embarrassing, but it teaches us an important lesson."

"And what's that?" asked Bobby.

"That the Giant's son isn't going to take second best. We are really going to have to work hard on this Learning Club."

"Hallelujah," grumped Bobby.

"Let me know what Mr. Gregory does in class. I guess you'll start learning about critical thinking tomorrow."

"Yeah. Everybody's so sick and tired of just readin' or writin', the change will be good," said Bobby. "I can give him some critical thinkin', if he wants it: his class really stinks."

"I don't think he meant 'critical' in that sense, but more in the way of clear thinking," said David.

"Ain't normal, botherin' us about whether we are thinkin' clearly or not. We just think. Whatever we think, we think. That should be clear enough to anybody," said Bobby.

"Well, listen carefully and try to report to me what you learn," said David. "Don't forget to take notes."

"We need to come up with some more programs," said Bobby.

"Yes," agreed David. "Why don't you see what the class wants when we meet on Thursday. I'll see if Mr. Pennythorpe can stay after with us. We can meet in his room as well."

"Hope everybody can come on Thursday," said Bobby. "I know at least five in the class have part time jobs. What if they ain't able to show up?"

"We can't have any backsliders," said David. "Tell them they've got to get permission to get off from their jobs. Why do they have jobs, anyway, when they're not doing very well in school?"

"Goin' through the motions," Bobby explained. "Ain't never had to do anythin' more than just go through the motions."

"You mean at school?" asked David.

"You bet," said Bobby. "Couldn't keep no job if they went through the motions at work."

"So why should school be different?" asked David. "When you're a student, going to school should be your *first* job. Everything else should come second."

"That ain't the way anybody I know sees it. Just the reverse. Ain't no gain from school. Nothing but the same old blah, blah, blah," said Bobby.

"Kids who graduate from high school do better than those who don't. Same with college and graduate school," said David.

"Yeah, I know. But even for most of them it's only the sheepskin that's important. Ain't the learnin', that's for sure. They should give us all a medal for just sittin' there and takin' the blather in year after year," answered Bobby, raising his hand to pull his ski hat tighter to his head.

"That's terrible. The way you describe it, learning is reduced to the barest externals. No wonder school feels empty. There's no satisfaction, because most kids don't work hard enough to discover satisfaction. Haven't you ever gotten excited about something at school?"

"Yeah. I get excited when the dismissal bell rings."

"School must pass pretty slowly for you," said David, testing a hunch.

"Like a river of stone," said Bobby.

"But don't you see, if you get involved in something, it becomes interesting. When that happens, time often seems to go fast, or even to disappear, because you've become genuinely engaged with whatever you're reading about or talking about."

"Ain't that way for most," said Bobby.

"It's going to be," predicted David.

"No way," argued Bobby.

"With the Giant's son, it's going to be that way or you're not going to get promoted," said David. "Trust me. I am sure of that much. He's not going to accept second best. You can be sure of that. Everyone's going to have to dig in and do some real work."

"Everyone's sick and tired of just readin' and writin'," said Bobby adding, "*Anything* would be better."

"Anything?" asked David.

"*Anything*," repeated Bobby.

* * * * *

On Tuesday, during their customary walk home, Bobby looked and acted totally withdrawn.

"I need some time to think about what went on in class today before we talk about it," Bobby confided to David.

"How about at dinner," David suggested. "Aunt Lillian will be interested, too."

The boys arrived home, had their ritual snack, checked to see if the mail had arrived, and worked on their homework. At six o'clock, Aunt Lillian called up the stairway, "Boys, time for dinner."

Bobby had been unusually reserved during their study time. David decided to try to draw Bobby out during dinner, which turned out to be a veritable feast comprised of beef stew, potatoes, carrots, and onions. Aunt Lillian ladled out large bowls for the boys.

"Bobby, what happened in English today?" asked David.

Bobby looked at Aunt Lillian and David, not knowing quite where to begin, but finally saying, "It ain't normal, that's what."

"What's that?" asked Aunt Lillian.

"All this tripe about clear thinking. If it ain't broke, don't fix it. We think clear enough already," said Bobby.

"Apparently the Giant's son doesn't see it quite that way," suggested David. "What did he talk about."

"I made some notes," said Bobby. "Lemme go get 'em."

Bounding up the stairway, Bobby soon appeared with two pages on which he had scrawled a lot of illegible notes.

"Have you ever heard of falsies?" asked Bobby.

"What's that?" asked Aunt Lillian

"Falsies," explained Bobby, "Things that are false, although at first hearing, you believe them."

David reached for Bobby's notes, saying, "May I?", examined them, then laughed, saying, "You mean fallacies."

"Whatever," said Bobby.

"No. It's important that you get it right. Say after me: fal - la - cies."

"Fal - la - cies," Bobby repeated. "So, what the hell are they?"

"Flaws in thinking, in language," explained David. "We studied some of those in the debate club I belonged to a couple of years ago at my old school."

Bobby looked at Aunt Lillian, as he pointed to his notes, saying, "These ain't natural. Worst damned things you ever saw, beggin' your pardon, Ma'am, but I ain't gonna sleep decent at night 'til we're done with these little critters. David, could you please help me with these?"

"Sure. They can even be fun," said David, only to receive a disbelieving glare from Bobby. "But tell us what happened in class today."

"The Giant's son comes in and says, 'Everybody: listen up! We're gonna get ready for your Learnin' Club, which will be a place where you discuss stuff, so you need to know how to enter into proper deliberations," said Bobby, checking his notes. "Yes, I wrote it here: proper deliberations."

"What happened after that?" asked Aunt Lillian.

"He goes off on all this jive about arguments and parts of arguments and fuzzy thinkin' and clear thinkin', enough so you'd just be gettin' real dizzy and sick to your stomach. Then he says, 'Zeke, answer this question for me,' as he draws three little boxes on the board. 'These boxes hold the same kind of medicine. Nine out of ten doctors recommend that you buy Box A. Which one will you buy?' And Zeke says, 'Box A.' 'But how do you know it's the best box?' asked the Giant's son. 'Because most doctors recommend it,' said Zeke. 'What kind of doctors are they?' asked Gregory. 'I don't know,' said Zeke. 'Maybe they ain't even medical doctors,' says the Giant's son. 'Maybe they represent only ninety out of a hundred, instead of ninety thousand out of a hundred thousand. This is a falsie—"

"Fallacy," corrected David.

"Fallacy," repeated Bobby. "Anyway, the Giant's son sure made a fool out of all of us. By the time he was done, no one knew if we knew *anythin'*. Our minds was just swimmin' around."

"He used the fallacy of false appeal to authority," said David. "It's a popular tool in debate."

"Give me a tool, and I'll dig myself a hole, and crawl right into it," said Bobby. "This falsie, I mean fallacy, stuff is gonna drive me nuts. I'll be sittin' in a padded room, wearin' one of them special white jackets. Zeke and you will be in there visitin' me, tellin' me what's happenin' in the real world, and all I'll ever want to know is if the Giant's son still lives, 'cause as long as he lives, I ain't comin' out."

"Bobby, these fallacies probably seem a little confusing. All you'll need is some help at learning them. David can do that, not just for you, but for the whole class," suggested Aunt Lillian.

"Yes, we have our first Learning Club meeting Thursday," said David. "Did Mr. Gregory give you a list of fallacies?"

"Tomorrow," said Bobby. "Probably just wants to make sure we lose our wits and nerve in the meantime. Probably gets a commission on the number of kids he can drive into the nut house."

"Did he go through any other fallacies today?" asked David.

"A whole mess of 'em, enough to sink a battleship," said Bobby.

"Can you remember any others?" asked David.

Bobby thought for a minute, checked his notes, and answered, "Yeah. I think I wrote most of 'em down. The Giant's son suddenly yells, 'Attention. You're all gonna learn these fallacies 'cause I'm bigger than you are, and if you don't, you'll be really hurtin'.'"

"Gosh," said David. "Didn't anyone object?"

"Object?" said Bobby, "Everybody believed him. Then he starts laughin', and tells that he just used a false appeal to force, and everybody gives a big sigh of relief 'cause nobody wants to get their ears boxed, especially by a Giant's son."

"Any others?" asked David.

"Argument against the person," said Bobby. "He roped Jiggs into that one. The Giant's son states: 'We can't believe whatever a drunk says 'cause he's a no good drunk,' and asked who agreed. Jiggs raised his hand first, and the Giant's son then says, 'That's an argument against the person. You can't reject the person's argument for personal reasons, even if those personal reasons are true.'"

"Any others?" asked David.

"Yeah. And this is what took the cake, as far as I'm concerned," said Bobby. "The Giant's son asked, 'Does anybody have an opinion of how I'm teaching this class?' So I raises my hand and says, "Yeah, I do. I think it stinks.'"

"Wow! What happened? I see you're still alive," said David.

"The Giant's son laughs it off, and says, "That's a fallsie...I mean fallacy. He says, 'You're beggin' the question.' And I says, 'I'm beggin' to get out of here.' He laughs again and says that the fallacy I committed was like sayin' 'it's so, because it's so.' So I tell him I still think the class stinks, and he laughs again so hard that he has to sit down in his chair."

"What was the class doing?" asked David.

"Just watchin', wonderin' when he was gonna kill me dead, and I almost wish he had, 'cause I wouldn't have to have no more truck with these screwy little fallacies."

"Let me go over these with you tonight, Bobby," David offered. "It will help me when I review them with the class during our first Learning Club meeting on Thursday. Please ask for an extra copy of the list he gives out to you tomorrow. I'll work really hard on them tomorrow night."

"What's worse," said Bobby, "is that the Giant's son wants us to memorize and be able to use all of these fallacies. Ain't no way our class can do that."

"Why do you have to memorize them?" asked David.

"For the big test on Monday," said Bobby.

"What kind of test?" asked Aunt Lillian.

"The Giant's son says he comin' in and is gonna speak to us, and if we can stop him and catch him in a certain number of fallacies, then that will offer evidence to him that we can begin discussin' both in class and in the Learnin' Club," Bobby explained, "but it ain't never gonna happen."

"Don't be too sure," cautioned David. "Let's wait and see what happens tomorrow. On Tuesday, I asked Mr. Pennythorpe if he could stay with us, and he can, but only until about a quarter after four. He has a doctor's appointment at four-thirty."

"Ain't gonna be a long meetin' anyway," predicted Bobby.

"Why not?" asked David.

"The whole class is gonna jump out the window," said Bobby, "just like in the Great Depression."

"It's only a first floor classroom," David observed, "but I'll lock the windows just in case."

"The fortunate ones will get cut on the broken glass and bleed to death," Bobby rejoined.

"My dear boys," said Aunt Lillian, "we must not yield to despair."

"Why not?" asked Bobby.

"Because it might interfere with the good job you are going to do," said Aunt Lillian, adding, "on both your homework *and* the dishes."

* * * * *

Zeke Minturn and Dana Foley arrived the next evening at seven o'clock, carrying notebooks.

Aunt Lillian had offered to do up the dishes so the four young people could lay strategy for what would become future meetings of the Learning Club.

"So, you came prepared," said David, noticing the notebooks that Zeke and Dana carried. "Let's sit around the dining room table."

Bobby joined them at the table, holding his head in his hands.

"Bobby," asked Dana, "are you okay?"

"This class is drivin' me crazy, all these damn falsies—"

"Fallacies," corrected David.

"Whatever," lamented Bobby. "And I think this Learnin' Club is gonna finish me off."

"No way," corrected Zeke, "*I'm* gonna finish you off, good buddy, pal of mine. And I promise you that it will be long and painful."

"Nothin' could be worse than this," sighed Bobby.

"Oh, I could think of something," teased David.

Bobby gave David a sullen look, as if to say, 'And?'

"You could be condemned to spend three years listening to the Giant's son harping about fallacies and poetry," said David.

"Gimme a gun," Bobby said to Zeke.

"Ya gonna end it all?" asked Zeke.

"No. I'm gonna shoot David," said Bobby.

"You guys are nuts," said Dana. "Should we begin to plan, or should we just sit here and gripe?"

"Okay," said David, taking out a yellow pad. "If we meet twice a week, and have most of our speakers on Thursdays, then we can talk about what they said the next Tuesday."

"No way we're gonna remember what they said that long," protested Bobby.

"But if you *could* remember, think of how impressive that would be for Mr. Gregory," suggested David.

"Yeah. Then he'd give us some memory test and we'd all ring up a huge zero," said Bobby.

"David's right," said Dana. "If it's worth remembering, we'll remember a lot longer than just until the next week."

"Okay, okay," sighed Bobby. "But what about our programs. Who will we invite to speak to us?"

"It could really be anybody," said Zeke. "Maybe even some of the club members."

"Are you out of your mind?" asked Bobby.

"No. Why?" asked Zeke.

"'Cause nobody in our class or club ain't a public speaker, and all you'd hear would be them say, "I dunno," followed by a frickin' hour of silence."

"Don't be so pessimistic," said Dana.

"I agree," said Zeke.

"Bobby's just a little choppy because of all these fallacies," said David. "Don't mind him being so negative. He'll get over it."

"What we need is some ideas," said Zeke.

"And some focus," agreed David.

"So, who'll we get?" asked Dana.

A short silence ensued.

"Hmm," thought David.

"Yes?" asked Dana.

"I wonder if it would be to your advantage to ask Mr. Gregory to speak more than just at the first meeting?" asked David.

"It would be death itself," said Bobby. "First these damn fallacies, and then some other hoopla."

"No," protested David. "I mean it. He's a really bright guy. We could we ask him to talk about lots of different things," said David.

"Maybe he could read some of his poetry," suggested Dana.

"No way," said Zeke. "The club's supposed to be interesting."

"We've already asked him to speak about learning," said David.

"Yeah," said Bobby. "Maybe we'll actually learn somethin'."

"We need different faces," said Zeke.

Dana nodded in agreement, "Mr. Gregory is really smart, but we get him every day in class. You know, too much of a good thing—"

"—Good thing?" questioned Bobby.

"Come on, Bobby," scolded Dana.

"Okay," said David. "Let's just leave it that Mr. Gregory will be our first speaker a week from tomorrow. Who will we invite to speak after that?"

"Since this class and club are drivin' some of us batty, why don't we try to get a shrink to come in?" suggested Bobby.

"We'd be ripe for the pickin'," said Zeke.

"You two already are," retorted Dana.

"Wow!" exclaimed David. "I just asked Mr. Pennythorpe this afternoon for suggestions about speakers, and he told me about a former college student of his, a Dr. Clarence Baker, who is a clinical psychologist and he doesn't live far from Midville."

"Sign me up," said Bobby.

"*I'll* sign you up," said Zeke.

"Have this psychologist dude come in to talk to us on all this clear thinking jive. After all this hooey from the Giant's son, we'll have old Clarence right in the bag where we want 'im," suggested Bobby, sharing a wicked grin around the table.

"He'll have *you* in a bag," warned Zeke, "or maybe a net."

"Okay. Second meeting will be on Clear Thinking, a talk given by Dr. Clarence Baker," said David.

"What else?" asked Dana.

"Can them psychologists hypnotize people?" asked Bobby.

"I don't know," answered David. "I suppose so."

"Let's ask Clarence back to give us a talk and a demonstration about hypnotism. I could use some. Maybe he could put me under and convince me I like the Giant's son's class before he saws Zeke in two," said Bobby.

"They always saw a woman in two," corrected Zeke.

"Well," said Bobby, opening his arms and shrugging his shoulders.

Zeke drew his fist back and was ready to drive it home to Bobby when David said, "Enough. Let's get this program down."

"Hypnotism is fine by me," said Zeke. "Maybe he can convince Bobby he has a brain."

"I have a brain that works," said Bobby. "Do you?"

"You two fight like brothers," Dana observed.

"Okay," said David. "Let's start with these two programs and see where they go. If we get off to a good start, the club will probably run itself."

"And if we ain't so fortunate, the Giant's son will drive the club right into the ground, and we'll be ridin' along with 'im when he does it," said Bobby.

"Bobby," urged Dana, "be optimistic."

"I'll try," said Bobby.

"Who will contact the psychologist?" asked Dana.

"I'll ask Mr. Pennythorpe to call Dr. Baker," said David.

"Shouldn't we ask him to take a letter or something from us?" asked Dana.

"Good idea. After all, it's *our* Learning Club," David agreed.

"We ain't got no fancy paper to write on," said Bobby.

"We do need stationery," mused David to himself.

"Hey. We ain't gonna become stationary," said Bobby. "At least, not as long as I'm president of this club. We gotta keep movin', or the jaws of failure will snap us all back into the ninth grade."

"Bobby," frowned David, "stationery, spelled s-t-a-t-I-o-n-E-r-y refers to a kind of formal letterhead that groups create and use. We should create our own."

"Better put a dunce cap on it," sighed Bobby.

"What could we use as a mascot or symbol?" asked David. "What do you all think of when you think of learning?"

"Ugh," said Bobby. "School."

"Reading," said Dana. "I like to read."

"Working on a car," said Zeke. "That's where I learn stuff that's really important."

"Well, so far Dana has the best idea. I suppose we could put a book on our letterhead," said David.

"No way," said Bobby. "We ain't readers, at least, most of us ain't. Dana, here, she's different. Ain't that right, Dana?"

"Yeah. Bobby's right. Only about three or four of us like to read, at least those of us in Mr. Gregory's class," Dana agreed.

"That still doesn't change the fact that a book is an almost universal symbol for learning," said David. "What we really need now is a second image that attracts attention."

"What's that?" asked Zeke, raising his left eyebrow.

"Look," said David. "Anyone can have a learning club with a book for a symbol. That's pretty simple. What we need is something that makes ours special, that calls attention to whatever we do or write or say. We need something no one would ever associate with reading or books, and then put that next to an open book."

"Are you crazy?" asked Zeke.

"Yeah," said Bobby. "He's real gone. Why do think Aunt Lillian invited me in here to live? Cheaper than the happy farm. I've gotta keep my eye on him."

"Yeah, yeah, yeah," said David, rising. "Let's go to the computer. We can make a really nice stationery that will floor everybody."

"Ain't safe if it's gonna floor the Giant's son. That would be some wicked earthquake. I hope I'm not around if it happens," said Bobby.

At the computer, the foursome scanned image after image, with none standing out the way David had hoped.

"Let's look at the section on animals," suggested David.

"Animals?" asked Dana.

"Yeah. Do you know any animals that read books?" asked David.

"Only my little brother," said Dana.

"Well, we need something to startle the reader, and the picture of an animal reading a book would catch anyone's attention," said David.

"Until they put the net over us and pack us off to Green Acres," said Zeke. "We don't want people to think we're nuts."

"They won't," protested David. "This is only a metaphor."

"Meta what?" asked Zeke.

"Wouldn't you like to clock him?" asked Bobby. "I get that all the time. He's just too smart."

"A metaphor is a way of describing or saying something using something else, like saying 'the water was a sheet of glass.' Now water isn't really like glass, but the metaphor lets us know that it was really smooth."

"Or shiny," said Zeke. "Maybe even like ice. Now I get it."

"What kind of animal?" asked Dana, as David, sitting at the computer, scrolled through the list, the others standing behind him.

"Got it," said David. "Let me bring it up."

Bobby, Dana, and Zeke suddenly felt mild surprise at the creature that appeared on the screen.

"What in heaven's name is—" Dana began.

"It's a platypus," answered David. "This little guy is a monotreme, one of the most primitive groups of living mammals. It's possible that his earliest ancestors walked with the last dinosaurs."

"No way!" exclaimed Zeke.

"Ryan'll want to shoot it," said Bobby.

"Unlikely," said David. "The platypus lives in Australia and is on the endangered species list."

"So are we," said Zeke, "Especially if we don't pass English this year. My old man will kill me, or make me wish I was dead."

"The platypus is one of only three mammalian life forms that still survives from the Paleocene Epoch, which began about sixty-five million years ago," said David, retrieving facts from his encyclopedic mind and grateful for his science class report on the megafauna last semester.

"Gosh!" exclaimed Bobby. "Finally, somethin' as old as Mr. Pennythorpe. Maybe they know each other."

"Be serious," said David.

"If it's been around *that* long, it shouldn't be readin' a book. It should be *writin'* one," suggested Zeke. "Probably multi-talented."

David mulled over Zeke's suggestion, saying to himself, "Well, it *is* a marsupial."

"I dare you to use that kind of language in front of the Giant's son; he'll knock you to Syracuse and back again," challenged Bobby.

"I didn't swear," said David. "The word 'marsupial' refers to those animals that carry their young in pouches, like opossums."

"Opossums ain't too bright," said Bobby. "I ain't sure I want to take after a mascot that's any relation to opossums."

"The platypus is different because scientists couldn't figure out at first whether it was a mammal or something else. It lays eggs, has a duck's bill and webbed feet, but it also has fur."

"Hey," said Zeke. "We're an English class that's *really* different. This is perfect. Have the plata ... whatever it is, read a book."

"Platypus," repeated David.

"I hope it ain't gonna scare off that psychologist friend of old Pennythorpe's. I'm gonna need my noggin' examined when he gets here," said Bobby.

"Don't worry," said Dana. "When he sees this stationery, he'll bring at least two nets with him."

"You don't like it?" asked David.

"I love it," said Dana. "And I think the others will, too."

"Who's gonna write the letter to the shrink?" asked Bobby.

"You're the president of the club, Bobby," David smiled.

"Oh, no. Not me. They look at every little darn thing and make a mountain out of it, whether it's there or not. No way. I'm not even gonna say 'boo' when this dude comes to speak."

"Why not?" Zeke asked Bobby. "You're overdue. They must have a couple of openings at the State Hospital as we speak."

"If I get one," said Bobby, "you'll get the other."

"What would *you* write, Bobby?" asked David.

"I dunno," said Bobby. "Probably somethin' like: 'Dear Sir, We are all nuts; how are you? Why not come on in an' speak to us and try out your best nets. You'll make a bundle if you can catch us. Reserve a really big padded cell for Zeke Minturn.'"

"That would get a quick response, I'm sure," said Dana.

"Then you write it," said Bobby. "But be careful: they look at every little dot you make."

"Don't be so paranoid," said Dana.

"I ain't," protested Bobby. "Fair warnin'."

"Psychologists try to understand people," said David. "It's just part of their training to notice as much as possible."

"They ain't gonna dictate nothin' to me," said Bobby. "I ain't gonna be told how to dress or speak by nobody."

"They don't do that," said David.

"One of 'em interviewed me at social services when my pa was drinkin' his brains out," said Bobby. "He looked at me an' said, 'Ya know, son, you'll go a lot further in this here world if you dress to advantage.' So I looks at him and see his three piece blue suit and gold watch chain and cufflinks and all that rich stuff and thinks to myself, 'An' just where have *you* gone, workin' for this crumby little rag of a social services hole that ain't got enough sense to blow its brains out?' but I stayed powerful quiet, 'cause they hold the keys to Happy Acres, and I ain't got no hankerin' to get locked away. School is bad enough all on its own."

"Dana," sighed David, "I think that as Secretary-Treasurer of the club that you should write the letter. Let me print some stationery up and give you some envelopes. How about a dozen copies?"

"Sounds good to me," agreed Dana, as David pushed the print icon on his computer program.

"Ya don't mean you're gonna have her write it out in cursive?" asked Bobby, astonished at David's innocence.

"Why not?" asked David.

"'Cause that beggar'll look at every little curly cue she makes and say 'this here 'y' means this, and this here 't' stroke means that,' and before ya know, poor Dana'll be carted away."

"I can't wait to hear you introduce Dr. Baker," said David. "You'll be shaking so much, you'll stutter yourself silly."

"Listen. I ain't gonna introduce no psychologist no where, no way, no how. Just remember, they have them photographic memories, just like that little hoodlum Dandy-Pandy tried to get locked away and, mind ya, some days I wish he'd-a-done it. Trust me. They have X-ray vision, too. If that there psychologist dude shows up, I'm just sittin' pretty and not movin' a hair on my head," Bobby promised.

"Well, Dr. Baker would probably think you were wrapped pretty tight," teased David, hoping to egg Bobby on.

"That's what I mean. Damned if you do, and damned if you don't. They say, 'Draw a picture of your own self.' So I draw one of them stick figures, 'cause *that's* how I draw. An' then he peers his big nose down at me and says, 'You're blockin' on me,' which I meant to take he thought I was holdin' somethin' back. So I says, 'This here is the way I draw.' And he says, 'You're gettin' passive-aggressive.' And I says, 'I ain't never aggressive 'cept when I gets real mad.' So he says, 'Here, draw a tree.' And I did, and then he says, 'I see what ya mean. That's okay.' Then he asked me a mess of questions, and my head was swimmin' before I got done."

"Bobby," protested David. "Dr. Baker isn't coming to examine anybody. He's only coming to speak to the members of the Learning Club."

"Just you wait," predicted Bobby, "until he gets a gander at our rinky-dink outfit. He'll run straight to the nearest phone and call out the militia, and maybe the National Guard on top of that."

"I want to be there when he does," David grinned.

"If he does, and we get packed away like sardines into some padded cell, you'll be coming with us on the big ride, Davey boy," Bobby promised. "I'll tell 'im you're the one who's really nuts."

"Here, Dana," said David, lifting sheets from his printer, "I made a dozen copies for you. I put an open book in front of the Platypus, so it looks like it's reading. Here are some envelopes. If you need any help, let me know."

"I'll be okay," said Dana. "So we'll invite Dr. Baker to come on the 22nd?"

"Let's see. Yes, the Thursday after Mr. Gregory gives the first talk to the club. Let's check the calendar."

Chapter Six
The Need for Critical Thinking

AVID SAT LOOKING AT THE MEMBERS OF BOBBY'S CLASS as they entered Mr. Pennythorpe's classroom. Many of them looked sullen and unhappy. Of course, very few, if any, were used to staying after school, except for those who had earned an occasional detention. But this was Thursday afternoon, and who wanted to linger after school on a Thursday, of all days?

After everyone was seated, Bobby announced that all present should give David their full attention. David, for his part, took his place at Mr. Pennythorpe's desk, since Mr. Pennythorpe was engaged in running errands, clipping articles, and putting up a new current events bulletin board in the rear of the classroom.

"Thank you all for coming," David began, adding, "I know that most of you are a little nervous about these fallacies that Mr. Gregory has required you to learn. As I understand it, your test this coming Monday is going to be whether you can catch him using them. Is that right?"

Several members of the class nodded.

"What is a fallacy?" asked David, looking for an answer among a sea full of blank stares.

"Okay," continued David, "a fallacy is a flaw in reasoning or a mistaken belief. It is a term used in the art of constructing arguments. Does anyone know what an argument is?"

Again, a desert of blank faces greeted David's question.

David thought to himself, —This is not an especially good beginning. These kids don't have a clue about argumentation, and they don't seem to care. They're only looking for some hints to help them accomplish the task ahead.

Clearing his throat, David continued, "Look. I know that you don't really care about the art of argument. Who needs to know what a premise is? Or an inference? Or even a conclusion? What you need to know is how to smell a rat."

"A rat?" asked Zeke. "What's a rat got to do with it?"

"It's the smell as much as the rat. To smell a rat means to have an inner hunch that something isn't as pure or good as it presents itself. Another cliché for saying the same thing is to say that 'something is rotten in Denmark.' Because they are based on false arguments, why don't we think of fallacies as dead rats, giving off an awful stench. Flaws in thinking would be another way of saying it. To recognize fallacies, or maybe I should say to smell them, will require a little focus and memorization—"

Moans and groans began to fill the room.

"Listen," said David. "I've got a plan that will require most of you to learn only two fallacies, instead of fifteen or twenty. The only problem is that everyone has got to stay really sharp and pull for each other."

Suddenly David felt as if he had secured everyone's undivided attention. Taking advantage of his temporary victory, he continued, "I'm going to try to help each of you to recognize these flaws in common statements, but you'll need to memorize one or two fallacies and their definitions and a couple of examples in order to know what you're looking for. When Mr. Gregory tests you, each of you will have become your own expert on one or two different fallacies, and for those who pay extra special attention, probably even more."

"Won't Gregory catch on?" asked Sheila Morrison.

"He never said you all couldn't do it this way, did he?" asked David, smiling at his quick repartee.

"No," said Dana Foley. "We just need to be able to catch him out on the fallacies that he uses this Monday. He's going to come in and start speaking to us, and we're supposed to interrupt him when he uses them."

"And if I understand the stakes correctly," said David, "once you've proven that you know these fallacies, then you'll be able to have regular class discussions again."

"It's also supposed to help the Learning Club," said Dana, "so let's go. I'm willing to learn my one or two fallacies. David, I'm still not sure I understand why you call fallacies *dead rats?*"

"Because when you hear them, if you're really listening carefully, part of you will know that something's not correct. In other words, you'll smell a rat, meaning that you'll know something is wrong, even though you don't know what it is."

"How do we smell the rat?" asked Tammy Young.

"By learning a few simple flaws in thinking and memorizing them and then by banding together. Each of you will be able to recognize at least two different fallacies, although they can be tricky. I suspect that Mr. Gregory will be more interested in your being able to recognize these flaws of logic and thinking, rather than being able to name them chapter and verse."

"You don't know him very well, yet," sighed Bobby.

"Well, then, you may have to learn their names as well. But I don't think Mr. Gregory expects you to learn or to use their Latin names."

"What if we smell a rat, but can't remember which rat it is?" asked Tammy Young.

"Good question," said David. "If that should happen, then start saying, 'I smell a rat.' Keep doing that until someone identifies it. How about that?"

"That is the craziest idea I ever—" began Tammy.

"Hey, let's cooperate," scolded Bobby. "David ain't here for his health, but to help us, and we all need it. He's a straight A student and has better things to do with his time. But he's doin' us a favor."

"Okay, okay," agreed David. "We'll prepare for the worst. Let me look this list over. I am going to assign each of you at least two. That way, with a couple of you protesting, it won't seem so ... staged. Everyone please regroup and sit in your assigned seats."

The class shuffled around into their normal positions. Once everyone was in place, David looked at the students in front of him. It was obvious to him that none of them wanted to be there, yet the fear of not being promoted into high school had driven them to the extreme of staying after school to learn these fallacies. It seemed wrong to assign fallacies; that would be too much like the traditional schooling they all hated. A small voice echoed in David's thoughts, —Let them pick. Let them pick.

"I'm not going to assign fallacies," announced David, drawing a rough seating chart, "I'm going to make up a record of which fallacies you all decide to pick. Please listen carefully. I will read the fallacy to you and then I will try to give you a reasonable example of it. If it calls out to you, raise your hand. The first two people to volunteer will be assigned that fallacy. Is that okay?"

The class members stared at David, flabbergasted at being given a choice or any discretion for that matter over their collective academic destinies.

"Sounds cool to me," said Dana Foley, with several other heads nodding their approval.

"Okay. Let's start. The first fallacy is called *ad hominem*, which is Latin for 'against the man'. It is nothing more than a personal attack, but it is done in a way to discredit an argument that someone is proposing. For example, Zeke's opinion on anything shouldn't be believed, because he's a bum."

"You got that one right," said Bobby, as laughter echoed through the class. "That ain't no fallacy."

"Yes, it is," David corrected Bobby. "And you know that, too. Why don't you take that one?"

"Okay, okay," said Bobby, begrudgingly.

"Anyone else?"

"I'll take it," said Sheila Morrison, lifting her hand.

"Very good," said David. "Next fallacy: *ad baculum*, which is an appeal to force. Try this example: 'If you do not agree that action must soon be taken to stop these riots, then we will all die.' As you can see, the appeal to force need not be directed against the opposing side. It can involve a third party. Yes, Zeke?"

"Hey. What if, say Bobby, says to me, 'Zeke, you'd better agree with my argument that the Yankees will win the pennant, or I'll break your nose. Is that a fallacy?"

"Ain't no way," said Bobby. "Zeke knows I'd do it, and his big nose would be even puffier when I got done."

Again laughter rippled through the room.

"You'd have to stand on a stool to reach it," retorted Zeke, noting Bobby's slighter stature.

"No way," retorted Bobby. "It's long enough to reach the darn ground, just like one of them long, snooty African anteaters."

This time David couldn't repress his own laughter at Zeke's and Bobby's banter. Their humorous slams and playful bristling had enlivened the gathering, bringing new interest in the topic as well as to the emerging drama.

"You two have just used the *ad hominem* fallacy," announced David. "Zeke made a personal attack on Bobby's height, and Bobby returned the attack by making fun of Zeke's nose. Neither issue has anything to do with whether or not Bobby's use of a threat would be a good argument for Zeke to agree that the Yankees will win the pennant. Neither argument had anything to do with baseball. A good argument would cite relevant evidence regarding the current Yankee team. Instead, it was all a sort of verbal tug of war."

"I smell two rats!" exclaimed Dana.

Laughter broke out again.

"Okay, okay," said David. "Who wants this fallacy of appeal to force? Okay, Tammy, and Joey. Let's go to the next fallacy: *ad numerum*, which means to try to persuade by appealing to the fact that because a lot of people hold a particular view, that only their view is correct, such as saying, 'Twenty million Yankee fans can't be wrong—'"

"They can't," said Bobby.

"Yeah, yeah, yeah," rejoined David. "Any takers? Gordie and Jiggs, good."

"Another fallacy, closely related to *ad numerum* is what is called *ad populum*, or the appeal to a large group of people. An example would be: 'Friends, because we are patriotic and love the flag, our country is always right. Politicians use this fallacy a lot. Any takers? Mickey and Danny, great. Next fallacy: *ad misericordiam*, the appeal to pity. This is where the arguer tries to evoke pity to win support. An example would be: 'You've got to accept my position because I've broken my leg, and it's hard for me to stand up here talking to you.' That's kind of obvious. I suspect that Mr. Gregory's examples will be a little more subtle but, at least, you get the idea. Who would like this one? Zeke, good. Who else? Sheila. Great."

"Wait a minute. I just figured somethin' out," said Bobby.

"What?" asked David.

"This appeal to pity jazz. That's what girls use all the time to get their darn way," proclaimed Bobby. "From now on, I'll just say, 'You are committin' a falsie, I mean fallacy.'"

"And probably get clobbered for your trouble," said Danny, looking back at Sheila. "Go ahead, Sheila, turn on the waterworks."

Sheila stuck out her tongue at Danny.

"Ain't that right, though?" Bobby asked David.

"Hey, I'm staying completely neutral on this one," said David. "You can go ahead and infer whatever you want."

"No pluck," said Mickey, using one of Mr. Gregory's descriptors.

"No luck," retorted David. "I'm not going to cross swords with any of the ladies. They have their ways."

"See," proclaimed Bobby. "I was right. I rest my case."

"You may be resting more than your case," said Zeke.

"Yeah. I might drown in all the tears," said Bobby.

"Hey, chump," warned Dana, who was sitting next to Bobby, "don't underestimate any of us girls."

"I ain't," protested Bobby. "I'm just sayin' that your cryin' is really nothin' more than ... than ..."

"Manipulation?" asked David.

"Don't go helping him," scolded Dana.

"Excuse me," said Zeke. "Forgive my leader's annoying ideas; he has only half a brain."

"At least it *works*," Bobby shot back as laughter echoed in the room. "All this reminds me that little kids must use fallacies all the time when they argue."

"Adults, too," said David. "Let's keep going. We've got a lot more to cover. The next one is *ad ignorantiam*, which means 'argument from ignorance.'"

"A natural for Bobby," jabbed Zeke.

"It assumes that 'something is true because it hasn't been proven false,' or it could also be the opposite way, too. A classic example is: 'The Loch Ness monster exists, because nobody has proven that it doesn't.' Of course, this fallacy doesn't apply in court, where the accused is presumed innocent until proven guilty. Who would like this one? Gloria, good. And Mickey. What's next? *Appeal to tradition*. Okay, this means that someone argues for doing something because it's always been done that way. 'We should keep school to Monday through Friday, because it's always been that way.' No consideration is given to Saturday school, as they do in some European countries—"

"Must be why they have all those revolutions," quipped Mickey.

"Or," continued David, "that perhaps students should go to school only twice a week."

"Right on," agreed Ryan.

"Any takers?" asked David. "Jiggs, good. Mickey? You've already got two."

"That's okay. These are fun," said Mickey.

"Thank you," said David. "Next fallacy: *post hoc, ergo propter hoc,* which means: 'after this, therefore because of this.' This occurs when someone argues that two events are related that may not share any real connection. One example would—"

"How about: 'I hit Zeke, and Zeke hits the floor?'" asked Bobby.

"Hits the floor laughing," Zeke corrected.

"Not exactly," said David. "My example is this: 'I failed the exam; therefore, I will fail the course.'"

"Hey, what if it's the final?" asked Dana.

"Then it wouldn't be a fallacy, especially if you had a low average," said David. "Let's see, maybe I can come up with a better one. Yes. 'The driver chose a bumpy road and got a flat tire the next day.' Any takers? Jiggs, good, and Dana. Thank you. The next fallacy is very similar to the last one: *cum hoc ergo propter hoc*, meaning 'with this, therefore because of this,' in other words, that two events must be tied together, leaving out any other possible explanations. Here's an example: 'The student failed to stay for detention and broke his leg walking home." Any takers? Gordie. Thank you. And Ryan. Good. Let's see what's next. *Petitio principii*, which is begging the question. As noted on the sheets Mr. Gregory passed out, this is also called 'circular reasoning.' It's like saying, 'It's so because it's so.' Here's an example: 'Politicians are elected to perform their duties honestly; a public office is a public trust.' Any takers? Jennifer. Good. And Zeke. Thank you."

"How will we be able to recognize these things?" asked Ryan.

"Through memorization and practice," David encouraged. "We'll do a couple of trial runs after we've learned them. Let's see. The next fallacy is called a *non sequitur*, meaning that 'it does not follow'. It happens when one statement is not logically related to another. Try this one: 'It rained all day in the desert; therefore, we will have a mild winter in the mountains."

"Hey, isn't that the after this, because of this one?" asked Dana.

"You're right," said David. "It's the form of the statement. Better that I should have said, 'It rained all day in the desert and the winter in the mountains was very mild.' You see, there's no logical connection between one day of rain on the desert and an entire winter season in the mountains. Good point, Dana. Sorry to confuse everyone. Any takers? Mickey and Dana. Hey, you guys are really piling them up. Let's see. Next is: *bifurcation*, or the either-or fallacy. Example: 'If you sign this Declaration of Independence, you will either hang as a traitor or die as

129

a soldier.' No other options are considered. Perhaps the signer would not die at all. Any takers? Jennifer. Good. Tammy. Thanks. Next: *sweeping generalization*, meaning when someone makes a statement as if it were universally true. Example: 'The tourist wearing the Hawaiian shirt is rude; therefore, all tourists are rude.' Not all tourists are rude. Any takers? Dana again. Good. Ryan. Good."

With a deep frown furrowed into his brow, Bobby raised his hand.

"Yes, Bobby?" asked David.

"You know, I'm beginnin' to think I ain't never gonna open my mouth again," said Bobby.

"About time," said Zeke.

"Hey," said Bobby, shooting a glance at Zeke. "I mean it. I'm beginnin' to realize that whatever I might say will be full of holes—"

"Just like your head," razzed Mickey.

"There might be an extra hole in your head in a minute," warned Bobby.

"Appeal to force," challenged Mickey.

"And it ain't no fallacy," said Bobby, making a fist.

"Okay, okay," said David. "Let's go back to Bobby's statement. In a way, it's true of all of us. If we gave real scrutiny to a lot of what we say, we'd discover that it doesn't make much logical sense."

"A wonder that we can understand each other at all," said Dana.

"You're right," agreed David, "but we also use gestures, body language, and facial expressions to help out. Let's move on to *hasty generalization*. This happens when someone maintains that something is so because of a single reason. Example: 'Zeke slipped on the stairwell; therefore, that stairwell is very dangerous and must be banned to all other walkers.' Perhaps Bobby shoved Zeke—"

"You mean knocked," corrected Bobby.

"Hey. Isn't that just like the after this therefore because of this?" asked Dana.

David thought for a moment, responding, "You're right. It's my wording again. All of these fallacies are closely related. They come in clusters. You'll notice shades of other fallacies in almost every fallacy you learn; that's because they share common flaws in logic. I should have said, 'Since Zeke slipped on the stairwell, it must be banned to all other walkers.' Maybe Zeke was wearing slippery shoes. Who wants this one?"

"I'll take it, since I would've pushed Zeke anyway," announced Bobby, giving a triumphant look to his friend.

"And Maureen," said David. "Very good. What's next? Oh, yes. *The Fallacy of Accident.* This is when a general rule is applied to a particular case, such as, 'Students generally dislike school. Therefore you all must dislike school.'"

"That ain't no fallacy, at least not in this room," proclaimed Bobby.

"Do all of you dislike school?" asked David.

Ten hands were raised, then another, and then one more.

"So, Dana, why don't you dislike school?" David inquired.

"It's okay, I guess. Better than just sitting around home doing nothing. I mean, I don't like all the work, but I like seeing my friends."

"And Mickey?"

"Same for me. I like seeing my friends. The work goes with it. So I can't really say I dislike school."

"So," concluded David, "my assumption, going from the general to the particular, didn't hold up, even in this class. Any takers? Danny, good. And, Jennifer. Thanks. Now, what's next? *Fallacy of Accent,* which is shifting meaning by emphasizing a certain word. For example, the statement, "Our friends are coming to our *rescue*," changes in meaning when we emphasize the word 'friends' like this, 'Our *friends* are coming to our rescue." The last casts doubt about whether the people are really

131

our friends. Any takers? Okay, Bobby. And Zeke. You guys should have some fun with that one."

Laughter again filled the room.

"I will have fun; *he* won't," strutted Bobby.

"I *don't* think so," retorted Zeke.

"Two examples as we speak," said David. "What's next? Oh, yes. *Tu quoque*, meaning: 'You're another.' Example: 'Why should we believe you? You're nothing but a liar.' Any takers? Bobby again, and Danny. Thanks. Next fallacy: *Slippery Slope*, meaning that if a certain thing happens, then all kinds of harmful things will happen afterward. Example: 'If students were required to go to school on Saturday, there would be a general rebellion and much damage to the school buildings in this community.' Any takers? Mickey, okay. Anyone else? No. Okay, the next fallacy is: *Complex Question*, meaning that the question assumes a definite answer to another question which hasn't even been asked. The classic example is: 'Have you stopped beating your dog?' The question asks whether you've stopped, but assumes that you have actually been beating your dog, which may not be true. Any takers? Larry, okay. And Tammy, good. Next fallacy: *Red Herring*, which is when something is introduced into an argument to divert attention away from the real argument. An example would be if you said, 'Learning is important,' and someone said, 'We can't afford to keep schools open in the summer so students can learn throughout the year.' Any takers? Larry and Sheila, good. Thanks."

"Ain't we ever gonna get done with these?" asked Bobby impatiently.

"Only a few more. But we'd better learn them all, or Mr. Gregory will surely find out."

"He'll smell a rat," laughed Dana.

"No. He'll smell a hole in students' preparation," corrected David. "Next one, and there are only a few more here, although there are more fallacies than these, is: *Straw Man*, which is when someone tries to misrepresent another person's position, and then tries to discredit that position. Say Mr. Gregory comes in and asks, 'How many say learning is important?' and you all raise your hands. Then he says, 'How can you suggest that learning quaint little facts is important when the world's wisdom is waiting to be discovered?' Do you get it?"

Class members nodded.

"Then who wants it? Maureen and Gloria. Thank you. Next up is: *Equivocation*, which is when a key word is used in two different ways, for example: 'Free market opportunities promote a free press and a free electorate and a free society.' Those involve different kinds of freedoms, the first is economic and the others are Constitutional, and they are not necessarily related."

"Hey. You lost us," said Ryan. "Could you say that in plain English?"

David thought for a moment.

"Okay. Ryan, your note to the attendance office says you were sick last Monday. What was your illness?"

"Huntin' illness," said Danny.

"Pretend you were sick, but not really sick," said David. "What was your illness? What were you sick of?"

Ryan brightened, saying, "I was sick. Sick of school."

"I think in that example the difference in meaning is implied, rather than stated directly. Let me try another. These fallacies are tricky little devils, aren't they?"

Everyone nodded grimly, studying their sheets.

"How about this one?" asked David. "Everyone in the fancy nursing home had great wealth, and the wealth of their experience allowed them to discuss their interesting lives.' I know that's not the best example, but I'm learning these along with you. Who wants the equivocation fallacy? Larry. Thanks. What's next? Oh, the last two: *Fallacy of Composition* and *Fallacy of Division*. These are related and they're easy. The Fallacy of Division has two different expressions. The first is when one assumes that a characteristic of the whole is also true of its parts. For example, 'You live in a neighborhood driven by drugs. Therefore, you must be a drug addict.' The second form is to assume that some aspect of a group is also true of a part of that group: 'Termites can destroy a house. Therefore, one individual termite can destroy a house.'

"The Fallacy of Composition also has two applications. One is when it is assumed that the qualities shared by the individual parts are also true of the whole, for example, 'This truck is made of light weight material, so the entire truck is light.' The other application is when we assume that what is true of one unit of something is shared by a larger collection of those items, for example, 'A car uses less gas than a bus. Cars emissions do less damage to our environment than buses.' Now, who wants these fallacies? Dana. Hey, go for it."

"I've got more than you do," teased Dana, looking at Zeke and Bobby.

"But not more than me," said Mickey. "We each have five."

"No way," said Dana. "My last two are split, so that makes two more. Right, David?"

"You guys have to work that one out on your own. Our job now is to get into groups to help each other learn these fallacies, and then I'll will pretend to be Mr. Gregory, and you'll try to catch me out whenever I use a fallacy. Okay?"

The class agreed, and soon each row of three were working together with great focus and diligence.

Chapter Seven
A Flock of Fallacies Found Wanting

ONDAY'S CLASS SESSION COULD NOT HAVE ARRIVED SOONER as far as members of the class were concerned. Most students were worried that their diligent work from the previous Thursday would be lost, owing to some of their number not having been able to remember the fallacies that they had attempted to memorize.

Having asked Mr. Gregory if he could sit in to observe the class session, David had situated himself in the rear of the classroom with a yellow pad, and waited to record the progress of the class.

Mr. Gregory, for his part, had dressed to the hilt for the occasion. Instead of wearing his usual dress trousers and sports shirt, he wore a three-piece blue suit, light-blue shirt, and red tie. No one had seen him display so much panache, and it almost seemed an incongruity for a published poet to look so affluent. But any real poet, like Nathan Gregory, broke all of the so-called rules most of the time anyway.

"Attention," he announced, his athletic frame rising to its full height as he rose from his desk, "this is the day we've been waiting for. David Andrews is sitting in the back to monitor your progress; I know that he coached you all last Thursday, and now that you've had the weekend to memorize the fallacies that we studied, let me test you to see how adept you all are in recognizing them and ferreting them out. I am going to begin speaking, and I promise you I will use many, if not all, of the fallacies you have learned. Your job is to stop me and point out each fallacy that I've used as soon as I use it. Any questions?"

Bobby raised his hand.

"Yes, Bobby?"

"I ain't quite got the hang of this yet, sir. Is the van from the funny farm waitin' outside to collect us after we've trashed our brains tryin' to figure these critters out?" asked the class president.

"You don't approve of clear thinking, then?" Mr. Gregory baited Bobby.

"Ain't got no notion of what's clear and what ain't clear, but whenever I get a notion if somebody's cheatin' me or lyin' to me, then I paste 'em a good one right in the nose," replied Bobby.

"Violence is never an acceptable answer, Bobby," observed Mr. Gregory.

"You and David should sit together," said Bobby. "These here falsies, I mean fallacies, ain't done us normal dudes any good. We ain't got no desire for this, and we ain't gonna be driven to it, so you might as well call the van to take us all to Happy Acres."

"I think you overrate the power of these fallacies," said Mr. Gregory. "Let's see how well you all do at recognizing them."

David sat in the back, grinning at Bobby's recriminations of fallacies. Late Sunday night they had conspired for Bobby to make this urgent protest, a strategy that would serve to dramatize the difficulty of fallacies and to engender in Mr. Gregory low expectations for the performance of the class. David only hoped that it would somehow soften Mr. Gregory's expectations of this particular group of reluctant learners.

Mr. Gregory walked over to look out the window closest to his desk, and announced, "Bobby, don't worry. The van is already out there waiting. If things go awry, I'll open the window and give them the signal to come in. How's that?"

Students next to the windows stood up to peek out and immediately laughed, with Ryan Baxter explaining, "Hey! There really is a white van out there. No kiddin'. But nothing's written on it."

"They move quietly these days," Mr. Gregory assured the class.

Most of the members of class then raced to the windows to observe the white van that might serve as their conveyance to Happy Acres.

"Ain't big enough to hold the whole group," observed Bobby.

"It'll probably make several trips," Mr. Gregory assured the class. "Anyway, this has been a great diversion, and I've enjoyed it as much as you have. I'm confident you'll do very well with our contest."

David sighed. The Giant's son had seen through Bobby's ruse, and now there could be little hope for mercy should any in the class fumble their fallacies.

"Everyone ready?" asked Mr. Gregory.

Class members looked agitated and unsure, but nodded in the affirmative, despite their uncertainty. Mr. Gregory cleared his throat, suddenly intoning in a loud voice, "You had better all agree that fallacies are important or you're going to be really hurting."

"Appeal to force," said Tammy Young, her swift response fully credited to her having suffered the intimidations of her older brother for many years.

"Very good," said Mr. Gregory.

David looked over at Joey Harris, who had also been assigned the fallacy of appeal to force. Unfortunately, it was obvious that Joey was in some other world; fortunately, he had only been assigned one fallacy. If Tammy hadn't come through, the contest between the Giant's son and the class would have been a very short one.

"We cannot believe anything that Bobby says because he's no lover of fallacies," continued Mr. Gregory.

Bobby's eyes shot wide as he looked around for someone to defend him, but then he remembered that he himself had been assigned the *ad hominem* fallacy, and raised his hand just as Sheila Morrison said, "That's an attack against the person. You're pretty rude to do that."

"And you're rude, too," responded Mr. Gregory.

"That's the 'you're another' fallacy," Bobby defended, glad that he could come to Sheila's rescue.

"This is an excellent beginning," proclaimed Mr. Gregory. "I was hoping to get the best of you, but I am not at my best today. I was up late last night helping a neighbor looking for his poor, lost dog, so I only got two hours sleep."

"You're appealing to pity," said Zeke Minturn. "Were you really up that late?"

Mr. Gregory laughed and shook his head, glad that Zeke had ferreted out the fallacy.

"Well, nobody has proven that I *wasn't* out that late," he retorted.

Mickey Drexel waved his hand, shouting, "Argument from ignorance. It doesn't wash. That's false reasoning."

Mr. Gregory nodded.

"Let's face it: public school is a good thing because the vast majority of Americans pay taxes to support it," said the Giant's son, changing topics.

"You're appealing to numbers," said Jiggs Stevenson. "You forget that people don't have a choice whether or not to pay taxes."

"It's also like the *non sequitur*," said Dana Foley.

"More than an appeal to numbers, Jiggs," said Mr. Gregory, "I think that my tax fallacy would be—"

"That's begging the question, isn't it?" asked Jennifer Lawler.

"Who knows?" said Mr. Gregory. "I will certainly not *embarrass* you because of your suggestion."

"That's undue accent," shouted Zeke, adding, "Yes!"

"Do you always shore up your guesses with such bravado?" retorted the Giant's son.

"Wait, wait, wait!" called Larry Jones.

"Complex question, complex question," Tammy Young agreed.

"Albert Einstein wouldn't recommend Brand X toothpaste," stated Mr. Gregory.

The class sat dumbfounded. David looked at his notes, and began to wonder if he had forgotten to cover the fallacy of false appeal to an authority.

"I smell a rat," said Mickey Drexel, stalling for time.

"I smell a rat," agreed Gordie Chase.

"I smell a rat," said Bobby Perkins.

"Hey, Einstein was no *dentist*," said Zeke.

David sighed in relief. It had been a close call. Thank heaven some of the class members had picked up on the rat smelling metaphor. That members of the class had recognized the fallacies they had been assigned was admirable enough, but that Zeke should have recognized one that had not been reviewed or assigned was nothing short of a miracle.

"We should only have to go to school for four months out of the year," continued Mr. Gregory.

"Appeal *ad populum*," said Danny Taylor.

"If this class favors only four months of school a year, then all classes favor the same thing," continued Mr. Gregory.

"Hasty generalization," called Maureen Grant.

Bobby also nodded his head.

"But if there were only four months of school, nobody would learn anything at all, and soon the entire society would crumble from pervasive ignorance," said the Giant's son.

"That's the slippery slope one," shouted Mickey Drexel, waving his hand. "You can't assume those things would necessarily follow."

'It's also a little like the 'after this, therefore because of it' fallacy," said Jiggs Stevenson.

"Fallacies mirror each other and some are very similar," continued Mr. Gregory, "but either you will identify it or you will not."

"That's the either-or fallacy. Bifurcation, isn't it? Maybe we'd just invent a new name for it or something like that," said Tammy Young, elbowing Danny Taylor as if to say, 'Agree with me.'

"Should I assume that just because one brick is easy to lift, that this school building is also easy to lift?" asked Mr. Gregory.

"Fallacy of composition," said Dana. "We can't assume that it's true of the whole."

"And if a herd of elephants could destroy an entire forest, then one single elephant could do the same thing?" rejoined Mr. Gregory.

"The opposite fallacy," said Dana. "Fallacy of division."

"How about the game laws in Africa?"

"That's a red herring," said Larry Jones, nodding confidently.

"I should give a written test on these fallacies because that's the way it's always been done," announced Mr. Gregory.

The class was momentarily stunned, until Jiggs Stevenson said, "That's false appeal to tradition."

"But that's what's always been done," argued the Giant's son.

"Prove it," challenged Bobby.

"Prove it false," retorted the Giant's son.

"That's the *ad ignorantiam* fallacy," shouted Mickey Drexel, giving a thumbs up and looking around for support.

"Yeah, that's it," agreed Gloria Adams.

Mr. Gregory sat down at his desk and smiled at the class.

"I am so proud of all of you. You've really done a good job with the fallacies I assigned. I think we're now ready to go to stage two."

No one in the room liked hearing about any 'stage two.'

Bobby raised his hand, "Sir, do you mean we passed our fallacies test?"

"Yes," confirmed Mr. Gregory. "And with flying colors."

"Ain't no need for stage two, then," prompted Bobby.

"Oh, yes, there certainly is. That's where we get into the real fun of applying what we've learned."

"What's stage two?" asked Dana.

"Public speaking, of course," said the Giant's son, at which point Gordie Chase almost went through the floor. An introverted and quiet soul, Gordie Chase's preferred personal stance was 'out of sight, out of mind.'

"No way," said Bobby.

"It's easy and fun. You'll see," urged the Giant's son. "Now I want you all to take out a piece of paper and begin thinking about a topic you know quite a bit about, preferably a topic which might be controversial in some way."

After a reasonable interval of three or four minutes, Bobby Perkins raised his hand, confessing, "Ain't no use pretendin' 'cause I don't know nothin' about nothin'.'"

"Which means that you know something about something," Mr. Gregory smiled. "What *is* that something, I wonder?"

"It sure as heck ain't grammar," shot Zeke, repressing a smirk, as Bobby coughed.

"Maybe it's about punchin' in your best friend's face," Bobby retorted, slamming his right fist into the palm of his left hand as he looked at Zeke.

"Now, almost everyone is ready for the next step. Here's your task: you've been asked to speak for five minutes about this subject which you know quite a bit about. Decide what position or argument you would like to take, and then organize your notes for your talk. Take about ten minutes to do this."

Students labored over their assignment.

Finally, Mr. Gregory announced, "Okay, when I call your name, you're to come up here and give your presentation. Begin by telling us your topic, and then make your argument ... that you are for or against a particular thing that relates to the subject you've chosen. The job of your classmates will be to find holes, or fallacies, in your argument. Let's see, who should we invite to speak first?"

"Why not the class officers?" suggested Mickey Drexel, giving an upset Bobby Perkins a confidential wink when he turned around to glower at his friend.

"Good idea. Dana, you first," said Mr. Gregory.

Dana had real pluck. Without hesitation, she strode to the front of the room and placed her notes on the lectern that sat on the teacher's desk. She was wearing a dark blue turtleneck over her light-faded-blue jeans.

"My topic is women's rights," she proclaimed, "and I favor equal rights for women."

Groans and sighs emanated from several males in the class.

"If two individuals perform the same job, those individuals deserve equal pay. Unfortunately, if one of those individuals is a woman, she usually receives less compensation than does a man. This is inequality and it is wrong."

"Hey, hey, hey," remonstrated Mickey Drexel.

"Hey what?" asked Dana. "I'm not a cow, you know. I don't like hay. What's your point?"

"My point is that, 'If you're the MAN, ya get paid, 'cause you're carrying the whole load. It takes a MAN to make the big decisions."

Dana composed herself as she challenged Mickey, saying, "That's *exactly* the kind of chauvinistic attitude that has made men so insensitive to women and to inequality."

"Hey," protested Mickey, "I'm all for equality. It's a woman's place to stay home and to raise the family and cook the meals. Talk about easy street, when the poor husband's out working his buns off in some dirty, noisy factory."

The temperature of the room had now risen by at least two degrees, as every eye followed this emerging debate on equal rights for women.

"Women are capable of doing anything that men are," said Dana, adding, "and just because they are women should not be the reason they are excluded from equal opportunity."

"I'll tell you where it went wrong," said Mickey. "It's when they got the right to vote. That's when they suddenly imagined they needed to hold an opinion other than their husbands', and it's gone downhill ever since."

"That's the 'after this, therefore because of this fallacy'," said Tammy. "Your argument is not logical, Mickey."

"Hey, I'm just tellin' you what went wrong," said Mickey.

"That's the fallacy that says 'it's so because it's so'," said Dana.

"Men are the stronger sex," protested Mickey.

"So why do women live longer?" retorted Dana.

"Because the men do all their work for them," said Mickey.

"You're a bigot," said Dana.

"Uh, uh. That's the *ad hominem* fallacy," said Mickey, "and you're one, too, for that matter."

"And that's the *tu quoque* fallacy," said Dana.

The class sat dazzled in the heat of their argument, never having before witnessed such fire and passion in an academic setting.

"I think that's enough," said the Giant's son. "Class, I have a small confession to make. I asked Dana and Mickey to stage this argument to show you how much fun fallacies and arguing can be. Their words do not *necessarily* reflect their real opinions."

"Mine do," shouted Mickey.

Dana glared at him and the temperature of the room dropped significantly.

"Just kidding, Dana, just kidding," he said, laughing to himself. "I have four sisters and, believe me, I *know* from their experiences just how rough it is for girls to get anywhere in this world."

"Thank you Dana and Mickey. You have managed to get everyone's blood up, so let's keep going. Who'd like to present an argument and face rebuttal?"

"I'll go," volunteered Zeke Minturn.

Mr. Gregory gestured to Zeke that the lectern was all his.

Zeke strode confidently to the teacher's desk, placing the notes he had scribbled on the lectern.

Clearing his throat, he announced, "My fellow students, it is time to shorten the school day."

Everyone sat silent because everyone agreed.

Zeke continued to pause, expecting someone to challenge his use of the fallacy of *ad populum*.

Instead, everyone wanted to hear more.

"Why must students spend so much time imprisoned behind these brick walls? Students need time to relax, time to think, time to consider their studies."

The reign of silent approval continued, although David started to scribble some notes on his yellow pad.

"Students get too much homework as it is, and between the time they spend in school and the time they take studying at home, they are left with little or no time for other interests or activities. Reducing their homework would reduce the stress they feel from school."

Again, silent approval led the way, with many students nodding.

"I think we should also shorten the school year," Zeke added, drawing a full round of applause from his classmates.

"That way, students could get jobs that would help to prepare them for the real world, not to mention earning a little cash to blow on stuff they like, like going to see the most recent flicks."

"If the school day and school year were shortened, students would be able to use the extra time to better advantage and would like school more. They would be grateful for the change. Thank you."

Applause greeted the end of Zeke's argument as he sat down.

"Are there no dissenters?" asked Mr. Gregory.

The entire class sat silent, lending its full approval to all of the sentiments Zeke had conveyed in his argument.

"Did anyone hear any fallacies in Zeke's proposal?" asked the Giant's son.

Again, unanimity of support shouted from the ensuing silence.

"His argument is full of flaws," said David.

Everyone turned to listen to this now unwelcomed intruder.

David stepped forward to the lectern.

"Just because we might agree with what somebody says doesn't mean that whatever that person says makes any kind of sense," said David.

Several hands shot up in protest.

"Let's give David a chance to rebut Zeke's argument," said Mr. Gregory. "David, it's all yours."

"Well, let me rebut what Zeke said in the order that he said it: first, Zeke, you argued that the school day should be shortened. You were appealing to students for popular support using the *ad populum* fallacy, and you also were saying that it should be so because it should be so, hence you were using circular reasoning; next you said that students shouldn't be imprisoned behind these brick walls, which is the fallacy of appeal to pity."

More hands shot up in protest.

"Let David finish, please," prompted Mr. Gregory.

"Next, Zeke, you again used the *ad populum* by advocating a reduction of homework so as to reduce student stress levels, but how do you know it would do that? What would happen when students found out that they weren't prepared to qualify for even the simplest jobs because they had not been required to learn anything?"

All hands were now up and waving.

"Finally, you suggested that if the school year were made shorter, students would use the extra time to better advantage. Well, I want to rebut every assumption you've made. First, you commit the fallacy of 'after this, therefore because of this' when you suggest that a shortening of the school day would give students more time to relax and to think and to consider their studies. How do you know that they would do this? Maybe they would just use the extra time to loaf around some more."

"Me, me!" yelled Zeke, waving his hand, wanting to rebut David.

"Not yet," smiled Mr. Gregory.

"Furthermore, school should be seen as preparation for the real world, not as a prison. What we do during these crucial years will help to determine how successful we become in the world. Your plan, Zeke, would condemn everyone to a minimum wage job and a lifetime of frustration and resentment. I guess I'm done."

"Zeke, go ahead," prompted the Giant's son.

"Davie, boy, you've got it wrong. You're making assumptions, too. How do you know that students would waste the extra time?"

"Because they waste the extra time they have now, don't they?" retorted David.

Zeke thought about it for a moment, replying, "Well, everyone needs to veg out a little now and again. We can't go like gangbusters all the time."

"Hey," protested Mickey, "we've got a right to do what we want, and if we want to waste time, we should be able to waste time."

"But what does that get you in the long run?" asked David.

"Mr. Dandy's job?" inquired Bobby Perkins.

The classroom erupted in laughter at the sly slight.

"I'm not saying that people can't choose what they do," explained David. Let's face it: people do choose to do what they want to do. What I'm saying is that what they choose is often NOT in their best long term interests. They grab at the fools' gold today and forsake the diamond of tomorrow, the diamond that comes from hard work."

"Are you calling us fools?" sputtered Tammy Young.

"Not at all. I'm just saying that students tend to be lazy and waste time. The school day provides a necessary discipline and routine and, even with that, they slack off and don't do their work."

"Hey. School is boring," said Danny Taylor.

"Only because students haven't worked hard enough to earn the satisfaction that comes from getting involved," said David, adding, "You should only expect to get back what you put in."

The class found itself dumbstruck by this disarming insight, for few, if any, had ever put very much into school, and the shoddy results of their many years of glib involvement now rose up to haunt them.

David seized the moment to his advantage, turning to Danny, "You say school is boring, Danny. That means that time drags on and on and on, doesn't it?"

"Yeah. I suppose so," agreed Danny.

"Is it dragging on right now?" asked David.

"Not exactly," said Danny, considering the engagement of his classmates in the current debate.

"That's because you're more involved than usual. That's part of the secret. At least, that's been my experience."

Members of the class sat silent, considering David's revelation.

"Yeah, but how often is school like this?" asked Danny.

"Usually teachers just yap at us," added Tammy.

"But that's the whole point. If we students took more responsibility, teachers wouldn't have to stand up there and yap. *We* could yap, and it's a lot more fun when *we* yap than when *they* yap," said David.

"This is an interesting digression, but does anyone have any more specific rebuttals to David's rebuttals of Zeke's argument?" asked the Giant's son.

David's words had left students speechless, for those words were powerful reminders to class members that, from their own experiences, they knew that his insightful observations carried more than a little truth.

"Well, if no one wants to argue any more with David, does someone else want to take the class on?" asked Mr. Gregory.

Jiggs Stevenson raised his hand, announcing, "I will."

Approaching the lectern, he decided to step out in front of it, since his relatively short stature impeded his view of the entire class.

"I'm here to advocate that more consideration be given to people who are both short *and* tall. These people have to suffer being squeezed or stretched to average sizes. Think of how hard it is for someone who is six foot ten inches to sleep in a regular bed, or how hard it is for me to peer over lecterns."

The class appreciated Jiggs' self-deprecating humor and laughed heartily.

"We need to be sensitive to those who are different. Let's give consideration to those of us who are shorter or taller than average. Thank you," concluded Jiggs.

Hands shot up, and Mr. Gregory said, "Jiggs, you call on them."

"Okay. Mickey?"

"Hey, little brother," began Mickey. "Do you know how much it would cost if companies had to accommodate all sizes? I mean, it's the average production that makes everything so reasonable."

"I'm just saying that more consideration could be given," said Jiggs.

"You're appealing to our *pity*, but I'm appealing to my *wallet*," retorted Mickey.

"Yes. It's not our fault that someone is shorter than average or taller than average," said Gloria Adams.

"I'm only asking for a little sensitivity," said Jiggs.

"I think that I would like to tell you all a little story about a man who became very rich," said the Giant's son. "It may not seem too relevant to our current topic, but please indulge me."

Of course, the class was always ready for any kind of diversion, including stories, although stories, since this was English class, fell near the bottom of the ladder, whereas fire drills were universally on the top of every ladder of every class diversion list, owing to the happy fact that they helped to liberate students from their stuffy classrooms.

"This is the story of Tony, a man who became a tycoon," began the Giant's son. He always had a good business head, and he invested wisely. Finally he was able to buy the most expensive penthouse in New York City. Each morning, he would always take the elevator to the first floor, where his limousine would be waiting outside for him; but each night, when he arrived home, he would have to take the elevator to the sixtieth floor, and then walk up five flights to the sixty-fifth floor. The question is, 'Why?'"

"'Cause he wanted some exercise after sitting all day in some stinking office," said Ryan Baxter.

"No. Sorry, Ryan," said the Giant's son.

The class pondered the riddle.

Bobby finally raised his hand, saying, "The little guy was too short to push the button for floor sixty-five."

"That's exactly right," said the Giant's son. "Does it make anyone a little more sympathetic?"

"Not me," said Mickey Drexel. "Anyone with that kind of dough could afford a little pointer or umbrella or servant to push the button for him, or a private elevator, for that matter."

"I admit that's very true," confessed Mr. Gregory, "but the real point of the story is to remind the listener that what most of us take for granted for convenience's sake is not necessarily the experience of those who are unusually short or tall of stature. I, myself, have trouble getting into small cars, and my bed had to be built especially for my height."

"Maybe we could suggest putting two different door knobs on doors or making all beds a little longer," said Dana Foley.

"But, but," started Mickey.

"Oh, hush," scolded Dana. "You and your precious wallet. Let a few of those moths fly out to get some fresh air. If the standard were a little larger than the norm, at least it would help the tall people."

"Good point, Dana," said Mr. Gregory, "thank you."

"She's just suckin' up," retorted Mickey.

"Not!" countered Dana. "May I please go next?"

"Certainly," encouraged the Giant's son.

Dana walked to the lectern as Jiggs sat down.

"My argument is a very simple one, and I hope that you are all listening," Dana began. "Good manners are a thing of the past, and it seems to me that society would be a much better place if we were to return to basic courtesies like saying, 'please' and 'thank you' and 'beg your pardon', and maybe bring back a little chivalry with some of the nicer guys opening doors for the ladies, and maybe people dressing a little better."

Most of the males in the class were smirking at each other as Dana was speaking, and she was not unaware that they were making fun of her proposal, but this did not deter her passion or her enthusiasm.

"It wouldn't hurt to be more polite; in fact, it would help. Thank you."

Danny Taylor's hand shot up.

"Yes," said Dana.

"Hey, why not let Jiggs here open the doors for everybody? That way there'd be no confusion," said Danny, elbowing Jiggs who promptly thrust Danny's arm away.

"Confusion over what?" asked Dana.

"About who'd be opening the doors," said Danny.

"Hey," objected Mickey Drexel, "who said guys should open doors for gals, anyway?"

"It probably goes back to the knights of the round table," said Dana.

"Why shouldn't it be the other way round?" asked Zeke. "Let the girls open the doors for us. After all, we're the superior sex."

"Superior egos, you mean," corrected Dana.

"Can anyone find any fallacies in these statements?" asked the Giant's son.

"It's the *post hoc, ergo propter hoc* one," said Jiggs. "Just because manners are brought back doesn't mean that our society will get any better."

"Yeah," agreed Zeke. "It might get worse. Some dude opens the door for the gal to walk through, and BAM, she's the one who takes the bullet instead of the guy."

"Give me a break," sighed Dana.

"Hey," objected Larry Jones, "why is it always equal this, equal that when the gals think they're not getting a fair deal, and then it's open the door for me, please, if you will?"

"It's just basic politeness," protested Dana.

"Why did men open doors to begin with?" asked Jennifer.

"Probably because the women were holdin' the babies," volunteered Ryan Baxter.

"Any other fallacies?" asked the Giant's son.

"Hey," said Bobby, "wait a darn minute. I just figured somethin' out, and I *really* smell a rat."

"What's that, Bobby?" asked Mr. Gregory.

"Seems to me that if we take these fallacy things real serious-like, they just bide their time to come back on us. Like, I mean, if I say to you, 'It's a beautiful day,' you could rise up and turn against me and say, 'What do you mean by beautiful? The day is ugly, unless you call that sunshine on the garden pretty, which it ain't. I mean, we ain't got nothin' to say to each other with these fallacy things hangin' over our heads. No matter what anybody says, someone can find a flaw."

152

"Bobby has latched on to an important truth about critical thinking and fallacies," admitted Mr. Gregory. "The truth is that language itself is very imprecise and unclear, even when used extremely well, and it is not too hard to make a fallacy out of almost anything. We have studied the more common ones, and their relevance and degree all depend on the context in which they are used. In other words, to say, 'The sky is red this morning; it will rain tomorrow,' might be a fallacy or it might not be. The old seafaring expression, 'Red sky at night: sailors' delight; red sky in the morning: sailors' take warning,' is based on experience and memory and might have some logic and credibility. Of course, if the morning sky is red because of some other reason, or if the standard weather patterns do not apply, then it is an unfounded prediction, thus becoming the fallacy of 'after this, therefore because of it.'"

"Then how do we ever know if we know anything?" asked Bobby.

Mr. Gregory gave a huge smile, responding, "There was once a Greek philosopher named Socrates who wondered the very same thing, Bobby. He asked others to explain to him things that he didn't understand. No one could, at least not to his satisfaction. Finally, old Socrates decided that he was a little clearer than his fellow philosophers, because he had managed to reach a point where he could admit that he *knew* he didn't *know*."

"Must've ended up in the looney bin," said Bobby.

"He was sentenced to death and made to drink hemlock," said the Giant's son.

"That's *one* way to get away from all these cursed fallacies," Bobby concluded. "Must have been pretty glad, too. Bet he took a big swig."

"Socrates was one of the clearest thinkers that the world has ever known," said the Giant's son.

"Then I bet he'd get a real rip out of this class," suggested Bobby.

"Perhaps he would," smiled Mr. Gregory. "Perhaps he would."

Chapter Eight
The Giant's Son Speaks of Learning

THE FIRST OFFICIAL MEETING OF MIDVILLE MIDDLE SCHOOL'S NEW LEARNING CLUB was fraught with anticipation and excitement. The club was open to all who were curious about everything, and David had invited Lisa, Mary, and Sean to come. Sean had also invited half a dozen of his friends. Even Mr. Pennythorpe showed up at the last minute and shook hands with the Giant's son, who was assembling a number of materials on his desk in preparation for his presentation.

It seemed only right that the club meetings be held in Mr. Gregory's room, for the club was, in fact, an inspired extension of class deliberations. Dana Foley stood next to the Giant's son, inquiring about when she should call the meeting to order and introduce the club's very first speaker.

After a few minutes, Dana stepped to the lectern, announcing, "My name is Dana Foley, and I am the Secretary-Treasurer of the Midville Middle School Learning Club. The reason that I'm calling this meeting to order and introducing our first speaker is because our notable president and vice-president don't have the guts to do it."

Laughter abounded in the classroom, although astute observers could notice that two faces, those of Bobby and Zeke, had turned slightly red.

"It is my pleasure to introduce to you Mr. Nathan Gregory, our English teacher, who is our speaker today. We have asked him to address us on the topic of learning. Mr. Gregory."

Striding purposefully to the podium, Mr. Gregory acknowledged the warm applause that followed his introduction, saying, "Thank you, Dana, and thank you everyone for your generous welcome. I congratulate you all on taking the time to spend a couple of hours after school to look into this curious question of learning, since learning is what school is about or, perhaps I should say, what school *should* be about. If the truth were told, school, at least from the perspective of most students, is more about seeing friends, playing sports, and avoiding genuine engagement in the learning process.

"Now, that may sound like heresy, especially to parents and school board members who fancy that schools are like the ancient Greek academies, where wisdom was sought for wisdom's sake. But not so today, since we live in a society that gives lip service to the value of learning, and spends very little money to back up its claims. Since actions are louder than words, we must conclude that learning, at least formal learning in school settings, is not a high priority in our society."

Those assembled had never heard such heresy, and they not only liked it, they agreed with it. Finally, *someone* had come forward with enough guts to tell the truth or, at least, part of the truth.

"Inherent in the formal schooling process, there can be found any number of factors which inhibit learning on many levels and in many ways. It would be sufficient today to address, in passing, only several of these, for the main focus of my presentation today is centered on learning styles, how individuals learn, and we will soon have some fun exploring those styles.

"Now, back to the consideration of some of the factors that inhibit learning, and these, I hasten to remind you, are taken from my reading as well as from my own limited experience. The first is fear. Fear is perhaps the most inhibiting force in our society, for we live in a world driven by fear.

"Now you might ask yourself, 'How could anyone be afraid of learning?' And that is a very good question. Let's look honestly at the kinds of peer pressure students put on each other. Is not one of those pressures the unwritten law of conformity? What do we call students who dare to excel, who dare to strive for excellence, and who succeed? We call them eggheads, brains, Einsteins, and we discredit them and their efforts through our ridicule.

"Now why is there such ridicule? Perhaps we see in their successes our own failures, for we really do envy them, don't we?"

Bobby Perkins raised his hand.

"Yes?"

"Sir, can we interrupt your speech with questions?"

"Yes, of course. What's your question?"

"More of a comment. I mean, I ain't a brain and I ain't dumb, but I think I can understand how some kids feel when they meet one of these here brains, I mean, it's downright furiating."

"I think you mean *in*-furiating," suggested the Giant's son.

"Whatever," shrugged Bobby. "That new word must mean 'mad as hell', 'cause that's what these little brains make most of us, 'mad as hell'. I mean, take for instance, just for example, a little seventh grade magpie genius who jabbers all the time and never shuts up. I mean, ain't that a bit much? It stymies the nervous system, and I've had my fill of it from time to time. But say, and this is just supposin', that some little seventh grade magpie has one of them incredible photographic memories and ain't afraid of nothin', not even the law itself—then, in truth, society is faced with the new problem of severe hoodlumism. Now mind you, appearances ain't what they seem—some of these little magpie seventh graders can look just like innocent lambs when it fits their purpose, but then they go around jabbin' little toy guns in people's backs when it suits their fancy."

Mr. Gregory smiled at Bobby's obvious passion for this particular subject, but asked, "I'm not sure I get your point, Bobby."

"That's 'cause I ain't got to the point yet," said Bobby.

"Please go ahead then," encouraged Mr. Gregory.

Bobby didn't realize that what he was doing was engaging in triangulation, speaking to someone through someone else, in this case to Sean through Mr. Gregory; needless to say, however, the little hoodlum sat in the rear of the room, all ears, committing to memory every single syllable that fell from Bobby's lips.

"Well, as I was sayin', you've got this little magpie menace that never shuts its little yappin' mouth, knows everything about everything, but needs to be stopped, I mean, *really* stopped, just so it knows that it ain't gonna rule this whole planet and all the people who suffer here for its little games and antics."

"What do you mean by *really* stopped?" asked Mr. Gregory.

"I mean *in its tracks*, but it ain't that easy. It's been tried. I mean, a whole gang of us boys tried once at a church. And there ain't a one of us today who still don't hobble around in pain; I mean, this little magpie just bent our toes back 'til we were blind. This little hoodlum is indestructible; that's what he is, but mind you, there's a growing lot who are plottin' his downfall."

Sitting in the back corner of the room, Sean for once resisted his fearless impulse to yell, 'Do it! I *dare* you.' Bobby's triangulation had put Sean's friends in stitches of laughter, which they were trying to suppress, especially considering that no one wanted to be rude in the Giant's son's face or to become involved in some dire contretemps.

"Bobby, your point still escapes me," said Mr. Gregory.

"This is it," said Bobby, "and I mean it, too. You spoke of some of us slower learners gettin' mad at the brains, and I'm givin' you an example. I mean, I would just like to put my hands around this little magpie's neck and start squeezin' *real* hard. Mind you, I wouldn't kill 'im, but he'd sure as heck never talk again."

"I hear you saying that a certain individual tends to upset you, and that you have even considered hostile responses to that individual's irritations," summarized the Giant's son.

"If that means I'd like to kill 'im," said Bobby, "you're right."

"Maybe there's a non-violent way you can settle your differences," suggested Mr. Gregory.

"Ain't no good in this case. Been through that with David and, I've got to admit, it worked with him. Nope. No satisfaction if I can't wring the little magpie's neck. It's just too smart for its own good, if you get my drift."

"I hereby appoint David Andrews as a committee of one to devise a fair and non-violent settlement of differences between Bobby and this other party," said Mr. Gregory, looking at Bobby and adding, "That means you've got to give a little to get a little."

"You ain't aware of the half of it," protested Bobby. "I mean, just before you came to this school, I was havin' it out with this little magpie right down on the first floor near the teachers' room. I *owe* him a big one, and I mean a *really* big one, and this has his name on it—"

Here Bobby clenched his right fist and held it above his head.

"—and he was bein' a pill to David last Christmas time and right into January, so I push him up against the wall and tells him he better stop makin' everybody so miserable. Then he looks up at me and gives me some guff and gets me so mad that I clench my fist and drive it home, expectin' to let him have it right between the eyes. The only problem is that the little magpie ducks, and I drive my fist right into the fire alarm box, making a frickin' bloody mess of my hand. And the fire bells start ringin' and ringin' as I try to keep my hand from spurtin' blood all over the floor. I give the little magpie some credit, though, 'cause he bandaged me up good 'til old Ferlinghausen could take me to the hospital. But it ain't right, and I still owe him a *really* big one."

"I think that with so complicated a history of involvement, I would defer to David's recommendation," suggested the Giant's son. "David, will you please take this issue on?"

David nodded his agreement to do so.

"Well, Bobby has given us a robust example of how easy it can be to dislike someone who seems to excel at something and, perhaps in this particular case, at *everything*. My point, though, is that we all have unique talents and gifts, and that we are ultimately only in competition with ourselves. Whenever we strive to do our very best, nothing is ever disappointing, no matter whether we succeed to the level of our expectation or not.

"If we *choose* not to risk, for fear that we might fail, then we adopt for ourselves a construct of non-growth, out of which can come *no satisfaction* because we have not tried our best. Yes. We may fear the ridicule of our peers if we show enthusiasm for learning, but why should their attitude control our choices and actions?

"There is a subtle, silent, leveling down of potential learning, one that grows from the anonymous majority of students, shouting the unspoken message that the 'pursuit of excellence in learning new things in school is *not cool*.' But I submit for your consideration that this posture grows directly from the fear of failure. If we avoid doing our best, or perhaps doing anything at all, we are able to avoid the possibility of *risking* and *failing*. Better that we should not try at all and fail on our own terms.

"Learning doesn't become interesting until we become *engaged* in its mysteries, its demands, its challenges. How can we hope to find meaning in something, anything, if we don't become involved? Why do we so often *choose* not to learn? Perhaps there really is an unseen 'union' of students, one where the unwritten rules prescribe that students refuse to do anything more in school than merely go through the motions."

Zeke Minturn raised his hand.

"Yes, Zeke?"

"But why learn something that isn't gonna help you in the future?"

"Could you give us an example?"

"Yeah. How about poetry?"

"How do you know that poetry might not be of some use to you when you get older?"

"*Believe* me, I know," said Zeke.

"That sounds like a fallacy," the Giant's son smiled.

"The 'it's so because it's so,'" chortled Bobby.

"Shut up!" Zeke warned Bobby.

"Okay," said Mr. Gregory. "How *do* you know, Zeke?"

"Hey. I don't like poetry and I don't understand it. Why should I bother with it? It's not gonna help me in my job. I'm gonna become a car mechanic. How will poetry help me there?"

"Does knowledge always have to be utilitarian?" asked Mr. Gregory.

"Utili what?" asked Zeke.

"Utilitarian means 'to stress the value of something's use or potential use over other considerations," explained the Giant's son.

"Yeah. Why learn something unless you can use it?" asked Zeke.

"But *how* do you, or does anyone else, ever know what he or she will ever use?" asked Mr. Gregory.

"Like I'm gonna use poetry when I'm fixing an engine," said Zeke, as members of the club erupted in laughter.

"Why not?" asked the Giant's son. "Poems afford us insight into life. Why not occupy your time with something that might help you to see life more clearly or in a richer way?"

"Because I don't understand it," said Zeke.

"But if you were to work at understanding it, then you would be able to muse over it. You also would have mastered a new area of learning, and that would help you with subsequent areas of learning," suggested Mr. Gregory.

"Hey. Why bother? I'd never use it," said Zeke.

"What if you met a girl you liked a lot, and what if she really liked poetry?" asked Mr. Gregory.

Zeke considered for a moment, saying, "I don't know."

"See. Already you're not quite sure that something you have rejected may or may not prove of some future importance to you," the Giant's son observed.

"Zeke, the poet," Bobby chortled.

"Bobby, the moron," countered Zeke.

"Okay, okay," warned Mr. Gregory. "Only time and experience will prove if what I'm suggesting to you has any merit," continued Mr. Gregory. "But I ask that you keep it in the back of your minds. I also ask that you give all new ideas a chance. Personally, I believe there's something of value in everything we learn, because learning is not an isolated event. It relates to all the other learning we might become engaged in, and it reaches us on many levels and in many depths. Already, thanks to the short time we spent on fallacies, you have a new understanding of what clear thinking is about. Today you noticed fallacious statements and arguments everywhere you looked; a few days ago you had not the slightest inkling of their existence, yet you made many judgments based on statements and arguments that, upon careful examination, carried little weight. Are there any questions before we proceed?"

The speaker's case had been so well made that no could think of a plausible objection.

"The focus of my talk today is not on the theory of learning, but rather on modes of learning. By mode, I mean the 'way' in which an individual learns. Researchers have discovered that all types of learning may be gathered into four major learning styles.

"But before we look further into that, I would like to propose a little experiment that will illustrate my premise better than any talk that I could give. I have here a short Learning Styles inventory that I would like each of you to take about ten minutes to complete. Once you've finished, please bring the paper forward. It will take me only a few minutes to score them, and then I will assign each of you to one of four groups. After we have formed into groups, I will then give you some tasks to accomplish. How does all that sound?"

Unaccustomed to being asked for their agreement or approval, everyone sat dumbfounded, looking at each other, wondering what the inventory would reveal. For lack of any objection, the necessary forms and response sheets were distributed and soon everyone was busy answering the questions.

After all the forms were completed and submitted, Mr. Gregory announced, "I will need only a few minutes to tally these sheets. Please take a short break. I'll call the meeting back to order when we're ready to continue."

Conversation erupted throughout the room, as students began to discuss the inventory they had just taken. Suddenly Mr. Gregory held his hand up, and the room quieted, "You don't have to remain in your seats. Why not get up and move around or go out into the hall for a drink of water?"

No sooner were his words spoken than all of the members of the club rose, as one entity, and then proceeded to mill about. Five minutes later, Mr. Gregory rose from his desk and flashed the lights in the room. Club members quickly resumed their seats.

"I appreciate the fact that we have guests here today," began Mr. Gregory, alluding to David, Lisa, Mary, and Sean and his friends. "I am going to divide my English 9 students into four distinct groups as would reflect their learning style preferences. The rest of you will receive your inventories back, together with information about these various styles. The reason I want to limit the working groups to my class is that I hope to build upon this procedure during class hours, and therefore today's club meeting will serve as an important beginning. But let me first give you all a brief introduction.

"Some years ago, a group of high-powered professional educators did some important research on the ways people learn. As mentioned earlier, they discovered that all learning styles could be combined into four basic styles. They also found that students' learning-style preferences are pretty well divided among the four groups. Most learners seem to favor one style over the other three. Nevertheless, it is essential and important that students, in their perceiving and processing, become comfortable with each learning style and be able to garner information and results through each mode of inquiry.

"Let me first reassign the seating arrangement of my English 9 students. The following students should form Group One back by Ryan: Jiggs Stevenson, Larry Jones, Tammy Young, Jennifer Lawler, and Gloria Adams. Here next to Danny Taylor, the following should form Group Two: Dana Foley, Mickey Drexel, and Gordie Chase. Over here where Zeke is sitting, the following students should form Group Three: Ryan Baxter, Bobby Perkins, Zeke Minturn, and Danny Taylor.

Finally, Group Four should form back where Joey is sitting: Joey Harris, Maureen Grant, and Sheila Morrison."

Students moved quickly to join their new groups.

"Now, let me tell you about the learners in Group One," began the Giant's son.

Bobby Perkins raised his hand.

"Yes, Bobby," asked Mr. Gregory.

"It ain't so good to be in Group Three," Bobby began. "I ain't a rocket learner, but I ain't the slowest sittin' here."

"The group numbers have absolutely nothing to do with native intelligence or I.Q., Bobby. They are merely arbitrary classifications for convenience. No one style is better than another, while each offers its own unique advantages and, I suppose, disadvantages. It's very important to become conversant in all of the styles, and not just the one in which you feel most comfortable."

"But why are all the best students in Group Two?" asked Bobby.

"Not all of the best students are," replied Mr. Gregory. "But all of the members of Group Two are good students, and the reason for that is that our traditional system of teaching favors the linear model, that of teaching facts and concepts. These three students prefer learning in that way, and since most schools prefer teaching in that way, it is a convenient match, a relationship of mutual advantage."

"You mean they ain't got to work as hard as we do?"

"Probably not, at least when learning facts and concepts," admitted the Giant's son. "Hopefully, school requires more than that from both them and you."

"It ain't fair," said Bobby.

"Life ain't fair," retorted Mr. Gregory. "We've got to get over all this fairness business and work to compensate for our shortcomings.

That way, our personal status is never anybody else's fault, but rather becomes *our* responsibility."

Bobby folded his arms and glowered his disapproval, but Mr. Gregory ignored his negative body language and continued.

"I think once we get into this, it will make more sense. Let me, at least from the information given on the learning inventories, introduce you to the members of each group, telling you a little about their learning preferences. The rest of you who took the inventory but who are not in these groups can follow along, for I have indicated which group you would be in.

"For Group One, we find a preference for a learning style built on imaginative learning. These students learn by feeling and watching, by opening themselves to learning from those around them, by becoming involved together in solving a problem or joining together in common quest for an answer. They like conversation, especially if it brings clarity. These students look especially for personal meaning, and the question they frequently ask themselves is 'Why?' Does this profile fit those of you sitting in Group One?"

Jiggs, Larry, Tammy, Jennifer, and Gloria all looked at each other, considering the words of the Giant's son and nodded to him as well as to each other.

"Remember, please, that we are painting with a broad brush stroke, and that these descriptions are meant to be loose overlays of preference. In no way does it box any of you in. Some of you might, in fact, like parts of other learning styles and do quite well with them. But, by and large, the inventories you took would suggest that your basic preference is for imaginative learning."

"Does that mean the rest of us ain't got no imagination?" bristled Bobby, raising his hand.

"Not at all," smiled Mr. Gregory. "We are merely looking at preferences. We all have excellent imaginations, and perhaps we should trust ourselves to use them more than we do. After I review some of the characteristics discovered about each learning style, I will talk briefly about how we all process information and perceive the world, which both deepens and connects all of the styles on a new level. Bobby, you may well be happy with the qualities ascribed to your group. Please be patient.

"Now let's look at Group Two. These are the students whom the universe has favored, for their learning style preferences most closely match most schools' teaching-style preferences. You are more interested in learning facts than anything else, because through facts you are able to master new concepts. You also like to listen and to think about information; you, in truth, are great detail people. The fancy name for this learning style is analytical, as in analysis. You want to learn the facts, after which you want to consider the new ideas those facts bring, and then you want to find out what the experts say."

Dana, Mickey, and Gordie nodded in agreement to all that Mr. Gregory was saying.

"For Group Three, we find a preference for a learning style built on common sense—"

"Hey, what's Zeke doin' in there?" asked Larry Jones. "He's real dangerous with a hammer."

"On your head, maybe," retorted Zeke.

"—students who are mostly interested in building and tinkering," continued Mr. Gregory, ignoring the interruption. "Those who prefer this learning style are most comfortable when they are building and fixing things. They combine thinking and doing in masterful ways, often by fixing things others can't. They combine theory and practice, and are very skills oriented. They just seem to 'know' how things work, how things are put together, and they love to experiment—"

"Can this here hammer hit my thumb?" said Larry, imitating the tone and character of Zeke's voice.

"Shh," scolded Zeke, who had become interested.

"—these learners," continued Mr. Gregory, "ask the question, 'How?' They make things usable. Do you all resonate with this description?"

Danny, Ryan, Zeke, and Bobby all nodded their heads.

"Ain't right to know so much about anybody," protested Bobby. "Have these here researchers been spyin' on us?"

"No. These are the findings of massive research studies and the wisdom of some of the finest minds in education and psychology today," explained Mr. Gregory.

"Now, to our last group. Group Four learners are called dynamic learners. They combine doing and feeling. They like to look beneath the surfaces and to explore hidden possibilities. They learn by trial and error as well as by self-discovery. Do these findings reflect your preference for learning styles?"

Joey, Maureen, and Sheila all nodded in agreement.

"Now, we have identified our learning-style strengths. We must also be mindful that we need to be able to identify and survive in the other styles, as well. Now what comes easiest is usually our preference. It's harder to give the extra effort required to accomplish learning in ways that we don't feel entirely comfortable and, in fact, that we may never feel comfortable. I suppose it's really more a matter of application, accommodation, compensation, and persistence."

"Does that mean trial and error?" asked Dana.

"I suppose it does," smiled Mr. Gregory. "Let me now speak briefly about the processing of information, which has two sides. The first is reflection. That's when we transform the knowledge we encounter into various kinds of structure and order. It is a highly intellectual process, and it often brings keen insights. The other side of processing information may be found in its application. This is called action. Our ideas are of little use unless they can find dynamic expression in external form. An architect's vision of a house is of little use unless he can set that design to paper; susequently, a builder is commissioned to build the house, thus bringing it to its fullest completion. This processing is a matter of testing our ideas in the world and adapting what we learn from those tests to the situations we encounter.

"John Dewey, the famous American philosopher and educator, believed that learning is real only if it instills purpose and direction in the learner, thus leading that learner to change and transformation."

"But school is so *boring*," said Maureen.

"Are you bored now?" asked Mr. Gregory.

"Well, no, but this is different," replied Maureen.

"Only because you have become engaged in our topic of conversation," suggested the Giant's son. "You have surmised that there may be purpose and direction to our inquiry, and you intend to test that. As a dynamic learner, you are taking the risk of integrating this new knowledge into your own world-view, which might or might not result in your re-thinking your belief that school is boring. Perhaps it is boring sometimes, even most of the time, but can we really say *all* of the time?"

Maureen thought about it, frowning to herself.

"I tend to learn by trying stuff out," said Maureen.

"That's part of your natural style," said Mr. Gregory.

"I don't do well in school," Maureen complained.

"Perhaps because you've never really tried," suggested the Giant's son. "At least, not from the advantage of being engaged in whatever was going on. Does school seem really slow to you?"

"Yeah, and much too repetitious," said Maureen.

"Perhaps it would become more interesting, should you ever decide to become engaged in the process," said Mr. Gregory.

Maureen considered this suggestion from the Giant's son, murmuring, "I'll think about it. Maybe you're right."

"Has anyone heard of the expressions 'left brain' and 'right brain'?"

"How about no brain?" asked Mickey. "Zeke knows all about that."

"You're just jealous because you're not in Group Three," retorted Zeke. "We're the ones who keep things running."

"We're the ones who—"

"—I think we will dispense with friendly rivalries during my talk," suggested the Giant's son, looming slightly over Mickey.

"Yes, sir," said Mickey. "Sorry, sir."

"Current thinking is that we process the information we receive from the world differently in each of these two brain hemispheres. The left-brain mode of processing is sequential in nature, meaning that it works in external, linear time. It is precise and uses reason and objectivity in its analysis and judgment of all information received. The left mode knows things that we can describe precisely, using classification, discrimination, and naming. Of the two modes, it is the one that is most adaptable to learning in traditional school settings.

"The right-brain mode of processing operates from feeling and intuition. It prefers images and patterns, wholes and relationships, as opposed to facts and figures. It is a very subjective mode and listens to its heart, as opposed to the logic of its head. Those who process information in this way know more than they can tell. Any questions?"

"Are you sayin' that we're one or the other?" asked Bobby.

"I am saying that each person tends to have a natural preference for one mode or the other. In point of fact, we all use both modes of processing. The best goal is to become double dominant."

"Double what?" asked Dana.

"Double dominant," explained the Giant's son, "which means that a person is equally versed in both modes of processing information. I would suspect we all prefer the mode which is easiest for us, but these distinctions, if anything, help to remind us that we all don't perceive the world in exactly the same way."

"I don't get it," said Zeke, scratching his head.

"Let me give this example: say Maureen back there has a natural preference for processing information through her right brain. That would mean that she is more comfortable in looking for patterns in relationships, looking at images instead of numbers, of looking for connections to the larger whole, getting subjective glimpses of how things work. She would tend to trust her intuition more than a facts-and-figures-data report; whereas, let's say Dana is more comfortable in processing information through her left brain, which means she would be much more analytical in her approach to things. She would also be linear, meaning that one would have to take things in order: 1, 2, 3, and so forth, whereas Maureen might skip from A to L to Z to S."

Bobby raised his hand, frowning in confusion.

"Yes, Bobby?"

"This here brain stuff is all hooey. It ain't nothin' but somethin' a group of them think-tank brains dreamed up to confuse everybody," Bobby concluded.

"Is there a fallacy in your statement?" asked Mr. Gregory.

"He's falling victim to the 'it's so because it's so, or circular reasoning," said Jiggs.

"Shut up, or I'll give your butler's head some circular reasonin' it won't soon forget," threatened Bobby.

"Appeal to force fallacy," Jiggs said smugly, raising Bobby's ire all the more.

"Now, hold on, there," scolded the Giant's son. "Let's be polite and calm down. Why are you so upset?"

Bobby thought for a minute, and then said, "'Cause I ain't got no clue as to what the hell you're talkin' about. I hate to be lost. I've always hated it, and I feel lost right now."

"Do you ever feel lost in school?" asked Mr. Gregory.

"Sometimes," snorted Bobby, looking around. "Just like everybody else here."

"Bobby, how do you know if something is true?" asked Mr. Gregory.

"I just *do*, that's all," said Bobby.

"Are you ever wrong?" asked Mr. Gregory.

"Not usually, but sometimes, yes," replied Bobby.

"So, you turn your mind to something, trying to figure that something out, and suddenly you understand it, a situation, a moment, or the way something works?" asked Mr. Gregory.

"Guess you could say so," admitted Bobby.

"See," said Mr. Gregory to the class, "Bobby uses his intuition to know things. And it's not that he can't use his reason; I would guess he uses plenty of that when he's trying to put something together. But he also listens to his heart, and he intuits answers to problems."

"Why ain't I able to intuit the right answers on tests?" asked Bobby, surprised that a chorus of laughter followed his question.

"I don't know," said Mr. Gregory, shrugging. "Perhaps because most tests are linear and factual. They don't accord well with intuition. Is it also possible that you may not have learned the required material?"

Bobby's face became red, as he murmured, "Yeah. It's possible."

"Intuition isn't a shortcut away from doing the required work. It's just a different *way* of getting information, as well as getting a different kind of information. I suppose someone *exceptionally* skilled in intuition would do quite well on tests, possibly without even having learned the information. But that sort of thing falls back on one, especially if it becomes a pattern," explained Mr. Gregory.

"No wonder I ain't no brain in school if I process with only my right brain," said Bobby.

"But we all use both," said the Giant's son. "You use both, but you probably favor your right brain. As I said before, it's important to try to become proficient in both modes of information processing."

"I feel dumb," said Bobby.

"But you're not dumb," said the Giant's son. "No one is. It's all too easy to become bogged down in these descriptions of processes, which appears to be happening right now, and that is not my intent for what I hope we will accomplish together today. Now that you've been placed in groups according to the information you gave on the learning styles inventory, let me invite you all to accomplish a task. The best learning is often about problems—solving problems. What is more enticing than a mystery? So ... I have one to give to your groups. I want you all to work with each other and come up with an answer. The answer need not be correct. The most important thing we're looking at right now is the HOW of what you do. I want someone in each group to monitor the process, or perhaps I could prevail upon some of our club members who are not part of my English 9 class to monitor group interaction. The problem is in these envelopes. Please take at least twenty and no more than twenty-five minutes to accomplish your task. We will then have reports to the larger group from each small group. Good luck. Oh, yes. Each group should elect a leader and a reporter."

With that concluding announcement, Mr. Gregory passed out the envelopes which contained the problem that was to be solved. Groups examined the contents, and began to work assiduously toward a solution.

Each of the envelopes contained the following task:

Your group is responsible for planning and constructing San Francisco's celebrated Golden Gate Bridge. Public funding is not an option for financing this project, and hundreds of millions of dollars are needed. Decide what will be the most effective first three steps toward the implementation of this project. A list of historical facts, figures, tables, and engineering information is given on the attached three sheets for your general information and planning strategies.

GOOD LUCK WITH YOUR PLANNING

The hum of conversation and debate filled the air. The Giant's son walked about the classroom, listening to the deliberations of each group and smiling.

After fifteen minutes, Mr. Gregory asked, "Do any groups still need more time?"

Almost all hands were raised.

"Okay. Take another ten minutes."

"That's not enough time," protested Maureen.

"We need to make sure that there's time to report back to the big group as well as to complete part two of this assignment. Do your best and don't worry, this is not for any grade or anything like that."

"What's it for then?" asked Zeke.

"Just for the satisfaction of figuring something out," said the Giant's son. "It should also lend insight into the four different kinds of learning styles."

After ten minutes, Mr. Gregory called the room to order.

"Okay, let's hear what each of the groups decided to do. I know that you may have had some help from our visiting members, and that's just fine. I'm most interested in knowing what you decided were the most important first three steps. How about Group One?"

"I was the reporter," announced Tammy Young. "We decided the first step was to figure out why a bridge like this would be important."

"What was your second step?" asked Mr. Gregory.

"Then we decided that if there was going to be a bridge, that it would have to be talked about a whole lot, and gain a lot of support among the people. So we decided to form a committee that would bring the possibility to the public through a lot of discussion, using the news media, talk shows, public forums."

"And your third step?" Mr. Gregory prompted.

"Then we thought we should try to raise the money, but we didn't come up with any ways how to do that, at least, not yet."

"Thank you, Tammy. Thank you, Group One. Now, let's ask Group Two how they would proceed."

"I'm the reporter for our group," announced Dana Foley. "We couldn't see any successful completion of this project until real plans and drawings were made. That would help people to get the idea of what we were talking about. So, we decided to form a bridge commission and borrow money to hire experts to do the initial planning."

"And then?" asked Mr. Gregory.

"Then we thought we would come up with ideas on how to sell the whole idea to the people of San Francisco, since they would be buying the bonds for the bridge's construction."

"Yes. Please continue," urged the Giant's son.

"Then we decided to do a business plan that would show how the bridge could pay for itself after many years."

"Great work. Group Three?" said Mr. Gregrory.

"I'm the reporter," said Zeke Minturn. "We decided that if we could show how the bridge would help others, how it would be useful, then we could get some start up money and hire someone to design it and someone to build a model. That was our first step."

"And then?" asked the Giant's son.

"Then we decided we would appoint a committee to figure out how to get the whole idea approved and the money raised."

"Good. And then?"

"That's as far as we got," said Zeke. "We were rushed for time. Rome wasn't built in a day, you know."

Mr. Gregory laughed to hear Zeke lob such an old cliché at him, retorting, "No. I think it took three days, didn't it? How about Group Four? What did you come up with?"

"We weren't convinced that the bridge was the right answer," said Sheila Morrison, "so we considered ferry boats, plane shuttles, and other alternatives to see if it would do the same job as the bridge does. None of the alternatives seemed to do as good a job, so we looked at how a bridge could be funded privately, with maybe half a dozen investors, and how much money it would generate."

"I see. You took an entirely different approach. What was your conclusion?"

"That the bridge really was the best solution after all, and then we ran out of time," responded Sheila.

"You have all done exceedingly well, and predictably well, too, if we compare your preferred learning style to your preferred approach to solving this problem."

"Wasn't it stacked that way," asked Zeke. "I mean, the way you put all of us together who like to learn in the same way, at least according to that questionnaire you had us fill out?"

"Exactly," agreed Mr. Gregory. "You are anticipating my next step, which is to divide the groups, so that at least one member of each preferred learning style will be present."

"Hey. We can't do that," objected Mickey. "Group Two has only three members, and we have four groups."

"Not to worry," said the Giant's son. "I will sit in on the group that doesn't have one of you three as new members. Now, let's see how we can reassign groups quickly and efficiently. Yes. Let one member of each group move to the next group. Good. Now, let a different member of each group move by two groups. Good, now by four groups. And, yes, I will join that group. Guess what our new task is. Any takers?"

"Probably the same problem," suggested Dana Foley.

"You got it, Dana. Congratulations. Let's see what solutions we come up with if our group members don't all see the presenting problem the same way. For this exercise, we will take half an hour. Please appoint a leader and a reporter for each group. Good luck."

The new groups proceeded in their deliberations, and a much higher decibel level resulted from their conferences as a passionate intensity inculcated their efforts to find the best possible solution to the assigned task. When it was time to report back, it was discovered that *all* of the groups had elected more balanced and sophisticated strategies, fully owing to their new diversity of membership.

At the conclusion of the club meeting, Mr. Gregory announced, "I am very proud of all of you for the good work you have done today. We will take up some new challenges in class tomorrow, related to a very interesting question, with which I hope I will be able to secure your input and help. Thank you very much."

Enthusiastic applause greeted his words of appreciation.

Chapter Nine
Strength in Diversity

THE BELL RANG, but Mr. Gregory was nowhere to be seen. Members of the English 9 class looked at one another. Any teacher's absence from a classroom was rare, but Mr. Gregory's absence seemed to bode a crisis or conflagration that went beyond all imagining. After all, wasn't this Nathan Gregory, the very son of Dr. William Gregory, the Giant who had come to Midville Middle School in January to address the entire student body on the rigors and raptures of education and learning? Dr. Gregory had captivated the entire assembly, and had spoken with eloquence and passion regarding issues about which students cared. The Giant had been death on the grading system and had come across as a practical, common-sense intellectual who, through trial and error, was attempting to work out better ways for teachers and students to enhance each others' lives.

"Ain't right," said Bobby, shaking his head.

"Something's wrong," said Zeke.

"Where is he?" inquired Dana.

"Class dismissed," shouted Mickey Drexel, the unpredictable and sometimes outlandish class clown.

Just as the words had been cast out, in through the door walked none other than the Giant's son himself, carrying a large white box with a brown paper bag floating on top of it, nestling itself against his chest. Smiling at the near insurrection that Mickey's shout had prompted, he announced, "Good morning. Sorry to be late, but I needed to retrieve this box for class."

"Must be a copy of our final," said Bobby.

"What's in the bag then?" asked Zeke.

"Smellin' salts," said Bobby.

"Come, now," scolded Nathan Gregory. "My final is always much larger than this. How could you have mistaken so small a box for my final?"

Bobby gulped, sorry that he had even brought the subject up.

"Let's not play guessing games, though, about what's in this box. I will tell you that whatever is in this box is for all of you if ... "

And here followed a very pregnant pause.

"If what?" asked Dana.

"If you help me with a little problem," said Mr. Gregory.

"I knew it," said Bobby. "I knew you'd come around to us if we only waited. Ain't no good denyin' it. I knew you'd come around."

The Giant's son, his eyes wide with wonder, looked quizzically at Bobby, asking, "Come around for what?"

"With that there little problem," said Bobby. "Ain't no use denyin' it, 'cause I know what it is, too."

"And what is the little problem, Bobby?" asked the Giant's son.

"Them there falsies—"

"Fallacies—"

"You and David, correctin' me day and night, has brought me to my wits end. But ya gotta give the devil his due. I predicted it, too."

"What?"

"That sooner, not later, sooner, those damn fallafalsies would turn your brain into *mush*, just like they're beginnin' to turn our brains into mush. Look at Zeke. He's *already* gone," said Bobby.

"Mush?" Mr. Gregory squinted at Bobby in puzzlement.

"Mush," reaffirmed Bobby.

"Mush," repeated Mr. Gregory. "Well, I guess so, then."

"Naw!" said Mickey. "Bobby can't be right, can he?"

"Mush?" asked Mr. Gregory.

"What's the real 'little' problem," asked Mickey. "Come on. We'll help you. We've just gotta know what you brought in that box."

"Mush," said Mr. Gregory, pointing to the box.

The class laughed; even Bobby laughed. It felt good to laugh, especially in school. Most of the students in the class couldn't remember when they had last laughed during school. It felt refreshing and good, like a shower of pure, warm water sweeping down and cleansing the entire class.

"My 'little' problem is this, and it's both simple and complex at the same time. I have agreed to make some specific recommendations to a certain select committee on education for what would constitute an ideal school and ideal learning. Since we're all in this learning boat together, I thought that I would open it up to the entire group, as a committee of the whole, and take your suggestions for possible inclusion in my report."

"Does this have anything to do with your dad?" asked Dana, who had only the fondest memories of the amazing talk the Giant had given to the student body in January.

"He does have a minor part in all of this," said Mr. Gregory.

"*Minor* part?" exclaimed an incredulous Bobby. "The man's a Giant, I mean a Genius, and they give 'im a *minor* part?"

"Well, do you want to help me out or not?" asked the Giant's son, calling the question.

"Do we get to say what we really believe?" asked Maureen Grant.

"Of course," said Mr. Gregory.

"Hey, why not?" asked Dana. "Anyway, I'm dying to see what's in that box."

"It's mu ... u ... u ... ssshhh," whispered Zeke.

Dana rolled her eyes in mock exasperation.

"So, do I take this response as your commitment to help me?" asked the Giant's son.

"Yeah," agreed Bobby. "We'll help."

"Okay, then. I'm not going to give you any directions, or any hints, or any suggestions. I just want to know what all of you would agree would constitute an *ideal school* and *an ideal education*. I will write down all of your suggestions on the board, but you *all* must agree, in other words, reach total consensus, for every item that remains on the board. Once an item is on the board, it may be argued about. I also want you to justify your recommendations. It's not enough merely to say what you would like; I need to have a good, solid reason in order to lend credence to all suggestions that are considered and kept. Does anyone have any questions? I'll write tentative ideas on this left hand board, and ideas that I agree to put in my report in capital letters on the right hand side."

No one raised a hand, since everyone was still trying to take in all that the Giant's son had said. Suddenly everything seemed harder than anyone had imagined.

Bobby raised his hand, "This ain't gonna be no lark?"

"This is serious," said the Giant's son. "It's *not* a game. I fully expect some debate, since we are dealing with at least three representatives from each of the four learning styles."

"No grades!" shouted Ryan Baxter from the rear of the room.

"Why?" asked Mr. Gregory.

A heavy silence settled over the class as students considered if there were any good reasons for advocating the elimination of grades. Mr.

Gregory suddenly erased the words NO GRADES that he had written on the front board.

"No grades!" shouted Larry Jones. "Give us some time, will ya?"

"Okay. Two minutes," agreed Mr. Gregory, who promptly sat down in his chair at his desk, intently studying the group.

"Why no grades?" asked Dana. "There must be some good reasons."

"What do grades do, anyway?" asked Zeke. "It's only a little symbol about how you've done in somebody else's eyes. I mean, what does an A really mean, or a B, or an F. And all teachers score really different."

"Grades are not fair," concluded Dana.

"Not good enough," said the Giant's son. "Ninety seconds."

"Why not good enough?" challenged Dana.

"Nothing in life is fair," came the response. "It's an empty argument. Fair as measured by whom or what?"

Dana could think of no way to counter Mr. Gregory's response.

"It robs satisfaction," said Mickey Drexel.

The Giant's son looked over at Mickey with great interest, waiting for a fuller elaboration on the statement, which the teacher appeared to be buying.

"Why?" asked Mr. Gregory.

"Because if I work my buns off on a project, and really learn a lot for me, maybe I'll only get a C or even a D, but that doesn't reflect all that the project has really meant to me."

"Okay. I buy that," said Mr. Gregory. "Educators would say that extrinsic motivations rob the student of intrinsic rewards and satisfactions."

"Competition," said Dana.

"How so?"

"A nasty competition can evolve with students trying to out do each other, thinking that getting the highest grade is the most important thing, when really the most important thing is *learning*," said Dana.

"I'll buy that, too," Mr. Gregory smiled.

He then wrote NO GRADES on the board that was reserved for the ideas and recommendations that he would take to the select committee. Encouraged by the teacher's agreement with their opinions and reasons, students stirred to find new recommendations for this so-called select committee on education. Perhaps their views would help their own future counterparts.

"No assignments," said Larry Jones.

"Why?" asked Mr. Gregory.

"They take away natural interest; if you've *got* to learn somethin', it sort of ruins it. Let the *kids* decide what *they* want to learn."

Mr. Gregory bit his lips as he considered the idea.

Students waited in expectation of some insight or quotation that would totally paralyze and kill off Larry's suggestion.

Finally, the Giant's son nodded and said, "I agree."

He then wrote NO ASSIGNMENTS on the board of the recommendations he would accept.

"What else?"

Again, an eerie silence fell over the class, but it wasn't because they weren't thinking. The wattage of brain power that was being applied to these considerations had risen to fearsome levels; the problem was that few, if any, had ever before thought about these questions.

"Is that it?" asked Mr. Gregory.

"Give us a break," pleaded Zeke. "We need more time."

"Okay," agreed the teacher.

"Only let kids learn who want to learn," said Jennifer Lawler. "Don't force people if they don't want to be a part of something."

"Don't force students' participation?" asked Mr. Gregory, writing those words on the board. "Why not?"

"'Cause kids can be stubborn," said Bobby Perkins. "If they ain't got a notion to do somethin', they ain't gonna do it. Instead, they just rebel and make *everybody's* life miserable."

"I agree," said the teacher, writing DON'T FORCE STUDENTS' PARTICIPATION in capital letters on the board of things that he would keep and recommend.

"Hey," asked Mickey Drexel. "How would you know if somebody passed a course? If we leave out grades and assignments, how do we measure who passes and who fails?"

"Color of their eyes," quipped Danny Taylor, "and Drexel: you lose big time."

"Yeah, yeah, yeah," said Mickey. "But really, I mean, how do we decide who advances and who doesn't?"

"Good question," said Mr. Gregory. "Any takers?"

The class sat contemplating this conundrum.

"Written reports by teachers," said Tammy Young.

"That would be the form, but how would student progress be *evaluated* by the teachers. What criteria would they use?" asked Mr. Gregory.

"Ain't gonna stay dumb long in this here class," said Bobby. "What the heck is a criter...ia? Is it like a cafeteria?"

"No. It means the standard or test or measure on which a judgment can be formed," explained Mr. Gregory.

"How about good looks?" asked Bobby. "I'd get an A+."

"For modesty, too," sighed Dana. "Come on, Bobby, we've got to stay serious."

"Why? Ain't school supposed to be fun? Why can't we laugh more? I mean, the little kids in the grades laugh it up all the time, 'til some ne'er-do-well like Dandy-Pandy scares it out of 'em."

Mr. Gregory wrote on the left side board, 'Presence of humor and laughter helpful to any meaningful learning process.'

"Is that what you're saying, Bobby?"

"No. That's what you said, but it's what I was aimin' at, and it's a damn sight better than what I muttered," said Bobby.

"I don't want to lose the question about criteria for evaluation, but let's first ask ourselves why the presence of laughter and humor is helpful to any meaningful learning. Anyone care to guess?" asked Mr. Gregory.

The class sat flummoxed, so removed from their experience was the idea of the possibility of a continuous feast of humor and laughter in any sort of learning forum, except perhaps when comedians taught each other. Understandably, there were no takers.

"My guess," began the teacher, "is because it is truly *healthy* to laugh. People who are genuinely able to laugh, both at themselves and the world, and I mean in a kind way, not a nasty way, live fuller lives, and probably longer lives. They encounter less stress, less tension."

No one rose up to deny the words the Giant's son had just spoken.

"Now I can't prove this with any hard facts, but it's my best intuitive judgment. I believe it's true. I could be wrong. But I'm going to keep it in, because I believe it deserves to be there," concluded Mr. Gregory.

Spontaneous applause filled the room.

"Okay, let's keep going. Let's go back to the criteria to be used in passing. Any ideas?"

In contrast to the eruption of applause that had just occurred, the silence that now invaded the classroom proved most uncomfortable.

"Make up a list of basic knowledge needed to pass every grade. If students can pass, great. If not, make them repeat," said Jennifer Lawler.

"Basic knowledge? Who would define what should be basic?" asked Mr. Gregory. "We already agreed not to demand any particular subject be learned or taught."

"Let the kids decide," said Jennifer.

"That's passin' the buck," said Bobby.

"So? It would be *their* school, wouldn't it?" retorted Jennifer.

"Why not have tests that could prove someone had learned something, but make them optional. That way, only those choosing to take them could be considered for promotion," said Maureen Grant.

"That's a dirty way of forcing people to do something," said Zeke. "I mean, if somebody didn't want to take any of the tests, that person could veg for years in the same grade. There'd be a lot of social pressure, not to mention a lot of fun made of anyone not makin' it each year."

Maureen considered Zeke's objections, answering, "I agree."

Zeke's mouth dropped open, especially to find such accommodating agreement from Maureen, whose acerbic and critical personality had alienated her from many of her classmates.

The Giant's son dutifully erased the proposed idea from the board.

"So, what criteria, if any?" prompted Mr. Gregory.

"Ain't it wrong to have promotion, if there ain't no hoops to jump?" asked Bobby.

"A good question," said Mr. Gregory. "Any takers?"

"I agree," said Dana. "If there's no basis for promotion, except maybe just age alone, then why not just forget promotion?"

"But there'd be chaos, wouldn't there?" said Mickey Drexel.

"Perhaps," said Mr. Gregory, "but everyone would either be engaged in learning or just sitting around."

"You know," volunteered Larry Jones, "I hate to admit it, but *this* class seems to be a lot less boring than before."

"Perhaps you're more engaged in what we're doing," suggested Mr. Gregory.

"Yeah," agreed Larry. "That's part of it, I'm sure. But it's more interesting, too."

"Don't things become more interesting the more we become engaged?" asked Mr. Gregory.

"Except math and science," Jennifer complained. "They stink."

"They may be a little drier than the humanities, but I think engagement there is still very possible, as long as one knows what one is doing, which usually requires a fair amount of work and memorization," said the Giant's son.

"This here business of promotion is a false issue," said Bobby. "That is, if we vote for a school with no grades or required learnin'."

"Good point," said Mr. Gregory.

"But what about the *real* world?" asked Sheila Morrison. "I mean, who's gonna hire us because we enjoyed learning, whatever we *did* learn."

"Make 'em give a test," said Bobby.

"And what if you fail?" asked Sheila.

"So you fail," said Bobby.

"But what if you want that job?" asked Sheila.

"Then you'd have to become qualified to get it," said Jiggs, "the same as everybody else."

"Yeah. But what good would school be? It'd be only a waste of time," rejoined Sheila.

"But must *all* learning be proven useful to have value?" asked Mr. Gregory. "And how do we know today what will be useful tomorrow?"

"I wouldn't care," said Tammy. "I mean, if school could be less boring, that's more important to me."

"What do you mean by less boring?" asked Mr. Gregory.

"You know, where kids get more involved, get interested," said Tammy.

"So, why are some kids not involved?" asked Mr. Gregory.

"I don't know. Maybe they're just lazy," said Tammy. "Or they just want to hang out with their friends."

"What's more important?" asked Mr. Gregory. "Learning something in school or receiving a diploma? How many say that it's the diploma?"

A majority of hands shot up.

"Ain't no hope without a sheepskin," said Bobby. "If you ain't got a high school diploma, business people ain't gonna look at you twice. Maybe not even once."

"How about somebody who had learned a great deal, but who didn't stay long enough to receive a diploma?" asked Mr. Gregory.

"The cards would be stacked against the person," said Mickey Drexel. "At least, until ability was proven."

"Yeah," argued Bobby, "but without the sheepskin, you don't even get a chance to get in the door to prove yourself."

Mickey shrugged, "Maybe. Maybe not. Who knows?"

"Ain't it a fact that kids without sheepskins get it right in the neck?" Bobby asked the Giant's son.

"Studies would show that their average earnings are far less than for those who do receive diplomas," answered Mr. Gregory.

"It ain't right," said Bobby. "I ain't a brain, but I ain't dumb, either. I know I could keep a job if I could *get* one."

"Probably it would depend on the job," rejoined Mr. Gregory.

"Society stinks," said Bobby. "That's what *I* say."

"How so?"

"It ain't fair. Just like in India with those casting systems," said Bobby.

"Do you mean the caste system?" asked the Giant's son.

"I mean those little men in the white coats and hats sittin' around on those filthy streets," said Bobby.

"Don't worry," whispered Zeke. "They're comin' for you right now. Just get ready for the *big* jacket after they net you."

"Shut up," Bobby scolded. "I'm bein' serious."

"The caste system in India *is* very restrictive," said Mr. Gregory.

"You're tellin' me?" said Bobby. "I mean: what a cruel director they must have, to say to them poor devils, '*You're always* gonna sit right here in the gutter and rot. That's *your* role.'"

"Director?" asked the Giant's son.

"Yeah," said Bobby. "Just like in the movies."

"Oh, I see," laughed Mr. Gregory. "You're equating the c-a-s-t-e, with c-a-s-t. The first is the restrictive Hindu social system; the second refers to members of a theater or movie company."

"I don't know nothin' 'bout no 'quating'. All I know is that it ain't only in *India* that us poor devils get it right in the *neck*. Untouchables. And that's just what we are, too: *untouchables*," groused Bobby.

"Well, if you *ever* took a bath—" began Zeke, stopping abruptly when he caught the fierce anger in Bobby's glare of reproach.

"This issue seems to be tapping into something that really bothers you, Bobby," Mr. Gregory observed.

"I ain't pretendin' to be nobody special," said Bobby, "not like some of them namby-pambies who put on airs. I'm just sayin' that it ain't fair the way people write you off, 'specially if you don't have the dough to dress sharp or the trainin' to speak right and proper."

"You're saying that's like a hidden caste system in our own country?" asked the Giant's son.

"Yeah," agreed Bobby. "And ain't that just a beast with horns on it?"

"He's right," said Maureen. "I've seen it before, too."

"Is there any way out?" asked Mr. Gregory.

The class paused to consider this question, wondering if there might indeed be a way to extricate themselves from this imagined prison of subtle rejection and inopportune assessment. For a while, it seemed that no way out could be envisioned. A blanket of doubt and depression began to settle over the class.

"How about learning?" asked the Giant's son.

"Learnin'?" asked Bobby.

"Yes. Learning," explained the Giant's son. "What you learn is one of the few things that others can't take away from you. It is one of the few things you can't lose, unless you suffer brain impairment. The more you know, the richer you become. The more you understand, the more you can do. It's like putting gold bars in an unseen knowledge bank, where they will draw interest as they wait to return to serve you."

"Ain't that just a snow job?" asked Bobby.

"Bobby, look at your own diction. It's very much a part of you, but as long as you hang on to words like 'ain't,' you will continually judge yourself, by your own words, as being a person who has not yet learned the correct, accepted way of speaking and writing. That will mark you as being 'ignorant,' like it or not, in the eyes of those who have achieved an acceptable mastery of language," said Mr. Gregory.

"What are you getting at?" asked Zeke.

"That refusing to do your best in school, in refusing to learn as much as you possibly can, you are only hurting yourselves," said Mr. Gregory. "And I hate to see people hurt themselves or others."

The class sat in focused silence, considering the teacher's words.

"So, you're sayin' that whatever we learn in school might help us down the road?" asked Bobby, his smirk betraying his skepticism.

"To be honest, I don't know," said Mr. Gregory, "nor do any of you. Who has a lens into the future?"

Typical of his droll sense of humor, Mickey Drexel began to raise his hand, but then put it back down his desk.

"Them there falsies that you made us learn," Bobby began, "I can see how they might help some poor devil *not* to be snowed who ain't got a prayer otherwise."

"Have you ever been snowed?" Mr. Gregory asked Bobby.

"Yeah, about as many times as anybody sittin' in this room. When David talked about smellin' rats, that's when I first really understood them falsies. I mean, sometimes when you're talkin' to somebody, and they is just comin' on real strong-like, you know that some new kind of cheatin' is comin' down the road and is gonna run right over you, just from the way the ugly dude is snowin' you with all his verbal diarrhea."

"Sounds to me as if you've dealt with salesmen before," the Giant's son grinned.

"Darn tootin', and proud of it," agreed Bobby.

"Well, the fallacies should help you even more, now that you are beginning to understand them. Language is not precise, and peoples' meanings can be very elusive."

"Don't know what e-loose-siv means, exceptin' if you're talkin' about a sieve that's not fastened proper-like to a house," said Bobby.

"The word 'elusive' means hard to grasp or to retain," explained Mr. Gregory.

"Well, there it *is*," said Bobby. "Decent language has been e-loose-siv to me since I started kindergarten. In fact, probably before."

'You've got to work at it," said Jiggs Stevenson.

Bobby puzzled for a moment, answering, "You do?"

"Jiggs is correct," said the Giant's son. "Now Dr. Baker is coming tomorrow. Perhaps we should ask him his opinions on all that we've been talking about."

"Yeah, and get snowed again," said Bobby.

"How do you know that?" asked Mr. Gregory.

"'Cause these shrinks flood you with questions, and by the time you've answered the first one, you can't even remember your own frickin' name. It's a trick to throw you off balance," said Bobby.

"Hey," said Zeke. "Remember, Bobby. We've studied fallacies. We can catch this guy out if he messes up."

"Zeke is right," said Bobby, "for the first time in recorded memory. I ain't pretendin' to be very quick about these falsies, but I'm sure as heck able to smell them frickin' rats, and we can lam into this dude if he tries any funny stuff."

"Sounds as if it's going to be a very interesting Learning Club meeting," said Mr. Gregory, looking at the clock. "It's almost time to go. Review the fallacies tonight so that you'll be ready for anything tomorrow."

"Guess we're gonna put the bag on the good ol' Dr. Dude," said Bobby.

"Dr. Baker," Dana corrected Bobby, as the passing bell rang and students began to gather their things, adding in a whisper, "Or maybe he'll put the bag on *you*."

Chapter Ten
A Psychologist Speaks

A WAVE OF EXCITEMENT AND ANTICIPATION CHARGED THE GIANT'S SON'S CLASSROOM, running swiftly through the members of the Learning Club as they sat waiting for the arrival of their speaker. This Thursday, the club's second official meeting, would mark the advent of a *real* psychologist, who had agreed to come to make three separate presentations to the members of the Learning Club on various topics of their choice. So confident had club members become at ferreting out fallacies of thought and language, they had collectively decided to employ this new armor of intellect in their deliberations with Dr. Baker. They had requested that he come to speak to them about the need for clear thinking, hoping to capitalize on all that they had learned.

"David," asked Maureen, who was sitting in front of him, "how did we get this psychologist to come?"

"He's an old friend of Mr. Pennythorpe," David explained. "When Mr. Pennythorpe heard how Bobby wanted to invite a psychologist, he suggested Dr. Baker. We invited him to come speak today, and he volunteered to come back at least two or three more times. His second talk is going to be about hypnosis."

"Cool. And he's a *real* doctor?" asked Maureen.

"Yes. He's a real clinical psychologist, with a Ph.D.," said David.

As the door opened, members of the club quieted immediately as they watched Mr. Pennythorpe escort Dr. Baker into the classroom.

Although Dr. Baker was of medium height, he still stood two heads taller than Mr. Pennythorpe. Dr. Baker had a full head of white hair, neatly parted on the right hand side. David was first struck by the kindness of the man's face, a face that harbored alert and sensitive blue eyes, which danced over a confident smile, the kind of smile that says, 'No matter what the problem is, we're going to navigate these stormy waters together.' Wire-rim glasses lent a professorial cast to the guest speaker, who was now removing his coat, surrendering it to the Giant's son to hang up. The speaker wore a three piece navy suit, the vest helping to amplify a professorial air.

Mr. Pennythorpe remained standing at the front of the room, pausing to catch his breath before speaking, still wearing his winter overcoat and scarf and buried under his furry Russian hat.

"Friends," began Mr. Pennythorpe, "I regret that I will not be able to remain here today to hear my dear friend speak to you, but I do hope to hear him on the occasion of his future visits. Clarence and I go back a long way. He was, in fact, one my best students when I used to teach at a small college. Unfortunately, the college eventually decided that it had no need of the luxury of a history department, and in one giant cost cutting swoop, we members of that department *became* history."

A small ripple of laughter echoed through the room.

"Nevertheless, I remember Clarence as one of my very best students. He is too modest to tell you that he graduated *summa cum laude* with two majors, or that he later went on to McGill University to earn his Ph.D. in clinical psychology. He has since built a large, prestigious practice, and he also teaches occasionally at the university. You may be interested to know that he is, among other things, a gifted hypnotherapist who has written dozens of articles on the use of hypnosis in counseling."

Mr. Pennythorpe extended his hand, which Clarence accepted, saying, "Dr. Clarence Baker, it is a privilege to have you as our featured speaker. I am already running late for my doctor's appointment, so I shall quickly be on my way. You'll enjoy this group. They're great kids."

With that salute, Mr. Pennythorpe quickly exited the room, leaving Dr. Baker at the mercy of the fallacy wolves. Considering the members of his audience, to whom he gave a warm smile, he cleared his throat, and began, "You, I am sure, hold Mr. Pennythorpe in as high regard as I do. He is a very generous man, both with his words and in his actions. When he gave me your letter and invited me to come to speak, he said that there appeared to be great interest on the part of at least one student to meet and visit with a psychologist. And please don't worry, I haven't come to psychoanalyze any of you."

"A *few* of them could use it," retorted the Giant's son, who was sitting in the back of the room. So pointed a suggestion, piercing deeply into the latent anxiety submerged in most minds in the room, caused a forced eruption of laughter and the release of enormous nervous tension. Zeke Minturn was looking at Bobby, nodding in agreement at the sly suggestion of Nathan Gregory that perhaps Bobby and several of his cohorts could indeed benefit from some psychoanalysis.

Dr. Baker noticed him and asked, "What's your name?"

Zeke immediately said, "Bobby Perkins."

"Liar," returned Mickey Drexel. This exchange brought a new round of laughter and mirth filled the assembly.

Smiling at Zeke's ruse with full knowledge of the shenanigans afoot, Dr. Baker continued, "I have also been told that you have shown great enterprise at learning how to think and speak clearly, how to identify various fallacies, and I commend you for that accomplishment. If I should commit any grievous errors, I would be grateful if you would kindly point them out to me."

—Have no fear, thought Bobby. —The fallacy wolves are here.

"But today I also want to challenge us all to look beyond mere fallacies of logic and language. I do not say that they are *not* important, for I believe that they are. However, I have come to believe that *clarity of self* is even more important, and I will take that as the subject of my talk today."

No other words could have served up a greater whammy to the class. Here they had been lying stealthily in wait for their prey, wolves who would ferret out all errors of logic and language, yet now this mysterious psychologist had thrown them an unexpected curve by suggesting that they focus on the need for clarity of self. It was enough to send a few of them right through the floor, had the floor been amenable to their departure from the classroom, which it wasn't.

"Now what do I mean when I say 'clarity of self'?" asked Dr. Baker.

No one leaped to volunteer an answer for, after all, they were now dealing with a very adept psychologist who had, in one fell phrase, scuttled their intended *modus operandi*.

"Anyone?" asked Dr. Baker.

"Clarity means to be clear," said David, "so I suppose it means to be clear about who we are."

"Yes," agreed Dr. Baker. "And who are we?"

This question threw the class for an even greater loop.

"We're human beings," observed Sean, who was sitting in the back of the room.

"Yes. And what are human beings?" asked Dr. Baker.

"Self-aware entities with fears, hopes, ambitions, feelings like joy and sadness," Sean continued, winning the lasting devotion of all club members who were reluctant to converse with a real psychologist. Sean, thanks to Midville Middle School counselor Melvin Dandy, had already conversed with a psychologist, especially about his love of violence and guns, and had been declared to be a perfectly normal seventh grader.

"Feelings," said Dr. Baker, "are an interesting and worthy area of exploration. Sometimes we suddenly find ourselves in a foul mood, all wrought up with anger for no apparent reason. Anyone here ever had that experience?"

No hands were raised until Sean lifted his, and soon all hands were lifted high, including Dr. Baker's.

"Is it possible for us ever to become clear about these kinds of foul moods that drive our actions beyond reason?"

The class stared in every direction, except, of course, at the speaker.

"Let's run a little experiment," suggested Dr. Baker. "I want all of you to close your eyes and to think back to a time when you were, for no good reason that you could understand, really upset at someone or about something. Take about thirty seconds to relive that anger or frustration, and then write down a little about the event, especially whether it's a recurrent event or pattern. After that, I'll lead us through a simple exercise that might prove helpful."

The members of the club sat in silence, recollecting an unpleasant moment of anger or frustration.

"Now, imagine yourself going down a path, searching to understand this anger which has boiled up inside of you. As you wind your way around a curve, you will suddenly see a structure that will represent and explain that anger. Take note of every detail of that structure, and decide whether or not you wish to enter it. If you enter it, take note of every single detail that catches your attention. Study the way the structure is built, what it made of, what it is designed for, the feeling that it gives you, the color or colors of the structure, the furniture inside, the kinds of windows, the type of environment in which it sits.

Now write down as much as you can remember. Who needs paper and a pencil?"

The Giant's son helped to pass out paper and pencils and after allowing ten minutes of time for students to write their responses, the papers were collected.

Zeke handed them to Dr. Baker, who said, "Thank you. What's your real name?"

"Bobby Perkins," said Zeke, drawing a rolling laugh from the class.

"No, it's not," corrected Dr. Baker.

"The laughter tipped you off," said Zeke.

"No. The way you moved your eyes tipped me off," corrected Dr. Baker.

"My real name is Zeke Minturn," confessed Zeke, turning red. "That's Bobby Perkins right there in the middle. He's our class president and he will answer all of your questions."

"When Mr. Gregory mentioned that a few people in this room might profit from psychoanalysis," Dr. Baker explained, "he was merely joking. In truth, we can, instead, learn to help each other, that is if we can only bring ourselves to trust each other. Your names are written on these papers. Does anyone have an objection to my reading these aloud?"

No objections were voiced.

"Very well, let me begin, although I may eventually pass these back to you in order to hear you read your own work," continued Dr. Baker, taking the first sheet and read announced, "Here's the event: 'I get mad when I'm told to do something I don't want to do. Now I am walking down the lane and turn and see a huge barn. The barn is bright red and I can hear chickens. I go up to the barn, but must walk through cow dung to get there. I arrive in front of it. It's in need of paint and parts of it are falling down. It feels like a place where I once played. It's sort of crumbling now. In the bright sunlight, I suddenly see a shadow next to the barn. It's the shadow of a boy I knew when I was about five. He was never very nice to me. He beat me up about once a week. I never liked him. I hated him bullying me, but I had no one to take my part.'

"How revealing this piece of writing is, my friends. The trigger for this person is being told to do something he or she doesn't want to do. The link, the shadow, that drives the anger comes from an old-patterned relationship, where someone bullied this person weekly. The images of the barn are interesting, perhaps red for anger, but let us not forget the chicken, perhaps a symbol of fear or cowardice, and walking through cow dung to get to the barn. The symbols are very graphic for the feeling. I also like the fact that the barn is falling to ruins, and that the sun now shows it up for being pretty shabby. That would suggest that the anger and conflict is abating with time. If my interpretation bears any insight, I hope it will help to hasten the complete dissipation of this bad memory. I also hope the interpretation is accurate."

"It is," said Larry.

"That was very brave of you to acknowledge authorship," observed the psychologist. "Shall I read another?"

The club members broke into applause, to demonstrate that they were eager not only to have all of their papers read, but also eager to see what Dr. Baker would say about them.

"Here's another: 'I get angry whenever my mother gets on my case about keeping my room neat. Now I'm on a brick road, and as I turn the corner, I see a brick house, sitting on a brick lawn, and even the trees are brick. I don't go into the house because I know that everything will be in perfect order, almost too orderly for the sake of sanity. It makes me feel very sad. I wonder who could possibly live there. Then I hear a child in the garden, and I go to the side of the house and see that the child is me, and I'm swinging on a brick swing. I get off the swing and walk toward the house, which is sitting under a huge cloud, no, actually a dark, dark shadow, and the bricks of the house are really cold to the touch. I go in, and I find it to be as harshly ordered as I had suspected."

"Once again," said Dr. Baker, "we are given a profound visual understanding of the presenting problem, which is an internal resistance to keeping one's room in order, and I might add that this propensity is quite a common thing among teenagers."

Shuffling could be heard in the room as many chuckled at Dr. Baker's aside.

"That's mine," said Tammy.

"Tammy Young."

"If you want me to, I will tell you what I think is going on, but I would appreciate your help. I would also appreciate it if my comments could be kept strictly within this room. Does everyone agree? Fine. Tammy, I see you as feeling very closed in, feeling that you have only a very few options, almost suffocating in an environment that has walled you in, together with your ability to be your own person as well, if that makes any sense."

Tammy nodded, affirming what Dr. Baker had said.

"I also see a mother who has been so deeply hurt by something, possibly an unexpected divorce, that the only way she has found to preserve her balance has been to apply an overlay of brick, for protection and strength, on almost everything around her."

Again, Tammy nodded her agreement.

"It is significant that you are able to swing on the brick swing, and that the swing is in the sunshine. I would also suggest to you that you might consider taking time to play with your mother. It could be games, or going shopping, or making cookies together. If you can give back to her that younger girl inside of herself, it will help her to leave all that brick behind."

"How come?" asked Bobby.

"Because she will need to come out of her protective shell to defend her daughter and to rebuild her life. The brick is only temporary, no matter how hard it may feel. As soon as your mother can reconnect with her emotions and feelings, the sooner she'll take all those bricks down. Does this bear any truth regarding your situation?"

Tammy blew her nose and nodded.

"There, there," said Dr. Baker, "go right ahead, because we've all needed to shed some tears, and we'd be a lot healthier if we did it more. There's a lot of hurt inside each of us that is just begging to be released. Our problem is how to become clear about what hurts us, where it began, and how to release it. It's like carrying a lot of baggage around. None of us needs to be strapped with an additional twenty, or fifty, or maybe even one hundred pounds. And if we spend most of our energy carrying such baggage, we have less and less energy to apply to things like school, homework, hobbies, friends, and jobs. I'm sorry to talk so much; I hope I'm not boring anyone."

"Read mine, read mine," came eager voices, hands waving for recognition.

"I think we've come far enough so that I'd rather have you read your own, those of you who want to share them," announced Dr. Baker, handing the papers back to Zeke, who began to return them to club members.

Once all of the papers were returned, Dr. Baker announced, "I don't want anyone to feel forced to read. And I also want to remind you that whatever is read, said, or discussed in this room remains here. Does everyone agree to that? Good.

"Who's next? Yes, your name, please," said Dr. Baker.

"Mickey Drexel. Should I go ahead and read?"

"Please do," answered Dr. Baxter.

"I hate it when someone pretends to listen to me but isn't really listening," Mickey announced, taking a deep breath as he got ready to read, and then continued: "My journey went like this: I find myself on a road in the forest, but it's morning and there's plenty of light. I walk and walk until I see a small cottage in a clearing off to the right. I hear a stream running as I approach the cottage. It looks old, like no one lives there, but suddenly my father steps out, and I see that he is sad about something, but won't tell anyone. I go into the cottage and see my mom making a wonderful meal for the family. I go upstairs and find my room, but have trouble opening the door because it's stuck. I hear Chocolate, my old Labrador who died a year ago, behind the door, so I keep pushing until the door flies open. I run in and she greets me with a huge kiss on my face. Then I hear my mom calling the family to dinner, and Chocolate suddenly barks at me and then just disappears. That's it."

Dr. Baker looked kindly at Mickey, finally saying, "I'm really sorry about Chocolate. Was her death unexpected?"

"She was really ancient. We knew we'd have to put her down some day, but no one is ever ready for it when the time finally comes."

"No one is," agreed Dr. Baker. "It seems that you were really close to Chocolate, Mickey."

Mickey didn't answer for a few seconds, as if trying to catch his breath. "Yes," he finally answered, and then hid his face in his hands.

Zeke Minturn, who sitting in front of him, reached his hand back to comfort Mickey as Dana Foley moved her desk over so she could rub Mickey's back. Jennifer Lawler found some tissues which she passed over, and which were gratefully accepted by Mickey.

"That's okay," said Dr. Baker. "It's healthy to cry, to let out all that pain and hurt, especially over loved ones that we have lost. Pets are an important part of families, and we lose more of them because they have shorter life spans. I'm sure most of us have lost at least one pet during our lifetimes."

Several students wiped tears that were now trickling from their eyes. Mickey composed himself, and said, "I guess I've needed to do that for a long time."

Dr. Baker nodded in agreement.

"Will you please interpret my walk?" requested Mickey.

"I'd be delighted to tell you some of things I heard and what I think they might mean. The forest is a common symbol for one's unconscious, so I suspected we would be uncovering something hidden, which was also given additional support because it was morning, and there was plenty of light to reveal whatever you would find. I also found it interesting that you identified the time as morning, for something told me that we should also consider the other spelling of the word: m-o-u-r-n-i-n-g, the state of grieving for someone who has been lost. The cottage, of course, represents both your physical home and your inner self. The stream symbolizes the present, reflecting the living waters of your current life. The cottage appears old because you have been away for some time, owing to your grief. That is why your father is sad. He knows and feels the depth of your loss, but it's hard for him to listen to you, for it reminds him of his own losses as well as his own mortality. I also sense that you are a person who tends to communicate through humor more than through sad emotions. It's especially hard for you when you need to share something that has made you sad. The reason that you get angry when people appear to listen to you, but really don't, is because you want to let out your grief, but can't; on another level, you have refused to listen to yourself, so you're angry with yourself as well.

The difficulty in opening the door reminds us of the curtain between this life and the next, and that Chocolate has died in this life. Your ability to greet Chocolate indicates that you are ready to honor that relationship by getting a new dog. Until now, you've been unable to let go. I see your insights, Mickey, as being very positive and growth fulfilling. I hope that you'll consider getting a new dog sometime soon."

Mickey nodded, saying, "I think maybe I'm finally ready to do that, Doc. Thanks."

"Thank yourself. It was you who wrote down the story that furnished all of the information; I only helped you a little by offering some possible interpretations. There's a great power in writing such stories, for they inform us about ourselves on many levels. Our job is to be open to what they are telling us. Dreams do the same thing, but in a more chaotic, symbolic way."

Hands shot up from the many students who hoped Dr. Baker would comment on their guided visualizations. Dr. Baker looked at the clock and smiled, saying, "I know that a lot of you would like to share what you've written, and I would certainly like to hear each one. My concern is that we may well run out of time, for I have come to share some insights from my many years of working with individuals that may prove useful. Why don't we plan to finish a little early, and those wanting to stay will be able to meet with me and share their experiences. Will this work?"

Class members nodded their assent.

"Well, then, let's look at the concept of clarity of self and what it might mean. Some of you have just experienced the sudden flash of insight, or clarity, that can come when we take courage to look inside of ourselves.

"Now I would wager that the real question in most of your minds is: 'How can one find clarity of self?' I would suggest that there are innumerable ways, depending on the individual. One way is to guard against presenting a false representation of ourselves to the world. Let the person that the world sees accurately reflect the person who each of us truly is. We blind ourselves when we lose congruence between the person we are and the person we let the world see. I know that the very real risk about doing this is the fear of rejection. It hurts to take on the courage of being oneself, only then to be rebuffed in some way.

"But look at it this way, better to be rejected for the person you actually are than for something that you're not. At least the first relationship is real on your part, whereas the second is merely a box of shadows. Let me illustrate on the chalk board."

Dr. Baker took a piece of chalk and drew a stick figure, saying, "This figure represents someone with whom you want to have a relationship. This figure next to it represents you. Both of the figures project images of themselves that are not fully congruent with who they *really* are. Our two core figures, therefore, attempt to have a relationship with each other that is doomed from the beginning, because the figures that they project are not genuine, and therefore cannot find a real relationship.

"Clarity of self comes from an acceptance of self, which leads us to accepting others. We all have warts and blemishes: no one is perfect. Ironically, even though that is an easy insight to remember, many of us fall victim to expectations or circumstances that drive us to seek perfection.

"Once we accept ourselves, in all of our complexities, because we are all mixtures of noble and less noble forces, we can then move toward self-direction, choosing what we desire, not on the basis of what others expect, but on the basis of what we truly want. And the last thing that any of us need on our respective journeys is somebody or something waving a finger in our faces, saying, 'You ought to have done this or that instead of…' and so on. Some of you look puzzled. Is anything that I have been saying unclear to you, or do you want to discuss it?"

"Why shouldn't we strive for perfection?" asked David. "We need to try to improve, don't we?"

"We always need to try to get better," agreed Dr. Baker, "but holding on to perfection as the standard through which we evaluate our efforts will only bring us disappointment."

"Why?" asked David.

"Because no one is perfect," answered Dr. Baker, "but that does not mean we shouldn't try to improve ourselves. In fact, I believe we are under obligation to grow, rather than to remain static. Let me tell you a brief story about one of my clients. It's about an interesting young child and his experience with schooling. Let's call this boy Charlie. He was an only child, having been born to parents who had finished high school, but who had never gone to college. He rarely saw his parents read anything except a newspaper or an occasional magazine, although both were successful in their jobs, which involved factory production.

"Charlie's school experience was troubled from the beginning. He found he reversed some of his letters when he read aloud or tried to write something down. He also had trouble reading and understanding what he had read. Owing to his struggles with language, he was placed in the slower sections, and largely forgotten.

"He was bright enough to get through on his own, compensating for his deficits, but never feeling very comfortable with book learning or the routines of school. He liked to take things apart and reassemble them. This he proved very good at, in fact, brilliant. He would much prefer to work with his hands than with words or concepts. School was boring, mainly because he had trouble keeping up with his peers, and soon he would tune school out entirely. Yes, he would be sitting in the classroom, but his mind and his heart would be elsewhere, most often thinking about some new kind of car engine he could dismantle and reassemble.

"Charlie's mechanical abilities were fully recognized by his school counselor, who arranged for him to take a number of tests, which qualified him for admission to a very prestigious technical school that taught advanced courses in mechanics and engine repair. Charlie flashed through that school like lightning, and got a very well-paying job when he graduated. He worked hard and eventually opened his own automotive repair shop. Eventually the school that he attended called him, wanting him to come and teach. He had always enjoyed teaching others how to discover the intricacies and challenges associated with motors and machine repair; it was like solving a big puzzle, and brought great satisfaction when one succeeded. Charlie wanted to take the job at his old school, but there was one catch. He didn't have a master's degree. In fact, he didn't have a bachelor's degree, only a two year certificate of mastery.

"But his old school knew him and really wanted him, and he wanted to accept their job offer, but the obstacles remained regarding his not having two college degrees. That's how I met him. He was referred to me by the president of the technical college for evaluation. After running about three days worth of tests on him, guess what I discovered? Number one: Charlie had an I.Q. of 130. By the way, I.Q. does not reflect how smart you are. It merely gives an indicator of how fast a person can learn something, and that usually relates to only a specified kind of learning. Number two: Charlie was a dyslexic, meaning that he had a neurological impairment, which caused him to process the information his brained received differently than did most of his peers. Number three: Charlie had attention deficit disorder. Number four: Charlie had resilience. If he decided to go after something, he would succeed.

"I reviewed the results of my tests with him, but he couldn't bring himself to believe that he had a superior I.Q.. Finally, however, I convinced him. Then he wanted to know why school had been so hard for him, and I tried to explain the problem that dyslexics and kids with A.D.D. face. He understood the symptoms well enough, for he had known them for his entire life.

"We talked about his goals. He had discounted himself as a candidate for the teaching job he really wanted, because he had convinced himself he could never earn the required degrees. So, I said to him, 'Charlie, you can get the degrees you need, but you are going to have to work harder than you've ever worked before.'

"He said, 'I don't have six years to give to getting two college degrees. Anyway, the job would be filled by then.'

"I assured him that the president of the school said they would wait for him, but that he must finish his bachelor's degree within two years. Fortunately, he had saved enough money to be able to dedicate his full time to school. With the help of some local educators, we found a school that would grant him two and one half years credit based on his earlier certificate and subsequent life experience. He relocated to where that school was situated and graduated a year and a half later. It wasn't easy. He had to hire tutors and to spend most of his time focused on his goal, but the important lesson is that he succeeded. He succeeded in accomplishing something that he had convinced himself years before that he could never do.

"After he got his bachelor's degree, the school hired him, and he was able to work part time on a master's degree at a nearby school, which he completed in three years. He's still teaching at the technical institute and is now married and has two children.

"My point in telling you this story is this: most of the time, we are all learning, whether we realize it or not. We tend to learn the things we choose to learn or like to learn, but there is no reason that we can't learn other things. It may only take us a little longer. All that is required is commitment, perseverance, and a trust in one's own self. Remember always what Socrates said, 'Know thyself,' and also what William Shakespeare admonished, 'To thine own self be true.' Are there other questions?"

Sheila Morrison raised her hand.

"Yes, your name, please?"

"Sheila Morrison. I wanted to ask you if all that stuff you told us about relationships and projecting images of ourselves that are not quite accurate has anything to do with how brief special friendships can be?"

"Do you mean special in the sense of dating?" asked Dr. Baker, with a twinkle in his eye.

"Yes. Dating relationships usually don't last more than a few weeks, at least not in ninth grade."

"I believe that we face an entire array of possibilities to explain the phenomenon you mention. One, certainly, is that each partner may not have projected an entirely accurate representation of self; another relates to our search to understand ourselves through our relationships with others, and once we've learned the lessons that we need to learn, we move on; a third factor might relate to what I call the impossibility clause."

"What's that?" asked Sheila with interest.

"If either partner, or both partners, in a relationship deny the possibility that their relationship will *ever* end, it's as good as conferring the kiss of death itself."

"I don't quite follow," said Dana.

"I am sure that we have all had at least one relationship to which we were so attached that we believed that it would never end," continued Dr. Baker, receiving several nods from members of the club.

"By denying the possibility that it *might* end, we stifle the freedom of that relationship to grow and to evolve. Such a mind-set is a sort of suffocating presence that ultimately dooms any friendship, forcing us to face the fact that we have unwittingly brought a relationship's end by ourselves by not allowing the other person sufficient freedom to be whatever might have been."

"Wow," exclaimed Dana. "That makes a lot of sense to me. From now on I'll just tell anybody I go out with, 'Listen, buster, this relationship is going to end, so don't get up any false hopes.' You're really smart, Dr. Baker. How did you get to be so smart?"

"Through a lot of pain," said Dr. Baker. "There can be no real growth without pain. The same is true in learning. We all tend to fool ourselves. We are especially good at avoiding looking at portions of ourselves that threaten or contradict our chosen self-image."

"Could we please talk to you about our visualizations?" asked Gordie Chase.

"Yes. Why don't we close here for today? I'm afraid I have not even covered a third of the material that I had hoped to share with you. Let me visit with the club's officers for a minute to figure out when I'm coming back, that is, if they want me."

Applause thundered its invitation for Dr. Baker's timely return.

After their short conference, Dr. Baker raised his hand and the room fell silent. "Attention, friends. Let me make sure this is what we've all agreed to: next week I'll come back on Tuesday to finish what I was not able to get to this afternoon, including listening to any guided walks that I may not be able to hear today after we disband. A week from today, on the very unusual day of the 29th of February, you have already scheduled a student, Mr. Sean Potter, who will address you on the subject of 'Fear and Death.' On March 12th, any of you are who are still alive will see my return, and I will talk to you about hypnosis and some of the things it can accomplish. I believe that you even want me to give a demonstration, using one of your club members as my volunteer. Anyone who wants to volunteer on that day must, and I repeat *must*, bring a notarized permission slip signed by one of his or her parents. Two days later, on Thursday, March 14th, we will do some additional work in guided imagery together. Now, how's all that?"

Applause and hoots thundered in the classroom, as Dr. Baker gave a cordial bow of appreciation to his audience. The Giant's son stepped forward to shake Dr. Baker's hand to thank him for coming. They conferred briefly at the teacher's desk, and then Dr. Baker announced, "I will be glad to stay for a while in order to listen to anyone who would like to tell me about his or her visualization from today's exercise."

Chapter Eleven
The Swami's Booth of Ten Thousand Screams

A N AIR OF EXCITEMENT FILLED THE ROOM, for it was February 29th, that elusive, special day that arrives once every four years, and during this particular year on a Thursday. Sean Potter's agreement to make a presentation to the Learning Club had club members and visitors abuzz about what he might say or do. A projector sat in the back of the room and next to it were more than a dozen of Sean's friends who had come to enjoy his presentation.

Sean was one of the most popular seventh graders, except when he broke the curves on math and science tests. Then he was the most unpopular, until he went to the respective teachers and pleaded mercy for his friends. He would remind his teachers that his abilities should not be compared with others in his class, for he had the advantage of having a photographic memory. Once, when asked for proof, he began to recite, verbatim, a lecture on rivers and lakes given two months previously. For all his efforts, the prevailing compromise was to extend to the rest of the class a generous curve when test scores plummeted.

"May I have your attention please," a feminine voice called at the front of the room. "My name is Dana Foley, and I'm the Secretary-Treasurer of... " and here Dana paused for dramatic effect and particular word emphasis, continuing, "*this here* Learning Club. I have been appointed the student host for these meetings supposedly because I have the gift of gab and like to talk. The real truth is that the President and

Vice-President are afraid to address groups of more than six people, so here I am stuck with the job."

Hoots, whistling, and applause filled the room.

"Today we are glad to have one of our own Midville Middle School students for our speaker: Mr. Sean Potter, a member of the seventh grade."

More hoots were heard amid a hearty round of applause.

"Some of his friends have come to hear him, but they also needed to help him find the room. You know these seventh grade rug rats. This is a big building, much larger than the grade school."

Boos and hisses greeted Dana's jab as she added, "They found it, too. Congratulations. Without any more fuss, I give you Sean Potter."

Applause and hoots again filled the room as Sean strode purposefully to front and center. He carried a small box, which he carefully placed on the teacher's desk behind him. Then he wrote on the board in large, bold lettering:

A PRESENTATION BY THEATRE-CREATURES, INC.

Turning and smiling, Sean looked toward his friends in the back of the room, nodding, and saying, "It gives me great pleasure that my hangers-on, sitting there in the back of the room, have followed me here today, with the obvious hope of learning something."

More boos and hisses emanated from Sean's coterie as Sean raised his hand, asking, "Any challengers?"

Hooter Reynolds, a blond-haired kid with an athletic build, jumped up in an earnest attempt to run to the front of the room to accept Sean's challenge to do battle, but was dramatically restrained by Brad Mallon.

"No, you'll kill 'im again, just like last time," Brad cautioned the eager fighter.

"Let me go," ordered Hooter, "let me go!"

"All right, then," said Brad, stepping aside.

Hooter stood in disbelief as if someone had just clubbed him between the eyes, eyes which became increasingly large in their shocked astonishment.

"What?" was all he could say.

"*En garde!*" yelled Sean, assuming a karate posture.

As Hooter looked at Brad and then back at Sean, the faintest semblance of a grin passed over his face.

"Fell for it," he laughed. "Didn't think I'd catch on, did you?"

"Well, done," Sean congratulated both of his friends.

All eyes were now riveted on the speaker, all ears straining to hear the meaning of the small drama which had just occurred. Surveying the class, as if to fix the position of each person in his mind, Sean cupped his left hand up to his left ear.

"Can you hear it?" he asked.

Everyone stared at him blankly, as if either he or they were nuts.

"Can you hear it? It's the big train, the big one, coming for us all, but it will be coming for us at different times and in different places. We each carry a ticket, although we don't know when the train will be stopping. We all hope it won't stop for a long time, but we still carry that ticket, because that was part of the bargain we made when we were born into this world. Some day, each of us will die. And that train is coming closer every minute, but all we do right now is to put it out of our minds and pretend it isn't there. Sometimes we deny that it even exists, hoping against hope, as we ignore its steady whistle.

"Aristotle said, *Luck is when the other fellow gets hit with the arrow,* and in some measure we feel the same way, although we don't think of it very often. A week ago today, we were privileged to hear a wise man, a learned psychologist, speak about the desirability for each of us, each day, to arrive at a greater 'clarity of self', thereby better able to face all of our fears.

"Dr. Baker helped us to discover within ourselves, and to devise publicly, a way of examining our journeys on this planet, including the obstacles we face and the fears that they might represent. And I submit to you that out of all of those fears, the ultimate, greatest fear is ... DEATH. Remember, too, what the famous Dr. Johnson said, that 'the prospect of death wonderfully concentrates the mind.'"

Suddenly Hooter Reynolds gave a heart piercing cry, as if murdered, as he struggled to get out of his desk, but instead falling noisily on the floor. All eyes were now turned on Hooter, who was trying to crawl a few feet, but then suddenly dropped his head limply on his left arm.

"Poor Hooter," said Sean. "He obviously didn't realize that the death train was coming for him today. What would his last day, his last week, his last month have been like if he had only known that the sands were falling briskly through his life's hourglass? Poor Hooter. Perhaps there's a lesson in his passing, a lesson that will help us to seize the moment, *carpe diem*, so as not to waste a single second on things like indecision or boredom or laziness or even the fear of failure.

"The word 'fail' comes from the Latin *fallere*, which originally meant to deceive, to escape from. A derivative of the original Latin is *fallan*, which means to fall. How can we better understand the meaning of failure and our relationship to it than by examining its original meaning? *What* is deceived? *What* is escaped from? *What* falls?"

A loud groan suddenly emanated from Hooter, who still lay lifeless on the floor, and brought subdued laughter from the class.

"Oh, sorry Hooter," Sean apologized. "I forgot you were still dead. You may resume your seat. I must have forgotten Hooter because in all of our airsoft battles, he's always the first one to take a lot of hits and then has to lie there dead, waiting for the rest of us to finish the war."

"NOT!" protested Hooter.

"So," continued Sean, "as I was saying, or asking: in our own relationship to failure, if we avoid the unpleasant prospect of failing: Whom do we deceive? Whom do we escape from? Who falls?"

Members of the Learning Club stared blankly, considering Sean's questions, with Larry Jones suddenly blurting, "You do."

"You mean 'ourselves and we do'," corrected Sean. "Now hear me out. I think I have a small insight here that may help all of us: real living is about seizing the moment, taking full advantage of every opportunity that presents itself, drinking in life in all its wonder and glory. If we avoid the possibility of failure by inaction, just as we try to avoid the possibility of death by not living life to its fullest, we deceive ourselves. We shroud ourselves in a funk of non-growth, just as Dr. Baker has suggested. We resist any kind of change that threatens to remove us from our safe, little worlds, although those worlds are decaying from the lack of any kind of challenge or fresh air. We fall prey to the old patterns that keep us from risking failure because they seem safe, but that is an illusion."

Sean paused to consider his audience, to catch each of their eyes and to make sure they were listening, and all were, before he added the whisper, "Failure ... is also an illusion."

Noticing that many seemed surprised by this revelation, Sean continued, "When we try our best at something, when we seize the moment, we never really fail, because we have given all we can give. That is my definition of excellence: to give the best that I can give. By trying to avoid this illusion called failure, we waste our energy evading phantoms of our own creation. I don't care who tells you that you have failed. If you have given your best, in the most important sense of the word: you have succeeded. Nothing is ever disappointing when we give our best effort, but that means work and diligence and commitment and even admitting that we might not reach our goal. And if we don't reach our goal, it doesn't mean that we have failed, for we will have seized the moment and will have *lived* the possibilities to their fullest. If you have ever felt bored, it's because you have not seized the moment of your situation. And the real beauty of it is that every situation is as different as every person.

"Now as to how all of this relates to the train of death, I think one clear example might save us having to hear many more of my words. May I have a volunteer from the audience?"

Quite sensibly, no one volunteered.

"Okay, then. Zeke, please come up here as a personal favor to me," Sean requested.

Zeke looked around at his classmates, several of whom nodded their approval that Zeke had been called upon to face this test, rather than they themselves. Cautiously, Zeke stood up and walked to join Sean at front and center.

"Now, Zeke, do you see this train?" asked Sean, taking out a toy train from the small box he had brought.

Zeke nodded.

"Zeke, I want you to turn around and pretend that you are walking merrily on your way through life, and you're being very careful to avoid any kind of real involvement. You're just cruising along, happily oblivious to the fact that this train is coming for you."

Zeke turned toward the door.

"Okay, Zeke, begin walking in place," instructed Sean.

Zeke began to walk in place.

"Tell me what your thinking, Zeke," Sean requested.

"Oh, nothin', except that I'm just movin' right along here in this same old rut, with no cares in the world," Zeke responded.

Sean removed a shiny dagger from the box and displayed it to the class, some of whom gasped.

"You see Zeke, there," said Sean, "going merrily on his way, having successfully denied that this train is coming for him, but the grains of sand are running out of his life's hourglass. He's young, so he probably won't die from disease. More likely, it will be from an unexpected accident, maybe a car crash, because we so deny our mortality that most of our deaths are quite unexpected."

Zeke kept walking in place.

"Now, Zeke, you will soon hear the train whistle. When you do, I want you to turn around and face me as quickly as you can," Sean instructed.

Sean poised himself with the dagger, waiting.

Zeke kept walking along merrily, until Hooter gave a very credible impersonation of a train whistle in the back of the room. Turning quickly, Zeke could only glimpse Sean's stealthy figure darting toward him. The knife was deftly plunged into Zeke's chest, blood spurting out on Sean's hand and on Zeke's shirt. The class gasped in horror and alarm, as it saw Zeke's eyes go wide in apparent pain and surprise, blood suddenly trickling out of the left corner of his mouth. The class sat motionless, shocked in horror, as Zeke fell limply against Sean and sank to the floor. Sean held the bloodstained knife up to the class in triumph, announcing, "So you see, death *does* come to us all."

The class sat stunned.

"Okay, Zeke, you can get up now," announced Sean. "Thanks for letting me murder you. I hope you had as much fun as I did."

When Zeke lumbered up from the floor, the class applauded in relief that the skillful homicide just witnessed had only been an illusion.

Returning the dagger to the box, Sean picked up the train, warning, "This train comes for us all. From the very moment we are born, it is dispatched on its journey, but not one of us knows the exact times of arrival and departure. We have heard within the walls of this Learning Club that some authorities believe that the most significant kind of learning has to come from experience. Part two of my presentation to you will not be here at school, but at my home, where all of you ninth graders are invited to come beginning this Monday. You will have the opportunity to face and name your fears in the Grand Swami's Booth of Ten Thousand Screams. Please turn the projector on, Mary.

"See this drawing? It is a crude sketch of the celebrated Booth of Ten Thousand Screams. It will give you a foretaste of what will become your moment of destiny, your moment to face and to name your fears. You will each soon be given a free coupon to come and visit the Grand Swami, who will prepare you for your journey."

Here a photograph of Sean wearing an orange turban filled the screen, but no one laughed, remembering well the presence of the dagger in the box next to where Sean now stood, together with how expertly Sean had thrust its blade into Zeke's chest.

"And, in this drawing, you will walk down the Hall of Footfalls, and if you turn around, you must go back and begin again, until you have reached Mary, who will be waiting for you at the far end. She will then take you into the Booth of Ten Thousand Screams. Here are my assistants," and a slide flashed up of Sean's friends, many of whom were watching from the back, "and it may well be their footsteps will haunt your walk down the Hall of Footfalls; in fact, they might be brandishing knives, perhaps real knives, to prevent you from arriving at greater clarity about your fears. But, no matter, if you should be stabbed in the Hall of Footfalls, my mom is an excellent ER doc and she might be able to save you, provided no vital organs are damaged, and some of you may need to be careful so as not to slip on your classmates' blood. So bear all that in mind when you come, and don't worry, life has no guarantees. Live each minute to its fullest. You may be dead in a week. And even if you're not, facing your fears and having experienced the terror of having nearly touched the great death, you will find a freshness to the water you drink, you will savor the food you smell, and you will be grateful that you have been given another day in which to become all that you are capable of becoming. Mary, the tickets."

Mary turned the projector off and passed out coupons.

* * * * *

As Sean walked home with Mary, he basked in her scolding.

"How could you?" she asked. "The class was really shocked when you thrust that dagger into Zeke's chest. It probably took a month off of everyone's life."

"I hope so," her brother responded, "the topic was fear, so I had to frighten them. Anyway, everyone signed up for coming to my Booth of Ten Thousand Screams before they left, didn't they?"

Mary walked in silence, frowning at the frozen chunks of snow that had been littered here and there by the sidewalk plow, partially upset by her brother's ruse and partially miffed that it had succeeded so well.

"Don't give me the silent treatment. I went to see Mr. Ferling-hausen about the whole presentation. At first, he was very reluctant to approve it, until we talked and talked about the importance and power of the dramatic in our lives. I think he still had some reservations, but I promised that I would give a subtle warning to everyone by writing that announcement about the theatre-creatures' presentation on the board. Guess I really took everyone in, eh?" Sean gloated.

"For all of a minute," Mary admitted.

"That's when I told Zeke he could get up. He played the part well, too," said Sean.

"Had you rehearsed it?" asked Mary.

"Only once in the bathroom just before the club meeting. That's when I gave Zeke the plastic capsule that held the fake blood. Didn't it look awesome when it sort of burst out of the side of his mouth after I stabbed him?"

"A little too awesome. I mean, that's what made it seem so real," Mary admitted.

"And how about the blood stain on his shirt and blood smeared on the dagger?" asked Sean.

"Very clever," snorted Mary. "How did you manage that?"

"It pays to get the best," said Sean. "That dagger cost me a lot of money. I bought it from the best theatrical catalog I could find. It not only cost me a lot of money, but a lot of lost sleep, because I knew I wouldn't know until it arrived if it was really top quality. There's even a little place you can pour in the fake liquid blood, so it spurts out when the blade retracts into the dagger's handle."

"Zeke had more blood on his shirt than that dagger could ever have given him," Mary observed.

"Right you are. I gave him two blood capsules for each hand, for him to crack open when he clutched his chest. Wasn't it neat how he made his eyes get a little bit bigger and he looked like he was in shock before he fell to the floor?"

"Yeah, and it completely horrified the club," said Mary. "You should have apologized."

"Maybe," considered Sean. "Any way, now they can face their innermost fears."

"When did you get the dagger?" asked Mary.

"About a month ago. I had planned to save it for my Swashbuckler Swords gang, but today was absolutely *perfect*."

"You're crazy," said Mary. "You know that, don't you?"

"We're all mad," retorted Sean. "That's what the Cheshire cat said, and he was right. Anyway, there weren't any heart attacks."

The twins walked on in silence, Mary considering Sean's words.

"Why did you tell Bobby's class that they couldn't come to look at their fears until this coming week?"

"This is Thursday and I need the whole weekend to get my booth ready," said Sean.

"Not the space ship," said Mary.

"You got it," said Sean. "It shouldn't be too hard to convert it."

"Why not? It's been everything else imaginable," said Mary. "How are you going to convert it?"

"Paint it black and red and give it gold lettering and put a dragon on it, baring its teeth," said Sean. "It'll look really forbidding. They'll be so scared, they won't even know anyone's listening to them."

"But's it not *big* enough for two people," said Mary.

"I'm going to crawl up inside under where the space controls used to be. My right ear will be directly under each visitor's mouth."

"Why not simply put in a microphone?"

"Not as effective. I want to be able to hear the slightest whisper," Sean explained. "Anyway, the loudspeaker behind each visitor will be able to play one of eight loops, at my command. I'll be holding the remote control. That way, I can gauge their confessions."

"Confessions?" asked Mary.

"Of their deepest fear or fears," sighed Sean. "Didn't you listen to any of my talk at the club meeting today?"

"Not after you stabbed Zeke," said Mary.

"I'm going to need your help, especially in greeting them when they arrive and preparing them for the booth. Will you help me?"

"For a price," Mary smiled.

"What is it, this time?"

"You wash the dishes all next week," said Mary.

"All week?" Sean protested.

"All week," Mary replied firmly.

"Okay," agreed Sean.

* * * * *

In a far corner of the basement of the Potters' rambling old nineteenth century house stood a once-and-future wooden space ship that Sean, several years before, had successfully wheedled out of a family friend, who also happened to be an expert carpenter. Originally designed as a compact space capsule, the device had witnessed a variety of services throughout Sean's expansive childhood and adolescence, including distinguished service as a military bunker, a medieval torture chamber, a British telephone booth like the one used by the great Doctor Who, a casket, a hidden alcove from which to shoot friends during airsoft wars, a backdrop for target practice with BB guns and, now, what would become Swami Sean's redoubtable *Booth of Ten Thousand Screams*.

With a diligent persistence characteristic of his sharp focus once he had embarked upon a course of action, Sean set himself to an entire weekend of meticulous work, preparing the stage for the following week.

The future Booth of Ten Thousand Screams had most recently been painted in camouflage, serving as the site of a number of violent skirmishes during a series of war games, resulting in many protracted deaths. The first job, however, was to find a new location for the booth in the basement. Students from Bobby's class would descend from the main stairwell, while at the same time Sean would have to scurry down a side entrance to the basement so as to enter the booth unobserved. After making careful measurements, the better to favor the angle of his entrance, Sean decided to place the booth behind the main stairwell, which would necessitate that students be escorted a short distance once they had reached the basement floor, a short walk that could be very disconcerting if conducted in the ominous hue of a faint red light.

Once Sean had repositioned the booth, with Mary's help, he treated it to two thick coats of black paint. Leaving the new paint to dry, he proceeded to perfect his costume as the Swami, which had been chosen from an array of refugee garments inherited after an ancient production about the Arabian nights. This forgotten wardrobe included an elegant dark blue silk shirt, red silk pants, and an orange turban, which proved perfect to his need.

Mary agreed to supervise the schedule, and to monitor the three students who would come each day after school, until the entire group would have faced their fears by Friday afternoon, March 8th. When each trio arrived, they would be escorted into the Potter living room to wait for their respective audiences with the Grand Swami. Mary would bring each student into the presence of the Swami, who would be sitting on an oversized pillow in the small room that abutted the dining room.

A game plan would be necessary, so the twins concocted the following procedure as a typical protocol: the Swami would prep each member of the class as to what would happen. Sean would conclude each initial interview by proclaiming — 'The Grand Swami has spoken and will now go and ring the bell of your entry' — after which he would fold his arms against his chest and exit to the kitchen through two old blue bed sheets rigged as curtains against the door. After exiting, he would ring an old cow bell and then immediately throw off his

Swami shirt and turban and race as fast and as quietly as he could down the back basement stairs as Mary escorted the student down the front basement stairs that were accessible from the foyer. At that point, each student would wait for Mary to cross toward the booth before embarking through the infamous Hall of Footfalls. If students turned when they heard the footsteps, they would have to go back and repeat their journey. Sean had rigged a recorder and several speakers that were cued by electronic sensors on the floor as students walked by. Mary stood near a floor switch which would activate and turn off the system. By the time she had conducted her charge to the Booth of Ten Thousand Screams, Sean would already have wedged himself up under what was once the space control panel. Students would sit in the darkened booth and speak into a funnel, which would lead directly into a tube that Sean would fit to his ear. The care taken to ensure that the Grand Swami could hear each student grew in part from the plan to have various screams and directions sounding from a loudspeaker behind the student's head. On Saturday, Sean adapted the eight feedback recording loops to his remote control and concocted several voice instructions complete with speech distortion and a choice of four bloodcurdling screams, equally distorted and enhanced through the wonder of echo recording technology. After each ordeal in the booth, Mary would escort the student back upstairs to the foyer to the Swami's receiving room as Sean raced up the back stairwell, donning his Swami shirt and turban and resuming his posture on the pillow, so as to appear that he had returned to meditate after leaving to ring the bell. The Swami would then unveil a crystal ball sitting on a pillow in front of him and proceed to look into the student's future, after which the student would be escorted out.

After taping the various pre-recorded loops to his satisfaction, having induced Mary to scream for him by promising a second week's worth of dish duty, Sean tested the remote control to make sure that the whole system was working properly. After giving it a dry run with Mary three times in a row, Sean set himself to painting a ferocious dragon on the front of the booth as Mary strung some more old bed sheets in the vicinity of the booth to make it look more mysterious. In addition to bathing the basement in a faint red glow, Sean erected a small spotlight that would shine on his dragon, which looked much like the one on the ticket he had given to each student.

By midweek, the twins had become so successful in their ruse that they had completely stymied class members. Part of the reason was that, although everyone smelled a rat, no one could discover where the rat lay. It occurred to no one that Sean could or would wrench himself into such a small space in the booth, his ear only inches from their whispers. The exit interviews also proved helpful to class members, thanks to Sean who, with his hard won insights, was deftly able to shine a positive light on their confessed misfortunes and fears. As the week passed, the mood of the class became less depressed, although everyone still smelled a rat, yet none could figure out how they were being hoodwinked, which bugged the dickens out of them, especially Bobby Perkins. It was an endless topic of speculation and frustration.

Thursday, however, brought a turning point through an invaluable insight. The last person to face the booth on that day was none other than Dana Foley. Spunky and determined, she was all ears when she entered the inner sanctum, intent on noticing every nuance of sound and visual clue that might disclose the secret to Sean's mysterious and uncanny success. The light was so dim that students were scarcely able to see where they had taken their seats, and the curtain was always closed by Mary. When it was Dana's turn, she resolved to open her senses as widely as possible to ferret out any clues that might fall her way, the better to understand the tricks of this irrepressible Swami.

"I am the Swami," came Sean's prerecorded voice, "and I will now give you three minutes of inward looking before I open the Dragon of Ten Thousand Screams. FACE YOUR FEARS!"

Dana sat in near darkness, contemplating her fears. She saw in her mind her worry that her parents might die in a car accident, a sentiment which grew out of a family car accident when she was only four years old. Another worry that surfaced was that of not being liked by her friends: image after image began to haunt her mind. A third fear began to intrude, somehow related to her cat, but before that could fully manifest itself, an ear piercing scream filled the booth, after which the Swami's voice, in full-echo majesty, intoned, "Open your heart, earthly mortal, and state your fear." Dana obeyed, whispering her inmost worries into the funnel that stood in front of her lips.

Another piercing scream echoed through the booth. The Swami's voice ordered, 'LOUDER.' Dana spoke with less hesitation, repeating her fears. A new scream descended, after which the Swami's voice announced, 'Earthly mortal, you will soon be escorted back to the majestic presence of the Grand Swami.'

Dana sighed, for any clue she had hoped to uncover had not been forthcoming, that is, until Sean gave an involuntary and muffled sneeze. If she had not been wide open, listening for every possible clue, she might have missed hearing a foreshortened kind of sneeze that Sean's mom, an emergency room physician, had taught him how to do years before, thus restraining him from sneezing on the family dinner as he sniffed its aroma in the crock pot. Subdued as his sneeze had been, it had been enough to inform Dana that the Swami was only a few inches from where she sat. Thinking it best that Sean not realize that he had unwittingly tipped his hand, Dana waited for Mary to come fetch her back to the Grand Swami's presence.

Upon entering the countenance of that majesty, Dana was seated as the Swami reviewed her fears, speaking of how natural they were, and how she could now cast them aside. Ironically, she suddenly found herself feeling a bit lighter and more optimistic from her experience, notwithstanding all of the theatrics. —Maybe just speaking one's fears out loud to oneself is enough, thought Dana as she walked home. Once home, she immediately called Bobby and Zeke, who in turn passed the news to other members of the class. Earlier in the week, Sean and Mary had bet the class that they would not be able to figure out the technical aspects of their operation. That bet had now been lost, but Jiggs Stevenson, Joey Harris, and Maureen Grant had yet to endure their respective visits to the Booth of Ten Thousand Screams the next afternoon. At least they could be clued in, which would be a triumph for the entire class.

After school on Friday, March 8th, Jiggs and Maureen walked home with the Potter twins. Zeke Minturn had to search for Joey and bring him a little later. It was decided upon his arrival that Joey had better be the first to venture into the presence of Swami, to ensure that the former could still perceive the Swami's presence, before zoning out. Joey would be followed by Jiggs and then by Maureen.

* * * * *

When Joey was ushered into the Great Swami's presence, Sean saw at once that he would have an uphill battle, for Joey's eyes betrayed the fact that part of him was somewhere else. Sean had heard Bobby's criticism of Joey's reliance on drugs, and he wondered if this rather theatrical ruse would serve any purpose, especially for Joey's greater benefit.

"Do you know who I am?" intoned the Great Swami.

Joey squinted, rubbed his eyes, staring at the exalted presence which had just addressed him.

"Well?" demanded the Great Swami.

"Is ... is that *you*, Sean?" asked Joey.

"SILENCE, MORTAL," thundered Sean, aggrieved that even in his perfunctory state, Joey had seen through his Swami persona.

Joey sat silent, wonder rising in eyes about the strange presence which sat in front of him.

"You will soon be taken to the Booth of Ten Thousand Screams," announced Sean. "Prepare yourself."

Standing up, folding his arms against his chest, the Grand Swami strode purposefully out of the room. Mary tapped Joey on his left shoulder, beckoning him to follow her. By the time he had seated himself in the booth, Sean was already in place and ready to rip. Mary bowed to Joey as she ceremoniously shut the door of the booth.

Sean pushed button number eight, which released the most terrifying echo enhanced scream of Mary's voice. A banshee wail could have instilled no greater fear. After the decibels abated, there was only silence in the booth.

—Better let him have another shot, thought Sean to himself. —This kid really needs a wake-up call.

Once again the horrible, wailing sound filled both the booth and the basement, and once again there was only silence in its wake.

Sean pushed button number three, and his echo enhanced voice ordered, "Listen, foolish mortal. Open your heart."

A short silence followed, and then Joey whispered, obviously quite taken by the entire experience, "Sean, *this* is so cool. So cool."

Sean pushed button number two, and the Grand Swami's voice could be heard commanding, "Mortal, face thy great fear and tell."

"I ... suppose it's, maybe, gettin' busted," said Joey.

"Why, mortal?" thundered the loudspeaker behind Joey's head.

"My mom would be really sad," said Joey.

Sean decided he had gone as far as he could, so he pushed button number five, and the Grand Swami's enhanced voice proclaimed, "We are done. You, mortal, will be escorted back to see the Grand Swami in his chambers."

When Joey entered into the presence of the Grand Swami, Sean could see both admiration and life in his eyes.

"Sean," he began, correcting himself, continuing, "I mean, your Grand Swami, sir, that is so cool, just so cool. What else can you do?"

"The Swami can do many things," Sean bragged. "Too many to tell you now, but know that you should never cross the Swami, or else a fate worse than death will await you."

"So cool," marveled Joey, as Mary escorted him out.

When Mary showed Jiggs in, Sean sat peering at him for a full minute, mainly because he was still miffed about what he considered to have been his failure with Joey. For his part, Jiggs wasn't going to give any ground to such treatment. After all, he had his dignity to think about. How could he ever carry himself with pride again if he let this little seventh grade upstart best him? Returning Sean's gaze, Jiggs finally said, "Well? Are we going to sit here all day staring at each other, or are you going to get off your little-seventh-grade duff and meet me down in that ratty booth you think is so grand?"

Jiggs was accustomed to bluffing his way through most arguments and confrontations. He had always been successful at using his sarcasm to throw off potential adversaries. Unfortunately, this tried and true method did not work now. As the depth of the insult took root, Sean's eyes grew as wide as they grew cold, causing a very deserved shiver to begin running up and down Jiggs' spine. Born under the sign of Aries, Sean was, if anything, a warrior, and a challenge so abrupt and direct invoked in him the desire to draw blood, but any violent brutalizing of Jiggs would be out of character for a Swami, especially a Grand Swami. In truth, Jiggs' in-your-face insolence to a so-called 'mere seventh grader' wasn't what had frosted Sean; rather, it was Jiggs' derisive reference to Sean's prized possession, the sacred booth of fun, play and imagination, which now caused Sean to consider carefully what part of Jiggs' body on which he would make his attack, Swami or no Swami.

Fortunately, Mary had overhead the challenge and, knowing that her brother was as impulsive as he was fearless and bloodthirsty, stepped between them, taking Jiggs by the arm and announcing, "Grand Swami, I will fetch this putrid excuse for a mortal down to the booth. He won't last long."

Sean glared at Jiggs, reluctantly restraining himself from an overwhelming desire to attack and pummel.

"You, foolish, miserable mortal," said Mary, looking at Jiggs, "are most fortunate that the Grand Swami has spared your worthless life. Otherwise, he would be wearing you for his shoes tomorrow morning."

Mary's unexpected humor and acknowledgment of his prowess brought Sean back to himself, and he bowed, folded his hands on his chest, and walked out.

As she escorted the miserable mortal downstairs, Mary shook her head and scolded, in dismay, "Jiggs, I can't believe you said that to Sean. Don't you know that he's got a brown belt in karate? He could break your neck in a heartbeat. And he *does* have a temper."

Mary didn't need to say anything more. Jiggs only had to remember the chills that had coursed up and down his spine as Sean had prepared to spring at him, for that chill of fear was the first intimation of terror that Jiggs had felt since he had been a very young boy and had been afraid to go to sleep in the dark. Unlike most of his compatriots, Jiggs appeared unfazed by the recorded footsteps. Actually, he was so rattled by Mary's warning, that he scarcely heard them.

Sean waited in the booth for his prey. Jiggs had thrown down the gauntlet and was now going to be given back a little of his own. After Mary had bowed and shut the door, Sean pushed button number eight, calling forth the worst possible wail, which he repeated three times, as appropriate openers for Jiggs' introspective look into his inner fears. If Jiggs had forgotten his early childhood terrors, those same hobgoblins had not forgotten him, and the dark shadows of the musty basement now caused those fears to return with a vengeance. Sweat began pouring down Jiggs' face as the voice of the Grand Swami thundered in the booth, followed by bloodcurdling screams and wails. Jiggs was also perspiring out of the realization that he had gone much too far with Sean during the interview. His normal off the cuff sarcasm had not served him well in the presence of the Grand Swami. The thunder rang louder and louder in the booth, as the Swami demanded to know about the subject's fears. During his confessional, Jiggs revealed that, as a young boy, he had been afraid to go to sleep at night, sensing a dark presence lurking in his closet. Sean silently wondered whether the so-called 'dark presence' had been Jiggs' clothes, for his current attire certainly conveyed that impression. At some time or another most children are afraid of the dark. Perhaps Jiggs had transferred that fear to some nebulous imagining in his closet. Sean doubted very much that Jiggs' had any pluck, either in his wardrobe or elsewhere, but he suddenly became determined in his own mind that he was going to find out. Accordingly, he decided to quickly terminate Jiggs' visit to the Booth of Ten Thousand Screams and raced upstairs to administer the test that had just flashed through his mind.

—Diabolical, Sean thought to himself, —but not without merit or reward, if I'm right.

Mary escorted Jiggs in to stand in front of Sean, who was also standing.

"The Swami permits the Jiggs to sit," intoned Sean.

Jiggs sat, careful to keep his large mouth shut.

"The Swami sees a short existence for the Jiggs in this crystal ball, a *very* short existence."

Jiggs swallowed hard and began to perspire.

"But service to others is what is needed to extend this life, possibly to as far as early middle-age. The Jiggs would do well to become of service to someone. The Grand Swami now wants to introduce the Jiggs to his assistant," the Grand Swami announced, bowing. "Soon I will go fetch him. His name is Sean. He is my bodyguard. He has killed hundreds of fools, fools who have dared to question him or me. He especially loves ripping their livers out and eating them raw. He tells me livers are delicious, especially if they're dripping in warm, sticky blood."

The Grand Swami bowed again as he stood, continuing, "I will go fetch him. He's in a bad temper over what some fool said to him earlier. Oh, I saw blood in his eyes. That fool may not have long to live. If so, I also may try fresh liver today."

Perspiration began dripping profusely from Jiggs' forehead.

"I will go fetch him," continued the Grand Swami. "He's only in the next room. Perhaps he's sharpening the liver knife. It's so shiny and thin, which is just perfect for slicing."

Jiggs began to breath heavily and to wet his lips.

"I will go fetch him," proclaimed the Grand Swami, turning to make a quick exit.

"NO!" begged Jiggs. "I'll do anything ... *anything!*"

Panic filled Jiggs eyes as he pleaded for mercy.

"There is one thing this Sean might accept," said the Grand Swami.

"Yes, what is it?" asked Jiggs. "Just name it."

"He needs a servant, a butler, who will wait on him hand and foot as he may venture to prescribe, merely by clapping his hands like this."

Here the Grand Swami gave two quick claps with his hands.

"Yes. What do you want?" asked Jiggs, breathlessly.

"I am not the Sean. You must ask him that when you see him. I will tell him, though. So he will know. And you will know. And he will know that you know, and you will know that he knows. And you will know that he knows that you know."

Here the Grand Swami clapped his hands again.

"Anything," begged the new butler.

"Go now and wait to do his bidding," instructed the Grand Swami, as Jiggs, relieved and still perspiring, turned and fled the room. As Jonathan Maplethorpe Stevenson rushed out of the house, barely giving Mary time to open the front door for his unimpeded exit, he gave a panicked and exasperated look at Maureen, who was sitting impatiently in the living room, feeling sorry for herself and aggrieved that the boys had gone in first and that she had been made to wait. Her wait, however, had also afforded her ample time to sulk, during which she had become clear about several things.

The first was that Sean made her nervous. His foolish little shenanigans were unsettling. She liked Zeke, who had always been kind to her, and she, for an instant, had worried that Sean had truly murdered him at Thursday's club meeting. She had also heard Bobby describing Sean as a little magpie to his friends, and this she added as another negative to Sean's personality. But perhaps it was Sean's talk to the Learning Club that had confirmed her intention to dislike him, for his acute and steady focus somehow made her feel very uncomfortable.

—Smarty pants show off, she thought. —He needs a good, stiff comeuppance to remind him of his real place. Maureen then thought of her place, and felt dark clouds roll over her smug rejection of Sean.

She knew that generally she carried herself like a thundercloud, wearing a sour-face for the world. And as sure as she was that she didn't care for Sean, an inner sentiment suddenly suggested to her the possibility that it might be a remote reflection that she also didn't care much for herself. Of course, she was slightly overweight, but only the mean girls took notice of that and made fun of her. Why did she crave eating all of the things that were not good for her, especially if she wanted to watch her figure? And why should *she* now have to wait when the boys went in first? Where were people's manners, anyway?

By the time she was ushered in to see Sean, Maureen resembled a smouldering bull in a bullpen; however, in his orange turban, Sean did not look much like a matador. If he had divined what was coming, he might well have picked up and run for his own sense of sanity and self. Instead, he looked Maureen over as she snorted her disapproval of him by fidgeting in her chair and paying him the discourtesy of inattention. This infuriated him, and he decided a good dose of button number eight might serve to bring this fickle Maureen back to her senses. Maureen, however, having heard of Dana's discovery, had not come unprepared. She was merely biding her time, for her own sake and for the sake of her classmates.

When Maureen was escorted down to the infamous booth, she, like Jiggs, had seemed unfazed by the footfalls, which had proven spookily successful with most students earlier that week. Perhaps it had been Dana's solving the mystery of the booth that had taken the uncertainty out of the larger gestalt of the experience. In any case, Maureen looked with growing disapproval at both the Hall of Footfalls as well as the Booth of Ten Thousand Screams. Mary noticed the rebellion in her eyes, but discounted it as an aggressive form of denial.

After the door to the booth was closed, Sean lammed into Maureen by giving her his best series of number eight recording loop screams, which amounted to four in succession. He couldn't see Maureen, but if he had, he would have tried to turn the volume of the speakers up, for she was holding her hands over her ears and studying the arrangement of the funnel device that sat in front of her lips. By the time the screams had stopped playing, she had figured out where Sean was crouching and what this funnel device led to: namely, to his right ear. A faint and diabolical smile crossed her lips and she waited to hear the Grand Swami's first injunction, which was, "Listen, foolish mortal. Open your heart."

A new series of screams echoed through the booth, although no one could see Maureen smiling as she clamped her hands over her ears. A new injunction from the Swami now ordered her to consider her fears, and during this interval of introspection, a brief interlude of silence ensued. Waiting for just enough time to pass, Maureen began to tell of her deepest fear, "I ... I don't know where to start. I am really afraid, and I don't know what to do."

"Continue, mortal," blared the loudspeaker behind her head.

As she continued to speak, she deliberately lowered the volume of her voice as she brought her listener up to the ultimate story climax. As she continued to speak ever more softly, her hand reached for a small object in the pocket of her sweater.

"And so, dear, wise, powerful Swami of the Booth of Terror, it turns out that my biggest fear is ..." The dim light reflected the flash of silver, and suddenly Maureen had her mouth clapped to a police whistle and was blowing it for all she was worth directly into the funnel that was connected to Sean's right ear. In self-defense, all Sean could do was hit button number eight, again and again, but that was merely a pyrrhic victory in the face of Maureen's whistle, which pounded in his ears like a sledgehammer with unabated fury. She continued blowing the whistle for all she was worth, just as Sean kept hitting number eight.

Sensing something was wrong, Mary appeared and opened the curtain to the booth, snatching the whistle out of Maureen's mouth and smashing it to the floor. Mary had seen Sean's ingenious funnel design, and she now worried that this monster who stood before her might well have deafened her brother or ruptured his eardrum.

"How dare you!" scolded Mary.

"Screw you," sneered Maureen. "Serves the imp right, trying to put on airs and lord it over us."

"He's trying to help you, if you could only see that. But you're too stupid to know that," countered Mary, who herself was not an inconsiderable fighter when it came to defending her family and friends.

"Show me out," ordered Maureen. "I can hardly wait to spread the news."

"First I'll show you back to the chambers of the Swami," said Mary. "Everyone else has done that before leaving, and so will you."

"All I need ..." began Maureen.

"Everyone else has done so and so will *you*," repeated Mary firmly, with cold ire.

When Mary led Maureen into the Swami's chamber, she could see the fury and pain in Sean's eyes. Mary was surprised that he had even returned to the room, yet knowing how much grit her brother had, she was certain that he had something appropriate planned for Maureen that would bring some justice to the situation.

Maureen sat smugly in her chair, basking in the glory of her triumph, but carefully avoiding any eye contact with Sean. Looking carelessly around the room, preparing to be inattentive to whatever Sean might say, she almost started to giggle, but suppressed the impulse.

Silence intervened, however, and its heaviness soon became increasingly uncomfortable. Maureen finally blurted out, "So, you finally got what *you* deserved."

The silence invaded the hollowness of her accusation, causing it to totter and crumble before her.

"Well, you did," huffed Maureen in defiance of the truth.

Again the silence revealed the emptiness of her accusation.

"Well, say something," she snarled at Sean, finally looking into his eyes. She immediately looked away, for she did not want to see what she had observed. She would never forget those eyes, the wounded innocence, the goodness betrayed, the sincerity crushed beneath the wheel of her whistling.

Sean said nothing, but only looked at her with his deep, penetrating, sad eyes. They haunted her actions, her very being.

In the face of their power, Maureen could only crumble inside like a wilted flower, tears pouring from her eyes, sobs burning her throat. Her jaw quivered and her hands trembled as she released her rage, a rage that had smouldered in her depths for years and that had desired to destroy everything that was of a greater quality.

She felt someone pushing soft tissues in her hands, and she applied them to the blur of tears that continued to stream down her face. She thought perhaps Mary had come in with the tissues, but when she looked out, she saw that it was Sean who was offering them to her. He looked very sad, and she knew his sadness was for her emptiness and for the anger and the pain that she felt, and that made her feel even more like the miserable worm she had convinced herself she was.

"That's okay," he said, comforting her. "That's okay. Mary, please bring us a glass of water."

Soon the water was being offered, as the sobs and tears continued, and Maureen suddenly found herself being hugged by both of the Potter twins, who simply held her in their arms, comforting her in silence.

Maureen had known little love in her life, and this outpouring of solicitude overwhelmed her. Even though, in its larger light, she felt like a miserable worm, there was no judgment or criticism in it as far as the Potter twins were concerned. They merely hugged and comforted and soothed.

Finally, Maureen wiped enough blur away from her eyes to see that all three of them were sitting, huddled together, on the floor. Looking at Sean, wanting to say how horribly sorry she was, Maureen couldn't find the right words, any words. But Sean did it for her.

"That's okay," he said, smiling. "I suppose I did deserve it."

Which, of course, made Maureen burst into tears again.

More sobbing followed, yet with it came the gentle, loving, embrace of friendship.

Finally getting some of her voice back, although it cracked when she spoke, Maureen looked at Sean and said, "Why didn't you yell at me or hit me?"

Sean smiled and put his hand on Maureen's knee, explaining, "You've already had enough of that, or else you wouldn't be hurting others so much. You must really have been hurting inside."

The words rang true down to the depths of Maureen's soul, although she scarcely was aware of what she might have been hurting from or why she had been so angry.

"Do you feel any better?" asked Sean.

Maureen reflected for a moment, answering, "Maybe a little lighter, but I don't know why."

"Anger and rage are irrational," said Sean. "It's hard to understand them rationally. It's hard enough even to know that they're sometimes there."

Maureen nodded, smiling.

"You have a beautiful smile," said Mary.

Sean nodded in agreement.

"Why don't you ever show the world that smile?" he asked.

Maureen shook her head, "I don't know."

"Well, it's easier to give a smile once you've received one," said Mary. "So, from now on, Sean and I are going to smile at you until we see yours. Is that a deal?"

Maureen grinned and nodded her assent, admitting, "I'm sorry I've been such an ass. Sean, is your ear okay?"

"It's still ringing, but I'm sure it will be fine."

"I can't say how sorry I am," said Maureen.

"Don't need to," announced Sean. "Apology accepted."

"Are you going to tell the class about the whistle?" asked Maureen.

"No," said Sean. "Are you?"

"What whistle?" asked Maureen.

"Sounds good to me," said Sean.

"I thought I was doing it for the class," Maureen confided. "But now I know I was doing it for me ... some perverse part of me."

"Not perverse," corrected Mary, "just hurting."

"You forgive me?" asked Maureen, looking at Sean.

Sean nodded, and a tear trickled down Maureen's right cheek.

"Let's make some hot chocolate," suggested Mary, rising to go into the kitchen.

After she left, Maureen looked at Sean and handed him the whistle, saying, "Please throw this away for me. I never want to see it again."

"Why throw it away? It's a good whistle; I mean, it really works," Sean smiled.

"It was in bad hands," said Maureen. "I never want to see it again."

"Where did you get it?" asked Sean.

"It was my grandfather's. He was a policeman."

"Wow! A real police whistle. Can I keep it?"

"Sure, if you want it. It's yours."

Mary called from the kitchen, "Come on in and make your hot chocolate. The instant hot water is instantly ready."

Sean and Maureen rose and went to join Mary.

Soon all were laughing about the Booth of Ten Thousand Screams, Maureen most of all.

Sean related his triumph with Jiggs.

"Serves him right," said Maureen. "He's been primming for the part of butler for years, and it has finally caught up with him."

"Don't think Sean won't use it," sighed Mary.

"One thing I don't understand," said Maureen.

"What's that?" asked Sean.

"Well, if you had held out the way you did with Jiggs, you might have gotten a maid out of it, too," Maureen laughed, pointing at herself.

The twins joined in laughing as Sean shouted, "I don't need a maid. I've got a sister."

A sturdy whomp was heard as Sean's smile strained a little.

"You two are brutal with each other," scolded Maureen.

"Of course," agreed Mary. "We're twins."

* * * * *

After Maureen had left, the twins took time to straighten up the kitchen, lest they incur the wrath of POTS the next day.

"Underling," asked Mary, "are you all right?"

Sean looked at Mary intently before answering, finally saying, "Yes."

"I was so upset with what Maureen did. Your ear must have been really hurting," said Mary.

"It felt like it was on fire. I guess I deserved it, with all those thunderclaps I threw at everybody this past week. Thanks for coming to help me when you did," Sean acknowledged.

"Oh, I know we have a lot of squabbles, both here at home and in public, but I won't let anyone hurt you, ever, if I can help it," said Mary.

"The same goes for me," confided Sean. "I won't let anybody ever hurt you."

"I know that you would've preferred a brother to a sister," said Mary, hesitating to share her fear.

"Naw," said Sean. "I would've killed a little brother years ago. This way, we can be pals, even though we sometimes fight like cats and dogs."

"You really mean it?" asked Mary.

Sean nodded. He wasn't used to talking about mushy things, especially with his sister. After the kitchen was straightened up and utensils put away, the twins retired to their respective bedrooms. Such moments between the twins were rare.

As Mary lay in bed, mulling over the day's events, she acknowledged to herself how very fond she was of her so-called underling, her younger twin by a matter of mere minutes. Sean was at the age where it was vitally important that the world know he was, at heart, a warrior; and, in fact, he was. But Mary knew about the soft spot in his heart; deep down under, he was a pussycat, although he rarely showed it. The last time had been when David's dog, Max, had been killed by Bobby Perkins' father. Sean had cried the hardest of anyone, and had not been ashamed for others to see his tears. Mary briefly wondered if a lot of her brother's bravado was for the sole purpose of hiding that soft, tender spot that she knew resided deep within him. No matter. They were twins, they loved each other, and if she had been born a male, she or he would have suffered fratricide years ago.

Chapter Twelve
Hypnosis Really Works

THE MEMBERS OF THE LEARNING CLUB HAD BEEN WAITING FOR OVER TWO WEEKS for Dr. Baker's return on this Tuesday afternoon of March 12th. The chosen topic of hypnosis was curious enough to hook everyone, although no one knew very much about it. The closest any of the group had ever been to formal hypnosis was watching stage hypnotists on television. Such experience, on their part, had only afforded them a theatrical view of the phenomenon. Now they had come to watch one of their peers go under the knife, to use a euphemism. With duly notarized permission slips in hand, all waited for the arrival of Dr. Baker.

Once again, Mr. Pennythorpe appeared at the door and showed Dr. Baker into the classroom. Sean's friends, who had come to cheer him on two weeks before, had also shown up, with signed permission slips in their hands. Like it or not, admit it or not, a fascination about hypnosis streamed like a mighty river through the combined psyches in this classroom.

As he removed his winter coat, it was interesting to note that Dr. Baker was wearing navy blue pants and a maroon turtle neck sweater, that his chosen attire at each subsequent presentation was becoming more informal. With him he carried several books and a small box. Placing them on the instructor's desk, he turned to those assembled, gave a wide smile and friendly nod, saying, "We'll begin in just a few minutes. I need a little time to get organized."

The members of the club shuffled a bit to become relaxed and comfortable for what was expected to be a lengthy and informative, and hopefully interesting, talk on the history of hypnosis.

"I am told," continued Dr. Baker, "that Mr. Sean Potter found an ingenious way to mix theory with experience, both during his talk on February 29th, as well as throughout this last week, with his much celebrated booth of one thousand screams."

"Ten thousand," corrected Sean, who was sitting in the back of the room with his friends.

"I beg your pardon," said Dr. Baker, smiling. "What's a scream here or there?"

"It was pretty lame," said Hooter, who was sitting next to Sean, and who immediately inherited a sharp elbow in his solar plexus.

"How many were frightened?" asked Dr. Baker.

Jiggs Stevenson raised his hand, looking around to see if any of his classmates would join him. None did. Wide-eyed, he began to lower it, until he saw Sean giving him the evil eye, and immediately he raised his hand even higher.

"Only one?" asked Dr. Baker.

"Well, we weren't scared as much as we were puzzled," began Zeke, "at how the little beggar could hear our every word and use them against us during the second interview."

"Against you?" puzzled Dr. Baker.

"Well, not really against us. Sean really did help most of us to face our fears, because he got us to say them aloud. I know I felt better after going, but it still bugged us all, because we didn't know how he was doing it, until one of our class members figured it out when Sean had to give a sort of muffled sneeze. Then we had the goods on him."

"But everyone still went?" asked Dr. Baker.

"We didn't figure it out until right before the last day. But the last three went because that was part of our bargain," Zeke explained.

"Better that Booth of Screams than some other method that forces your whole life to pass before your eyes," said Bobby. "I've had 'em both, and I'll take the Booth any day, like the choice between the whirlpool and the monster?"

"Scylla and Charybdis?" asked Dr. Baker.

"That's it. I heard about that pair last year. Ain't it true that some say that no matter which one you end up with, you wish you had gotten the other?"

"Some say that, I suppose," said Dr. Baker.

"Well, if Scylla is the little toy derringer, I'll take Charybdis any day," Bobby concluded, folding his arms and sitting back in his chair. Most in the room had heard of how Sean had actually caused Bobby's life to pass in front of his eyes in the library workroom in the fall.

"You'll have to explain that to me, sometime," said Dr. Baker. "Now let's turn our attention to hypnosis. Has anyone here ever seen anyone hypnotized?"

Several hands were raised.

"Was it on television?" asked Dr. Baker.

The students nodded in the affirmative.

"Yes. Stage hypnotists tend to give this whole field a sort of checkered reputation. That poses a significant problem. Let me assure you that no one can be forced into a hypnotic state, or forced to do anything against his or her will while under hypnosis. Let me also promise you that I will not ask anyone here to bark like a dog or to squawk like a chicken."

"Hooter!" yelled Sean's friends in the back of the room, laughing. "Hooter will."

"Hooter won't be asked to do so," corrected Dr. Baker.

"What if that person *is* a chicken to begin with?" asked Sean, to the delight of his friends.

Dr. Baker ignored the merriment emanating from the back of the room, while the Giant's son moved closer to Sean and his friends and whispered a few words. Suddenly a pall of sobriety descended on their raucous fraternizing and they became all attention, looking as one entity at Dr. Baker, hanging on his every word.

"Regarding hypnosis, I would caution you always to remember three things: one, no one can hypnotize another person, especially against that person's will; two, all hypnosis is merely self-hypnosis; and, three, hypnosis is nothing more than a state of heightened relaxation, wherein the subject becomes more amenable to suggestion. Hypnosis, therefore, as best I understand it, is an altered state of consciousness that is different from our normal waking state of consciousness. It is also an integrated state, for scans reveal that it is comprised of alpha, beta, and theta brain waves. There are many different kinds of hypnotic trance as well as different levels of relaxation. If you have ever caught yourself daydreaming, you have entered into an altered state of consciousness. Sometimes people, when driving long distances, will suddenly realize they have driven many miles without being aware of it. They, too, entered an altered state of consciousness, although they were not aware of it at the time. I suppose that daydreaming in front of a television set or in class at school represents additional altered states of consciousness, where the person has somehow left the present reality."

A stirring ripple of laughter affirmed the club members' knowledge of Dr. Baker's last example.

"Now, to elaborate a little on what I've already shared with you: to be hypnotized is to be neither awake nor asleep. Rather, it is to enter into a heightened state of relaxation, wherein the subject feels refreshed and clear-minded, while at the same time becoming more open to suggestions. Furthermore, as mentioned earlier, no one can force a person who is under hypnosis to do something against his or her will. There is often a sense of time disorientation for those who are hypnotized, many of whom are surprised to learn that forty-five minutes have passed, when it has seemed, for them, only like twenty minutes. Hypnosis has also proven itself as an effective tool in helping athletes reach their maximum level of performance. It has also aided students who have endeavored to use it to better their progress in school. Under hypnosis, a subject can often take in details of a normal setting that escape the attention of most people, and can repeat those details upon request. In part, I believe it shows how *very* observant some part of our psyche is, a part which stores a lot more information than we would normally ever realize. Finally, intent is important. Hypnosis relies on the power of words, the power of suggestion. The subconscious is very literal, and great care must be taken in how such suggestions are formed and given. Words are very powerful, and our intent is also not lost on a subject. Hypnosis, in psychotherapy, has also proven itself an effective tool at revealing truth that is sometimes masked by our conscious minds. Any questions so far?"

Bobby raised his hand, saying, "I saw in a movie once how this dude got a girl and made her lie stiff as a board between two little tables. Was that hypnosis?"

"Probably illusion more than hypnosis, although a subject's body can be made to do some astounding things under hypnosis, including giving the arms and legs greater strength. Any other questions before we proceed to a brief overview of the power of suggestion and the history of hypnosis?"

Club members sat absolutely riveted to their seats, totally focused on what they were learning, eager for the much anticipated demonstration.

"If anything, hypnosis is suggestion, suggestion given to a subject who is in a highly receptive state of consciousness. I believe there is great truth to the maxim that we become what we think we are, that the our conscious minds and subconscious minds can work in our favor if they are trained to do so. Post-hypnotic suggestion can work to the greater good and better health of a subject, whether it be formed to help that individual conquer a recurring and negative habit, or formed to help that individual see through to the reality of greater potential of self-fulfillment. While hypnosis can't make a major league baseball player out of someone whose skills are quite average, it can certainly help any athlete to his or her peak performance, perhaps even setting the *necessary* stage and discipline for even more advanced accomplishment. Why not, I ask you, use the recurrent power of suggestion for our greater good? It only waits to serve us, if we are willing to allow it.

"As for its origin, much of what I will now share with you comes from my many years of studying the history of hypnosis. It so happens that some of the earliest records regarding the use of suggestion come to us in accounts left by the ancient Egyptians. A stone pillar, whose origin dates to at least one thousand years before Christ, gives details of how induced sleep was used to help cure patients of various ailments. The Egyptians created sleep temples, and those coming to be healed would be put in trance, and suggestions would be made for the curing of their various maladies. The success of these Egyptian sleep temples led to their introduction into Greece, where they were flourishing by the fourth century B.C.. In Greece, the sick were placed in a hypnotic sleep and instructed to see heavenly visions and to experience a cure for their various ailments. A century later sleep temples appeared in ancient Rome and continued there during its golden age.

"By the beginning of the sixteenth century, the well-known physician Paracelsus was successful in obtaining cures through what he called sympathetic magnetism, which I interpret to be hypnotic activity, and one of his writings describes in detail how monks from a cloister near Karnter Ossiach healed patients by getting them to gaze into a crystal ball until they fell asleep.

"Perhaps the earliest beginning of modern hypnosis can be traced to the work of Franz Anton Mesmer, who was born in 1733. Although his ideas and writings about what came to be known as mesmerism are now mostly discredited, we must acknowledge and thank Mesmer for his astute insight that remarkable curative powers reside within human beings and that these powers can be summoned forth to bring physical and emotional healing.

"Still considered a charlatan, most of Mesmer's problems were brought on by his own immodesty and outrageous antics. He would seat his patients around a large magnetic bath, filled with iron filings and with iron rods protruding from the sides, encouraging his patients to touch the rods and receive the magnetic flow. As they did this, he would strut about his clinic, attired in a lavish, purple robe, touching a glass wand to the patients. Many were cured of their so-called illnesses, but probably only those illnesses that had evolved from hysterical maladies, rather than from organic origins.

"You may be interested to know, as a sideline of interest, that Mesmer, during his studies of medicine with a Jesuit priest in Vienna, became friends with the parents of Wolfgang Amadeus Mozart. Marie Antoinette was also one of his celebrated patients.

"Becoming so successful that his clinic could not accommodate all who came for cures, Mesmer took to 'mesmerizing' various objects, convincing his patients that if they only touched these objects, they would be healed.

"The French medical establishment had no use for Mesmer, and in 1784, under the authority of the French Academy of Science, the King appointed a committee to investigate his practices. Do any of you know the famous American, then residing in Paris, who was a member of that committee? It is the same American on whom Oxford University bestowed an honorary doctorate for his discovery of electricity."

"Benjamin Franklin," said Sean.

"Correct. In any case, when the committee made its unannounced visit to Mesmer's clinic, they found him mesmerizing trees, after which dozens of hysterical patients would throw themselves at these trees, touching and stroking them in order to absorb the special energies. The members of the inquiring committee, as it worked out, were very observant and noticed that several of those who were cured had not been touching any of the trees. They concluded that Mesmer's cures were merely from his patients' 'imaginative fancy' and they recommended that the practice be outlawed in France. Poor Mesmer retired immediately and lived out the remainder of his days as a breeder of canaries. Still, others in Europe explored the ground he had broken.

"The Marquis de Puysegur noted that Mesmer's magnetic bath and the creation of convulsions in patients were not necessary to produce a hypnotic state, and thereby restored to the world the ancient knowledge once held by the Egyptians, Greeks, and Romans.

"A famous London surgeon named Dr. John Elliotson began using mesmeric-magnetic applications to prepare his patients for surgery. His findings spurred others to new discoveries, and soon the birth of modern hypnosis occurred when Dr. James Braid, a Scottish eye surgeon, went to see a mesmerizing show with the goal of debunking its star, a certain Monsieur La Fontaine. By examining those subjects mesmerized by La Fontaine, and conducting his own experiments, Dr. Braid figured out that eye fatigue was an essential part of producing trance, and that a person's potential to be hypnotized increased in accordance with how high that person's expectations were that something would happen. Dr. Braid, in fact, published a book on hypnosis in 1842.

"Dr. Braid also recommended new hypnotic procedures for the application of hypnosis as an anesthesia during surgery. In those days, surgery was little more than the whacking off of diseased or wounded limbs, or perhaps grubbing inside someone's intestines—"

"YES!" rejoiced Sean from the rear of the room, sitting himself to full attention so as not to miss any new details about nineteenth century blood and gore.

"—and a survival rate of fifty percent was not especially encouraging," continued Dr. Baker.

"A friend of Dr. Braid, a Dr. James Esdaile, who practiced in India, was so successful at using hypnosis as an anesthesia that he came under the suspicion of the prevailing medical establishment. A government committee was appointed to investigate but, in contrast to what happened to poor Dr. Mesmer, this committee gave a very favorable report and encouraged Dr. Esdaile to continue his research. It was found that hypnotic anesthesia caused less bleeding in patients and reduced the rate of mortality from fifty to five per cent. There was also no post-operative shock to the system and wounds healed more rapidly than through conventional methods. You can imagine how astounding these findings were.

"It is, I believe, extremely unfortunate that just as this new hypnotic anesthesia was becoming accepted and common, chloroform was introduced into surgery in 1847. When this anesthesia was used on Queen Victoria during childbirth in 1853, it obscured the proven advantages of hypnosis.

"It also didn't help that Sigmund Freud declared hypnosis useless around 1889. Instead, he touted his own technique of free association for those working in the area of psychoanalysis. Some suggest that Freud was a very poor hypnotist, and that he condemned the technique merely because he could not excel at it.

"The Germans used hypnosis during World War I when their drugs for anesthesia were exhausted. It was also used to help shell-shocked victims after the war. By the late 1950s, hypnosis had become recognized by the British and American medical societies. Today it is used successfully to cure many people of phobias, addictions, and unwanted habits. It is also used, in the form of focused mental imagery, to help patients rid themselves of their diseases. Now, I've been talking a fairly long time. I would suggest that we take a five minute break, after which we'll regroup so that we can watch one of you become hypnotized."

Applause filled the room, which Dr. Baker acknowledged with a cordial bow. No sooner had the applause abated than he was surrounded by students eager to know more about the subject, each with specific questions.

After the break, a hush fell over the assembly when Dr. Baker resumed his place and announced, "If you would be willing to volunteer to be hypnotized, please raise your right hand."

Every right hand in the room suddenly lifted high, including the hands of Mr. Pennythorpe and the Giant's son.

"For those still willing to be hypnotized, please lift your duly notarized parental permission slip in your left hand," continued Dr. Baker.

Mr. Pennythorpe and the Giant's son dropped their hands, sighing in disappointment.

"Now, for those of you with hands raised, I wish to conduct an experiment in suggestibility. You may now lower your hands, but please listen and follow my directions as closely as possible. Please stretch both of your arms out in front of yourself at shoulder level. Close your eyes and imagine that you are holding a bucket in each hand. The bucket in your left hand is made of cardboard and is very light; in fact, there is nothing in it. It is very easy to hold. The bucket in your right hand, however, is made of steel, and is very heavy. The bucket in your right hand, in fact, contains several rocks. Feel how heavy the rocks are, for they are beginning to weigh down the bucket, and you are having trouble holding it at shoulder height. The bucket in your right hand is becoming heavier and heavier, for more and more rocks are being dropped into it. Heavier and heavier, the bucket in your right hand is beginning to drop, more and more, heavier and heavier, you can hardly keep on holding it, it has become so heavy. You feel it pulling your arm down, more and more. You can hardly hang on to it now, it has become so very, very heavy. Down it goes, down, and down.

"All right. Very good. You may all open your eyes now. We have just done a preliminary investigation to find out those among us who may prove to be the easiest subjects. I suspect that most of you, if not all, could be hypnotized fairly easily, should you choose to be. But for the contributing factors of a live audience, especially the distractions of peers, I think today that I will choose one of you to be my subject, so that the others might see hypnosis demonstrated. Assuming that you would all volunteer, since you all raised your hands, I will go to the person who performed the best on our little test, although there were several of you who also came quite close to her mark. Sheila Morrison, would you please step forward."

If the class had considered Sheila's selection on the basis of her high suggestibility score, they would have quickly remembered that she always had her ear to the ground for the latest gossip about the current dating relationships at Midville Middle School, information that she kept tabs on and that she appeared to believe without question upon first hearing, even when various portions of that information were obviously self-contradictory.

"Sheila, here is the instructor's chair, which I am placing in front of his desk. Please take a seat. Are you comfortable?"

"Yes, thank you, Doctor," Sheila responded, obviously delighted to have become the focus of the club's attention.

"Do you have anything you'd like to work on together this afternoon, Sheila?" asked Dr. Baker.

Sheila thought for a moment, then asked, "Like what?"

"Perhaps a persistent fear or a particular phobia," explained Dr. Baker.

Sheila closed her eyes for a moment, then exclaimed, "Spiders. I hate spiders. I don't want to be afraid of them anymore."

"Okay. We'll see what we can do. Let me ask the class to be perfectly silent and still during the induction, for I don't want you to be distracted from our purpose.

"Do you see that small nail on the rear wall, to the left of the flag?"

"Yes."

"I want you to fix your total attention on that small nail. Begin staring at it with all of your powers of concentration. Do you still see it?"

"Yes. It's still there, but I'm beginning to see a little haze of light around it."

"Excellent. Don't take your eyes off that little nail. And as you stare at it, I want you to listen to the sound my voice, for it will be your guide. Please take a few deep breaths, and then begin to breathe slowly, in and out, in and out."

Here Dr. Baker's voice took on a lilting, sing-song quality that was soothing to the ear. Sheila began to feel her eyelids becoming heavy as she stared at the fixed spot on the wall and listened to Dr. Baker.

"Your eyelids are becoming heavier and heavier, Sheila, and that is fine; in fact, it's quite normal. You may also sense a tiredness or heaviness in your limbs. That's normal, too. Nothing to worry about. And as I speak to you, please keep on looking at that spot on the wall. It's there to help you fall into trance, for your eyes are getting even heavier and you are finding that your breath is slowing down even more. Yes, your eyes are so heavy now that they want to close, but whether they close or not is entirely up to you. The spot on the wall is there to help you, to serve you. You may feel as if weights are pulling your eyelids down, even as you find yourself breathing slower and slower. That is quite normal and nothing to be worried about. Your eyelids are almost closed now as you find yourself going deeper and deeper, yes ... heavier and heavier ... and deeper and deeper."

Here Dr. Baker paused and looked carefully at Sheila, who had tilted forward slightly in her chair and whose eyes were now completely closed.

"Do you hear my voice?"

"Yes," said Sheila.

"Yes," said Joey Harris, sitting with his eyes closed at his desk.

Immediately Dr. Baker rose and went over to look at Joey. He carefully studied how deeply Joey was breathing and turned to Bobby, and asked, "What is this student's name?"

"Joey Harris."

"Joey, do you hear my voice," asked Dr. Baker.

"Yes."

"Joey, I want you to go into a deeper trance and to wait until I call on you again in a few minutes. You will not hear what I am saying to Sheila between now and then, and you will not be distracted or wakened by any noise or movement in this room. In fact, any such noise or distraction will cause you to fall only deeper and deeper into trance. Do you understand?"

"Yes."

"Go deeper, then, until I come back to call you out," said Dr. Baker, walking back to Sheila.

"Sheila, do you hear my voice?"

"Yes."

"Sheila, I want you to imagine that you are standing in front of an escalator, which is traveling down. In fact, it is one of the longest escalators in the world, and I want you to step on it, and as you ride down the escalator, you will fall deeper and deeper into trance. Down, down, down. Deeper and deeper. You will continue to go deeper until I ask you another question, at which time you will have fallen ten times deeper into trance than you now are. You will not hear my voice again until I address you directly by name. Do you understand?"

"Yes."

"Then keep traveling down on that escalator, deeper and deeper and deeper."

"Thank you, friends, for remaining so still and quiet," said Dr. Baker. "As you noted, Joey also fell into trance, and I will work with him after Sheila and I have explored for a while. Any questions so far?"

"You mean to tell me they can't hear you?" asked Dana. "I mean, I can hear you."

"Under hypnosis, sensory abilities are often heightened. But I have given them the express instruction not to respond to my voice again until I address them directly. I am sure that they can hear my voice, but I would rather guess that the meaning of my words is not being processed in the usual way. If I were to tell a funny story right now, and then wake them both up, they would not have remembered hearing it."

"Wow," exclaimed Jiggs.

"Sheila, do you hear my voice?"

"Yes."

"Have you finished your descent on the escalator?"

"Yes."

"When did you finish?"

"Just now."

Dr. Baker rose and lifted out a small bottle of cola from the box he had brought and several plastic glasses. He also took out a small container of bottled water.

"Sheila, I'm going to give you some soda. You will taste it and describe it. You may open your eyes."

Sheila accepted the plastic glass of soda.

"What is it?" asked Dr. Baker.

"Cola," said Sheila.

"Very good. Anything else that you drink from now on will taste like cola, until I tell you that your normal sense of taste has returned. Here, what is this liquid?"

Dr. Baker handed Sheila a glass of the bottled water.

"Cola, just like before," said Sheila.

"And this?" asked Dr. Baker, giving her an empty glass.

"It's empty."

"Okay. Sorry. I have just filled it. Please try again."

"Cola, just like the other times," said Sheila.

"Very good. Now Sheila, look in front of you and you will see a group of three movie theaters. I want you to go to the ticket window and purchase a ticket. You will see a spider printed on the ticket. On the reverse side will be a letter, either A, B, or C, and that letter will indicate the theater that you are supposed to enter, because in that theater we will see a movie that will explain to you and to me your fear of spiders. Is that okay with you?"

"Yes."

"Proceed. Where are you now?"

"I'm getting my ticket."

"What color is it?"

"Baby blue."

"Is there a spider on it?"

"Yes."

"What letter is printed on the reverse side?"

"B for theater B."

"Proceed to theater B," instructed Dr. Baker, adding, "Are you in the theater now?"

"Yes."

"Then watch the movie and please describe what you see," Dr. Baker requested.

"I see myself as a little baby, maybe two or three years old. I'm playing in my crib. My mama is near me. She's really big. I see a big black spider on a little music box in my crib. It plays a song about a little girl eating cheese curds, and then a spider comes to frighten her away. My mama loves to wind it up and play it for me. She has just done that, and I hear the music and the words. Now my mama is grabbing her belly, and I see my daddy taking her out of the room. I'm very frightened that something is wrong. Next I hear a baby screaming. It's my new baby brother, home from the hospital. He took my mama away from me."

"Very good, Sheila. Allow the movie to advance a little further into the future to help you to understand your dislike of spiders," urged Dr. Baker.

A brief pause ensued.

"I'm in my room trying to sleep and I'm scared because of something I think is in my closet. I'm panting, I'm so scared. The door to my room opens a little. My baby brother is climbing on my bed. He's holding a little plastic spider. Before he can reach me, I'm screaming, and my mama has come to see what has happened."

"How old is your brother?"

"About four, maybe three," said Sheila.

"Allow the movie to fast forward to the next most significant event that helps to explain your fear of spiders," said Dr. Baker.

"I'm at summer camp. I'm about eight years old. It's my first time away from home. I'm running through the woods, being chased by some friends. It's evening. I suddenly run right through a huge spider web, and then I'm on the ground screaming, trying to brush the webs away, but there are no spiders. My friends are trying to help me," said Sheila.

"Are there any more events we need to look at, Sheila?" asked Dr. Baker.

"The screen is empty."

"Okay. You've done very well. I want you to take a well-earned rest. Please tune out until I call you by name. Okay?"

"Okay."

Dr. Baker looked at the class and said, "What do you think of what you've just seen?"

The class sat in awe.

"Fascinating," said David. "I mean, do you think that she really got in touch with the sources of her spider fear?"

"Yes, I do," said Dr. Baker. "Do you understand what's going on?"

No one dared to venture a guess.

"Do you want to know what I see?"

Everyone nodded in the affirmative.

"Sheila is suffering from early separation anxiety from her mother, whom she identifies with the spider. She feels displaced by the arrival of her baby brother. The separation anxiety theme is further emphasized by the episode at summer camp and, please note, it was the first time she had ever been away from home for so long, running into the spider's web, becoming hysterical, but no real sign of spiders."

"How do you explain the fear of whatever was in the closet?" asked Dana.

"The closet represented Sheila's repressed emotions, both her anger at her mother as well as at her brother. We don't like to look at those moments when we harbor ill feelings toward those whom we love. The brother's advent into the bedroom with the plastic spider served to exacerbate her condition, connecting all three parties again."

"How can you say that her fear of spiders came from her feeling displaced by her younger brother?" asked Jennifer, adding, "Isn't that just an assumption?"

"How about the theater ticket," Dr. Baker explained. "What color was it?"

"Baby blue," answered Jennifer.

"And what theater did she need to go to?"

"Theater B," said Jennifer.

"Blue for boy and B for boy," Dr. Baker concluded.

"You don't miss a thing, do you?" asked Jennifer.

"Oh, I miss a lot. I'm just grateful that enough is usually given that the puzzle eventually becomes clear," replied Dr. Baker.

"How do you help Sheila get over her fear of spiders?" asked Gordie Chase.

"By helping her to see that she identified her mother with the spider on the music box at a time of enormous emotional upheaval, a time when she felt displaced by her baby brother," answered Dr. Baker.

"How do you do that?" asked Zeke.

"Watch. We'll try. Sheila, I am now speaking to you once again, and I want you to forget everything that you may have heard us talking about since I last spoke to you. Let's go back to the moments you described when you were in a crib, and your mother was winding up a little music box for you, a music box with a spider on it. This time, Sheila, when your daddy takes your mama to the hospital, I want you to go with them. I know you didn't go with them when this really happened years ago, but now I want you to go with them in your mind. What do you see?"

"I see our old car. Daddy's helping mama in. He looks worried. He's driving really fast. They get to the hospital and they put Mama on a stretcher. She goes to a special ward. The doctor comes to see her, and then leaves. Then the doctor comes back. Now they take Mama to a special room. They're going to have to cut her open. I see them begin to do it. Now they're pulling—"

"Yes, Sheila," said Dr. Baker.

"They're pulling a big spider out of her tummy. It's my baby brother."

"Sheila, look at your mama. Look carefully. What do you see?"

"I see my mama."

"Look even closer," urged Dr. Baker.

"A spider, like on the music box. I see a big spider," said Sheila.

"Sheila, now look in front of you. You will see a large mirror. I want you to look at yourself. What do you see?"

"A spider. I'm a spider, too."

"Mother spider loves both of her little spiders, Sheila. She didn't want to be away when your baby brother was born, but she had to go to where she and he would be safe. Can you forgive her for having to go away?"

"Yes."

"Please do it, then," urged Dr. Baker.

"Mama, I forgive you," said Sheila, tears trickling down her cheeks.

"Now, Sheila, there is a wonderful story about a mother spider that I want you to read. It's by an author named E. B. White and it's called *Charlotte's Web*. You will read that story and learn about the great love that this mother spider has for her baby spiders as well as for all of the friends she meets. Reading the book will bring you a sense of healing and completion, and you will no longer be afraid of spiders. I will arrange for Mr. Gregory to give you a copy. Do you understand?"

"Yes."

"And you will remember nothing that has happened here this afternoon, and you will be unable to move from your chair until I say to you, 'Jack Robinson'. You will also keep tasting only cola until I say to you, 'Jack Sprat.' Now, please return to the escalator that you took when you went deeper and deeper into trance. Find it. It will now be moving upward. Is it now in front of you?"

"Yes."

"I want you to step on it and ride back up, and as you ascend, you will come out of your trance. By the time I count from ten to one, you will be completely awake, and you will have forgotten all that we have done here. You will also feel very rested and relaxed, and you will open your eyes and yawn just once when you're completely out of trance. Ten, nine, eight, seven, six, five, slowly now, four, three, feeling wider and more completely awake and refreshed, two, and now one."

Sheila opened her eyes and yawned.

"How was it?" asked Dr. Baker.

"I ... I don't remember anything, but I feel rested," said Sheila.

"Sheila, you may go back to your seat now," said Dr. Baker.

"I don't want to," said Sheila.

"I am asking you to go back to your seat," requested Dr. Baker.

"I like it here," said Sheila.

"I'm instructing you to return to your original seat, Sheila, now, please," said Dr. Baker.

"This is my seat," said Sheila.

"Jack Robinson," said Dr. Baker, and Sheila rose and returned to her seat.

"Sheila, please come here and take a drink of this bottled water," said Dr. Baker.

Sheila came forward and took a sip, and a frown formed on her face.

"Anything wrong with the water?" asked Dr. Baker.

"It tastes just like cola," said Sheila.

"Jack Sprat," said Dr. Baker. "Try it again, please."

Sheila sipped again, and a new frown formed on her face.

"Yes," prompted Dr. Baker.

"Now it tastes like water," said Sheila, mystified.

"Thank you, Sheila," said Dr. Baker, "you may return to your seat now."

"Now let's wake Joey up," said Dr. Baker, walking over and standing next to Joey Harris.

"Joey, do you hear me?" asked the psychologist.

"Yes."

"Without opening your eyes, I want you to look straight in front of you until you see a tree, a tree that will have all kinds of fruit on it, including apples, oranges, grapefruit. Do you see it?"

"Yes," answered Joey.

"It is quite a remarkable tree, isn't it?" asked Dr. Baker. "One never sees a tree like that in this world."

'Yes," agreed Joey.

"Now, Joey, this is a magical tree that will help you to know more about yourself. I want you to go to the tree and shake the trunk. After you have done this, one fruit will fall, and I want you to go and pick it up and tell me about it. Go ahead, and let me know what you're doing."

"I'm going to the trunk and am shaking it. It's really hard to shake, but one fruit just fell behind me. I'm turning to pick it up. It's every color of the rainbow. It looks sort of like an apple, but it has all these beautiful colors," said Joey.

"Good. I want you to take a bite out of this fruit," said Dr. Baker. "After you do, you will see yourself doing something. Please describe to me what you see yourself doing. Go ahead, take the bite."

A short pause ensued.

"I see myself flying through the air and visiting beautiful castles in the clouds. The fruit has also given me the power of being invisible. So I can fly anywhere without being observed. There are so many pretty colors to the things I'm seeing, and I'm flying around them. Wait. They're beautiful birds, and now they've just turned into bubbles, and now they're circles of water with rainbow colors. I can't really describe them, but they're cooler than anything I've ever seen."

"Have you ever flown like this before?"

"Kind of, but this is really great. Before things got weird and I wasn't sure of who I was or where I was going. This is really cool."

"Joey, I want you to take your right hand and place it on your left shoulder. Good. Now, in the future, if you want to return to this place and fly around a little here and there, if you put your right hand up on your left shoulder the way you're doing it now, it will serve to help you remember this experience so vividly that you will be able to find your way back to it. Do you understand?"

"Yes," replied Joey.

"And refrain from doing it at times when you need to be paying attention, such as in school or at home, but only during your own spare time, and only if you feel the need to explore again in this way," said Dr. Baker. "Look at the tree again. Can you see it?"

"Yes," answered Joey.

"Look at it carefully and it will transform into something that will prove important to you. What do you see?" asked Dr. Baker.

"A bed. It turned into a bed, but I don't know why," said Joey.

"Never mind. Just remember, and later it will become apparent," said Dr. Baker

"Okay," said Joey.

"Now, Joey, I'm going to count backwards from ten to one, and at the count of one, I want you to wake up from the trance fresh, alert, rested, and satisfied. Ten, nine, eight, seven, six, now slowly relaxing our way back to this classroom, five, four, three, two, eyes beginning to open, and one. Welcome back."

"That was so cool," observed Joey. "I want to go back."

"Not today, but some other time," Dr. Baker encouraged. "You see, my friends, altered states of consciousness can prove very helpful to us, provided we know the right questions to ask while in trance. In two days, this coming Thursday, we will experiment a little more with creative visualization, and pair off into groups of three in order to discuss our experiences. If time permits, I hope to be able to escort you through two exercises. I see that our time is almost up for today's meeting. Just as I did two weeks ago, I will remain for a few minutes to answer any questions; however, Mr. Pennythorpe and I need to be moving along in about twenty minutes, since we are meeting our wives for dinner. They are shopping as we speak, and I dare say that your very own Mr. Pennythorpe and I have become virtual paupers during these last two hours, as mediated by whichever VISA or Master Card our wives are using today. Who invented credit, anyway?"

The class sat still, warmed with Dr. Baker's none too subtle humor, wondering if he would have been as forthright had his wife and Mrs. Pennythorpe been standing at the door.

Deciding in the affirmative, the club rose to adjournment.

Chapter Thirteen
A Journey into Guided Imagery

EMBERS OF MIDVILLE MIDDLE SCHOOL'S LEARNING CLUB WAITED EAGERLY FOR THE ARRIVAL of the now celebrated Dr. Clarence Baker, who had successfully hypnotized two of their number on the previous Tuesday. Although today's topic was on the effective use of guided imagery, which wasn't quite as dramatic as a full-hypnotic induction, club members were still curious as to what might happen. Even Sean Potter and his friends had returned to witness and to participate in the proceedings.

The door opened, and Dr. Baker was once again escorted into the classroom by his former teacher and old friend, Thatcher Pennythorpe.

"It is my pleasure to give you Dr. Clarence Baker," announced Mr. Pennythorpe, who proceeded to take a seat in the rear of the classroom next to Mr. Nathan Gregory, club advisor.

"I feel a little like Willie Wonka today," began Dr. Baker, "for he would say we have too little to do and too much time, but then he would reverse that, meaning: we have much to do together and very little time. On Tuesday, you observed my inducting two students into hypnosis, one who had been selected, the other who entered into trance on his own. You have had a very small sampling of what hypnosis can do. But it is only one of many kinds of altered states of consciousness. Today I would like to continue to explore the value of guided imagery. It is a process where I will invite you all to relax, and then I will guide you through a journey, a journey where it will be most important for you to notice as much detail as possible, because all of the information that you will receive will be helpful and relevant in some way. As soon as we have finished this exercise, I want you to write down the details of your experience. Is there some paper? Who needs pencils?"

Zeke and Bobby passed out the necessary materials so that those assembled could make detailed records of their journeys.

"Now, please sit back in your chairs, close your eyes, and become as comfortable as possible. Take a deep breath and hold it for a few seconds, and then slowly release the air through your mouth. And let's do that again, and as you do it, you will find yourself becoming increasingly comfortable. Release any tension that you may have in your shoulders by shaking them gently. Let any tension drain out of your jaw and neck; imagine all of your tension flowing down through your body and out into the floor like water. Take in that deep breath again, very slowly, and now exhale through your mouth.

"Now I invite you to pretend that your eyes are locked shut and to imagine a white light just above your head. As you breathe in slowly, imagine that light entering the top of your head and moving down your neck, into your shoulders, down through your arms, as well as into the center of your body, now down into your legs and feet. That light has entered into you to help you retain inner clarity and harmony; it will also help you to relax more and more. Now, once again, take that deep, deep breath in, and now exhale slowly through your mouth. That's it. You're all doing very well.

"I now invite you to imagine yourself on a path, a trail, in a forest. You have an important journey to make, and you have already embarked upon it. Take note of the kind of forest that you are in, the time of day, the vegetation that is there, if there are any animals. What kinds of sounds do you hear? What kinds of smells can you smell? Now, continue on this journey, and keep enjoying this path that you are walking on. Take note of the kind of path that it is. Is it a natural path, or perhaps one made of stones? As you move along your way, take note of everything that happens.

"As you turn a corner on this path, you will suddenly find yourself confronted with an obstacle. Take note of what kind of obstacle that it is. Look at it very carefully. Is it a tree? Perhaps some branches? Is it a large stone? Is it a brick wall? Look at this obstruction once again, and see if it gives you any hint of its nature, its purpose for being there. Now study it very carefully, and then ask yourself how you may best bypass this obstruction, the better to continue your journey. As you look at it, you will realize what you must do.

"Now, if you were given information on how to proceed, please do so. And as you do, remain vigilant about all that is happening. You are hoping to arrive at a small cottage not too far ahead of you. See if you can do it. For those of you who are not able to bypass the obstruction in the road, continue your journey in whatever direction seems best, and remember all of the details of your travels. You may also still arrive at this cottage quite unexpectedly.

"Now when you arrive at this cottage, before entering it, look at it carefully and remember the kind of feeling it gives you. Is it welcoming, warm, cozy, or is it a little sinister? Is it made of wood or stone or perhaps something else? Once you have taken in all that detail, proceed to enter, and look around on that first floor, remembering all that you are seeing. Look at the kitchen, the bedroom, the living room. What are they like? What kind of feeling do you get from each?

"I will wait a few minutes now as you collect as much information as possible. When I speak to you again, I will invite you back to this classroom."

The class sat in silence for a few minutes, which seemed a long time to some, but to others seemed only a fraction of a minute.

"Okay. Let me invite you back from this cottage, this forest path, back to the Learning Club at Midville Middle School. As you make your return journey, you will remember all of the significant details that you will soon write down. As I count backwards from ten to one, you will gradually return to this Learning Club, and with each number, you will become clearer about all that you experienced and what you need to write down. Ten, nine, eight, seven, six, five, slowly waking, slowly returning, four, three, remembering all that you will need to know, two, and, finally, one, and now able to open you eyes. Welcome back," said Dr. Baker.

Members of the Learning Club opened their eyes. Several students scratched their eyes, while a few others yawned.

"Now, please, take ten minutes to record your journeys. Remember to include as much detail as possible. Everything you saw was important, as we shall soon see," instructed Dr. Baker.

All present took pen or pencil to paper and began writing furiously.

After ten minutes, Dr. Baker announced, "Time's up."

"No, not yet."

"Not done."

"Wait."

"More time," requested many present.

"All right. Five more minutes, but no more," said Dr. Baker.

Five minutes later, everyone had finished.

"Now I would like you all to divide into groups of three. After you have formed your groups, please read or share your experiences. And after you've shared your journeys, see if you can interpret the meaning of each journey to the others in your group. They will also be able to lend insight, especially where you might find yourself stuck. Plan to report back to the larger group when you have all finished."

"How do we interpret?" asked Dana Foley.

"Attention, everyone," called Dr. Baker. "Dana just asked an excellent question, so before we break into groups, let me give you a case history of one of my clients. The recounting of her journey and the meaning of the symbols that she encountered may help you when we begin looking at your unique journey. So, the question is: how do we interpret the symbols we encounter? Symbols can mean different things to different individuals, but some may mean the same thing to almost everyone. The example that I now offer to you is of a journey that one of my clients experienced in a similar visualization not long ago. Let's call her Mary, although that is not her real name.

"During her visualization, Mary found herself on a worn path in an overgrown forest. As she followed the path, she noticed that the light was dim, as one would expect at twilight. The curious thing is that the light didn't vary. It got neither brighter nor darker. She worked her way along the path, which meandered back and forth through the brush and trees. When she encountered her obstacle, it proved to be an ancient tree that had fallen across the path, possibly many years before. It was rotting away, and she could see the termites ravaging its bark and wood; however, even though they consumed the tree furiously, the tree did not get any smaller. She looked to see how she could travel beyond the rotting tree, and she could see no way around it in either direction. Finally, she decided to try to crawl over it. As she did so, she fell into its crannies and hollow spots, and she had to brush the termites off as she went. Gradually, she arrived at the other side. When she finally jumped off the tree, the sun came out and illuminated the forest. She suddenly felt as if she had a lot of new energy she had not had before, especially when she was trying to crawl, and that was her exact word, to crawl up over and through the tree that lay in her path. She turned to look at the tree and it was gone. It had vanished. Mary continued to search for the cottage, and soon came to a clearing, which had several beautiful flower gardens in it. She entered the cottage, which was a beautiful white stone dwelling, and everything was fresh and clean and waiting to be used. She noticed that her bed had been turned back. When she first entered the cottage, she smelled the wonderful aroma of fresh bread, and there was a new loaf on the table next to a knife and some herb butter. She sat down and ate the bread, which was the best tasting bread she had ever eaten. After she ate, she decided to go to sleep. And when she emerged from her visualization, she was just beginning to fall asleep in her newfound cottage.

"Now, what did her journey mean? For me, it meant that our course of therapy together would prove important and successful. As it worked out, the journey was a wondrously transforming experience for Mary. It helped her to liberate herself from some of her old patterns and negative self-images."

"But what did all of those symbols mean?" asked Dana.

"Good question. Let me interpret them as best I can, although I caution you that symbols are never subject to merely one or two interpretations. A stone, for example, can mean a million different things, depending on context. Now that you've all participated in this exercise in guided imagery, I can tell you a little more. The forest, of course, represents your inner self, your psyche. The journey is your current journey. The identification of an obstacle leaves open the possibility of analyzing anything that might be impeding you from your intended course, and I hasten to add that some participants never encounter obstacles. But back to Mary: the overgrown quality of the forest would suggest to me that we were being given a glimpse of some pattern or problem that was impeding Mary's growth. I find it instructive that the light does not change, for that kind of static repetition is very typical of a neurosis that has paralyzed a personality. And isn't it interesting that the 'ancient' tree could not be consumed by the termites. The description of the tree as ancient offered a hint that whatever was driving this neurosis, it happened a long, long time ago. Since there's no way around the barrier, Mary decides to crawl over it and through it. Isn't that an interesting word choice: crawl, as opposed to climb or scramble or heave. Crawl would suggest the need for regression, in order to face and remove the obstacle. And isn't it an interesting, good sign that the sun comes out once she's through, and that the old dead tree disappears? Her cottage is also welcoming and cozy, and the fresh bread would symbolize to me the sign of new growth, as would her desire to sleep after partaking of the nourishment that her true home, true center, has offered her.

"You see, Mary's central struggle was to remove from her inner self a false image of who she was. That negative self-image had said to her for years, 'You're fat. You're overweight.' In point of fact, Mary wasn't as fat as she had allowed her neurosis to dictate. She was merely what I would call 'pleasantly plump'. Nevertheless, she was convinced that she was fat and ugly. The tree in the forest represented that lie, and her neurosis drove her to a state of continual self-loathing. Isn't it revealing that no matter how much the termites ate, the rotten tree would never go away. Mary had convinced herself that she was fat and ugly, and for years she had failed to dress to advantage or to be careful with her diet. She had become, in fact, a compulsive eater, but I remind you that she was in no way as unattractive as she had led herself to believe.

"Her crawling through the tree represented our future sessions of hypnotic regression, where I would induct her into a state of medium to deep trance and invite her subconscious mind to take us back to the first moment of imprinting, to the very first moment her negative self-image took root. The image of crawling could also suggest that during late infancy Mary formed an unconscious dependency, or oral fixation, on food. Mary and I returned to those some dozen moments together, and relived them to see them for what they really were, relived them several times in order to remove their power, and by the time we were finished, Mary was much more objective about what she thought about herself. She had won for herself a new lease on living.

"The centeredness of the cottage, the warmth, the nourishing meal, those symbols speak for themselves. Needless to say, Mary came closer to her true center and was able to throw off unhelpful eating habits and to feel better about the person she truly was. Now, I want each of your groups to share and to analyze your guided walks in the same way. I will circulate to each group in case there are any questions. Please have someone in your group keep a record for when we report back to the entire Learning Club. Why don't we take about forty-five minutes? That would give fifteen minutes for each member of each group. First you will share your walk, then your impression and your own interpretation of your walk and, finally, you will listen to the insights of your two partners. Good luck."

After quickly forming into groups, the members and visitors of the club were sharing their various experiences, hoping to glean new insights from their peers. Dr. Baker visited with Mr. Pennythorpe and Mr. Gregory for a few minutes before groups started raising their hands as a signal that they desired consultations with him.

Forty-five minutes passed very quickly, too quickly for most of those assembled. Dr. Baker assured everyone that there would be time for general feedback and questions, and he clapped his hands to summon participants to refocus for that purpose, announcing, "Let's hear some of the more unusual symbols from our respective journeys, as well as any that you still may have questions about."

Joey Harris raised his hand, saying, "None of us understood the barrier that I encountered."

"Please read to us the beginning of your journey," requested Dr. Baker.

"All right. I find myself in the middle of a dark woods, although there's a little shaft of sunlight shining through. I think it must be morning. I walk down the trail. I see a lot of moss and stones. The trees look lonely. The bushes closest to the path look mad. There seem to be mean faces looking out of them. I get scared and keep walking. Suddenly I come to the barrier. It's a stream, a huge stream, and the waters are running really fast," Joey read.

"A stream," Dr. Baker contemplated.

"Yeah. What does it mean?"

"And you said you felt lonely in the woods?" asked Dr. Baker.

"Yeah. It felt a little creepy, too. Everything seemed a little out of focus, if you know what I mean," said Joey.

"What are your associations with water?" asked Dr. Baker.

"I take a shower every morning," said Joey, a little indignantly.

"No, I mean what do you think of when you think of water?" Dr. Baker clarified.

"It's for getting clean and for drinking," said Joey.

"How did you feel when you suddenly saw the stream? Did it surprise you?" asked Dr. Baker.

Joey thought a minute, saying, "You know, it's kind of funny, but it almost seems that I was expecting it, in some way."

"Did it seem friendly?" asked Dr. Baker.

"Yeah. It did, even after I fell in," said Joey.

Some of the class laughed.

"Fell in?" asked Dr. Baker.

"Yeah. I tried to crawl across the stream on a branch of an old, dead tree that had fallen between the two banks, but half way over I slipped and fell into the stream. The water was rushing really fast, and it carried me right along with it," Joey explained.

"And then what happened?" asked Dr. Baker.

"I finally was swept over some waterfalls but I was able to crawl up on the land. I was a little bruised up, but I could still walk. I was out of the woods by that point, so I walked up this little bank and into a meadow where there was a really cool house."

"And what made the house so cool?" asked Dr. Baker.

"Well, it was there part of the time, and then it was gone. It was sort of shimmering, but I knew it was my house. I went up to it and waited until it was visible, and then I opened the door and walked in," said Joey, adding, "It's funny how big it looked inside 'cause on the outside it didn't seem that big. It felt good, though, and I was glad to be home."

"That's very interesting," said Dr. Baker. "What do you make of it?"

"I don't know. What do you think? You're the doctor," said Joey. "Having heard you talk these last few weeks, I know you think *something* about it, but maybe you don't want to tell me, which is fine."

"You're very perceptive," admitted Dr. Baker which, of course, aroused the entire club's curiosity.

Joey sat, staring at Dr. Baker, waiting for an answer.

"Perhaps we could talk privately about it later," suggested Dr. Baker.

"No way," said Joey. "Others have risked in here, and I'm gonna do it, too. I don't mind knowing what you think, 'cause I know you'll be fair and honest, and I respect you."

"Thank you," replied Dr. Baker. "In that case, I will tell you what I believe your journey into guided imagery was trying to tell you. I believe that you are being warned to desist from the path that you are now following, whatever path that may be. The waters seem to promise refreshment and cleansing from whatever you may be struggling with. If I were to guess, I would say that you are one of those individuals who seeks thrills beyond the five senses on which most people rely. In short, you have found taking certain drugs to be a cool trip, or whatever they call it these days. That impression was formed last week when you slipped into trance so easily. It seemed to me that you'd been in altered states before. Hypnosis is one of many ways to produce such altered states of consciousness. Tell me if I am wrong."

After a short silence, Joey looked directly at Dr. Baker and murmured, "You're not wrong."

"Then, it seems to me that you are being told that you will somehow be deterred from your present course. I have no idea how, but that stream you encountered seems to want you to arrive at your true home from a different direction than the one you're now traveling. Does that make any sort of sense?"

"Maybe. That's only *your* take on it," said Joey.

"Yes. And I could well be wrong. It's not easy to give up things that we've become accustomed to, especially if we like them," said Dr. Baker.

Joey sat silent, contemplating all he had heard.

"Let's have some other symbols. Yes?"

"Hi. My name is Jiggs Stevenson."

"Hello, Jiggs," said Dr. Baker. "Is Jiggs a family name?"

"No, sir. A nickname. Some people say that I would make a good butler," said Jiggs.

"And why, pray tell?" said Dr. Baker.

"Because they say I'm a little on the formal side," said Jiggs, as several of his classmates began coughing.

"I see," said Dr. Baker. "And what was the symbol that you want to share with us?"

"It's the barrier in the road. Mine was a really tall brick wall," said Jiggs, "and I don't have a clue as to what it might mean."

"Did you get past the wall?"

"Yes. I walked around to one side and found some steps and climbed all the way up one side and down the other," said Jiggs.

"And what was it like on the other side?" asked Dr. Baker.

"The sun was shining. It had been drizzling where I was. I couldn't believe it. And when I finally came to the cottage, it was a lovely little stone cottage with a brown oak door. I went to open the door, but it was locked. Then I saw a little note on the door, and it said, 'Humor is the key.' So I started laughing, and the door opened by itself."

"What a marvelous experience," exclaimed Dr. Baker.

"So what was the brick wall all about?" asked Jiggs.

"To me it would represent something artificial, something foreign to the forest, and therefore not essential to the person. What kind of feeling did it give you?" asked Dr. Baker.

"Sort of cool and rude," said Jiggs.

"Did it seem excessively formal?" asked Dr. Baker.

"What do you mean by formal?" asked Jiggs.

"Stiff, unresponsive, very much by the book," said Dr. Baker.

"Sort of," said Jiggs, studying the notes he had made.

"It may well represent a current part of your personality that one day you will simply walk away from. Do you laugh much?" asked Dr. Baker.

Jiggs thought a moment, and then answered, "Not really."

"Try to laugh more, Jiggs. I bet you'll feel better about yourself. And don't take the world and life so seriously. Roll with the punches."

"Yes, sir," said Jiggs, as he returned his attention to his notes.

"Who else?" asked Dr. Baker.

Maureen frowned and raised her hand, "Me. I'm Maureen."

"Yes, Maureen. I remember you from Tuesday. It does help, though, if you would all kindly remind me of your names when you speak. Eventually I will learn them all and be able to call you all by your correct names. What was your question?"

"My barrier was a mountain of books," said Maureen. "I hate to read and I don't do very well with language, although I'm a fair speaker. Do you think the mountain of books is a warning to me that I should start to read more?"

"What do you think?"

"I don't know."

"There are many different ways of knowing and learning. Books constitute only one avenue of many, albeit a popular and time-honored path. I would think that the presence of the mountain perhaps hints at the disadvantages you may encounter for not having become as widely read as others," explained Dr. Baker.

"I hate to read," said Maureen.

"That's quite all right. If you hate it, don't do it," said Dr. Baker.

"But I need to pass school," said Maureen.

"Are you dyslexic?" asked Dr. Baker.

"What's that?"

"It's when one reverses letters, like b's and d's, when one reads or speaks," explained Dr. Baker.

"I don't know. I don't think so. It's just hard for me to make any sense out of words on a page. It's like there are just so many symbols, and I feel unable to make sense out of all of it," said Maureen.

"You seem to be very articulate now," said Dr. Baker.

"Yes. I'm great when it comes to speaking, but horrible when it comes to writing."

"I don't know what to tell you, except that your journey into guided imagery seems to be suggesting that written language will continue to be a struggle for you. Perhaps some day you will find a way to overcome this obstacle. There are a number of helps that are available through bio-feedback programs. I'll be glad to send you some information. *That's* the important thing, to move beyond the obstacle," said Dr. Baker.

"That would be really great," said Maureen.

"Anyone else?" asked Dr. Baker.

No hands were raised.

"Very well. Then I think we have time enough for another exercise, provided that you all want to participate," said Dr. Baker.

All heads vigorously nodded their assent.

"Then settle back into your chairs again, and become as comfortable as possible. Having done this once already this afternoon will make this journey even easier. Take a deep breath and hold it for a few seconds, and then slowly release the air through your mouth. And let's do that again, and as you do it, you will find yourself becoming comfortable. Release any tension that you may have in your shoulders by shaking them gently. As you inhale, take note of any part of your body that is tense. As you exhale, relax that part of your body, as well as your entire body. There is a wonderful energy of light above your head. As you breathe in now, that energy flows into your head, down your neck and arms, down through the middle of your body, down your legs. It brings refreshment, and clarity and well being. Draw that light in again, as you go deeper and deeper into trance.

"Now you will find yourself standing alone in a special room. Look around to see what you notice. What does the room feel like? If you look closely, you will see a table in front of you and on that table a box. It might be a large box, or a medium-sized box, or a small box; I do not know. Only you know, because you are now looking at it. What does it look like? What color is it? What kind of feeling does it give you?

"You are now walking up to the table. You will soon open the box in front of you, but before you do, you need to know that this box is going to tell you something important about your future. Inside of it will be an object or symbol that will give you some very important information about something that will happen to you within the next few months. Now go ahead and open that box. Take out whatever is there and study it closely. A lot of information is going to be passed along to you, so make sure you notice every single detail. Also notice how the object or symbol makes you feel. When you have finished, please say 'thank you' to your subconscious for its having helped you in this way, and then return the object or symbol to the box. Leave the box on the table, turn around, and as you walk out of this special room, know that you will begin to return to this classroom. As I count down, beginning with ten, you will make your way back here, remembering everything that you have seen and felt and heard, ten, nine, eight, seven, thinking about every bit of information that has been given to you ... six, five, four, three, beginning to wake, now ... feeling refreshed and rested ... two, and, finally, one. You may now open your eyes."

The members of the club opened their eyes, some blinking a bit.

"Please write down everything that you can remember as quickly as possible. We'll take ten minutes, then break into the same groups as before, finally reporting back to the entire group. Good luck," said Dr. Baker.

Everyone present wrote assiduously, trying to capture as many details as possible of their respective experiences. Even Mr. Pennythorpe and the Giant's son wrote their impressions.

Within fifteen minutes, the classroom was abuzz with the sound of students sharing their journeys and insights. Dr. Baker sat with Mr. Pennythorpe and Mr. Gregory, listening to their experiences, occasionally asking questions and making comments.

When Dr. Baker resumed his position in front of the classroom, he looked a little worried and tired. He wiped his brow with his handkerchief, and then announced, "These insights can be very intense, especially if one is privy to knowing what they mean. Would anyone like to share his or her experience?"

Jennifer Lawler raised her hand.

"Yes?"

"I'm Jennifer Lawler, and when I opened my box ..."

"Jennifer, please read to us what you wrote to make sure we don't miss any of the images," requested Dr. Baker.

"Okay. I'm in a medium-sized room with light green walls and lots of windows. The table is circular and made of oak. The box is not that big, but it is the prettiest shade of green I've ever seen. I approach it and open it, and inside is a lovely gold necklace. I pick it up and look at it, and can see the pretty writing on it, but I can't read the writing. It's in a strange language. Inside the box is also a small photograph of two little kids I've never seen before, but they look happy."

"Anything else? What kind of feeling did you get from the box?"

"A good feeling. It was like opening a Christmas gift," said Jennifer, "but for some reason I kept thinking about Thanksgiving and turkeys and I could smell my mom's dressing."

"Well, let us know if anything happens that might give indication that what you saw gave you a glimpse of something important in your future," said Dr. Baker. "Who's next?"

"Me," said Bobby, raising his hand, "I'm Bobby Perkins—"

"The class president," noted Dr. Baker.

"Uh, yeah. That's right. I am. Anyway, I was in this room, lookin' somethin' like a classroom, except that it ain't like a normal classroom, not havin' no chairs or desks, and the large white box was on what was like a teacher's desk. So, curious as anything, I opened it. I reached inside and took out a graduatin' hat," and here Bobby looked toward the rear of the room to catch the eye of the Giant's son, who gave a look of mild surprise, pursing his lips out a little.

"I would say that your guided fantasy is both promising and optimistic," Dr. Baker smiled.

"Wait. This is the worst part," Bobby hastily added, "When I went to try the hat on, it disappeared into thin air."

"Not so promising, then," said Dr. Baker. "What kind of feeling did you get?"

"Not bad. It seemed a natural thing to happen. I didn't mind the graduatin' hat disappearin'," said Bobby. "I just don't understand what it means. Ain't got a clue. Can you clue me in, Doc?"

"Such information is often paradoxical, at least at first glance. Perhaps the next two or three months will make clear what this information was trying to communicate," said Dr. Baker.

Bobby scratched his head, looking at his classmates.

"It may mean something or nothing. Only time will tell. If our subconscious minds can get a glimpse into one of our possible futures, only time will tell whether that information was accurate or not."

"Have you known this exercise to bring accurate predictions?" asked David.

"Yes, I have," said Dr. Baker. "And may I add, predictions or clear insight in the most amazing and unexpected ways. The most frustrating thing is that it isn't usually recognized until after the events transpire."

"That's awesome," said Sean.

"What was yours?" asked Dr. Baker.

Sean looked at his notes and began to read, "I was in a large room that had tall stone columns on each side, like a huge castle. The table at the front was huge, almost the size of a room. I had to walk up twelve steps to get to it. The box was also huge. I tried to open it, but it was locked. Then I remembered, I needed a key. So I looked in my right pocket, and there was a beautiful golden key. So I took the key out and tried it in the lock, and it worked. And when I opened it, guess what I saw—"

"POTS," whispered Mary to Lisa.

"Shut up," said Sean, giving the evil eye to Mary, and then turning back to Dr. Baker, apologizing by saying, "Sorry, sir. My sister was just being smart."

"Go ahead," urged Dr. Baker.

Sean took a breath and was just about to resume when he noticed how Mary sat listening, perhaps a little too eagerly, hanging on his every gesture. Something inside of him warned him that he would be far more likely to achieve the promise of his special box if he were to keep its contents to himself.

"No. I'm *not* going to tell," Sean said firmly. "I think it best if I refrain from revealing what I saw."

"That is always one's prerogative," Dr. Baker agreed.

Sean glared at his sister, whispering so all in the room could hear, "Time will tell."

Mary suddenly looked uncomfortable, as Sean sat down smiling.

"Let me remind everyone that no one is obligated to share his or her experience," said Dr. Baker, "as has amply been demonstrated just now. Often times, it is perhaps best to keep these revelations private. I will leave that entirely to your discretion."

All who were present quickly evaluated their own experiences, testing them as to whether they should be subjected to potential public disclosure.

"Anyone else care to share?" offered Dr. Baker.

"I'm Gloria Adams. My box had a diary in it. It was a pretty little red diary, with a golden lock. There was also a key in the box, so I put the key in the lock and opened it, and when I opened the diary, nothing was written in it. So I locked it and held it for a little bit, looking at it, turning it over in my hands, feeling the leather and looking at the pretty decorations. Then something told me to try to open it again, so I put the key in, turned it, and opened it, and guess what: it was full of notes. But only a little of it was in my handwriting. So I locked it again and put it back in the box. I don't understand what any of that means. Do you?"

"Are you a person who can keep secrets?" asked Dr. Baker.

A muted snort was heard from Maureen Grant, and Gloria gave her a dirty look.

"Sometimes," she said, in a most non-committal way.

"Perhaps that experience is suggesting to you the need for a new method of operation," said Dr. Baker.

"How so?"

"I would interpret it to mean that it is one thing to have secrets, but quite another to keep them, and that to have any secret implies an obligation to keep it."

"Oh," said Gloria, not quite understanding.

"Do you see?" asked Dr. Baker.

"Not really. I mean, I like talking to my friends. We have our secrets, and I think that we need to," observed Gloria.

"Yes. And it's very important not to violate another's trust. So, having secrets is just fine, as long as they remain secrets," said Dr. Baker.

"I still don't think I understand," replied Gloria.

"Another clue to consider," said Dr. Baker, "is the presence of the secrets in written form, instead of oral form. Perhaps the images given are suggesting that you should keep a tighter lock on your secrets."

Gloria glowered at the good doctor.

"I don't mean to suggest that you don't," he added. "Just consider the import of the images you received. You'll become clear about it sooner rather than later. If you'd like to talk with me about it at another time, I'd be glad to."

"Okay," said Gloria, tentatively.

"Any other experiences to share?" asked Dr. Baker.

The group continued sharing and discussing symbols for over half an hour, at which point it was decided to adjourn.

Chapter Fourteen
They Can Because They **THINK** They Can

J UST AS THE TARDY BELL RANG THE NEXT DAY, Mr. Gregory entered English 9 carrying a large black box, smiling as he asked, "Does anyone know what day this is?"

"Friday," said Bobby.

"March 15th," said Dana.

"The *Ides of March*," announced the Giant's son, "the day that Julius Cæsar was assassinated in 44 B.C., hence coming to mean a day when the most terrible and frightful things happen. I promise you that I'll do my best to keep that tradition alive; in fact, Bobby and I have been having several very productive meetings recently, and I will announce the results of our secret deliberations at the end of the period. The announcement should suffice to etch the Ides of March permanently into your memories."

"I *knew* it," said Zeke, expecting the worst, whatever that worst might prove to be. Looking toward Bobby, Zeke became even more alarmed, for he could see the nervous tension in Bobby's posture.

Turning to the now curious class, Mr. Gregory proudly announced, "The last two meetings of the Midville Middle School Learning Club have been most remarkable, both for their quality as well as for their content. I would like to pick up on what Dr. Baker has given us, although I am certainly no psychologist, nor do I pretend to be one."

"At least he ain't nothin' like that ne'er-do-well Dandy," Bobby Perkins whispered to Dana Foley.

"I believe, however, that I know enough about guided imagery to lead you all on an important journey today," continued the Giant's son. "Does anyone object to our exploring together in this way?"

No objections were tendered.

"What's in the box?" asked Zeke Minturn, hopefully.

"It's a surprise," said Mr. Gregory. "It may prove helpful to us, but probably not in the way any of you might be thinking. I will only tell you that the box will take something from you and give something back."

"But we ain't even got a clue as to what's in the box," said Bobby.

"Animal, vegetable, or mineral," Dana teased.

"All in good time, my friends," said Mr. Gregory.

Pointing to an envelope that he had placed against the chalk board, the Giant's son announced, "In this envelope I have written on a sheet of paper the target for our journey. I will not tell you what that target is, but the images and content of your guided walk inside yourself will give you important information about that target that will help you to face particular fears, to rise to specific challenges."

"We ain't gonna wait for Dr. Baker?" asked Bobby.

"No. Dr. Baker and I talked about this exercise last night after the Learning Club meeting. He's thinks you're ready for it right now, and so do I, but only if you're willing to do it," Mr. Gregory answered.

"Why not?" said Dana. "I'm game."

"Me, too," said Zeke, looking at Bobby as if he should also agree to join in the guided imagery exercise.

"Okay, okay," grumped Bobby. "At least it ain't English."

"Now, be aware, please," began Mr. Gregory, "that the target of your guided journey is not in the present. It's in the past. The nature of that target will be different for each of you, because you have all had different experiences growing up. The images that you get, the details of this first journey, are very important to unlocking an even deeper door, one that should prove most helpful to us in our common quest."

"Do you want us to write any of this down?" asked Jiggs.

"Yes. Please take out a sheet of paper and a pen or pencil, and as soon as we have finished this journey in guided imagery, please write down every single detail that you can remember. At that point, we will hear from those who would like to share their journeys. After we have done that, I will read the target destination that already has been written on a sheet of paper in the envelope that I placed on the chalk board. Then we will see if the symbols and imagery encountered in your journeys have relevance to the selected target," explained Mr. Gregory.

"Ain't this ass backwards?" asked Bobby. "If we ain't got no clue as to where we need to go, how can we get there?"

"As Dr. Baker explained yesterday, Bobby, our subconscious mind knows the target already, as well as the symbols that will be helpful for us to understand that target and its influence on our lives and attitudes. We have actually witnessed that already in Dr. Baker's presentations. Let's just trust ourselves to the larger process and see what happens," the Giant answered.

"Okay by me," said Bobby, "although I ain't got a clue as to what I'm supposed to do."

"That's okay. Just make the journey and write down as many details as you can remember. Okay? Everyone else ready?"

Heads nodded their assent.

"Okay. Please put down your pens and pencils and relax in your seats. Stretch and yawn, if you need to. Rub your eyes and then place your hands on the desks or on your laps. Please close your eyes and take a deep breath, counting to three. One, two, three, that's it. Good. Now do that again and hold your breath for three seconds before letting go. One, two, three, and one, two, three, exhale. Very good. As you breathe in, notice how relaxed you're getting. Any tension that you feel anywhere in your body is going to begin to drain away during your next breath. Ready, one, two, three, hold, now, exhale, and let all the tension go.

"Now I want you to imagine a pure, clear white light hovering directly over your head. This light brings clarity and truth. I want you to imagine this light entering your head. It also brings healing and peace. Imagine it swimming around in your head, bringing peace and contentment. Now imagine this same light beginning to course through all of the other parts of your body, bringing healing, peace, light and clarity. You may feel your palms getting warm, or you may feel a tingling in your toes. That often happens, or you may feel nothing at all, which also happens.

"Look around you, and notice that you are now standing in a wooded area, in a lovely forest. You are on a path. Notice the details of the path and all that surrounds the path. This path represents the journey of your life. You are now facing the future. I want you, however, to turn around and face the past. You know this road, for you have traveled it. It is marked in the pain and joy of your experience and memory; it is also marked with your successes and failures, your hopes and disappointments, your strengths and your doubts. The target that we search for is found in the past, your past, and I want you to start walking back on this path until you find the target that we are searching for. Be sure to remember all of the details that you notice for later recording and understanding. I will pause now as you walk. If you reach your target before I begin again, please wait for me, and then we will all begin together."

Mr. Gregory rubbed his own eyes and turned to the next page of the script he had been reading. Looking at the clock, he decided to wait for four minutes before proceeding. An eerie silence of focused meditation pervaded the classroom.

"Okay," resumed the teacher. "All of you, by now, have reached the target. It might be many things, including an obstacle that has haunted you ever since you encountered it, but perhaps one that you failed to recognize or to notice at that time. Look at it carefully, and you will see that you are fettered to it in some way, either by a thread, rope, chain, or some other device that hampers your belief in what you are capable of doing, of what you can really do, when you put your mind to a task. The target may not be entirely clear to you. If it isn't clear, move closer until it comes into better focus. Take note of its every detail and, remember, we are looking at symbols, metaphors, for something that actually happened earlier in your life to slow your progress, to place a shadow over your abilities. Now remember as much of this walk as you possibly can, because I will soon call you back to the present, at which time I want you to write down in detail, all that you have noticed and experienced.

"You will now feel yourself coming out of this guided meditation. I will count backward, beginning with ten. Ten, nine, eight, seven, six, five—now you're beginning to come out of your relaxation, more and more—four, three—you will wake refreshed and with new energy—two—coming up at whatever speed you need to, and, finally—one. You may now open your eyes."

Class members opened their eyes. Some yawned; others stretched. Soon all were furiously writing their recollections on the sheets of paper in front of them. Mr. Gregory looked at the clock, and resolved to allow them to write for no more than five minutes.

"Everyone done?" asked the Giant's son.

Only half of the hands lifted in response to the teacher's query.

"Okay. Three more minutes," announced Mr. Gregory.

Those who were finished were stretching their hands, several of which had suffered muscle fatigue from such fast writing.

"Who would like to share first?" asked Mr. Gregory.

Maureen Grant's raised her hand.

"Yes, Maureen, please go ahead," the Giant's son encouraged.

"I don't really understand any of this, but this is what I saw. I found myself on a path in the woods you described and, when I turned around, I saw that there was more light where I had come from rather than in the direction I was going. So I followed the path. The farther I traveled, the greener the moss became and the brighter the trees. I came to an old rotted out log, which had fallen across the trail. Suddenly I noticed that where it had fallen had been the original trail, and the trail I was following back was not the original one that I had been on. Does that make any sense?"

"Yes, please continue," requested Mr. Gregory.

"So, I looked at this log, this rotted out tree. It had maggots on one side and icky things growing on the other. It also had a big number 2 on it in bright red paint, or maybe it was blood. I stepped in to take a better look, and part of the log had been shattered into little pencils. Number 2 pencils. Then, water started to flow out of these little pencils, just like they were crying or something, and I started to get sick. I turned to run away, and I saw some butterflies, so I followed them to the original path I had left after I had encountered the log."

"Anything else?" asked Mr. Gregory.

"That's it," said Maureen.

"Can you make any sense out of it?" asked the Giant's son.

"Not really," said Maureen.

"Well, let me read the target information," as he removed the envelope from the board and opened it and read: "Your target is an event, place, person, or situation in your life which caused you to lose confidence in your ability to learn when you were younger. It need not be the first such event, but it should be a prime example."

Looking at the class, Mr. Gregory added, "We *all* have such events in our lives. More often than not, we repress them, but their power over us can continue. This exercise was designed to help identify and remove some of these negative shadows. Maureen, can you make any more sense out of your journey now?"

Maureen looked at her notes again, and sniffed, as if she had a cold. Gulping once, she answered, "When I was in the second grade, I had a really mean teacher who pinched us if we were bad. Sometimes she pinched us if we didn't do something her way, like..."

Maureen was looking at Mr. Gregory, but it appeared she was also looking far beyond him, far back into her past.

"Go on, Maureen. It's okay," encouraged the Giant's son.

Maureen shook her head, not wanting to continue.

"Let it come out, Maureen. It really wants to. Let it come out," said Mr. Gregory.

"Like the way I held my pencil," blurted Maureen, tears beginning to trickle down her face.

Mr. Gregory immediately took several tissues from the box on his desk walked to the back of the room and handed to Maureen, saying, "That's okay. Tell us more."

"She was mean, this teacher. I hated her eyes. She stopped one time to tell me I was holding my pencil the wrong way and showed me her way. It didn't feel right, so I held it my way. She got mad, and she pinched me so hard it really hurt and left a horrible, little red mark. After that, I was afraid to hold my pencil the way it was most comfortable. It was an awful year."

More tears came, and Maureen wiped them away.

"Maureen, is there anything else?"

"I think I shut down that year. I didn't want to be hurt again, so I remember building a pretend wall between myself and my teachers, myself and school, myself and people."

"Maureen, that wall is asking to come down. In fact, I think it already has. Remember the butterflies in your journey?"

"Yes," said Maureen.

"Well, did they not lead you back to the real path that your journey was first on? The log is gone now; you're no longer on that path. The butterflies led you back to the path where there is more light."

Maureen nodded, wiping a stray tear on her cheek.

"Maureen, it took great courage to go first. I salute you and thank you for that. We don't have enough time for everyone to share with the entire class, but now that you know what the target was, I want you all to go back and look at your experience, and see if you can make new sense out of it. Anyone want to interpret a journey?"

Tammy Young raised her hand.

"Yes, Tammy," said Mr. Gregory.

"My journey took me back on a road that I didn't think I had ever been on. But the road came to an intersection, and at the intersection was a sign. The sign post for the road that I had been on had a big K on it, and little wooden play blocks had forced me away from the real road. Now I remember that when I was in kindergarten, there was a mean kid who didn't like me. She always said nasty things to me. One day I had built a pretty castle with the wooden blocks and she came up and knocked it all apart and looked at me and said, 'You're not very pretty, are you? And you're really dumb, too. You're not even going to pass kindergarten, are you?'"

"That must have been very painful," said the Giant's son.

"I wanted to cry, but I didn't give her the satisfaction. But I remember that I never played with the blocks again, and I'm always worried I'm going to fail."

"Isn't it amazing how we all fall victim to such negative experiences, such cruel words? Don't they seem to take on a life of their own, retaining a subtle and silent power over us?"

Tammy nodded in agreement.

"Who else?" asked Mr. Gregory.

Jiggs Stevenson raised his hand.

"Yes, Jonathan," said Mr. Gregory.

"My road took me back to a spot in the road where a big tree had fallen. I climbed over the tree and I saw two huge rocks on each side of the path, with a fallen log stretched over them. Both the tree and the log were rotting. Then I noticed a bright, shiny whistle at the bottom of the fallen log, and I picked it up and pitched it into a river that was flowing next to the trail," said Jiggs.

"Anything else?" asked Mr. Gregory.

"No. That was it," said Jiggs.

"Can you make any sense of it?" asked the Giant's son.

"Yeah. It's crazy, but it really does fit the assignment. The whistle reminded me of the whistle of my grade school gym teacher who made fun of me because I couldn't jump over a gymnastic bar. I mean, the bar wasn't that high, but everyone else could jump over it. I'm not very athletic, and I know it. But it still made me feel really lousy, and from that point I just hated going to gym class. I still do," explained Jiggs.

"What does your tossing the whistle into the stream mean?" asked Mr. Gregory.

"I think it means that I'm done with feeling inadequate because of a stupid thing like that. I may not be very athletic, but that's not the only thing in life. My dad is a draftsman, and he's been teaching me how to draw all kinds of things, which I really love to do," said Jiggs.

"That's great. Anyone else want to share a journey?" asked Mr. Gregory.

No one volunteered.

"Is there anyone who couldn't understand the symbolism that a journey gave after the nature of the target was understood?" asked the Giant's son.

Zeke Minturn raised his hand.

"Yes, Zeke?" said Mr. Gregory.

"My journey was kind of weird. I turned and went into the past the way you told us to, and as I walked down the trail, everything got bigger and bigger," Zeke began.

"So everything got bigger as you walked along?" asked the Giant's son.

"Yeah. So, I turned and walked back down this huge hill or mountain. I kept walking and walking and everything kept getting bigger. The moss and ferns were at least six feet high and the trees were huge, I mean, hundreds of feet high. I finally got to a spot where a blue and white bird's egg had dropped from its nest. I looked up and could see the bird's nest, way up in the tree. I was going to try to climb the tree and put the egg back, but then I noticed that it was cracked. It made me feel real sad, so I climbed the tree anyway to see if the other eggs were okay. When I got to the nest, there were three other eggs, but the funny thing is that they were pink and white, instead of blue and white. So I wondered if I had gotten to the right nest. Then the mother bird was suddenly behind me, and I felt her claws on my back, and she started pecking at me, and I fell from the tree, all the way down, smashing the blue and white egg that had fallen on the trail. I was on the ground for what seemed like years and years. That's when my journey ended," explained Zeke.

"Any thoughts about the meaning of those symbols?" asked Mr. Gregory.

Zeke shook his head, pondering the question.

"Well, it would seem to me that everything getting larger as you regressed in time would indicate that the event happened when you were quite young. The change of size would also suggest to me that in some way you identified with the egg you found on the trail, since finding it made you feel sad. Does any of that resonate?" asked Mr. Gregory.

"Kind of," said Zeke, frowning as he thought.

"Anything happen to you like that when you were really young?" asked the Giant's son.

Zeke reflected for a moment.

"In second grade, I was in a reading group with three girls, and they were all good readers. I liked the pictures in the reading book more than the words, although I knew most of the words. One day we were taking turns reading, and I was looking at the pictures instead of following, and my teacher came up behind me and put her hands on my shoulders and told me to continue. I couldn't find my place, and she scolded me, and then she put me in a different group. I think she liked girls better than boys, and I remember stumbling over words after that in a way I hadn't done before," said Zeke.

"Isn't it amazing how such seemingly small incidents can later become huge shadows that haunt us for years?" asked Mr. Gregory.

Jennifer raised her hand, saying, "I just figured mine out. I don't know if it was something you or Zeke said when you were talking, but I sort of just got a picture about what mine was about."

"Please tell us about it," requested the Giant's son.

"My road took me back to a grove of peacock feathers," said Jennifer. "They were growing right out of the ground and the eyes were all alive and staring right at me. I looked at the path, and it was all slippery with something black and oily, and I was suddenly afraid I would fall. In the middle of the peacock grove was a huge pacifier. Then I remember something I haven't thought about in years: when I was in nursery school, I was very, very shy. I understood what was required, but it took me a while to respond. One day one of my teachers became very impatient with me, because I hadn't responded quickly enough, even though I knew what she wanted. I must have been sucking my thumb, because she grabbed my hand and pulled it out of my mouth and shouted, 'Grow up!' I was so embarrassed. Everyone was looking at me, just like the eyes in peacock feathers. It made me feel that I was the slowest, dumbest kid in the nursery school. After that, I was always last in line for anything we did, and I really hated going to the place. I started having problems at night, too, for a long, long time."

"Thank you, Jennifer," said the Giant's son. "Who's next?"

One by one, all shared their journeys. Concern and support could be felt growing among class members, as stories were told. The tissues were occasionally passed back and forth, and no one was disdainful of anyone's need to use them.

Finally, after all journeys had been shared, Mr. Gregory announced, "This black box which I brought in today is empty because it is waiting for you to discard the pain which has afflicted you for years. I want you all now to fold your papers, and as you do so, think of all of the pain and grief these forgotten, now remembered, moments have caused you. As you fold these sheets, again and again, you are wadding that pain into a little bundle which you will soon discard into this black box. Once you have thrown it away, you will feel light and free for having done so. Go ahead, fold away, and know that you will soon be able to get rid of these limitations that have haunted you and that have held you back for years. And please remember what I promised at the beginning of the period. You will give something to this black box, and it will give you something in return."

Students folded their papers and then, as Mr. Gregory took the black box around to each one, they tossed their wadded sheets into the box. Some gave sighs of relief as they did so; others looked stoic and resolved to rid themselves of these recollected shadows.

"This is an important day, my friends," announced the teacher, "for you have all taken on the courage to face some of the fears that have haunted you for many years. I congratulate you, and I hope that our exercise today will encourage you to trust in your own abilities and powers. You have the ability to accomplish whatever you choose, so long as you trust that you can. One of our worst enemies is self-doubt, much less the doubt stirred in us by others. Doubt and worry create *obstacles*; hope and confidence build up *ability*.

"Years ago there was an overemphasis of value on people who had high I.Q.s. People wrongly equated a person's I.Q. as representing that person's degree of intelligence. The truth is that it represents only one form of intelligence, or perhaps several forms, if the tests take into consideration spatial perception and things like that. Always remember: persistence is the key to achievement. I admire people with average I.Q.s who work hard and persist until they have reached their goals. There is no degree in this world that any of you can't have if you become determined enough to earn it. Don't be buffaloed by doubt or worry. Instead, realize that you can actually accomplish your goals, especially if you *think* you can."

Bobby raised his hand, saying, "That ain't what we been told over the years. We ain't smart, that's what we been told."

"Did you buy into it, or did you know that it wasn't true?" asked the Giant's son.

"Ain't no arguin' with failin' grades," said Bobby.

"Remember, school is geared to serve and measure only one quarter to one third of the student population. All of the others are better skilled at learning in different ways, other than the linear model," explained Mr. Gregory.

"I ain't sayin' I bought into it, but my grades did," said Bobby.

"Grades only reflect your ability at certain kinds of learning. Language may not be your strong suit," said Mr. Gregory.

"Or his weak suit, either," said Zeke.

"*Listen* to the man," Bobby scolded Zeke. "You might learn somethin'."

"So, please don't doubt your ability to attain your goals. Just remember that we are all born with different abilities, strengths and weaknesses. It may take longer to achieve success in an area that doesn't come naturally, but that's just the way life is. You will find that the *joy* comes in the *effort*, the *struggle*, not in the victory. This sentiment is well expressed in the Latin phrase: *Gaudium Evenit Nitendo*. Any accomplishment will seem sweeter the more difficult it is to achieve. But success never comes from avoiding one's shortcomings, or denying them. That will only make one's path more frustrating and more confusing.

"If I am not mistaken, I remember reading once that Pliny the Elder, the Roman general and writer who perished in the famous eruption of Mount Vesuvius in 79 A.D., said of the athletes of his day, 'They can, because they *think* they can'. Always remember that assertion, for you, too, *can*, if you *think* you can."

The class was so captivated by what Mr. Gregory was saying that the passing bell startled everyone, several students jumping slightly in their seats. Several began to shuffle their books together.

"*Please* don't move. We have taken from the black box, and now we will receive. Bobby and I thought about what we could do for a memorable surprise on this Ides of March. We thought of lots of things, but Bobby finally agreed that my idea would best serve the class, at least in the long run. William Shakespeare memorialized the Ides of March in his play *Julius Cæsar.* As I now reach into this black box, I will probably draw out one of your worst unrealized fears. Yes. I've got it. It's not the play I mentioned; instead, it's Shakespeare's *Macbeth.*"

And the Giant's son waved the paperback copy of the play high over his head.

"Oh, no," sighed Dana. "Guess we're going to have to read it."

"Yes," agreed the Giant's son, "But there's more."

"We're probably gonna have to memorize some passages," said Zeke.

"No," replied the Giant's son. "There is a different 'more'."

The class sat in silent contemplation. What would be one of their worst, unrealized fears? A picture began to form in many minds, and the picture was not at all attractive.

"You've gotta be kiddin'," said Danny Taylor.

"No," said Mr. Gregory. "You're going to produce this play. We will start working on it Monday. I've got copies for you to take this weekend, so you will be able to get a head start on becoming familiar with the lines."

"We're gonna just read it in class?" asked Danny, hopeful to the bitter end.

"Certainly not. You're all going to act it out, to stage it, right in our own auditorium," said Mr. Gregory.

The concept of baptism by fire had never been entertained by any of the members of the class, but they now found themselves embroiled in a conflagration not of their own choosing, and one that played upon some of their deepest insecurities and worst fears.

Bobby felt his face turning red, and it was because not a few of his friends were looking daggers at him for selling them all out. Flushed with embarrassment, he started coughing so hard that he had to leave the room to get a drink of water. And as much as most of the students were on the verge of lynching their class president, what kept him from becoming the anathema of the class was that his peers also realized that Bobby had probably put up his best fight to stay off the forthcoming theater production. They intuited correctly that Bobby had been mere putty in the Giant's son's hands.

"Don't worry," encouraged Mr. Gregory. "We're going to do a good job, and we're going to have a lot of fun. In fact, we will do more a little later, especially in the way of helping you all to believe that you can successfully stage a production of *Macbeth*."

"Lunch is being *served*," protested Ryan, not wanting to miss the cafeteria's celebrated rubber hot dogs or the opportunity of sitting with his girlfriend.

"Lunch will soon arrive," corrected the Giant's son. "In the theater, there is a tradition of having a cast party after the final performance. We're only going to stage this play one time, and we're going to have our cast party right now. And it's on me."

Students looked at each other in confusion, attempting to divine the meaning their teacher's announcement. A knock was heard at the door, and a man wearing the cap of a famous pizza company entered the classroom, carrying six large pizzas. A helper followed him, bringing in six two liter bottles of various kinds of soda pop and some plastic glasses. The Giant's son took out his wallet and gave the delivery men an unknown number of twenty dollar bills.

"Only starvin' moths would've flown out of Dandy's wallet," Bobby whispered to Dana.

"My friends," began Mr. Gregory. "I am so proud and pleased with the good work that you have done, with the courage that you have demonstrated, that I decided it was time to celebrate. We will first have the feast of food and drink, which will then be followed by the feast of certainty, for I am going to lead you in another guided imagery exercise suggested by Dr. Baker that will help you to feel confident about staging *Macbeth*. Let's eat!"

The students needed no invitation to devour their favorite food items, which had just been delivered. Dana wryly noted that the boys were, true to their reputations, ninth-grade boys, eagerly shoving their way in to get their slices of pizza and glasses of soda.

"Not a gentleman in the bunch," growled Dana.

"It's like the Titanic," apologized Mickey, taking a huge bite of his first slice of pizza, "every man for himself."

"But they let the women and children go first," protested Dana.

"Bad mistake," retorted Mickey. "They never got their pizza."

"Oh, forget it," sighed Dana.

Fortunately, enough pizza and soda had been ordered so that everyone ate and drank well, and no one went hungry. Mr. Gregory took his pizza and soda last, and was congratulated by Dana, who said, "Well, chivalry still lives."

Dana's male classmates were too busy gorging themselves to hear her compliment to Mr. Gregory as well as her subtle knock on their poor manners. After the feast, Mr. Gregory called the class back to order, for only about ten minutes were left, asking them to sit in a relaxed posture.

"Now close your eyes and imagine yourselves sitting down, as a class, to make plans for our staging of *Macbeth*. Remember, we've identified many of your learning preferences, so see yourself engaging in preparations that relate to those strengths. Look and see us reviewing the play together, making sure everyone understands it. Look closely and you will see that you are helping each other to learn your words, your roles, your responsibilities. Look and see us preparing the stage, selling tickets, rehearsing for the final presentation. Look to see how successful we are at all of these things, for it is true that we *can*, if we *think* we can.

"As we embark upon this play journey together, you will be required to do things that you never expected you would be required to do, such as reading lines on a stage before a live audience. Nevertheless, see yourself doing that just now, and notice how easy it is."

Suddenly Gordie Chase was afflicted with a violent coughing fit, turning beet red, and becoming so embarrassed that he hid his face in his arms, placing them on his desk. The spell was now over, and Mr. Gregory seemed to take its unexpected dissolution in stride. Looking at the clock, he announced, "Before you all go, we have just a couple of minutes. I want you all to take this poem, a poem that I have written for each one of you, and read it to yourself every evening before you go to bed. I hope that you like it, and I hope that you will also read it every morning before coming to school, at least until the end of this school year."

They Can Because They Think They Can
(A Pantoum)

They can because they think they can;
Please do not misunderstand—
New thought has brought into their plan
Smart rigor to this growing band.

Please do not misunderstand—
Before they thought there was no chance,
Smart rigor to this growing band
Came of their choice to make advance.

Before they thought there was no chance,
Their fortunes tossed by circumstance—
Came of their choice to make advance,
The heart to seize the victor's lance.

Their fortunes tossed by circumstance,
New thought has brought into their plan
The heart to seize the victor's lance:
They can because they think they can.

Chapter Fifteen
Assembling the Parts

THE FOLLOWING MONDAY THE GANG OF FOUR SAT TOGETHER at lunch, ready to compare notes regarding the new ordeal faced by Bobby's class.

"I can't think of anything more daunting to them than a play," said David. "It's just not in their experience, and so many of them stumble over words."

"I can't believe the Giant's son conned Bobby into agreeing to it," said Lisa.

"Bobby says that Mr. Gregory can be *very* persuasive, in a sort of 'wouldn't it be nice if we could just manage such and such' way. Bobby argued against it until he was blue in the face, but for every point he made, the Giant's son turned the tables on him. Bobby said it was sort of like arguing against goodness itself. He wants to resign as president, but I talked him out of it, at least for the moment," said David.

"Gregory's asking a lot," said Mary.

"But they don't even have to memorize their parts," protested Sean.

"But even when they just read lines, they mess up," sighed David.

"Practice makes perfect," said Lisa. "They will really need to work. I can't believe there wasn't a major rebellion."

"It was a pretty slick deal," said David. "Gregory swore Bobby to absolute secrecy. Once the Giant's son had railroaded it over Bobby's protests, they both called on the local theater and got them to agree to lend a stored castle set that will be perfect for most of the play. Gregory convinced Bobby that they should wait until it *was* the Ides of March to spring it on the class, and then the Giant's son treated them all to their own cast party, even before the play was produced. Under that combination of circumstances, what could any of the kids do except grin and bear it and hope for the best?"

"Assassinate Gregory," said Sean.

"How and with what?" asked David. "The guy's a tank."

"I could figure it out," announced Sean. "I just don't have access to the right weapons, not that I'd want to off him anyway. Personally, I think the dude is really cool, but I can't believe he's getting away with all this. But when you think about it, this whole play business is probably the best that could happen to Bobby and his class. Hey, I need a different fork. I'll be right back."

"Sean's right, for once," agreed Mary. "Although, I hate to admit it. More to the point, what can we do to help Bobby and his class?"

"We'll need to do a lot of coaching," predicted David. "Oh, by the way, Bobby's coming over to join us midway through lunch to see what we've come up with to help them. They're busy trying to arrange the set, because it was dropped off in a hundred pieces. So far, they've done an amazing job."

"That's because you insisted that responsibilities be divided up, David, according to the four learning styles that Mr. Gregory told us about. That way, everyone can work from a point of natural advantage," said Lisa.

"It's great that Mr. Gregory lets them work in the auditorium during class and even goes in with them," said Mary.

"Banzai!" shouted Sean, returning with a new fork and tossing it on his tray, pretending to give it a resounding karate chop. Mary started and Lisa jumped back a little in her chair.

"Sean, grow up," demanded Mary.

"Got to keep you on your toes," replied her brother.

"Sean, we're going to try to brainstorm some ideas to help Bobby's class pull off their play production," said David.

"I heard that they have a set already," said Sean.

"Yes. It's from a recent production of Macbeth at the community theater that the Giant's son knew about," explained David.

"Sweet!" exulted Sean. "I'll start sharpening my swords."

"How can you sharpen plastic and plywood?" asked Mary, casting doubt on the reliability and authenticity of Sean's weapons.

"On your teeth, once I've tied you down," retorted Sean.

"Could you and your Swashbucklers Swords please instruct our future actors on how to fight?" asked David.

"Gladly. Do you want us to do a sword fight before the play?" David mulled over Sean's offer.

"I'm not sure. It could really upstage them. Let's wait and see."

"Understood. We'll be ready just in case," said Sean.

"Is everyone still complaining about the play?" asked Mary.

"Yes, although on Friday they actually seemed more confident than I would have expected them to be," said David, "but I still think they're at least a little terrified underneath the surface of things, probably some more than others."

"But Mr. Gregory did help them prepare themselves with one of those guided imagery walks that Dr. Baker showed us," observed Lisa. "And there is the poem that he wrote for them, too."

"They're probably still in shock," said Sean.

"Are the kids really mad about having to do Shakespeare?" asked Lisa.

David shook his head, answering, "I don't know. I think they're mostly mad about having to do any kind of play. It really exposes some of their weaknesses."

"Not after we coach 'em," said Sean.

"I'm sure that will help," said David. "And it's obvious Mr. Gregory is determined to convince them that they can do this *because they think they can*. He's been very insistent that they believe that they are capable of this feat. I bet he's glad it's a humdinger, too. If they can pull off this play, it will be a real boost to their self-confidence."

"It shouldn't be too bad, if we all lend a hand," Sean yawned.

"I hope you're right," said David. "At least *Macbeth* is one of Shakespeare's shorter plays."

"You know, the play could turn out to be a really good thing," said Lisa. "The few that I've been in have brought a real bonding among cast members. I bet that could happen here, if they can get over a few humps, like petrified stage fright."

"Lisa's right," David agreed. "We're sitting on a perfect bonding device for the class, but we need to help them far enough into the process of play production until the whole thing takes on a life of its own. That's when the magic really begins to happen. I've been in a couple of plays myself, but quite a few years ago."

"It's Howdy Doody time," Sean began to sing.

"Stow it," ordered David.

"Here comes Bobby," said Mary.

"Bad news, David," said Bobby, as he approached the table.

"Have a seat and tell us about it," invited David.

"No time. Part of the castle we put up before lunch just fell all the hell down so some of us are leavin' lunch to try an' fix it. Gregory's already there, waitin' for us. It's discouragin' after we thought we had put it up proper-like," said Bobby.

"It probably just needs a little bracing," said David. "Good luck. Let us know if we can help."

Bobby left with Zeke and Danny for the auditorium.

"They really do know how to put stuff together," said Lisa confidently. "Now all they've got to do is figure out how to assemble the castle so it will *stay* together."

David laughed.

"What's so funny?" asked Mary.

"Better that the castle fall down now, today, than during the play performance," he answered.

"David, you're becoming hysterical over the theater arts," Lisa observed, shoving her tray at him.

"I promised that we'd all go listen to them run through their first full rehearsal after school today. Okay?"

"I need to get home today," said Lisa, "but I'll stay next time."

"We'll be there," said Sean, looking at Mary who was nodding her agreement.

"Great," said David. "Any other ideas beside the possibility of having Sean's Swashbucklers knock the heck out of each other before the play?"

"Who else is coming to the play?" asked Lisa.

"As few as possible," quipped Sean.

"That's not fair," said Lisa. "People need to know about it and should be able to make their choice."

"I sort of had the impression it was just something for the class," said David. "But maybe it's meant to be for everyone."

"I mean, why all this scenery fuss?" asked Lisa. "It's getting to be a real production. Did you ask the Giant's son?"

"No. Bobby should, since he's president, but I think he's afraid to meet with Mr. Gregory alone any more, for fear that he'll be bamboozled into something else. After this play was sort of railroaded down his throat, he's really skittish about any kind of meeting."

"Why don't you go with him?" asked Sean.

"I'll offer, but maybe it should be Zeke and Dana," said David.

"At least you could advise them," said Mary.

"Okay. Maybe I'll try that, but the question of how public the play will be needs to be settled now," said David.

"Why now?" asked Sean.

"Now for several reasons: one, if the Giant's son insists that it be really public, then a lot of preparations need to be made; two, if it is going to be public, the casts' collective blood pressures are going to go off the chart. We'll need to do a lot of rehearsing and unruffling of feathers," said David.

"You're right that Bobby shouldn't be sent in, David," said Lisa. "He's taking all the heat for the play being produced, so let Zeke and Dana go."

"I agree," said David. "Let me go over now. I see them talking with some of the others at that table. I think they're going over their lines."

David left to consult with Zeke and Dana.

"You know," observed Mary, "if this whole thing goes public, maybe we should plan to sell tickets and make some money."

"Great idea," chimed in Sean. "The money can be given to the famous Swashbucklers Club."

"Yeah, yeah, yeah," said Mary, "fat chance."

"Or maybe to the library to buy books," said Lisa. "That would certainly be an endorsement for their learning to love learning for learning's sake."

Sean laughed.

"What's so funny?" asked Lisa.

"You," said Sean.

"And why, pray tell?" asked Lisa.

"You reminded me of Sidney Greenstreet in *The Maltese Falcon*, where he tells Bogie, 'I like talking to a man who likes talking about talking.' Maybe we could do a funny little parody of it when we give the money to the library."

"For once, you've had a good idea," said Mary.

"Ahead of you, at least," retorted Sean. "We'll book the parody."

"When would we donate the money?" asked Mary.

"Right after the play, don't you think?" said Sean.

"No. You can't just hand it over. It has to be done in a formal, dignified way, with the Giant's son there to see how much the class is supporting learning."

"How about an awards dinner?" asked Sean. "The sports kids get them all the time."

"Why not?" Lisa agreed.

"Why not what?" asked David, returning to the table.

"We want to have the play go public and sell tickets and give the money to the library for new books," explained Lisa.

"Hey. Great idea. But we should wait to see if it's even got to go public. If the Giant's son decides to keep the play within the class, then that will take a lot of pressure off. I'd be glad to donate money to the library for new books just for the relief of not having to see everyone really stirred up for these next few weeks," replied David.

"And who's going to pay good money to hear a bunch of ninth graders muff up from their scripts?" asked Sean.

"Parents?" asked Lisa.

"Yeah, but Sean is right," agreed David. "We'll need to ensure that the house is full if the play is going to be public. That means community support as well. Maybe we could get the mayor to come the way he did for Mr. Pennythorpe's reading of *A Christmas Carol*."

"I bet we could," said Lisa.

"How else did we sell tickets?" asked Mary.

"Dandy-Pandy," said Sean.

"Mr. Dandy?" asked Lisa.

"Don't you remember? He threatened to call every eighth grader in for an interview who didn't show up. Almost *everybody* came," David laughed. "Isn't that called negative reinforcement, or something like that?"

"It *did* work. Maybe if he threatened to breathe on them, they'd come to see Bobby's class do *Macbeth*," said Sean dryly, remembering his encounter with the counselor's breath of death when opening his student locker.

"Why don't we make a big deal out of it and give out awards?" said David, adding, "The class will deserve awards by the time they're done with all of this, and maybe we could come up with a phony-funny award, some sort of private ruse, just for an in-class joke. That would help to solidify the bonding of the class, which is probably one of the most important secondary outcomes to the production of the play itself. You know, kind of a 'Here's a little joke that only *you're* privy to. Don't tell. It's *our* secret.'"

The Gang of Four mulled over possible awards that could be given.

"Why don't we give an award to Dandy-Pandy," suggested Sean. "For the seller of the most tickets. We'll call it the 'Don't Breathe On Me' award, or maybe just a comparative citation which states, 'Melvin Dandy, your breath is just like a lobster's fart'."

"That's *mean*, Sean," said Lisa.

"But true," countered Sean.

"If we're going to give an award as a private ruse, it seems that our esteemed counselor would be just the one to receive it," said David.

"But what?" asked Mary.

"I've got it," said David. "We'll call it the YARB award, for 'Youth Annual Recognition Benefit,' which is our secret acronym, meaning 'You Are *Really* Bald'."

Mary looked at Lisa and rolled her eyes as Sean nearly fell out of his chair laughing.

"It would be awful if he ever found out," said Lisa.

"He won't," said David. "It will be our little secret."

"Little secrets have a way of getting around," warned Lisa.

"Trust me," said David. "This will work. Let me run it by Bobby."

* * * * *

That night, after dinner, as David and Bobby washed up dishes, David shared the gleanings of his Gang of Four.

"What?" exclaimed Bobby, "An award for that little Rumpelstiltskin? I'd rather give it to my worst enemy, or maybe to a brick wall."

"I suppose we could include Gertrude Coachman," David mused to himself, as he noticed the glint of fire that ignited in Bobby's eyes.

"Then you'd have a sorry pair," Bobby snorted. "Two of a feather, for sure. If you put 'em both in a bag and shook it, you'd be lucky to get half of a real person out of it."

"We can't include Mrs. Coachman," David reflected, "She isn't bald."

"She'd shave her ugly head if she thought she'd get an award for it," said Bobby. "You're just tryin' to get me goin', aren't you?"

"Actually, the YARB award is on the front burner," said David.

"Well, put it in the damn oven and turn up the broiler," said Bobby.

"How can we modify it so that you, as president of your class, would approve of it?" asked David.

Thinking for a moment and drawing the letters Y, A, R, B in front of him, Bobby replied, "Yeah, add A and D to make it YARBAD. That'll do it."

"And what does YARBAD mean?" asked David.

"You Are Really Bald And Dumb," said Bobby.

"We couldn't," protested David. "It's too mean."

"It's too true, you mean," said Bobby.

"*Yar* bad," teased David, proud of his pun.

"Just consider ..." said Bobby.

"No one is *ever* dumb," interrupted David. "Not in the sense of being stupid. We've already discovered that people learn differently."

"Well, that little Rumpelstiltskin ain't gonna learn unless his little head's in a vice-grip, I'm tellin' ya, and that ain't no joke," said Bobby.

"Maybe we should think of giving the YARB award to a couple of other people, too," suggested David. "You know, to a couple of other men who *are* really bald, but who don't have to hide it."

"Who? Who's *really* bald?"

"Mr. Pennythorpe," said David, adding, "*and* the Mayor."

"Maybe," said Bobby, considering and protesting, "but maybe not. We ain't been told whether this play's gonna be a public spectacle or not. I ain't gonna go alone to see the Giant's son again, ever! God help Zeke and Dana. They said they'd call to let us know his answer. I hope they did better than me."

At that instant the telephone rang.

"Speak of the devil," said Bobby as David reached for the phone.

"Hello. Oh, yes, Zeke. We were just talking about that. How did it go? You did? He did? He didn't? He did? You did? He did? Okay. Thanks. See you tomorrow, Zeke," said David.

"Well?" asked Bobby.

"Well what?" said David.

"That's it," said Bobby, stretching his dish towel and starting to roll it into a rat tail.

"Okay, okay," said David. "I was just kidding. Here's the long and short of it: the Giant's son wants the play to be a community event. He also loved the idea that Lisa and Mary had about selling tickets and donating all the proceeds to the school and village libraries. Mr. Lowery liked that, too."

Bobby stood scowling, finally saying, "You know, they're all going to be on my case for this."

"No way. That's why we sent Zeke and Dana in. It also proves that the Giant's son is pretty persuasive with everyone. In fact, Zeke promised him that your class would guarantee a full house," said David.

"The Giant's son is convincin' all right. Just let me tell you when you're sittin' in front of that human wall and it wants you to see somethin' in a certain way, you just see it that way, like it or not. It ain't right. It's like brainwashin', that's what it is," protested Bobby.

"It's not brainwashing," David protested.

"I ain't gonna take kindly to havin' to be in a play in front of a mob," said Bobby. "I never once *chose* that, I'm tellin' ya."

"But you asked that question about Mr. Dandy during that big assembly program when the Giant's son's father came to talk to us about education," David reminded Bobby.

"But that was different 'cause that little Dandy ne'er-do-well had it comin' to him for puttin' on all those airs. The Giant agreed with me, too, didn't he?" asked Bobby.

"Yes. He did," said David.

Taking the notepad from the refrigerator door and holding it out toward Bobby with its corresponding pencil, David announced, "Bobby Perkins, future star of stage, screen, and television, may I please have your autograph?"

"Sure," said Bobby, "but you ain't gonna like the autograph you're gonna get."

Having heard that cue before, David bounded into the living room and plopped himself down next to Aunt Lillian. Bobby raced in after him, slowing a bit when he almost ran into the chair where Aunt Lillian sat, reading a book and sipping at her evening tea.

"Oh, boys, I'm so glad you've come in to join me," said Aunt Lillian. "Shall we play some cards tonight?"

"Fine with me," said David. "How about you, Bobby?"

"Ain't no time. I have a mess of homework," said Bobby.

"Well, deal me in, Aunt Lillian," said David, as he rose to go fetch the canasta cards and card tray.

"Bobby," asked Aunt Lillian, "How's your play shaping up?"

"It just took a turn for the worse," said Bobby. "David'll explain."

"Oh, dear," said Aunt Lillian. "Let me know if I can help you."

"Thanks," said Bobby, venturing upstairs to do his homework.

* * * * *

The next day at lunch hour the Gang of Four discussed play preparations and how they could help Bobby's class.

"How was rehearsal?" asked Lisa.

"A real struggle," sighed David.

"That's an understatement," corrected Sean. "I mean, you should've seen everybody falling all over the words."

"It was lacking," Mary agreed.

"What's wrong?" asked Lisa.

"I don't think they understand the meaning of the words that they are trying to read," said David. "If they understood the meaning of the words, they would read them differently. Right now, the words are just so many meaningless sounds. They might as well be reading numbers or formulas."

"Has anyone gone over the play with them?" asked Lisa.

"Not that I know of," said David. "We could suggest that they ask the Giant's son to do that, I suppose."

"Why don't we?" asked Lisa.

"Yeah," agreed Sean. "The play's full of juicy killings and murders. They'd really like that. Maybe we could do a modern version."

"Fat chance with the castle scenery they're putting up," said Lisa.

"I mean in sort of modern dress," said Sean. "It would be what's called an anachronism, but it can work, provided it's done well."

"I think that would be asking too much of them," said David. "Let's just confine it to a traditional presentation of *Macbeth*. Do we know anybody who really knows the play?"

The Gang of Four pondered David's question.

"Hey," said Sean, "I remember a lady at our church, Mrs. Prince, telling another lady about how she loves the theater, and this Mrs. Prince went to see the community presentation of *Macbeth* last fall. What did she say? Let me think. Oh, yes, she said, 'Lavina, I like to get one of the best seats in the first or second row so I can smell the blood.'"

"Really?" asked David.

"Yeah. Really. That's what she said. Maybe she would be willing to come and talk to the class about the play and what it means," said Sean. "Maybe she'll even show us how she smells the blood. That would be *really* cool."

"You don't need any help with that," retorted Mary.

Sean started sniffing in Mary's direction.

"Oh, stop it," she ordered.

"Do you know this Mrs. Prince?" asked David.

"Not really. I mean, she's one of the Sunday school teachers. She's listed in our members' directory. I'll call her tonight," offered Sean. "Maybe she'll help us, or maybe she won't."

"We need someone like that, especially if she likes the theater and knows something about it."

"Maybe we could rent some videos of the play," suggested Lisa.

"Great idea," agreed David. "Why don't we plan to have a showing of at least one of the versions this weekend. Aunt Lillian would be glad to host the gathering, including popcorn and all the works."

"Shouldn't we also invite Mrs. Prince to come so she can sit near the television and smell the blood?" asked Sean.

"You can't smell the blood from the television," sighed Mary.

"How do you know?" asked Sean. "Maybe *she* can."

"Invite her to come Saturday," urged David, "so she knows what she'll be up against if she decides to help us."

"Okay. I'll find her name in our church directory and call her. I'd also better order some more fake blood from my supplier," offered Sean.

"We'll need a lot of it," agreed David.

"Maybe I should order an extra little flask for Mrs. Prince, so she can smell it any time she wants," Sean thought aloud.

"Oh, Sean, you're impossible," said Mary.

"Can you afford the quantity of blood we'll need?" asked David.

"I'll tell my mom it's for school," said Sean.

"Sean," scolded Mary.

"Well, it *is* for school, in a way, isn't it?" argued David.

"Oh, all right," agreed Mary.

"I can think of a cheaper source of blood a lot closer to home," said Sean, eyeing Mary intently.

* * * * *

Saturday afternoon brought Bobby's class, armed with their copies of *Macbeth*, to Aunt Lillian's, together with the Gang of Four, and a certain Mrs. Edith Prince, a veteran Sunday school teacher at the Midville United Methodist Church and a longtime aficionado of the theater, preferring plays by Shakespeare and Ibsen. Mrs. Prince, short of stature but durable in body, wore her raven black hair tight back on her head, forming it into a little bun on top. The slightest hint of gray now colored her hair, lending a distinct dignity to her presence. Mrs. Prince's round face was simple and sincere, and she carried within her bearing an intensity of personality hidden beneath a quizzical smile, which made her seem a little odd on first meeting. Nevertheless, it was obvious to anyone meeting her that she was not only bright, but would also be very competent at any task she might embrace. Having attended university, taking a degree in literature, she had become a local promulgator of the arts, which had proven to be pure missionary work in Midville. It was even rumored in the Homecroft Circle at her church that Edith Prince had doubtless read every biography ever written about anyone of any consequence. Here, in Aunt Lillian's living room, sat this remarkable lady, local bastion of arts and letters, come to lend aid to a novice group of players, who in sheer desperation and utter terror, were soon to launch into a community production of *Macbeth*.

When everyone was seated, David welcomed the group and announced that they were going to watch a DVD of *Macbeth* that had been recommended by and borrowed from the public library.

Looking toward the back of the room where Mrs. Prince sat next to Aunt Lillian, David asked, "Mrs. Prince, we appreciate your coming, and we hope you will consider helping Bobby's class stage their version of this play. Do you have anything you'd like to say before we watch this version?"

"Why yes, thank you," said Mrs. Prince, looking at the small assembly that sat before her. "I know only a few of you by sight, remembering that I've seen you at church. When Sean called, I was very touched that you might actually want my help. I must confess that I have never studied the theater arts, nor have I acted in any play, but I do love theater, especially the plays of Shakespeare and Ibsen. I would be delighted to help you in any way with your project. David tells me

319

that he thinks one of the big hurdles you'll have to get over is that of Shakespeare's language. I believe we could do that together. Anyway, I'm delighted to be here. Thank you."

"Anything else before we begin?" asked David.

Sean, who was sitting in the front row, raised his hand.

"Yes, Sean?"

Rising and turning to face Mrs. Prince, Sean asked, "Mrs. Prince, would you like to trade seats with me, so you can come up here and smell the blood?"

Mrs. Prince smiled, a twinkle in her eye giving full approval to Sean's question, and answered, "No, thank you. You go ahead and smell it for me today."

David gave Sean an exasperated look as he started the DVD player. Zeke turned out the lights.

The group then watched an excellent rendering of *Macbeth*. During the select scenes where bloody swords were displayed and used, Sean could be heard sniffing for all he was worth. After the video had concluded, Sean turned around and winked at Mrs. Prince, confessing, "It really works. I smelled the blood."

"Good for you, Sean," said Mrs. Prince. "Can anyone tell me what Shakespeare's *Macbeth* is about?"

The class sat dumbfounded, not having expected so specific yet general a question.

"It's about power, isn't it?" asked David, hoping to start the ball rolling.

"Yes, but more specifically, what is the relationship of the Macbeths to power?" asked Mrs. Prince.

"They want power," said Dana.

"Yes. How badly?"

"Enough to kill for it," said Zeke.

"So, the play is not just about power, but also about ambition, is it not?" asked Mrs. Prince.

The class members nodded.

Bobby raised his hand.

"Please give me your names when you speak," requested Mrs. Prince, "so that I can get to know you. Yes?"

"My name is Bobby Perkins, and I ain't able to make sense of Mr. Shakespeare. To me, this language is nothin' more than a lot of hooey. It ain't normal to speak like that."

"I quite agree," said Mrs. Prince. "Shakespeare was writing at a time when our English language was still emerging, still taking form. There was no real standardization of spelling until Dr. Samuel Johnson published his famous dictionary in 1755."

"So *that's* who we shoot," concluded Bobby, his sentiment catching the nods of Ryan Baxter and Danny Taylor. "Where do we find the ne'er-do-well?"

"Do you mean Dr. Johnson?" asked Mrs. Prince.

"Yeah. The one who put the damn dictionary together, beggin' your pardon Ma'am, but our lives ain't been easy facin' down one spellin' test after another all these years. That damn ne'er-do-well has made our lives into a living hell. Where can we find him?"

"Dr. Johnson is buried in the Poets' Corner of Westminster Abbey," said a perplexed Mrs. Prince, raising her thick eyebrows.

"He may soon be joined by another poet," predicted Bobby, adding, "if you catch my drift, Ma'am."

Mrs. Prince didn't exactly catch Bobby's drift, but she saw most of the students nodding their heads in agreement. Feeling that Dr. Johnson had borne some sort of slight in the conversation's undercurrent, she decided to defend his remarkable personage, for she had read a number of excellent biographies.

"I hasten to add," she started, "that Dr. Johnson was born almost dead and was very sickly as a child. In fact, if I remember correctly, he suffered from scrofula."

"Sounds like the beggar deserved it," said Bobby mercilessly, "whatever that is."

"It's a sort of tuberculosis of the lymphatic glands, especially in the neck," explained Sean, whose encyclopedic memory had won him both love and hate, "and it was also called 'the King's evil'."

"Poor Dr. Johnson was left with unsightly scars on his face and neck and became nearly blind in his left eye. He also had very distracting tics."

"Ain't those the little buggers that run amuck in the woods and give the unsuspectin' Lyme disease?" asked Bobby.

"No. That's tick, spelled T-I-C-K. I mean tic, spelled T-I-C, which is an affliction of involuntary moment of muscles, often facial muscles. Dr. Johnson had a difficult life," continued Mrs. Prince. "In fact, until he began to speak, many believed that he was an idiot."

"He was, if he put that stinkin' dictionary together. He just wanted to make the world suffer 'cause he had suffered," Bobby proclaimed.

"He was a man of great courage and intellect," Mrs. Prince countered, adding, "and a man whose accomplishments lived after him. He allowed us to standardize our language."

"Ain't no use to us," said Bobby. "I say we shoot him."

A ripple of applause could be heard from the room's least able spellers.

"My dear, you are speaking of the author of the *Rambler* essays," rejoined Mrs. Prince.

"I would've run, not rambled," Mickey Drexel piped up, gaining a much needed round of laughter.

"I still say we shoot him," said Bobby.

322

"Dear boy," cautioned Mrs. Price, "the poor man is already dead."
"Then let's dig up his bones and shoot them," said Bobby.
"YES!" cheered Sean.

"I take it you are not a particularly good speller," Mrs. Prince speculated, looking closely at Bobby.

"Never claimed to be," Bobby responded.

"I could help you to spell better, if you'd like," offered Mrs. Prince. "Perhaps we could talk about it a little later. My concern now is to talk to you about Shakespeare and the language that he used, as well as about his play *Macbeth*. You might be interested to know that Dr. Johnson wrote some of the first criticism of Shakespeare's work; in fact, it was published in eight volumes."

"Ain't as bad a dude as I thought, maybe," said Bobby, looking around to see if anyone else agreed.

"In criticism, I don't mean 'to criticize'," Mrs. Prince hastened to correct any false impression, "but rather literary criticism, which seeks to bring new meaning out of any work by analyzing it in some particular way."

"Ain't no use wastin' our time any more on this ne'er-do-well Johnson, 'specially when we got a bigger one to deal with, namely this here William Shakespeare," suggested Bobby.

"What I want you all to do," said Mrs. Prince, "is tell me the parts of the play you don't understand."

A quick inventory revealed that most of the class felt that they understood very little of the play as written, although most had captured the essential story line.

"Then we are going to have to translate, line by line," concluded Mrs. Prince. "Does anyone have an extra copy of the play?"

"Right here," offered David.

"All right. Please begin reading. We are going to go through the meaning of each line, line by line, word by word, syllable by syllable, until you've got it."

The group, in fact, ordered pizza that night, and, by midnight, Mrs. Prince had helped each of them to 'get it.' And 'get it', they did. For the first time, they had begun to understand the meaning behind the words they had been trying to utter. With that new understanding came better articulation and rhythm as well as greater clarity. Mrs. Prince even promised to come and coach them after school until the play was produced. The group gratefully accepted her offer.

* * * * *

On Monday morning, the 25th of March, the Gang of Four descended on Midville Middle School's guidance office instead of reporting to lunch.

"Do you think Mr. Dandy will have finished reading the paper yet?" asked Lisa, for it was an open secret in school that the counselor spent much of his time perusing the columns of the *New York Times.*

"I should hope so," said David. "The day's almost half over."

Mrs. Amelia Fullerton, Mr. Dandy's severe and overly efficient secretary, sat typing a letter when the students entered the office. Mrs. Fullerton looked and murmured, "Oh, dear."

"We would like to see Mr. Dandy, if he's available," David requested.

"Let me buzz him," Mrs. Fullerton obliged, picking up her telephone and pushing a button which caused a raucous sound inside the counselor's office. The students could hear him answer and noted the long pause that followed the announcement of their arrival. Finally, the counselor murmured a few things to Mrs. Fullerton, who immediately cast an appraising and not entirely laudatory glance at

Sean, and then responded, "Yes, sir. I understand. Perfectly. I'll give them the message."

Turning to the Gang of Four, Mrs. Fullerton said, "I'm sorry, but Mr. Dandy is suffering from a rather severe headache, one that I think may have just fallen on him. He's not up to seeing more than two or three of you, and he suggested that Sean see him at a later time. The three of you may go in."

"That's okay," said Sean, turning to look at David. "I understand. Just tell him I've gone to the auditorium to practice smelling blood."

David looked at Sean, giving him a confidential wink.

The door to the counselor's office opened a crack and, as soon as Sean left, it opened wide, with Melvin Dandy coming out of his office, "Sorry not to be feeling tip top today. Come in and we'll see what I can do for you. I think I can grant you five minutes, perhaps ten at the most." Although short of stature, the counselor walked with an air of authority that not only emphasized his importance, but also lent a pompous impression to his bearing.

After the students entered and were seated, David said, "Sean asked me to tell you that he was going to go to the auditorium to practice smelling blood, but that he would be back to see you sometime in the not too distant future."

"Must he?" asked Mr. Dandy, a little shaken, then correcting himself, by saying, "Oh, yes. He must. He must."

The counselor sat in silence, trying to get his bearings, quizzically weighing David's words.

"Why would he, or anyone, be practicing smelling blood?" asked Mr. Dandy.

"For the play that Mr. Gregory's ninth grade English class is going to be staging," explained Lisa. "Bobby Perkins is president of that class now, as well as the newly-formed Learning Club. They're planning to produce *Macbeth*."

"Oh," said Dandy, appearing to believe her news, "*Macbeth*, eh?"

"Mrs. Prince, a nice lady from the twins' church, volunteered to help the kids deliver their lines," explained David.

"But isn't *Macbeth* a bit ... ah ... advanced ... for that group?" asked the counselor.

"They don't have to memorize their parts, but only read them with meaning, clarity, and conviction," said Mary.

"Still a tall order for that outfit," concluded the counselor.

"We bet that they can do it, sir," said David. "And so does Mrs. Prince. She's the one who told them about smelling the blood in the first place."

"Oh, I see. So now Sean wants to smell the blood, too?" asked the counselor.

"Yes. He's been practicing ever since she mentioned it," said Mary.

"I don't doubt it," said Mr. Dandy, suddenly taking notice of some scratches on Mary's neck.

"Is everything all right?" asked Mary, who couldn't fail but remark upon the counselor's sudden interest.

"I was just going to ask *you* the same thing. Everything all right at home? Those scratches look pretty nasty. Has anyone been mistreating you? I know that your parents wouldn't, but siblings sometimes get carried away and need to be reined in."

"These were from two of our six Burmese cats," said Mary.

"Ah, yes. That's the *official* story. But you can tell me the truth, the *real* story. I can help you, you know. Before you could ask, 'What happened,' we'd have that little outlaw behind bars, and after I got done talking with the authorities, they'd throw the key away."

Mary sat in silence, contemplating Mr. Dandy's most attractive offer, until David, noticing her interest, exclaimed, "Mary!"

"Oh, no sir. It really *was* two of our cats," said Mary.

"Yes, yes. I know, dear child, I know," said Dandy, winking at her. "Perhaps you would prefer to stop by a little later for confidential chat in private, and I can arrange for Mrs. Fullerton to be the witness, I mean, to take notes. Just drop by, *any* time."

"Thank you, sir," said Mary.

"The reason we dropped by today," said David, "is that we need your help again in convincing students to attend this play. Mr. Gregory wants the eighth graders to see it. That will only happen if you do what you did for us before Mr. Pennythorpe's Christmas reading. That brought out *all* of the eighth graders, except those who were traveling with their families."

"And why should I endorse this so-called play, without knowing its quality?" asked Mr. Dandy shrewdly.

"Because a group of kids in this building is actually doing something directly related to learning and to theater," said David. "That's worth supporting, no matter how poorly or how well they'll do. We also plan to sell tickets and donate the proceeds, half to our school library and half to the town library."

"A worthy goal," said Mr. Dandy, "Lowery must be rubbing his hands already, eager to order all those new books."

"Will you help us, sir?" Lisa asked.

"I'm not sure. I'd look like a fool to endorse a play that flopped. I can't risk doing anything to undermine a reputation that I've carefully built up over the years," replied the counselor.

"Sir," pleaded Lisa, "it's for a noble cause."

"Yes, and often those who are for noble causes get it right in the neck," bemoaned the counselor. "I mean, we have a history, don't we?"

"Yes, sir," agreed David. "But all's well that end's well."

"You can understand my wariness. Part of me always worries and wonders about hidden agendas. Just once, I would like to know about a hidden agenda ahead of time," said Mr. Dandy.

The students sat studying the counselor's fictitious hairline.

"Sir," said David. "We hope to sponsor an awards dinner after the play; that's when we'd give the money from the play to the respective libraries. At that dinner, we plan to recognize three very important individuals who have aided our school and community. We're planning to give each of them what we are now calling the YARB award, which means: the Youth Annual Recognition Benefit award."

"Who are the other two individuals?" asked Mr. Dandy with interest, generously counting himself in the running before being told he was even a candidate.

"Mr. Pennythorpe and the Mayor," said David.

"The Mayor?" said Dandy. "Well, that puts a different light on the whole thing. Do you think I'd fit in to that lofty company?"

"You're a natural, sir," said David. "Believe us: we *know*."

"Bless your hearts. I'll do it. I'll lam into every eighth grader at this school to insure that all of them will attend your play and, if they don't pay enough to get in, we'll make 'em pay to get out. After all, we don't want to give measly little gifts to either library."

"You're very generous, sir," said David. "Thank you."

"No. I must thank you for considering me for this YARB award. Are you sure I'm a qualified candidate?"

"No one could be *more* qualified, sir," said David.

"I'll be glad to help. Whenever you've determined the date and time of the play, bring 'em by and I'll begin making my rounds."

"Thank you, sir, that's wonderful. We should know the date of the play and the awards dinner within the next few days," said David.

"Ah ... how can I put this? ... will there be complimentary tickets for the intended award winners and their spouses?" asked Mr. Dandy.

"You'll be our guest at the dinner," said David.

"And the play?"

"That, too," said David.

"Splendid," said Mr. Dandy. "Can't wait to tell the Missus."

"Thank you for your time, sir," said David, rising with the others to leave.

"You know," said Dandy, "Maybe I've been too cautious. I admit that I am wary of your little Gang of Four because of some of our past troubles, but today, for the first time, you have come in here with a noble request and generous acknowledgment, with no strings attached, no hidden agendas. So, I'm going to rethink my position. Maybe I have misjudged you after all," said the counselor.

David could only smile and bow in deference as the three left.

In the hallway, Lisa scolded David, "That's just awful. Sitting there and telling him about the YARB award, without his even suspecting that it means, 'You Are Really Bald'."

"He'll never know," said David. "It's going to be an in-class secret. The Learning Club is bonding in a lot of ways, and they're becoming excited about what they're doing. A little levity and humor helps along the way."

* * * * *

After practicing smelling blood near the front of the set, Sean met his three gang members in the cafeteria for lunch, where they promptly filled him in on what had happened.

"What a cheapskate!" exclaimed Sean. "I mean, did you hear that? He was begging for free tickets and wanting to make sure the dinner wouldn't cost him anything."

"At least he's going to help us," said David.

"Yeah. After he found out he would get an award," retorted Sean.

"We all like to be recognized," said David.

"Let's announce what YARB really means at the dinner," Sean suggested.

"No," said Lisa. "You can't do that."

"But who could argue it? The Mayor is as bald as a BB," said Sean. David looked sternly at Sean.

"Okay, okay," said Sean, "I won't. I promise."

"Good," said David. "And we'll be sure to keep it that way."

"All right, all right," said Sean.

"Mr. Dandy's help is going to bring in a lot of money," said Mary. "I mean, last time he must have been solely responsible for the sale of at least one hundred and fifty tickets."

"And at three dollars a pop, that's almost five hundred bucks," said David.

"You know how he does it, don't you?" asked Sean. "He walks into the English classes and says, 'I'm telling you all something for your own good, and that's that you're all going to go to this play. And I'm going to be right there, taking attendance. And, if you don't go, I'll be calling you into my office for hour-long discussions on the need for civic responsibility and school spirit."

"He doesn't," scolded Mary.

"Does so," argued Sean. "And, by that time, everybody's ready to pay double for a ticket, and he lays the final whammy on: 'And if I think we have a little problem, you can count on at least three one hour sessions where you can look into my ugly puss and smell my lobster breath. And when I start preaching, that's when the breath stinks the most, because it's generated by the hottest air. And I'm talking as hot as it is on the sun. It's so hot, it's a wonder I don't turn into a hot air balloon, except that all that hot air goes right up out of my little bald head. Mighty severe, it is, on the toupee, which at one time looked like real hair, but that was before the moths struck. Now it's nothing but a rats' nest. Fumigation isn't cheap, mind you, but *I am*. And since I've become a real nasty, little Napoleon in my amber years, I might as well wear a rats' nest on top of my head as anything else. Cheaper than a new hat,'" Sean intoned, in imitation of the counselor's best stuffed shirt voice.

"Oh, Sean," said Mary, "you're absolutely awful."

"Thank you," said Sean. "That's better than what you usually say."

David rolled his eyes, wondering what life would be like without the Potter twins, concluding that it wouldn't be anywhere near as interesting or as much fun.

"Should we arrange for some small gifts or plaques for the three award winners?" asked Lisa.

"Good idea," said David. "One of Aunt Lillian's former piano students runs a sporting goods store and they sell trophies. I'm sure he'll be able to give us a good deal. I bet Aunt Lillian would even underwrite that part of the expenses, as well."

"She does an awful lot, David," said Lisa.

"Well, she's got an awful lot to do an awful lot with," said David.

"Just as long as we don't play that card too many times," said Lisa.

"Okay. I'll check into the plaques," said David.

"How about presents, or would plaques be enough?" asked Mary.

"I think we should give them all presents," said Sean. "Why don't we ask Ryan to help us? He's a hunter and trapper. I bet he could get us some beaver pelts. We could put one pelt in each box and say that it's something to keep for a rainy day or to keep the drafts out."

"Sean, you're impossible," said Mary.

"But wouldn't the pelts be great?" asked Sean. "We could put a little tag on the bottom of each: FEAR NOT, NO MORE BOUNTIES; WEAR WITH PLEASURE."

"Someone will wear your little tongue with pleasure some day," said Mary.

"Do it! I dare you," said Sean, sticking his tongue out.

"It wouldn't help. Even if I did, it would never stop wagging," Mary grinned.

Sean gave Mary the evil eye as David and Lisa began laughing.

Chapter Sixteen
Play Preparations

O N TUESDAY MEMBERS OF THE LEARNING CLUB REMAINED AFTER SCHOOL to finish the final preparations of the set for *Macbeth*. The Giant's son gave an overview of the play and invited students to consider the parts for which they would like to audition. There were more than enough roles to go around, and several members of the class would have to do double or triple duty. On Wednesday through Friday the class would watch a different version of the play, to help further their understanding of its themes and plots.

On Thursday, the Learning Club would meet as usual, and Mrs. Prince would arrive to help class members determine their respective parts. Sean was glad that his Swashbuckler's Swords club would perform only before the play, thus enabling him to sit in the front row throughout the performance and smell the blood. Perhaps Mrs. Prince would even sit next to him.

David decided to ask Bobby to call a special meeting of the class after school on Wednesday. At Bobby's request, the Gang of Four had made plans for the banquet, which was going to be held in the school cafeteria and catered by Lisa's parents, who owned and operated a local restaurant. A generous menu had been approved, and now the Gang had to collect ten dollars from each class member. Typical of her generosity, Aunt Lillian had quietly requested that she underwrite the dinner tickets of all honored guests, with more than a dozen expected to attend, including the Professor and Doctor Potter. Bobby agreed to call a meeting for Wednesday, but expressed reservations about the ability of many in the class to pay for their own dinner tickets.

"They'd better cough it up," said David. "At the rate we're offering it, this dinner will be a steal."

"I ain't complainin'," said Bobby. "I'm only sayin' that a lot of the kids ain't got much dough."

"They seem to have it when they need it," observed David, "like whenever they want to go the movies."

"Some have their ways," admitted Bobby. "But an awards dinner ain't in their general vocabulary or means, if you catch my drift."

"Well, they're going to go, and they're going to *pay* to go," David determined. "I will have a little chat with each one of them, if it comes to that."

"Better you than me," said Bobby. "Recently I ain't been a very popular president. Next, I expect they'll peach me."

"*Im*peach," corrected David.

"No, peach," said Bobby. "Ain't that where they stand you in the middle of a circle and throw a bushel of peaches at you to teach you how to be a better president?"

"If it were only that easy," said David. "But being the president of anything is a really thankless job. Let's just review the class list. I want to know who's going to be trouble. I want to be prepared. And I want you there, too. If I'm going to be the bad cop, you can be the good cop."

"No desire to be a cop, unless I could arrest that little hoodlum, clap 'im in prison for life, and then resign," said Bobby.

"Bobby, we have to stick together on this. I don't mind being the tough guy, but you've got to support me," said David.

"Okay. But wait. You'll see how hard it is for some of 'em to come up with any dough."

"All I know is that your class is going to have to show its total support in what it's doing, or the Giant's son is going to be very unimpressed," warned David.

* * * * *

It was decided that the meeting would be held in the auditorium. Most of the class could inspect and admire the finished set, when David and Bobby met with the potentially troublesome students in a remote dressing room.

The first student called into the presence of David and Bobby was Joey Harris. Looking sickly as usual, he looked even paler under the soft light, behind the stage dressing area. The three of them were sitting at a work table, and Joey sat across from David and Bobby with his arms folded.

"And you mean to tell me," David asked Joey, "that you don't even have ten dollars for a ticket for this awards dinner?"

"Not required," said Joey. "The play is the important thing."

"It's only ten dollars," said David, "and you're *going* to be there."

"Who died and left you boss?" Joey asked David, looking in question at Bobby.

"David is speaking for me, too, Joey," said Bobby.

"Then you can both stick it where the sun don't shine," said Joey, rising to go.

Bobby stood up and grabbed Joey by the lapels of his shirt and threw him back on the work table, leaning over him, scowling with anger, saying, "You ain't gonna go nowhere 'til we tell you to go, and you ain't gonna miss no awards dinner."

"I got better things to do with my money," protested Joey, squinting up at Bobby.

"Like gettin' blitzed on drugs," snorted Bobby.

"None of your business," said Joey.

"Look," said David, appalled at Bobby's strong armed tactic, "I'll pay for your ticket, Joey. Just be sure you're there. Okay?"

Bobby released him.

"Okay," said Joey, lifting himself off the table, preparing to leave.

"Oh, one more thing, Joey," said David. "Bobby tells me that you aren't going to accept a role in the play. Is that right?"

"Yeah," said Joey. "What of it?"

"Do you wanna go back on the table, Sport?" said Bobby, raising his hands toward the lapels of Joey's shirt.

"I'm just not gonna do it," said Joey, looking at David and Bobby with contempt, adding, "and nobody can make me. I know my rights. I'm not gonna do it, and that's that."

Bobby reached to grab Joey by the lapels again, but David stopped Bobby, looking at Joey and saying, "If you don't take a part, we're going be in real trouble. We already have too many parts, and there just aren't enough people to fill every role."

Joey shook his head vehemently, saying, "No way. No way."

"You're gonna let the whole class down," said David.

"Too bad," said Joey, looking disdainfully at David. "No puny eighth grader's gonna tell *me* what I'm gonna do or not do. So there."

Bobby lost his temper and pushed Joey violently against the table.

"Ow! My side. That really hurt!" said Joey.

Bobby advanced, shoving him hard on his left shoulder, saying, "Okay. Let's go. We're gonna finish this here and now."

Joey looked in desperation at the exit and then at David.

"Come on," urged Bobby. "Take a swing so I can kill you."

"Bobby, please stop it," requested David. "Joey, whatever role Mrs. Prince assigns you will be the one that you will play. We'll help. But you must participate. If you don't, then all of our efforts are in vain."

"No way," said Joey.

"Get out of here," said Bobby, pushing Joey toward the door.

Joey glared at both of them as he departed.

David shook his head, "You know, I don't think that went so well."

"Nope," agreed Bobby, "he should've left with a pair of black eyes. That would've been really instructive to the others we're gonna call in. Let me call 'im back and finish the job."

"No. It's obvious that we're going to have a lot of trouble with Joey. Let's talk it over later and review our options. Who's next?" asked David.

"Sheila Morrison," said Bobby.

"The social butterfly," asked David. "Maybe she should hold off on buying all that makeup. Let's have her in."

Not knowing what had transpired with Joey, Sheila sat in Joey's chair with her legs crossed and arms folded.

"So, Sheila, I find it hard to believe that you can't come up with ten dollars," said David.

"Hey. I've got my expenses, and who wants to go to an old, stupid dinner anyway. It's going to be BOOORING."

"Look, Sheila," David implored, "we need you to come to the banquet. It's going to be a little on the dull side, so we need you to wear one of your gorgeous dresses and to help us liven it up a bit. What do you say?"

"Well, I got a nice dress my aunt gave me for Christmas. But ten bucks is still a lot of money for a stupid, old dinner," said Sheila.

"I'll lend you the money. You can pay me back a dollar every week," David offered.

"Okay," agreed Sheila, "but payments don't start until *after* the dinner. And it had better be a *good* dinner, at that price."

Both boys nodded in agreement as Sheila rose and walked out.

"Who's next?" asked David.

"Gloria Adams," said Bobby.

"Oh, the complainer. Don't worry. I'll take care of her," said David.

Bobby escorted Gloria in to the dressing room. Flinging herself into the chair both Joey and Sheila had occupied, she too folded her arms and glared at David.

"Is anything wrong, Gloria?" asked David.

"Plenty," she scowled.

"Plenty?" asked David.

"Not bad enough doing all this play folderol, but *now* we have to attend an awards banquet. The smart little seventh and eighth graders think you're just so swell, coming to our rescue and all that drivel. First it's fallacies, then the Learning Club, now the play ... and here you go off planning an awards banquet to top it off. You need jobs, real jobs, that's what you need," huffed Gloria.

"Do you have a job?" asked David.

"I used to," Gloria glowered. "Had to cut my hours way back because of all this nonsense. Now I only get four hours a week, and who can afford ten dollar dinners on that? I work as an assistant at a local beauty parlor that my aunt runs and I only make minimum wage."

"That's okay," said David. "You don't even have to come to the awards banquet."

"I don't?" asked Gloria.

"No. Don't bother. If you don't want to, I don't want you to."

Gloria reflected for a moment.

"Well, maybe if I saved up for a couple of weeks—"

"Don't even bother," said David. "You're excused."

"I don't want to be excused. I can pull my own weight in this class. I'm not going to be told what to do. If I want to attend the awards banquet, I will."

"It's expensive, and will be just a silly dinner," said David.

"No, it won't," said Gloria. "Mr. Pennythorpe is the featured speaker, and it's worth going, just to hear him."

"I couldn't agree more," said David. "Perhaps you could just tiptoe in after the dinner. Nobody would notice."

"I don't *want* to just tiptoe in," Gloria remonstrated.

"We could make some special arrangement—"

"Stuff it," ordered Gloria. "I'm coming, and that's *that*. Nobody's gonna order *me* around. I'm a *free* agent."

She gave a huff and walked back to the stage.

Bobby looked at David in genuine admiration, shaking his head, saying, "Nobody'll ever believe it."

"Nobody will ever know," corrected David. "We don't tell what goes on in here. Understand?"

Bobby thought about his near altercation with Joey and nodded.

"How did you know about Gloria?" Bobby asked.

"Easy. She's a grumbler. Not happy unless she can grumble about something. She doesn't believe that she has much of what psychologists call a *locus of control*. From her point of view, everything in life happens *to* her, making her the victim so she can grumble. All I did was try to take away any feeling of being victimized."

"She played right into your hands," said Bobby.

"Probably thinks I'm pretty bossy—" began David.

"Come quick!" shouted Zeke. "Joey's having a fit or something."

All three boys raced to the stage, where they found the members of the class surrounding Joey, watching him writhe around on the stage, babbling incoherently, spitting, his eyes dull and frozen, as if he were having a seizure.

"Joey," began David, "are you—?"

"Snakes! Get 'em away from me," shouted Joey, lurching away from David, and panting to catch his breath.

"He won't let anybody touch him," said Dana.

"Call Mr. Gregory," said David.

"We already did," said Dana.

"Joey, we're here to help you," shouted David.

"Turn the lights off. I see all kinds of lights, flashing on and off. Turn off the lights. My backbone is burning up. The snakes, get 'em away. Get 'em away."

"Joey, your eyes are closed. No lights are flashing. Open your eyes!" said David.

Soon Mr. Gregory came running up to the stage. Having no better luck than David at communicating with Joey, he instructed David, "Go to the office and have them call 911 for an ambulance."

David obeyed immediately, and soon members of the Midville Ambulance Corps were hoisting Joey up on to a stretcher, where he still writhed around and babbled incoherently. Mr. Gregory went to the office to get Joey's mom's number and to ask her to meet them at the hospital. In light of all that had happened, it was decided that it would be best for the class to adjourn for the day, and soon most were on their way home.

* * * * *

At the behest of the boys, Aunt Lillian called Dr. Wayne Smith who, in turn, called Joey's physician. Dr. Smith also called Joey's mom and asked her permission to convey news of her son's condition to the members of his class. Mrs. Harris agreed and asked him to request that members of Joey's class pray for him.

"Wayne says that whatever happened seems to have been from a flashback from a drug trip, possibly LSD," said Aunt Lillian. "Mrs. Harris is apparently quite shocked, not having been aware of Joey's alleged habit."

"Everybody at school knew," said David.

"What are they callin' it?" asked Bobby.

"Nothing yet. He's being kept for observation, although he seems to be very remote, even to his own mother. He still keeps talking about seeing snakes on the floor and spiders on the wall."

David shook his head sadly.

"Wayne said that the tentative diagnosis is for some sort of psychotic breakdown," continued Aunt Lillian. "It doesn't look as if Joey's going to be returning to school this year."

"Oh, no," said David. "We needed him for the play."

"It doesn't look good for that right now," said Aunt Lillian.

"I wonder if Dr. Baker could look at him?" asked David.

Aunt Lillian shrugged her shoulders, "Joey already has two doctors. What does he need with a third?"

"He knows Dr. Baker," said David. "That could make a huge difference."

"Should I call his mother to inquire?" asked Aunt Lillian.

"Please. And please tell her we will do all that we can to help," said David.

Aunt Lillian borrowed the class list and left to call Mrs. Harris. Returning a little later, she said, "I think she must still be at the hospital. I might just drive over. Do you boys want to come?"

David and Bobby thought of how they had treated Joey earlier, looked at the floor sheepishly, saying, "Not tonight. Maybe later."

After Aunt Lillian left, David said to Bobby, "The last thing Joey Harris wants to see is you and me walking into his hospital room."

"Do you think we caused it?" asked Bobby.

"Don't know. We did apply quite a lot of stress to him today," said David. "I sure hope we weren't the cause."

"Well, if he's seein' spiders and snakes that ain't there, he'd think we were two gorillas walkin' in if we visited him."

"He'd probably think we'd come to finish the job," sighed David.

Returning about two hours later, Aunt Lillian looked in on the boys, who were finishing their homework.

"How's Joey?" David asked.

"Apparently not much different. The tests are contradictory and Joey is still having hallucinations. He's also complaining of headaches and some sort of heat moving up his back and all through his spine. Not one of the medical tests that they administered so far has been conclusive. It's certainly turning out to be a mystery. I'd call Dr. Baker, except that it's quite late. I'll try him in the morning. He was planning to go to see Mrs. Prince cast the class. Why don't I come over about that time, and maybe you both could fill him in on the details of what happened to Joey. I could take him to the hospital to meet with Joey's mom. Joey spoke highly of him, so I'm sure she'd be willing for him to lend whatever help he can."

"Great, Aunt Lillian. Thanks," said David.

"Good night, boys," said Aunt Lillian

"Good night," came their response.

* * * * *

On the next day, March 28th, Aunt Lillian arrived prior to Mrs. Prince's casting, hoping to consult with Dr. Baker, who had also arrived early. As soon as Dr. Baker saw David and Bobby, he walked over to speak with them and Aunt Lillian.

"So sorry to hear about Joey," said Dr. Baker. "Could you tell me more about what happened?"

"Sure," said David. "But you should also talk to some of the other kids who saw the whole thing."

"Please have them come over. I'll talk with everyone individually during Mrs. Prince's casting. Then I will follow your aunt over to the hospital to meet with Joey's mother."

"David and Bobby, do you want to come to the hospital with us after the casting?" asked Aunt Lillian.

"Nope," said Bobby.

"No thanks," said David. "We've both got a lot of homework. We'll just walk home. We've got a key."

Mrs. Prince arrived carrying a large yellow legal pad on which to make notes, several books about the play, and her crotchet paraphernalia. Students were astonished at how she would sit there nonchalantly, focused on her crocheting, and then suddenly make telling comments and suggestions, although she appeared not to have been listening. It became apparent that Mrs. Prince wasn't interested in smelling the blood during the casting process, for she sat in the last row of the auditorium, next to David, Bobby, and Dana.

"Attention everyone," announced David. "Before parts are assigned, Mrs. Prince wants everyone to read one of two speeches. Boys will read Macbeth's lines in Act Two, Scene 1, lines 30 through 64. Girls will read Lady Macbeth's lines in Act One, Scene 5, lines 1 through 25. We will go in alphabetical order, which means Gloria Adams goes first. Go ahead Gloria."

Gloria looked around at the class, as if she had just been offered poison, scowling as if everyone had betrayed her.

"Gloria?" David prompted.

"All right, all right. I'm going," she responded, walking to center stage, leafing through her copy of the play for the correct lines.

Gloria found her place and began to read.

"Louder, please. Remember to project," requested Mrs. Prince.

Gloria's reading proved positively undistinguished.

"Ryan," called David.

Ryan took center stage and began his part. As Ryan read the part of the assigned speech that talked about seeing a dagger floating before him, Bobby whispered to David, "Good thing Joey ain't here. Can you imagine how that would set 'im off, 'specially since he's been seein' spiders and snakes that ain't there."

"Shh," whispered David, noticing that Mrs. Prince had cupped both of her ears to hear Ryan.

"Louder, please. You absolutely *must* speak louder," requested Mrs. Prince. "I know that most of you, if not all of you, are anxious about being on stage. But we don't have to memorize our lines; we only have to read them as best we know how. That, my dear friends, is going to take some considerable practice. Owing to our extended session last Saturday, I know that the story of the play and its lines are clearer to you than before. Now we have to make it *live* for the audience. Ryan, you are a tall, strapping youth, and I'm sure your voice can be louder than that. Don't be afraid of speaking the words. Belt them right out. I want you all to pretend that I'm your little old great-grandmother, sitting back here, trying to hear your every word, partially deaf, and without benefit of hearing aids. Try it again, Ryan."

"Again?" complained Ryan.

"Yes, dear. And with a little more volume and gusto. I know that you can do it," encouraged Mrs. Prince.

After Ryan had read again, Mrs. Prince applauded, saying, "Much, much better, Ryan. You've set a standard for everyone else to emulate. Please keep Ryan's excellent work in mind when your turn comes everyone."

"Gordie," announced David.

Gordie Chase took centered stage, looking extremely nervous. Bobby had warned David that Gordie hated public speaking and that he was going bonkers over having to be in a play.

"Should I get the barf bag?" asked Bobby.

"It's not going to be that bad, is it?" asked David.

"Ain't gonna predict," said Bobby.

"Now Gordie, I can see that you're nervous. Forget that anyone else is out here except your little old great-grandmother. I want to hear every single word you say, so don't forget to speak up. Just pretend that it's only little old me out here; forget everyone else," instructed Mrs. Prince.

This stratagem seemed to effect its own peculiar kind of magic. Gordie began to read, and read loudly, if a little erratically, but nevertheless got through his lines without losing his lunch. When he finished, everyone present applauded. At first he seemed astonished that anyone was even sitting out in the auditorium, except for his little old virtual great-grandmother in the persona of Mrs. Prince, yet the applause of those present brought no smile to his face, and he abruptly left the stage fully red-faced and in panicked embarrassment.

"He's going to be a really tough sell on acting," David observed.

"That was amazin'," said Bobby. "Just amazin'. Never thought I'd see Gordie stand up on a stage."

"I wonder if he'll ever get on one again," David wondered.

"Ain't a problem. Me and Zeke have got our ways of convincin' the fainthearted."

"I can only imagine," David returned, as he looked down at his roster, calling, "Mickey, you're up."

In florid contrast to Gordie's painful bashfulness, Mickey Drexel took center stage and bowed three times, once to each third of his audience. It would have been obvious to any newcomer that here stood the self-appointed class clown.

"Earn your bows," shouted Mrs. Prince.

The smile on Mickey's face faded slightly, but he looked fiercely back at Mrs. Prince, proclaiming, "I just want everybody to know that I am going to give the best darn reading of anybody in Bobby Perkin's gang. They don't have the pluck to match my style and dramatic presence, much less better it."

With this surprising gauntlet thrown down, Mickey began to read, and read extremely well, with dramatic pause and theatric flare, until his final words, 'Hear it not, Duncan; for it is a knell/ That summons thee to heaven ... or to hell.'

Enthusiastic applause greeted Mickey's surprisingly good reading, thus challenging and bringing all subsequent readers to a new level of competition and excellence.

Bobby looked at David, whispering, "Ain't like Mickey to go against his fellow gang members in that way, or any way, for that matter. I smell a rat. Ain't normal."

David tried to suppress his budding grin, and Bobby caught the faintest hint of satisfaction in his face.

"Did you put Mickey up to that?" asked Bobby.

"Ask me no questions; I'll tell you no lies," said David.

Mrs. Prince had finished making notes on her yellow pad and had resumed her crocheting.

"Dana," announced David.

Dana walked to center stage with new purpose and confidence. Facing her audience, she began her part. Her voice was strong and steady, and she halted only over a few words. It was obvious that she, too, had worked with diligence on her part. When she had finished, another wave of affirming applause greeted her efforts.

"Maureen," announced David.

Maureen Grant walked up on the stage and looked at the audience, giving a tentative smile. David was immediately taken by the apparent change in her personality, which used to be surly and malcontent in nature. Now she seemed more composed and self-assured. It was obvious she was nervous, but nevertheless willing and confident about what she was going to do. Her reading was both heartfelt and focused. Warm applause again greeted her efforts, and she gave a slight bow of acknowledgment before leaving the stage.

David looked at the next name on the list, which read 'Joey Harris'. Looking over to where Dr. Baker was still quietly interviewing students, David announced, "There will be a five minute intermission."

Everyone began visiting about their respective performances and how nervous they had felt, ribbing each other and laughing, as David walked over to confer with Dr. Baker.

"Yes, David?" said Dr. Baker.

"Sir, do you think that Joey will be able to participate in this play, or should we simply write him out?"

"Oh, I wouldn't write him out. In fact, from what I'm hearing about what happened yesterday, I am becoming convinced that Joey has been misdiagnosed. I will soon leave for the hospital to meet with his mother and his two physicians."

"It sure would be great if Joey could help us, " said David.

"I'll tell you more after I've talked with Joey," said Dr. Baker, "but I do know that what appears to be happening to him is something of which many physicians are unaware."

"What's that?" asked David.

"I need to see and talk with Joey before I can be sure, but so far it has all of the signs. I'll let you know my diagnosis when I'm positive," said Dr. Baker.

"Okay. Good luck," replied David.

Returning to Bobby, David whispered, "Aunt Lillian and Dr. Baker will soon leave for the hospital, so we'll walk home after these auditions, as previously discussed."

"Fine by me. I'd just as soon go now and be done with it," said Bobby.

"Not before you read. You're the class and club president," said David. "And remember, Mickey's challenge was to everybody."

"Seems to have worked a miracle," observed Bobby.

"You may be right. How do you feel about your reading?" asked David.

"Nervous," said Bobby. "Butterflies in my gut, but I'll be okay. I'm not gonna let that little wuss of a Drexel upstage me."

Readings resumed, with students Larry Jones and Jennifer Lawler distinguishing themselves by virtue of their passion and accuracy. The class was beginning to bond even more, eagerly anticipating Mrs. Prince's decision on which roles would best be served by whom. Meanwhile, Mrs. Prince continued to crochet and to make notes on her large legal pad. She no longer needed to encourage everyone to project, since the standard had been firmly established by Mickey Drexel.

When David went to read Zeke's name, Bobby motioned with his arm for him to pause, whispering, "Wait. I'll do it."

By this time Zeke was looking over at David for the anticipated cue. Bobby cleared his throat, announcing, "Ezra Ezekiel Minturn."

Zeke's eyes grew dark as he stood up, and for a moment he seemed torn between walking to center stage or advancing to the rear of the auditorium to throttle Bobby. Everyone felt the tug of war at work inside of Zeke and watched carefully to observe what would transpire.

David finally raised his arms, as if to say in apology, 'I didn't know he was going to do that. Sorry', and motioned Zeke toward the stage.

This seemed to satisfy Zeke, who then mounted the stage and found the correct lines. Zeke's performance embodied a very real kind of suppressed anger, which helped to intensify his reading, which was met with warm applause.

"Sheila," announced David.

Sheila strode center stage and gave an unfocused, but heartfelt, reading of Lady Macbeth's lines, as applause affirmed her efforts.

"Bobby," announced David.

Bobby walked to center stage, opened his script, looked up, announcing, "I ain't against readin' this part of Macbeth, but I really want to get assigned the part of King Duncan, the one who gets killed real early-like. That way, I'm out of the play."

"Cheap, cheap," yelled Zeke. "Just tryin' to get out of readin' more lines. How do you know you'll be named the King?"

"Why? 'Cause my butler-servant is followin' me up here," said Bobby.

When the others realized that Jiggs would read after Bobby, laughter echoed throughout the auditorium. Not to be outdone by Bobby's reference, Jiggs was on his feet in no time, shouting, "I won't be anybody's butler."

Mrs. Prince became mildly interested in the interchange, and appeared to understand its import after David explained Jiggs' nickname to her.

"Bobby," said David. "Let's have your reading, please."

Bobby looked at his lines and began to read. It was a little rough, not unlike Bobby's character, but it was, once again, sincere and heartfelt. Warm applause greeted its conclusion.

Bobby bowed to the audience and resumed his seat next to David, noticing that Zeke was making a mock-slash-across-the-throat gesture instead of applauding.

"Zeke's still pissed off," Bobby whispered to David.

"Good for him," said David. "He has a fine name. He should be proud to be named for his great-grandfather."

"Better than for his great-grandmother," quipped Bobby.

Jiggs followed Bobby, who was then upstaged by Danny, who was then followed by Tammy Young. All gave credible readings, although it was clear that Danny was doing his best to beat Bobby and Mickey. The entire group took a twenty minute break to allow Mrs. Prince time to complete her recommendations for casting.

Since it was Thursday, David, Dana, Zeke, and Bobby decided that after Mrs. Prince announced her choices, rehearsals would be adjourned until Monday, in order to give cast members a chance to review their lines. No memorization was being required, but genuine familiarity with the words of the text, and most especially the meaning of each passage, was vitally important.

Mrs. Prince stepped to center stage to announce her choices, saying, "Everyone, please come sit here in a semicircle and I will indicate which parts I think you will all be most comfortable playing. I must emphasize, however, that these assignments may change, owing to unforeseen circumstances or need.

"As you will note from the list of *Dramatis Personae*, we have too few players for too many roles. With a little creative adaptation, and some additional favors from Sean's formidable *Swashbuckler Swords*, I feel that we can be successful in our presentation.

"Before I announce parts, let me say a huge 'thank you' to all of you for reading so well. Now, let me see. Oh, yes. Here's my list: Duncan, King of Scotland: Bobby Perkins; Donalbain: Gordie Chase."

At this announcement, Gordie's face became so red that David began to worry that he might suffer a stroke. His eyes also seemed to glaze over. —We're going to have trouble with Gordie, thought David, making a mental note to talk to Bobby about Gordie's reaction.

"Malcolm: Larry Jones," continued Mrs. Prince, "and I was especially pleased with the volume of Larry's voice, which was very much improved; Macbeth: Mickey Drexel," at which point Mickey stood and bowed like the ham that he was, "Banquo: Zeke Minturn; MacDuff: Jonathan Stevenson."

Mrs. Prince paused to study her notes, looked up, and announced. "And here I think we will prevail upon Sean Potter to ask his friends if they will kindly do double duty and serve as the Noblemen of Scotland. They will also be Swashbuckler swordsmen before the performance.

"Fleance will be played by Ryan Baxter; Danny Taylor will play Siward as well as Young Siward; Seyton will be played by Joey Harris; the Boy, son to MacDuff and the two doctors will also be played by Sean's friends as will the Old Man, Soldier, and Porter. Lady Macbeth will be played by Dana Foley; Tammy Young will play Lady Macduff; the Gentlewoman will be played by Jennifer Lawler. Lisa Jones has agreed to play Hecate, and the Three Witches will be played by Maureen Grant, Gloria Adams, and Sheila Morrison. I think that is going to work out just fine."

Club members applauded each other, although David noticed that Gordie Chase did not applaud or show any sign of emotion, except for the telltale glint of terror in his eyes, just like that seen in eyes of a caged animal shortly before it tries to win its freedom.

* * * * *

Upon arriving home that evening, Bobby and David prepared a light supper and waited until Aunt Lillian returned home.

"How's Joey?" asked David.

"We're not sure," said Aunt Lillian. "Clarence thinks that Joey may have been misdiagnosed, but won't be sure until he conducts some more interviews regarding Joey's experience of what happened. I invited him to come over for dinner some evening once he's satisfied, hoping that he can help us find ways to provide assistance to Joey."

"Ain't no help for somebody who's gone bonkers," said Bobby.

"Dr. Baker doesn't believe Joey has gone 'bonkers', so let's wait and see what is discovered," Aunt Lillian replied.

"What does he think it is?" asked David.

"I'm not at liberty to say, at least, not yet. But if what he suspects proves true, then Joey is going to have some real adventures in store for himself. Dr. Baker hopes to help Joey navigate through his new experiences."

"New experiences?" asked David.

"I'm afraid that I've already said too much. Dr. Baker promised that he would let us know his findings, with Mrs. Harris's permission, but that may take several days," said Aunt Lillian.

"Gosh!" exclaimed David. "Will Joey be able to be in the play? We really need him."

"I don't know. It seems rather soon for anything like that," said Aunt Lillian. "Let's wait and see."

* * * * *

On Monday, April 1ˢᵗ, as members of the cast assembled in their assigned places after school, Bobby approached David, who was reviewing a list of proposed cues with Mrs. Prince, and whispered, "Gordie skipped out. Sheila saw him get on the bus."

Mrs. Prince looked at David, appealing for his help, "David, would you mind filling in for Mr. Chase today? Since he has left us in the lurch, I will assume your duties and call out cues, if necessary."

"Sure," agreed David, turning to Bobby, "Is there any reason Gordie skipped out?"

"He's got a job at one of them fast food dives," said Bobby. "But I think he's just petrified to be in front of people. He's a real loner, not very sociable. Don't worry, me and Zeke will pay 'im a little visit tonight just before he gets off work. He should've arranged not to work 'til the play's done with."

After the first night's rehearsal, Bobby and David reviewed the cast's progress. There had been a number of glitches, but there would be ample time to correct them. Perhaps the most important and gratifying event was that students had read their lines with understanding, thus they were able to communicate the meaning of their parts to their listeners. Mrs. Prince had been especially pleased, since the good readings were in large measure because of her steadfast efforts to review and elucidate the play for club members.

But first, Gordie Chase's absence would have to be addressed.

Bobby had arranged to meet Zeke where Gordie worked around eight-thirty p.m..

* * * * *

Bobby returned home shortly after ten o'clock.

"It's kind of late," said David, descending the hall stairwell in his bathrobe. "How did it go?"

Bobby grinned, announcing, "Gordie's gonna make each and every rehearsal we have from now on, and he's gonna come on performance night as well, 'cause Zeke is gonna escort him."

"Guess that's one way of making sure Gordie's there. How did you get him to agree to come back?" asked David.

Bobby looked at the floor, searching for the right words.

"Well," demanded David.

"Guess Zeke and I sort of work like the mafia," said Bobby.

"You didn't rough him up, did you?" asked David.

"No way," protested Bobby. "We only talked to him about the future, meanin', if you get my drift, *his* future."

"His future?" asked David.

"Yeah, I mean, like, if he was even gonna have one," said Bobby.

"That's threatening," said David.

"Ain't right, I know," said Bobby, "but Gordie showed a little more pluck than Zeke an' me expected."

Bobby proceeded upstairs past David.

"Hey, you've got to tell me more than that," David implored.

"Better that you ain't in the know," said Bobby.

"Look," asserted David, "I *need* to know. So cough it up."

Bobby sat down on his bed and looked at his step-brother.

"Okay. Zeke and me gets there and go up to the counter normal and decent-like and order up some french fries and coke. Gordie waits on us, but ain't got enough courage to look us in the eye. We see that he's real worried from the way his eyes avoid makin' any real contact with our eyes. Shortly before his shift is over, Zeke and me go outside to wait. About ten minutes later, out Gordie waltzes, thinkin' we've gone on our merry way. So he says, 'What do you want?' And I says,

'You know what we want.' And he puffs himself up and shouts, 'I *ain't* gonna be in any play.' So then Zeke grabs him by the lapels of his shirt, real firm-like, and says, 'Listen to Bobby, little boy, before somebody rubs those little freckles off your ugly, frickin' face."

"I've heard *that* before," sympathized David. "Poor Gordie."

"So Gordie says, 'Try it, Champ, I dare you.' So Zeke clenches his fist and heaves it back, ready to give Gordie the old GOOD NIGHT, IRENE, but I says, 'Zeke, don't hit him. Ain't worth goin' to jail. And, remember, Gordie's under David's protection. That means absolutely no violence.'

"Then Gordie gave Zeke a smirk as if to say, 'Try forcin' me now, buster,' so I says, 'Gordie, our class is dependin' on you. You're lettin' us all down. Gordie says, 'So what?' So I looks at Gordie and says, 'You ain't gonna be able to come to work with your toes bent all the way to hell and back again. We're gonna keep our promise to David *tonight*, which means absolutely no violence. If *that's* the way you want it, that's just the way it's gonna be.'

"And Gordie says, 'What do you mean?'

"And I says to him, 'We're gonna call in our silent partner.'"

"Silent partner?" asked David, frowning.

"Hey. I was desperate. I heard somethin' once 'bout a silent partner who was a hitman in a gangster movie, so I said it. And thinkin' of the gangster movie made me think of that cursed little magpie," said Bobby.

"Sean?" laughed David. "He's anything *but* silent. What did Gordie say?"

"Gordie says, 'So who's your silent partner? David? I'm just *so* scared.' So I tells him straight out that it's Sean, and he laughs again, saying, 'I *ain't* afraid of him. He's just ridin' 'round on that overrated karate belt.' So I says to Gordie, 'Oh, yeah? Let me tell you what happened when I went to his MYF one time.' And Gordie says, 'What's an MYF?' And I explains, 'Methodist Youth Fellowship.' We were all gonna go see some religious musical. Sean and his sister invited me and David.' Gordie shrugs and says, 'So what's that got to do with me?'"

"You didn't," said David, grinning.

"I did," nodded Bobby. "I looks at Gordie and says, 'Just listen to my story. David and I gets to the church. No sooner do we walk in the door than six of Sean's friends come up to us and say, "Sean is gonna get his tonight. We're gangin' up on him, but we need your help. You need to lure him into the bathroom so we can mug him." David says he's not interested and I says I'll help, 'cause I owe that little hoodlum a big one from last October when he made my very life pass in front of my eyes. So I give 'em five minutes, and then find Sean and ask, "Where's the boys' room?" And he says, "Follow me." So we get to the door and he goes in first and says, "Hey. This light should be on." And then there's a rush of wind and bodies and everybody is on the floor holdin' Sean down. So I piles in on top of the whole bunch to help 'em nail the little beggar, who's squirmin' around on the bottom of the heap. Then one of the kids below me says, "Hey, somebody's untyin' my sneaker." And real sudden-like that kid just starts floppin' around like a fish out of water, screamin' at the top of his lungs and tryin' to get out from under the pile, finally falling out on the floor groanin' and writhin' around. Then another kid says, "Somebody's untyin' my sneaker, too." And damned if he doesn't start hollerin' and screamin' and floppin' around, and the same thing happens again and again until, finally, I feel some-body untyin' *my* shoe and slippin' it off, and then I feel the biggest pain I ever felt in my whole life in my right middle toe, pain that would blind any normal person, so I started floppin' around and yellin' in pain, hopin' that somebody will put me out of my misery. So everybody is writhin' around on the floor, groanin' in god-awful pain, just like the little hoodlum had machine-gunned us down but, instead, he just bent our frickin' toes off. And as we lie there floppin' around in pain, the little beggar has the nerve to walk out as if nothin' ever happened. When we got on the bus a few minutes later, all seven of us was quite the pretty group, real awesome-like, just like cripples hobblin' around tryin' to walk."

"At the time, I wondered what had happened," David reflected. "At least you could still come to enjoy the musical."

"Ain't got much recollection of it," sighed Bobby. "All any of us poor devils could do there was grip our seats an' nurse our achin' toes, wonderin' if they were gonna fall off or not before intermission, hopin' to hell that some day, somewhere, we might walk normal-like again."

"So what did Gordie say to all that?" asked David.

Bobby looked with exasperation at David, "Can you stand it? He said, 'That ain't got nothin' to do with me. Sean ain't gonna hurt anybody who don't bother him.' And I knew he was right."

"So, what did you do?" asked David.

"I found a new angle," announced Bobby, proudly, "hopin' to scare the livin' lights out of Gordie."

"Obviously it worked. What did you say?" asked David.

"I says, 'Me and Zeke are gonna tell Sean that the reason you are so quiet at school is 'cause you spend most of your time readin' about funny things, like those dudes in India who walk barefoot across the hot coals. We're gonna tell Sean that you need his help, 'cause you want to walk across some hot coals yourself, but you ain't been able to toughen up your feet. And what you need is someone to help you learn how to resist pain by bending your frickin' toes off your feet.' So then Gordie gets real pale and worried, and says, 'You wouldn't say that. I mean, I never said that.' And I says, 'So what? It ain't got nothin' to do with us.' And Gordie says, 'Sean wouldn't do that.' And I says, 'Yeah. I know what you're sayin'. He's wild, but he's not mean. That's why Zeke and me will frame it up so that he thinks he's helpin' you. The louder you scream and the more you writhe around, the more he's helpin' you.' Gordie looked at the sidewalk like he had just lost his best friend and wanted to run away, and then back at me, sayin', 'Sean wouldn't believe you.' And I says, 'Oh, yes, he will. I'll even tell him that you're gonna deny that you want his help to toughen up, like them there Spartans in the olden days, but that you really want him to bend all your toes back 'til you go blind with pain, with me and Zeke holdin' you down the whole time.' Then I see that Gordie is considerin' the truth of my words, so I shut up. He finally looks at me and says, 'Okay. I ain't gonna miss any more rehearsals.' And I says, '*Or* the performance.' And he nods, and me, Zeke and him shake on it. So that's it."

"Do you think he really will come back?" asked David.

"If he ever wants to walk again he will," said Bobby blandly.

"Maybe he'll get cold feet again," said David.

"We got insurance," said Bobby.

"What kind of insurance?" asked David.

"Zeke is gonna pick him up and escort him to every single rehearsal as well as to the play," said Bobby.

"You guys certainly turned Gordie around. What a bluff," said David.

"It wasn't no bluff, Davey boy, and Gordie knows it, too," said Bobby.

"I don't know. Sean is pretty quick," said David.

"Hey. Zeke and me would've convinced Sean that he was giving a service that Gordie really needed and wanted, so that Gordie could eventually toughen up and walk on them hot coals. I would've said to the little hoodlum, 'From all your readin' about torture, and from what you did to us when we ganged up on you at the Methodist Church, you are the master of torture and pain, and we need your help to get Gordie into shape to walk on them coals, but he's just too shy to ask. He really wants you to play his toes like a cash register, and me and Zeke will hold him down as you ring up them bills."

David shuddered in sudden realization that Bobby's ploy probably would have worked, and that Gordie might never have walked normally again. David realized that he had, once more, underestimated Bobby's cleverness.

* * * * *

That Sunday, after a weekend of unseasonably warm weather, Dr. Clarence Baker and Mrs. Robin Harris joined Aunt Lillian, David and Bobby for dinner. Joey's mother appeared to be a little sparrow of a woman, not unlike Aunt Lillian, although approximately twenty years younger. Her chin was weak, though, and in her bearing she conveyed a sense of uncertainty, rather than authority. It was easy to surmise how an adolescent male could find wayward paths to follow under a home rule wrought in confusion and indecision.

"Glad that you could both come," said Aunt Lillian. "How's Joey?"

"Much, much better," said Mrs. Harris, smiling for the first time. She had looked a bit worried when she entered, her brown eyes betraying a clouded anxiety. She wore a drab brown skirt and light green blouse and her hair looked slightly unkempt, as if hastily combed.

"So glad to hear it," replied Aunt Lillian.

"And all because of this wonderful man, Dr. Baker," Mrs. Harris added.

The guests were shown to their respective places and, after a short blessing, Aunt Lillian began to dish out her famous Hedges' casserole, an easy and simple dish that could feed numerous guests with minimal preparation and modest ingredients. David poured and filled all of the water glasses.

"It must be very gratifying to you that Dr. Baker discovered Joey's misdiagnosis," said Aunt Lillian.

"More than I can say," said Mrs. Harris. "I'm a single parent with two boys, and Joey's the oldest; I have my hands full, in addition to trying to hold down one full time and one part-time job."

"Dear, dear," said Aunt Lillian, "how ever do you manage?"

"Rather poorly," said Mrs. Harris. "Dr. Baker has been counseling me as well as Joey. There are some things I'm going to have to do to become a better parent, including becoming more consistent. One of the first will be to quit my part-time job."

"How will you make ends meet?" asked Aunt Lillian.

"We'll just tighten our belts," said Mrs. Harris. "Now knowing some of the things my oldest son has gotten into, I need to supervise him more carefully."

"How's Joey been since his release from the hospital?" asked David.

"He's been very quiet and he sleeps a lot. Sometimes he reads from the books Dr. Baker gave to him about the kunda..."

"Kundalini rising," said Dr. Baker.

"Yes. He's become very interested in that since it's now part of his experience. Dr. Baker thinks he'll be able to return to school next Wednesday," said Mrs. Harris.

"Two days before the play. Great! We really need him," said David.

"Do you think Joey's participation in a play would be advisable?" Aunt Lillian asked Dr. Baker.

"Depending on the part. I wouldn't want to add any unnecessary stress to his life right now. If his part can be minimal in its demands, I would let him try it, just for the benefit of his joining in with his classmates," said Dr. Baker.

"Trust me," said David. "I'll see that he gets a part that's a real breeze."

"He ain't even done that for *family*," grumped Bobby.

"Well, Joey's been hospitalized," said David.

"Then I'll step in front of a school bus," said Bobby, "if it means I ain't gotta have a big role."

"Yeah, yeah, yeah," said David.

"You know how brothers are," said Aunt Lillian, looking at Mrs. Harris.

"Only too well, I'm afraid," said Mrs. Harris. "Jake is only three years younger than Joey. They seem to fight constantly."

"Where's Jake tonight?" asked Aunt Lillian.

"At a friend's house. Dr. Baker thought it best if only he and I accepted your kind invitation to dinner. Joey's home sleeping," replied Mrs. Harris.

"Yes, I understand how he must need his rest right now," said Aunt Lillian. "We all want to know what we can do to help Joey. Could you please fill us in?"

"Gladly," said Dr. Baker. "The symptoms of Joey's experience are often confused for psychosis or schizophrenia, in part because many physicians and neurologists are not yet privy to understanding the unusual circumstances which caused those symptoms."

"I don't understand," said David.

"For many years I have been interested in Eastern mysticism and yoga, and have done a considerable amount of reading in that area. One of the East's insights into human development is a description of a phenomenon they call *kundalini rising*. We all have these kundalini energies, and they lie dormant in our bodies waiting for release. Some experts suggests that the release of these kundalini energies, which navigate up the spine, opening the energy chakras, marks an important advance in our spiritual evolution, where we become privy to higher states of consciousness. The energy itself has been described as a liquid fire, which rises from the base of the spine, thus activating and transforming each chakra as it ascends to the head."

"Chakra?" asked David.

"These are energy centers in the body that Eastern medicine and Eastern spiritual practices describe. Each one represents a separate area of influence on different portions of the body and personality. Kundalini energies are normally released only after long preparation and deliberate practice, such as are found in the study and pursuit of certain kinds of yoga. However, there are other ways these energies can be released: one is through a sudden and extremely powerful, jarring bump to the lower spinal area. These energies can also be triggered through the use of certain drugs, including LSD."

"Wow!" exclaimed David. "You mean that the hallucinations that lots of people on drugs go after can be found through these kundalini energies?"

"I'm not sure I would call them hallucinations," said Dr. Baker. "People who release these energies often find that their sensory and extrasensory abilities are greatly enhanced. After all, what is real? Should we limit ourselves to believing that only what we see, touch, hear, taste, and smell is real? X-rays can't be seen, but their existence can be proven through the use of certain kinds of cameras."

"You mean the things that Joey saw were real?" asked David.

"Not in the sense that you or I could touch them. In fact, they may even have been symbols that relate to issues that Joey has to work out," answered Dr. Baker.

"Do people who have these energies flowing in them see strange things, then?"

"Sometimes. Perhaps it would be helpful to think of these energies as having a foot in at least two different worlds. Eastern mystics tell us that the release of these energies is a necessary and time-honored path to greater spiritual awareness, especially if one truly hopes to find enlightenment and understanding," explained Dr. Baker.

"Why did Joey see snakes?" asked Bobby.

"Probably because he thought he felt snakes crawling slowly up his body toward his head. Classic accounts of the kundalini phenomenon indicate that first the person feels intense heat at the base of the spine, which then works its way up the back, and finally throughout the whole body. Sometimes the body begins to shake, and the creeping sensation gives the impression of ants crawling or snakes wriggling up the body. Others experience things like birds hopping or monkeys leaping."

"Gosh!' was all Bobby could say, his eyes wide with fascination and his mouth hung open.

"These kundalini forces have traditionally been seen as energies that cleanse the body and mind, finally resulting in a sort of cosmic consciousness," continued Dr. Baker.

"What *is* cosmic consciousness?" inquired David.

"It's a vaulted state of consciousness where one perceives and feels at one with the entire interconnectedness of all realities, including the one we're living in at present. It is also a state where one can see extremely lucidly, for example, realize or know in ways beyond knowing that consciousness is the source of this external reality that we currently inhabit."

"You mean this universe?" asked Aunt Lillian.

"Yes. The most recent theories about reality, especially those about its holographic nature, would suggest that energy follows thought, and that we live in what is called an explicate, or material, plane of reality, which, in turn, folds infinitely into countless implicate orders of reality, which constitute ever higher orders of energy."

"That goes *way* beyond me," said Mrs. Harris.

"And I can't confess to understanding much of it myself," said Dr. Baker. "Although I find it absolutely fascinating."

"Does that mean Joey has cosmic consciousness?" asked David.

"No," replied Dr. Baker. "Or, perhaps I should say, 'not yet'."

"Joey talked about seeing lights," said David.

"Yes," agreed Dr. Baker. "That is also very common. Many devout adherents to Eastern philosophies, who know a lot more about this than does Western culture, work their entire lives to attain enlightenment. One path is the release of these kundalini energies. One of the problems that occurs is when they are released before the individual is ready for them. If there are blocks, or points of stress, along the energy pathways, the kundalini forces work away at them until they dissolve. But this process can result in physical pain and psychological fallout. There can be persistent tension headaches, nightmares, lack of sleep, moments of disorientation, and many other symptoms. Some poor souls, not prepared for the transformation that is occurring, fall into what appears to be various kinds of psychosis."

"Wow!" said David. "What else can you tell us?"

"A person's thinking may be accelerated or decelerated or brought to a near standstill. There may also be moments of profound and lucid insight as well as moments of irrationality. There is sometimes the problem of detachment, wherein a person seems to see from a distance what is happening inside. The Sufi tradition speaks of a 'fire of separation' that might allude to this phenomenon. There is also sometimes a dissociation which leaves the person delusional, believing that this experience is the sign of being chosen for a divine task."

"Are there other symptoms besides these?" asked Aunt Lillian.

"There are many. Although there are certain, standard common possibilities, the phenomenon is also idiosyncratic to each person. Out-of-body experiences and extreme enhancement of psychic abilities is not uncommon, but Western medicine does not recognize any of these phenomena as being anything but delusions, although I believe that this prejudice is now in decline, in the light of recent research," Dr. Baker explained, adding, "The allopathic community is, bit by bit, throwing off its fetters to a mechanistic world view. Scales are beginning to fall from a few precocious eyes."

"I don't understand much of this, either," admitted Aunt Lillian, "but it's very interesting."

"The real question is how to help Joey," said Dr. Baker.

"Yes," agreed David. "What can we all do?"

"Patience and understanding will go a long way," said Dr. Baker, "especially if he acts strangely. I have been sharing a lot of this with him, so he knows what he can expect. We also talk daily by telephone and I will see him every third day in my office."

"Should we ever call you if he goes ..." David began.

"Bonkers," interrupted Bobby.

"Of course. If there's ever a problem, please call me," said Dr. Baker. "By the way, Lillian, this is one of the finest dishes I've ever had. Do you share the recipe?"

"It's extremely easy and simple. I'll write it out for you before you go. Would you like some more?

"Yes, please. A large helping, in fact. Thank you."

"Do you have any books I could borrow about this kundalini thing?" asked David.

"Yes. Most of them are now in the hands of Joey's two physicians, but I have a few left," laughed Dr. Baker. "The next time I'm coming by your house, I'll drop some off."

"Thanks," said David.

"I hate all this," announced Bobby.

"Hate what?" asked Mrs. Harris.

"It ain't right. I *mean* it. Just as soon as a fellow thinks he's got his bearings, then WHAM, some new darn thing steps up to the plate. This kundalini thing ain't catchin', is it Doc?" asked Bobby.

"Oh, no, Bobby. Don't worry. You aren't apt to catch it; at least, I don't *think* so. Remember, this is something that usually happens only after years of devout meditation and concentrated yoga practice. As I mentioned before, harsh accidents to the base of the spine occasionally will release these forces. Unfortunately, the use of drugs such as LSD can also release these kundalini energies, often before individuals are ready to recognize or to cope with the new worlds that they encounter."

"I am so grateful for Dr. Baker," announced Mrs. Harris, "for he has convinced Joey to swear off of drugs."

"Great!" exclaimed David. "But, how?"

"In our talks, I simply pointed out to him that there are far safer and better ways to reach altered states of consciousness. Hypnosis is one example. Meditation is another. With Joey's permission, I have already begun to train him in the art of self-hypnosis, and we will be exploring various kinds of meditation."

"We'll keep a careful eye on Joey at school," David promised.

"Let's *all* keep a careful eye on him," suggested Dr. Baker. "He'll be fine, especially if he's sure he has our understanding and support."

"Cherry pie and ice cream for dessert," announced Aunt Lillian, rising to take plates. Bobby and David assisted, after which the adults enjoyed some decaffeinated coffee as Bobby and David washed the dishes.

Chapter Seventeen
A Play is Presented

IMMEDIATELY BEFORE MONDAY'S REHEARSAL, David met with Mrs. Prince, the Learning Club officers, and Mr. Gregory. "We really need every day this week to fine tune the play. But I'm still glad we scheduled it for Friday, April 12th. Didn't the Titanic sink on the 14th or 15th of April?" asked David slyly.

"*Thanks* for the vote of confidence," grumped Bobby.

David smiled at the strong reception his allusion had received, and continued, "All of the advertising announces that proceeds will be divided between the school library and the village library. Mrs. Grant and Mrs. Adams are arranging for us to have the correct costumes, and they will be assisted by Mrs. Stevenson and Mrs. Foley, who will also oversee props and be our stage managers so that players will not be late for their entrances. Publicity is out and programs are printed. Mrs. Baxter said ticket sales are flourishing, especially among the eighth graders. Every member of the Learning Club is also expected to sell at least five tickets, at three dollars each."

"Nobody'll want to come and see *us*," said Bobby gloomily.

"Hey," corrected Zeke, "let's be *positive*. If Mr. Dandy can get the eighth graders to come, we can get the rest."

"I think Zeke's right," agreed David. "With Mr. Dandy's support, we're guaranteed at least one hundred and fifty eighth graders."

"Is he gonna take attendance the way he did in December?" asked Zeke.

David nodded as everyone suppressed bemused smiles.

"Eighth graders purchased tickets very briskly last December," said David. "Most of them have *already* purchased tickets for *Macbeth*."

"Is it true that some seventh graders even want tickets?" asked Zeke. "I heard Sean Potter was doing something to get sales."

David rolled his eyes indulgently, answering, "Well, you all might as well know. When Sean saw the success that Mr. Dandy was getting, he started imitating him, pushing smaller seventh graders up against the wall and peering down at them and telling them they'd better get tickets and attend the play or he would have individual conferences with each one of them."

"You've got to be kidding," said Dana Foley.

"I'm serious. And the funny thing is that his imitation is *almost* letter perfect," said David.

"Except for the lobster breath," added Bobby.

"Bobby," scolded David, but none of the adults present seemed to have taken notice or offense at the comment.

"The paper gave your efforts a positive spread," said Mr. Gregory.

"David's got awesome connections down there. I just hope people aren't expecting a *real* play performance," Dana worried aloud.

"The publicity is quite clear in stating that students will read from their play books as they engage themselves in the play's action. I don't think anybody's going to expect all that much," said David.

"I hope not," replied Dana. "I'm already getting nervous."

"Sean has an idea for how to double or triple our take," said David, looking around at his listeners.

"How's that?" asked Zeke.

"At the end of the play, we announce that Mr. Dandy is going to give a two-hour speech, and that anyone not wanting to listen to it is going to have to *pay* double to get out," David laughed.

"We could make a fortune," said Zeke.

"Well, Mr. Dandy is assuring you of at least one hundred and fifty tickets, is he not?" asked Mr. Gregory.

"Yes, sir. And without that support, we wouldn't have much of anything to give to the libraries. I know we have our little jokes here and there, but it's all in good fun," replied David.

Mr. Gregory merely smiled in acknowledgment.

"Mrs. Prince," asked David. "What do you think our major obstacles are from this point on?"

"The lines are coming, and I am much relieved about that. We did ourselves a favor when we went so carefully through the play. But I think dramatic timing may pose a challenge to us. Students need to develop a sense of when they walk on and off, without any stage managers having to shoo them here or there. That will probably come in time; at least, I hope it will. Students will also have to project more. I will continue to sit in the very back of the auditorium during our rehearsals, but I insist that I get front row center during the night of the performance. I promised to teach young Potter how to smell the blood, so we're going to sit together and do *just* that."

"Sure, anything you'd like," said David, as everyone gave their consent by nodding their heads. The play needed Mrs. Prince, and one thing was certain: nobody was going to dare cross her. After all, she said liked to smell the blood, and who could ever guess where that might lead?

'Thank you," responded Mrs. Prince. "I appreciate your courtesy."

"You're very welcome," said David, rushing to give a response since he saw that Bobby was about to make some derogatory comment about the little hoodlum. "Let us know how it goes."

"I see that almost everyone has assembled," replied Mrs. Prince. "Shall we get started?"

Soon everyone had taken a seat in a semi-circle and all were listening to Mrs. Prince's instructions. It was clear that Act I would be emphasized, although there might be time to run through the other Acts.

Sean Potter sat next to David, who sat next to Mrs. Prince. Sean whispered to David, "Mary told me that there are witches in this play. You could've saved three parts if you had asked POTS to play the witches. She's big enough to play all three at once."

"Your nanny would kill you if she ever heard you say that," retorted David.

"You won't give me away, will you?"

"Don't tempt me," said David. "How's your *Swashbuckler Swords* group coming?"

"We'll be ready. We rehearsed for two hours last Saturday. It's going to be great. I think everybody will love it."

"Are you going to use your trick dagger?" asked David.

"Of course. Hooter's going to try to stab me with his sword, but I'm going to get him with my knife. I'm going to be sure to win for my team, even if they get me in the end," said Sean.

"Not like you to be the victim," observed David.

"On my terms, it's okay," said Sean. "Anyway, each of my friends is putting up ten dollars for this library cause, just for the privilege of trying to do me in."

"I thought your sword group carefully scripted the outcomes of your battles," said David.

"No way. That would be really boring," objected Sean.

"Have you read the play?" asked David.

"No. I saw it on video, though," said Sean.

"I bet you can recite every word of it," David wondered.

"Almost. I wasn't paying full attention when it was on," said Sean.

"Please read it, Sean," requested David.

"Why?"

"Because if we are down any characters, guess who will fill in?"

"Not me. I'm going to be out in the middle of the first row with Mrs. Prince smelling the blood."

"I'm talking *emergencies*," David reassured.

"No girl parts," warned Sean.

"Okay," agreed David.

"It had better be a *real* emergency," said Sean. "I'll do my part at the beginning, but I really want to enjoy this play."

"Okay," said David. "I don't think we'll need to call on you. Gordie Chase had a real bad case of stage fright. The only reason he's here now is that Zeke is escorting him after his last class, so he can't escape from the building. You might consider warning him not to duck the performance."

"Do you really think he might?" asked Sean.

David shrugged, saying, "Who knows? I'm just saying that a word from you would work miracles."

"Why me?" asked Sean, suddenly suspicious.

"You've got the gangster reputation around here, like it or not. When you threaten some poor devil, that person listens, because it has become legend how very resilient you are. You can conquer a whole horde and walk away without a scratch," explained David.

"Like that little MYF caper?" grinned Sean.

"Bobby's still talking about it. It's almost become an obsession. I think he can still feel the pain in his toes," said David.

"No way," said Sean.

"Just a word from you to Gordie would cinch it," said David.

"Naw. I'll send my butler over," said Sean.

"Your butler?" asked David.

"Yeah. Jiggs is my new butler. Watch," said Sean, clapping his hands. Immediately Jiggs left where he had been standing and presented himself at full attention, saying, "Yes, master."

"I don't believe it," said David.

"What is your pleasure, master?" asked Jiggs.

"Go and tell Gordie Chase that if he dares to miss any rehearsals or the performance, he's going to have to answer to me, because I don't want to have to fill in for anybody. I want to sit in the front row next to Mrs. Prince and smell the blood."

"Yes, master," said Jiggs, walking directly over to Gordie and giving him the message. It must be admitted that Gordie took it well. For all the pressures that were building inside of him, this unexpected notice might have been the last straw except, like Macbeth, Gordie now thought he was in so deep, he might as well cross over the river of blood rather than turn back. Not wanting Sean to have to smell any other blood than that which would be let on performance night, Gordie gave a forced smile and frail nod signaling his agreement to the message Jiggs had just delivered.

"Places, please," called Mrs. Prince.

Everyone obeyed immediately.

"We'll start with Act I: Scene 2," continued Mrs. Prince, explaining, "The witches are going to rehearse their lines and special movements under the supervision of Mrs. Jones back stage. Curtain, please."

Although the grand drape had not been drawn closed, everyone interpreted Mrs. Prince's request to be a metaphor, which was meant to signal the beginning of the scene.

An awkward pause ensued, until Mrs. Stevenson's voice could be heard to give a loud whisper, "Bobby, you're on."

Bobby Perkins walked to center stage with Larry Jones, Gordie Chase, and several of Sean's friends, only to meet another of Sean's friends who staggered toward their party. No costumes or props were yet ready, so they were only holding their play books. Stopping and staring out at Mrs. Prince, Bobby began, "What bloody man is that? He can report, as seemeth by his plight, of the revolt the newest state."

"STOP THE MUSIC!" shouted Mrs. Prince, jumping out of her chair and running over to the stairs and clamoring up the right side of the stage. On her way up, though, she tripped and went flying out on to the proscenium. Several students rushed to her aid, although Bobby and his fellow actors stood motionless, temporarily shocked by her reaction to their entrance, wondering exactly what 'music' she had heard, for they themselves had never been inclined to singing. Picking herself up with great dignity and the help of those who now attended her, Mrs. Prince wiped stage dust off of her black skirt and marched purposefully toward the cast members who had just made their entrance. She turned to those watching from the wings, and announced, "Everyone out, please. Everyone come out here for a meeting."

When everyone had gathered in a semi-circle, Mrs. Prince looked at them with great fondness and pleaded, "My dear friends, you've got to forget that you're on a stage whenever you make your entrances. Otherwise, all the audience sees is you giving them the *impression* that you're on a stage, *trying* to act out a play. The play, the story, must come alive. You must step into it, as if into a real world. When you step on this stage, you *become* the character that you're playing. So when you walk out here, always remember, you're not walking out on a stage. You're either coming into the castle or going out of the castle."

Mickey Drexel asked, "How about the wood?"

"We don't *have* a wood," growled Mrs. Prince, who herself was now playing the very credible role as a frustrated director of a play. "But we need one. I forgot about that. Any ideas? Anybody?"

Everyone pondered the problem. The castle set, which had been accepted on loan from the community theater, was definitely more than adequate for most of the play's scenes; in fact, it was a tad oversized for the relatively small middle school stage. The need for a wooded area had been either forgotten or ignored.

David suddenly was seized with an inspiration, one that would kill, or save, two birds with one stone. For the last two weeks, David had encountered Gordie Chase throwing up no fewer than half a dozen times in the boys' bathroom. He was pale, sick, and nervous, and that these last two weeks of rehearsals hadn't killed him was nothing less than a miracle, not to mention a great complement to the staying power of certain threats. David now knew that he could get Gordie off the hook, and would Gordie ever owe him, big time.

"Mrs. Prince," he began, as everyone turned to listen to him, "I think I've got the perfect solution, although it will mean a little shuffling in the cast."

"Yes, David, what is it?"

"At the end of the play, the wood moves. Why not have it move at the beginning?"

"Rewrite Mr. Shakespeare!" exclaimed a horrified director.

"No, no, no," David hastened to add. "All we need to do is have two cast members who are dressed to look like trees. When we need to have action on the heath, where the witches are, we'll just send one tree out and let the cast play around and in front of it. At the end of the play, when old Birnam wood moves toward the castle, we'll send two trees out, and Sean's Swashbucklers can walk between them, with one tree leading and one following. It would be a totally unspoken part, and the people playing them would have to remain dressed up as trees throughout the entire play."

"Hmm," mulled Mrs. Prince. "It might just work, David. That's an absolutely brilliant suggestion. It helps us to triumph over these exceedingly poor staging conditions, even with such a fine and imposing set. I fully agree with David; I think we should try it. Are there any volunteers for these two tree roles?"

Every cast members' hand shot up immediately, with some raising two hands and waving them wildly for all they were worth.

This presented Mrs. Prince with a new dilemma that she had not expected, for she had assumed the opposite would have occurred, that no one would have wanted to surrender a speaking part. She forgot, however, that she was dealing with a ninth grade English class, many of whom were reluctant to speak in class, much less on a stage.

"Oh, dear," she said, holding both of her hands to her lips, looking over desperately at David for some sort of suggestion.

"May I please pick?" asked David.

"Why, of course, please do," Mrs. Prince encouraged.

Now the hands waved more fiercely than ever, with many of the cast shouting 'me, me, me' at David.

"I pick Gordie Chase—"

"YES! THERE *IS* A GOD!" exclaimed Gordie, jumping up with his arms flung wide open, apparently giving thanks to a newly discovered deity.

"And ...?" prompted Mrs. Prince.

Hands waved more wildly than ever, now, for the last life boat to sheltered obscurity was now leaving.

"Joey Harris," said David without hesitation.

"Joey?" asked Mrs. Prince. "Oh, the poor boy who had the seizure. How is he?"

"He'll be coming back to us before the play," said David. "Dr. Baker is working with him every day. This will be a perfect part for him because he's still going to miss most of the rehearsals."

Everyone in the cast nodded; David had picked well. For many, the sought after illusion of safe haven in the harbor of quiet anonymity now faded into the recesses of what might have been.

"We must ask the lovely Mrs. Stevenson to create two marvelous tree costumes," announced Mrs. Prince, looking at Jiggs.

"I'll ask her tonight. I'm sure she'll be glad to. Just give me the measurements," said Jiggs.

"Places everyone," said Mrs. Prince. "Back to the wings. We'll get this production off the ground yet. We'll start from the beginning. And no talking in the wings. We can even hear the whispering out here."

With Gordie Chase now recast into a non-speaking role, Sean volunteered two more of his friends to assume Gordie's former role of Donalbain, and Joey's two roles as Seyton and Ross. The Swashbucklers, except for Sean, would also play soldiers and noblemen as required.

Larry Jones had volunteered to bring in his synthesizer, which offered what Sean Potter had described as a real, wicked thunder sound. Actually, the sound was intended to simulate an explosion, but when several of the lower keys were pushed at the same time, the thunder effect came through remarkably well. Maureen Grant also arranged to borrow her uncle's photography lamp, which gave a convincing imitation of lightning, on demand.

Maureen Grant, Gloria Adams, and Sheila Morrison worked very hard to perfect their witches' scenes, meeting each night after rehearsal at each other's homes, eventually memorizing all of their lines. They had also introduced such wonderful cackles into their voices that Sean Potter had opined that POTS, his nanny, must have given the girls private lessons on how to act and speak like a real witch. On remarking on how credible their performances had become, Sean had quipped, "Now, if you could only *look* like POTS."

Hooter Reynolds was assigned to play the very important role of Porter in Scene Three of Act Two, which he accomplished with great charm and wit. Cast members worked hard to support each other and, by the second week of rehearsals, things were proceeding so well that Mrs. Prince insisted that the cast relax on the Tuesday before Friday's play night and join together in watching another version of the play.

"Now, remember, my dears, if the story of the play is clear to you and you understand what the words you're saying actually mean, the sense of the words will take care of themselves, for you'll read them with real meaning."

And, to the astonishment of most of the cast, they discovered that she had been correct. The clearer they had become about what their parts were in the larger story, as well as what each of their words actually meant, the more smoothly and clearly the play flowed.

Dress rehearsal was scheduled for Thursday evening, to simulate the actual time of the play, which was to begin at exactly eight o'clock Friday evening. The Swashbucklers rendered their violent attacks on each other for fifteen minutes before play time, as the cast assembled itself in the wings, waiting for Dana Foley's announcements before giving this last rehearsal their very best.

Costumes were well-tailored, thanks to the several mothers, most especially Mrs. Stevenson, who had lent many hours to procuring them or making them. Joey Harris had returned to school on Tuesday, and was able to see the video of the play. Gordie coached Joey on his new role as a tree, a relatively easy role, since Joey had only to come on at the very end of the play. Dr. Baker had assured Mrs. Prince and David that Joey would be just fine.

Mickey Drexel was a clown at heart, and his casting in the *dramatis persona* of Macbeth had centered on his lack of stage fright, his ability to read well, and his normal habit of being a natural ham. The part, however, had been trying for him, for Macbeth never laughs, and Mickey was used to laughing a lot, every day. As dress rehearsal arrived, when Mickey saw all of his friends attired in their costumes, he began to giggle. What was most funny to him, though, were his closest friends, Zeke, Bobby, Danny, and Larry wearing ornamented gowns.

Danny, who played both the young and old Siward, delineated the latter character by placing a gray mop on his head, the better to symbolize the gray laurels of the old Siward's wisdom and age. For some reason, this gray mop, in particular, caused Mickey to go into hysterics. And worse, Mickey's laughter was so heartfelt that it was infectious to all who heard it. Terrified at this unexpected prospect of his ruining the play by laughing at some inappropriate time, which for the character of Macbeth, would be at *any* time, Mickey begged his friends to help him remain focused and serious by doing to him what his older brother's high school football coach did to his brother's team if they were losing at half time, that is, to slap their faces *really* hard, so as to bring forth both a focused anger and the killer instinct.

Bobby's gang of friends had been buddies for many years, and it should be no surprise that there was now a long line, all waiting to slap Mickey, each friend especially eager to help his old class-clown cohort, as well as to enjoy his full turn at giving Mickey the old one-two, one-two *really* hard.

The cast's dress rehearsal proceeded in a very credible way.

"David, what is that slapping noise off stage?" asked Mrs. Prince.

"I don't know. Let me go see," said David.

Returning a few minutes later, having been apprised of the potential problem, and witnessing Mickey begging his friends to keep him focused, David reported to Mrs. Prince, "I don't think there's anything we can do about it, at least, not just now. We may have to live with it."

"Don't you think it's a little distracting?" asked the director.

David nodded, whispering, "Yes. But it's a lot better than what we might get if we weren't hearing it."

"I don't understand, but I'll take you're word for it," said Mrs. Prince.

The dress rehearsal continued without a hitch, to the marvel and satisfaction of all present. David sat, wondering and worrying: could Mickey get through the dress rehearsal without breaking up? Could he get through the actual performance? Bobby had informed David backstage that since he and Zeke would be murdered off fairly early in the play, they could focus their energies on keeping Mickey from bursting into unrestrained laughter.

Bobby's prediction had proven true, for after he and Zeke had each been done in, the slapping from offstage became louder and longer. All proceeded well, however, until the final act. When Mickey entered upon the stage for Scene 5, Act V, his face appeared flushed. The slightest traces of a hand mark could be seen when Mickey's face caught just the right angle of light. In this scene, he would be told that his wife, Lady Macbeth, had died. This news would then lead him into reciting one of the most famous soliloquies in all of Shakespeare. Mrs Prince had challenged the principal cast members to memorize these famous lines, hinting that some sort of culinary treat would be their reward were they to master these special parts. Not being one to spurn food on any occasion, including even wakes and funerals, Mickey had memorized this soliloquy. A servant, one of Sean's friends entered, announcing, "The queen, my Lord, is dead."

Mickey closed his eyes, and looked as if he were in real pain, which David knew to be only too true, and began his speech:

She should have died hereafter;
There would have been a time for such a word —
To-morrow, and to-morrow, and to-morrow,
Creeps in this petty pace from day to day,
To the last syllable of recorded time;
And all our yesterdays have lighted fools
The way to dusty death.

Placing his hands over his face, Mickey continued, crying:

Out, out, brief candle!
Life's but a walking shadow; a poor player,
That struts and frets his hour upon the stage,
And then is heard no more:

Everyone was captivated by the intensity of Mickey's performance, which grew directly from a very real physical pain, a smarting sensation that still tingled on both sides of his face. Mrs. Prince could be heard to whisper, "Marvelous" to David and Sean, as she sat in the deepest admiration of Mickey's intense portrayal of these lines.

Then Mickey made his fateful mistake. He took his hands away from his face as he began the last two and one half lines:

It is a tale
Told by an idiot, full of sound and fury,

At this very instant Mickey found himself looking directly at Danny Taylor, who stood off stage watching Mickey's performance, waiting to enter the next scene to play the old Siward, the gray mop flopped right on top of his head, dangling in and out of Danny's ratty blond hair.

Mickey suddenly wondered if Danny, owing to his long, stringy hair, had perhaps been wearing such a mop for years, one that nobody had ever noticed. The immediacy of this image, coupled with the stringy-blond moppy hair, which was intertwined with the real gray mop, created an image of incongruity that Mickey could not suppress. Had he not just talked about life being a tale told by an idiot? And, now, Danny stood in front of him, looking very much just that, or so it seemed to Mickey, for he had never seen a real idiot before. Rather than conclude his soliloquy, until now so marvelously rendered, Mickey bit his tongue, for he knew what was coming, and he suddenly rued the day he had ever consented to play a role on this God-forsaken stage, for his stinging tongue gave him no respite for what now was boiling up inside of him. Desperately he wanted to utter the final line, 'signifying nothing'. Everyone was waiting for it, anticipating how it might be delivered. One last glance at Danny's foolish gray mop and the intertwined flaxen strings of real hair, caused Mickey to quiver and quake, as the laughter began to erupt. If Mrs. Prince had been alerted to this potential eruption of unrestrained laughter, she might have been able to coach Mickey into making it look like a fit of crying and agony, for real emotion can be finessed by an accomplished actor to play out in almost any way. Unfortunately, Mrs. Prince had been left out of the loop, although she would soon find herself in the middle of it.

Mickey fell to the stage floor, laughing uncontrollably at the incongruity his imagination had spun as a result of his inadvertent glance at his buddy Danny, the innocuous and innocent old Siward. So rollicking was Mickey's mirth, that he shook as he gave way to unabated laughter, writhing on the floor of the stage. His laughter was also highly infectious, and soon everyone was laughing, despite all attempts at restraining the merry beast that sought release. Now it was only Mrs.

Prince who was not laughing; rather, a frown had appeared on her brow, as she stood in disbelief, peering at this unexpected spectacle.

David wondered if they would lose their director, either through resignation or stroke. Mrs. Prince proceeded up on to the stage and now stood over Mickey, looking with puzzlement at his convulsive merriment. No doubt, she wondered if what had happened to Joey was perhaps now happening to one of her principal cast members. Mrs. Prince must have been inwardly torn as she tried to ascertain Mickey's condition, for Sean Potter, owing to his remarkable photographic memory, had agreed to play any male part that might be required in the event of an emergency. And *this* certainly was an emergency. But Mrs. Prince had also been looking forward to teaching Sean how to smell the play's blood and she truly wanted him at her side.

Mickey looked up at Mrs. Prince's inquiring face, and burst into an entirely new fit of laughter, which many others joined, despite their failed efforts to retain in their outward person an appropriate decorum.

"Mickey," began the director, "that soliloquy, that last line, wasn't supposed to be funny. What's so funny?"

Mickey looked over at Danny, laughing again, hardly able to answer, but finally blurted out, "I talked about a tale told by an idiot, and I looked at Danny, and he really looked just like an idiot with his gray and blond hair and mixed up together."

Again Mickey rollicked with laughter.

For all of her outward dourness, Mrs. Prince could enjoy a good laugh, just as most people can. Although she didn't fully understand what had so tickled Mickey, she knew it had been real. She quickly concluded that this release of energy might well be in lieu of the typical stage fright that someone playing a leading role might feel. Deciding that it was a case of Mickey's being overworked and more than a little nervous, Mrs. Prince answered, "But, my dear, you can't laugh *there*, because you're going to be *dead* soon."

Another surge of hilarity rose in Mickey, for Mrs. Prince loomed over him, like a black widow spider, her ominous presence and zeal for smelling blood suggesting that *he* might soon be dead, indeed. This outlandish notion wove a new image of incongruity into his mind, and he bit his tongue to avoid laughing in Mrs. Prince's face. What must he do to redeem himself? Blotting the new image from his mind, he bowed his head, as best he could while lying prone on the floor, apologizing, "I know. I'm really sorry. I just couldn't help myself."

"That's all right, dear. We're *all* a little tired. Everyone, let's take a ten minute break and resume where we just stopped. Or, better yet, we'll resume beginning with the next scene."

During the ensuing break, David and Mickey had a private conference with Mrs. Prince, during which they explained all that had happened. She was remarkably appreciative of the boys' honesty and concern, giving her swift approval to any necessary slapping that might be required backstage on performance night, acknowledging that she herself might well make a visit backstage before curtain time just to administer to Mickey five or six of the old one-two, one-two's, in order to establish the proper decorum for the play.

After the break, the cast gathered and resumed the dress rehearsal, all of the final scenes going without a hitch. At their conclusion, Mrs. Prince gathered her players together again on the stage, saying, "My dears, you have all done an excellent job, and I am *very* proud of all of you. I believe that we are truly ready to give our audience tomorrow night a very credible and passionate performance of this play. I would only ask David, Bobby, and Mickey remain. The rest of you may go, with my blessing and thanks."

With a flurry of relief and satisfaction, cast members hung up their costumes backstage, and proceeded to meet their parents, many of whom were waiting in cars outside the building.

After everyone had left, Mrs. Prince looked at the three boys she had asked to remain and smiled.

"Do you want *me* to slap him up or do *you* want to?" asked Bobby, pointing at Mickey.

"I'll leave that to you and the others tomorrow night, if we even need it. I think tonight's hilarity has released a lot of nervous tension for all of us. I think I'm even glad it happened. No, what I want to go over with Mickey is how to convert any impulse to laugh into crying or pain. If the emotion is there, you'll be able to translate it. So, Bobby and David, stand over there and get ready to make Mickey laugh, and I will work with him right here."

"But it was Danny who got him going," said Bobby.

"Well, then, pretend that you're Danny, Bobby, and go over there and get ready to put that ridiculous gray mop on your head.'"

After several instructive hints, Mickey mastered the art of translating emotion on the stage and felt very confident that any impulse to laugh the next night would be quickly transformed into his character's agony and despair, grieving and torment. Mrs. Prince was pleased with how quickly he could adapt, and how convincing his performance was.

Some of the principal cast members elected to absent themselves from school on Friday, and had been encouraged to do so both by the Giant's son and Mr. Ferlinghausen. With the performance a few hours away, energy needed to be conserved.

This would be the very first performance of *Macbeth* ever to grace the boards of Midville Middle School's stage, or even the former high school stage, for that matter. It would be a performance greeted by a full house. The evening's largest audience majority was composed of eager and rambunctious eighth graders, knowing in the secret depths of their hearts that they, by virtue of their faithful attendance, had spurned the dire threat of this hour, successfully avoiding an hour-long interview with their old-ignominious-lobster-breath guidance counselor Melvin Dandy.

On the program, before the listing of the play and its respective acts, was this notice:

The Swashbuckler Swords
⚔ Programme ⚔
A fighte to the deathe,
⚔ featuring Sean Potter & his Peers ⚔
against Hooter Reynolds & his Peers.
⚔ Beware for your lily-livered life, hateful mortal. ⚔

Fifteen minutes before curtain time, a procession of two teams of knights, in full regalia and armed with wooden shields and swords, made its way to the stage. As these knight errants stood looking at the audience, a piece of painted wood resembling a hunk of raw meat was tossed into the center of their company, an object for which they began severely to batter one another. As they clobbered each other with studied and practiced blows, each responding in kind to his enemy's assault, David, who was sitting in the front row one seat away from Mrs. Prince, whispered, "I forgot how good these seventh graders really are. They're going to steal the show."

Mrs. Prince, who was saving the seat between them for Sean, who would soon come to edify himself under her instruction at the proper way to smell the blood, gave a quick study to the theatrics now raging in full vigor on the stage.

"No," she reassured David in a kind whisper, "they're good, all right, but Shakespeare is even *better*."

"I wasn't thinking of the play," said David.

"The words, my dear, the words. Words carry so much meaning and power, especially when we choose to allow them to live. Trust the bard. He's a master storyteller. Trust the bard."

Mrs. Prince always had a way of making everything sound vaguely mysterious. When she handed out rainbow ribbons to her Sunday School students after they had read about Noah and the flood, one could almost hear the flood waters running and swear that those ribbons were wrought from Noah's original rainbow itself.

Meanwhile on stage, ten seventh graders continued to clobber each other with great glee and élan. Finally, after about ten minutes of intense and passionate fighting, wherein grunts and heavy breathing could be heard, each of the five pairs of peers who had been fighting managed to kill each other off in grand style. Where one peer might suddenly make to thrust his sword into another's back, he himself would then turn around to receive a similar sword thrust into his belly. The costumes, highly colorful, had, in their own way, created a spectacle, a drama, wherein the audience had become totally transfixed and fascinated by the swordplay that cascaded in front of their very eyes. Suspension of disbelief was at its crowning height by the time Sean and Hooter, the two leaders, faced each other. In typical knightly fashion, each threw off his head protector, thus revealing a disarming rage that could only lead to a fight to the death. A bristling of swords clacking against each other stirred the audience to new heights of passion. Hooter managed to knock Sean's shield from his left arm, but missed his chance to finish him owing to Sean's uncanny stealth at avoiding Hooter's sword thrust. Dropping his sword, Sean drew out his knife, the very same and celebrated Hollywood knife that had seemed to take

Zeke's life during Sean's presentation to the Learning Club. Many skipped heartbeats in this world owed their existence to that knife and, most especially, to the warrior hand that held it.

Hooter raised his sword above his head, as if relishing this moment of opportunity to decapitate his adversary. Sean, for his part, positioned the knife in his right hand and held it forward, as if looking for an opportunity to slash at poor Hooter, who was now clearly not as fast or as stealthy as Sean, yet the two continued to circle each other fiercely, swinging and slashing. Finally, Hooter lunged forward, hoping to decapitate his enemy, but missing by inches; unfortunately for Hooter, Sean had taken advantage of this failed attack to thrust his knife upward into Hooter's lower belly, at which connecting instant Hooter gave a rueful half-cry, his eyes bulging out, followed by the classic trickle of blood flowing from his mouth.

Sean pulled the gory dagger out of Hooter's gut, as the dying knight stepped forward a couple of paces before falling to his knees, trying to keep his entrails from spilling out on the stage floor or, at least, that's what it looked like. Mrs. Prince, for her part, went into action immediately, smelling for all she was worth at the first glint of gore. Sitting next to her, David immediately concluded that she and Sean would make an ideal team. For only an instant, David wondered whether Mrs. Prince may have been, in an earlier incarnation, a spider who waited for prey to become caught in her web. With Hooter now on his knees, Sean stepped up and, placing the gory dagger against his victim's throat, swiftly administered the coup de grace slash that felled Hooter's body to the stage floor.

The audience burst into fervent applause at the spectacle they had just witnessed, many of them certain that Rome could not have done better except, of course, that Rome had never even once considered using Hollywood daggers or wooden swords. And now all of the

Swashbuckler Swordsmen had returned for their final and most deserved bows.

As the stage was cleared and cleaned, Sean slipped stealthily into the front row seat Mrs. Prince and David had been saving for him.

"How was it?" he asked.

"Great," said David. "Thanks so much."

"My dear, it was superb," said Mrs. Prince. "But, please, a little more blood next time. Either I'm getting older and can't smell it the way I used to, or there needs to be more."

Of course, this request to Sean to arrange for more blood the next time was like inviting a famished wolf into the sleeping chicken coup.

"Ladies and Gentlemen," announced Dana Foley, who had walked to center stage. "We members of the Midville Middle School Learning Club thank you all for coming. All proceeds from our ticket sales to this event will be divided between our school library and our village library. As you know, we are reading this play, for it would have been far too difficult to memorize, at least, for the short time we have had to get it ready for production. We have enjoyed preparing it, and we have learned a great deal. I would like to give special thanks to several people. The first is Mrs. Edith Prince, who has coached us from the beginning. Mrs. Prince, please stand."

Mrs. Prince stood and received an enthusiastic ovation.

"And, now, thanks to Mr. Gregory, our club advisor, who has also helped us from the beginning," continued Dana.

As Mr. Gregory stood to receive a resounding ovation, David was gratified to notice that Dr. & Mrs. Baker were also in attendance.

"Finally, many thanks are owed to the one person who is responsible for our having sold more than four hundred tickets. The eighth graders know the person I'm talking about. Let's give a round of applause to Mr. Dandy."

The counselor, who had been taking attendance at the rear of the auditorium, was caught by surprise. A smattering of applause soon swelled to a louder ovation, with several boos thrown in by some of the rowdier eighth graders, especially from several who had yet to cultivate a taste for the celebrated plays of William Shakespeare. Melvin Dandy quickly craned his neck in every direction to determine from whence these several boos had originated, for he would make those ungrateful rascals pay for their fun at his expense. Fortunately for these rowdy youth, Mr. Dandy could not locate his detractors.

"And now, it is my pleasure to say, 'On with the play,'" Dana concluded, turning and walking regally off the stage.

David sat in expectation next to Sean, who sat next to Mrs. Prince. Their work was now done. They could only wait and hope for the best. Great volumes of tickets had been sold; a larger than anticipated audience had been brave enough to attend; the cast had labored with diligence to render a smooth and well-read play, one which would honor and give focus to the play's themes and subplots; the mothers of many participants had labored long and hard to create or acquire costumes and props; Sean's Swashbucklers had created a wonderful dramatic tension and expectation in the audience; appropriate thanks had been rendered before the performance to three adults who had been especially helpful in different ways; and Dana Foley had distinguished herself as both a master of ceremony and an announcer: the die was now cast, the spring wound—what would be the combined results of their collective labors? No one knew. And, as every play is like a newborn babe, every play grows, in its own way, to a unique perfection that is rarely understood or fully appreciated.

The house lights were turned down, and three shadows could be seen flowing over the dark stage. Lightning flashed and thunder roared as, suddenly, a red stage light illuminated three witches inspecting a black cauldron. A lone tree, or some semblance of a tree, stood behind them. The first witch intoned, "When shall we three meet again? In thunder, lightning, or in rain?" Again, lightning flashed and thunder unleashed its deep roars. The first witch was answered by the second and within seconds, all three were chanting one of the play's most prominent themes, "Fair is foul, and foul is fair: Hover through the fog and filthy air." More lightning flashed as its thunder rolled, and stage lights came up to show the entrance of Duncan, Malcolm, Donalbain, Lenox, and their attendants. All looked as if they were indeed walking into an encampment, the setting for that particular scene. Mrs. Prince's counsel had been well heeded.

From that moment, David knew that all would go well. As the play uncoiled itself, revealing its many themes and interrelationships, David became prouder and prouder of his friends. One would have to take special notice that they were holding play books, their readings were rendered with such precision and feeling. It was obvious that they knew what they were saying, and how their words fit into the greater tapestry, the larger whole. Again, Mrs. Prince's counsel had been faithfully kept.

After the discovery of Duncan's murder, when the bloody daggers were brought on to the stage, including Sean's celebrated Hollywood dagger, David noticed that both Sean and Mrs. Prince started breathing deeply, trying their best to smell the blood. He wondered, in fact, if they could. Throughout the remainder of the play they continued to smell the blood together, no doubt forging a lasting bond.

Sean's friends proved themselves invaluable as stage hands, their expert labor minimizing the length of the intervals between critical scenes and acts.

Occasionally, a series of slaps could be heard offstage, and David correctly surmised that Mickey had taken note of Danny's gray mop and had begged his friends to keep his attention focused and his demeanor solemn. Probably for insurance against anything as untoward happening as the laughing spectacle from the night before, the number and volume of offstage slaps seemed to increase immediately before the critical scene where Mickey had lost his composure during the prior evening's dress rehearsal.

During the following scene, when Macbeth is told that Birnam wood is on the move, Gordie Chase and Joey Harris unexpectedly entered the far corner of the stage, dressed, of course, as trees, and although Gordie remained still, Joey endeavored to hop when mention was made of Birnam wood moving.

David and Mrs. Prince gave a huge sigh of relief that Joey's improvisation had not imperiled the tone of the play. Very shortly after, in their sword play, Mickey unintentionally broke Danny's sword, who was playing Young Siward. Danny looked at the remaining half of his sword, unable to speak his lines, which would have been, "Thou liest, abhorred tyrant: with my sword I'll prove the lie thou speakest." During this dramatic pause, both boys looked at each other in astonishment, wondering what to do. Mickey suddenly gave a bloodcurdling war cry as he lunged at Young Siward, running him through.

Immediately Mrs. Prince and Sean inhaled deeply, as they heard Mickey jeer at the falling Young Siward, "Thou wast born of woman:—", turning to the audience to add, "But swords I smile at, weapons laugh to scorn, brandish'd by man that's of a woman born."

MacDuff entered on cue, and the ensuing sword play and killing of Macbeth caused even deeper breathing next to David, especially when the paper machê model of Macbeth's head, which actually did look a bit like Mickey's head, was brought in, all gory and dripping in blood, as Sean had insisted it be, having coached his friends on how to prepare it. This was, for Sean and Mrs. Prince, the grand finale, and they sniffed for all they were worth.

Soon the final scene was concluded and the entire cast stood before an approving audience, which thundered its applause and volleyed shouts of bravo. Dana motioned for Mrs. Prince to be escorted to the stage by David and Sean, where she was given two dozen blood red roses for all of her time and help.

As the final curtain closed, many cast members, on stage and off, found tears welling up in their eyes, for this spectacular journey into the galaxy of theater, into the universe of story, had left them all transformed in new and enduring ways. For the cast, their journey had been one full of adventure, anxiety, hard work, trepidation, laughter, and joy. A bond had been forged that would forever unite them in that larger domain of theater art.

Chapter Eighteen
Awards and Plans for an Awards Dinner

"THE MAYOR *IS* COMING," announced David, looking up from the note he had just opened. "Here, look."

THE VILLAGE OF MIDVILLE

Office of the Mayor

Dear Members of the Learning Club,
    It is my great pleasure to accept your kind invitation to the YARB (Youth Annual Recognition Benefit) awards dinner and ceremony.
    I am especially honored to be named one of the three recipients by the awards committee.
    It will also be a pleasure to accept, on behalf of our village librarian, your generous check for new books at that facility.
                     Very truly yours,

William Perry
(The Hon.) William Perry

"That's absolutely marvelous," said Aunt Lillian.

"Don't tell me," grinned David. "Mr. Perry is one of your former piano students?"

"Goodness gracious, no, dear child," said Aunt Lillian. "Why, I've never even met the man. But I've heard some very good things about him. They say that he is both fair and progressive."

"What's he doin' in Midville, then?" asked Bobby.

"He's doing good things, of course," said Aunt Lillian.

"Did you vote for him?" asked David.

"That is a private matter, my dear," said Aunt Lillian.

"Come on, you can tell us," David teased.

"And if I do, it will be the first thing you tell the poor Mayor when he comes to the awards banquet," said Aunt Lillian.

"No, it would be the second," said David. "First, I would tell him that I have the most generous aunt in the whole world."

"But then he would ask me for a donation," sighed Aunt Lillian, adding, "A very large donation."

"And I bet you'd give him one, too," predicted David.

"That, my dear, is another, private matter," rejoined Aunt Lillian. "Is everything arranged for the banquet, now that you have three honorands to attend?"

"Ain't never heard of no honor-ran," said Bobby. "Anyone running from honor ain't deserve no award, and that ne'er-do-well Dandy ain't got no place to stand up there with two real gentlemen, if you get my drift."

"But that's the whole point. It's for the private class ruse," David reminded Bobby.

"What ruse?" asked Aunt Lillian.

"YARB is an acronym for 'You Are Really Bald'," explained David. "Mr. Pennythorpe and the Mayor don't hide it, but Mr. Dandy does. So we decided to invent an award that would become a special, private, little class joke, for the sake of class bonding."

"You won't explain the real nature of the award, then?" asked Aunt Lillian.

"No way," asserted David. "Everyone, except the class, and now you, thinks it means 'Youth Annual Recognition Benefit'."

"I'm afraid it would simply shatter your counselor if the truth were discovered," Aunt Lillian observed.

"I'd like to shatter him to hell and back again," said Bobby.

"Bobby, let bygones be bygones," urged David. "You'll have, I mean, we'll all have a confidential laugh when Dandy stands up to accept his award along with Mr. Pennythorpe and the Mayor. Maybe we'll even have to bite our tongues to keep from really laughing, like Mickey."

"The floor will be flowin' with blood up to our ankles," predicted Bobby.

"Let's just hope no one falls prey to give a sudden cackle," said David. "It could set the whole room off."

"I am so pleased that Lisa's parents are going to cater the banquet. We know first hand what fine cooks they are," said Aunt Lillian. "Will they bring the appropriate finery with it?"

"Finery?" asked David.

"China, silverware, goblets, candlesticks, you know ... the works," explained Aunt Lillian.

"Gosh. Nobody thought to budget for that. We just couldn't afford it anyway. It would cost a fortune to rent all that stuff," said David.

"I'd be glad to cover the expense," offered Aunt Lillian.

"You're already paying for half of it now," said David. "That's more than generous."

"It would dress things up a little," said Aunt Lillian.

"I don't know," said David. "Bobby, what do you think?"

"Ain't nothin' but a waste of finery to me and to those like me. Ain't got the know how to use all those fancy little forks and things."

"I suppose you're right," agreed Aunt Lillian. "We want the banquet to be a celebration of that wonderful play you all staged, rather than a new obstacle to conquer."

"There must be *some* way we can dress the banquet up," groaned David. "It deserves something better than the usual. It's also in the auditorium. That'll remind everyone of the play."

Bobby mulled over David's suggestion, nodding in agreement.

"Are students dressing up?" asked Aunt Lillian.

"Yes. We have insisted that dresses and ties and jackets are required," said David. "That alone will help."

"Ain't none of us gonna recognize each other," Bobby laughed.

"Are the adults dressing up as well?" asked Aunt Lillian.

"I don't know. I assume so," said David.

"Then, let me suggest that you ask your three honorands to dress up with tuxedos and black tie. It would make an ever so impressive photograph for the newspaper," said Aunt Lillian.

"I've never seen the Mayor in a tux before," said David. "I wonder if Mr. Pennythorpe has one he could wear?"

"Probably the *original*, the first one ever made, like maybe from the time of President Lincoln, or maybe even made by Betsy Ross herself," said Bobby.

"How about Mr. Dandy?" asked David.

"If he had one, he'd likely sleep in it, or wear it to school to impress his ditzy secretary. Ain't no good havin' a tuxedo if it's half moth-eaten, which I bet it is, if he's even got one," said Bobby.

"We'll just have to ask and see," said David.

"Ain't a mystery any more 'bout all them damn bugs he's got in them ugly glass cases in his office. They're the moths that did it, I bet you a million bucks," Bobby laughed.

"Poor Mr. Dandy has certainly been the butt of many of your jokes, boys," said Aunt Lillian.

"Bet his little old ne'er-do-well ears are burnin' as we speak," chortled Bobby. "Ain't no excuse for havin' to endure the preachin' of a little Rumplestiltskin like that. He ain't gonna talk, is he? Please tell me he ain't."

"Each recipient will say a few words, but Mr. Pennythorpe will give the real talk," said David.

"Do you have a Master of Ceremonies?" asked Aunt Lillian.

"That's the job of the learning club president," said David slyly.

"What?" cried Bobby. "In front of all those dignitaries? I'd shoot myself before I stood up in front of that outfit."

"David's teasing," said Aunt Lillian.

"Mr. Ferlinghausen has agreed to do it," said David. "I wish we could give him an award, too, because he's really bald, but we need someone of importance to hand out the awards, to shake hands and to pose with the recipients for photographs. Let's face it, Bobby, you're going to have to be in at least a couple of pictures."

"Better the newspaper than the post office," Bobby smiled.

"Bobby, I swear your wit has sharpened since your first association with David. Do you hear yourself saying funny things?" asked Aunt Lillian.

"I ain't nothin' but a shadow of my former self," said Bobby.

"Yeah, yeah, yeah," said David.

"Ain't nothing to blame it on but these cursed fallacies. See, I got it right, finally. No more 'falsies' for me. Then the play put the frostin' on the cake. I may be one step away from the nut house, but at least I'm ahead of that little counselor ne'er-do-well. He's been nuts for years," said Bobby.

"I would say nervous more than nuts," suggested David.

"Call it whatever you want," said Bobby. "He's still nuts."

"What do you think, Aunt Lillian?" asked David.

"I think poor Mr. Dandy has had a lonely life and just needs someone to make a fuss over him now and again. I'm sure his wife does, but it's different when it comes from the world," said Aunt Lillian.

"I'd sure like to send his wife a gun for Christmas," said Bobby. "But that would be murder *indirect*."

"How so?" asked David.

"'Cause the poor woman would face a ... a ... condubdrum," said Bobby.

"I think you mean conundrum, a riddle?"asked David.

"Yeah. Should she shoot the little Rumplestiltskin and go to jail, or should she shoot herself and go to hell?" explained Bobby.

"Bobby, you've got to bury the hatchet some day," said David.

"And I know *just* where," said Bobby.

"You boys are too much," said Aunt Lillian.

"Omigosh!" said David.

"What?" asked Bobby.

"We've got to do something for Mrs. Prince for all she did to help us make the play the success it was," said David.

"Those flowers on play night ain't nothin' to sneeze at," said Bobby.

"I know, but she gave us so much help and time. Let's create a special award for her and make its presentation a surprise on banquet night," suggested David.

"If she shaved her head, we could give a YARB award," said Bobby.

David gave Bobby an exasperated look.

"Let's give her a nice plaque which calls her a promoter of arts and theater and all that. What's that fancy word for supporting the arts?"

"Promulgator?" asked Aunt Lillian.

"Yes. That's it. We will say that she has been a 'model *promulgator* of theater arts in this community.' I bet she'd really like that," said David.

"You can't say *that*," exclaimed Bobby. "People'll think you're swearin' at 'em."

"No, they won't," laughed Aunt Lillian.

"Plans are running really smoothly," David smiled. "Bobby's class has become a real force these last few weeks. Everybody knows how to work together for a common goal."

"That darn play ruined us," said Bobby. "Ain't right to be so organized. Ain't it against student union rules? The class still laughs a lot about what happened."

"How's Mickey's face doing?" asked David.

"Mickey's face?" inquired Aunt Lillian.

Bobby explained how Mickey Drexel had begged his friends to slap his face, hoping it would prevent him from having a fit of giggles during play night. Aunt Lillian laughed as Bobby recounted the dress rehearsal fiasco and the close calls during the play.

"Memories of such moments of bonding last a lifetime," observed Aunt Lillian. "Your class is much richer for the adventures they have shared on their journey together."

"Sounds just like the Giant's son," said Bobby, looking at David and pointing to Aunt Lillian.

"But not as tall," smirked David.

* * * * *

The YARB Awards dinner arrived with much fanfare and pomp. David even arranged for a photographer to come from the Midville *Courier* to take pictures of the award recipients.

The head table sat directly in front of the stage. All of the tables had fine, linen tablecloths and school silverware had never looked better. Fancy green and gold paper napkins adorned the table. Students sat closest to the head table, members of Bobby's class being given preferred

399

seating. David, Lisa, Mary, and Sean sat with some of Sean's friends who were seated toward the back of the auditorium, not far from where many of the parents sat, including Aunt Lillian and POTS, who sat with the Professor and Dr. Potters. Behind the head table, the stage itself now seemed empty for the absence of the *Macbeth* set, but two large vases of flowers, anonymously donated for the occasion, dressed up the proscenium.

Colorful posters showing many quotations about learning from famous thinkers were displayed on six large portable chalk boards. The walling off the dining area made the entire affair seem more intimate, despite its location in a large auditorium. Extra tables and chairs were neatly stacked on the west side of the cafeteria. On the opposite side of the auditorium from the head table was the buffet line.

Mr. Ferlinghausen walked to the speaker's podium, which was at the center of the head table, and announced, "May I have your attention? Thank you. We are gathered tonight to celebrate the many achievements of Mr. Gregory's ninth grade English class, which also comprises the majority membership of Midville Middle School's new Learning Club. As you know, one of the goals of the club was to raise money for new books, and I am pleased to announce that checks for the sum of six hundred and fifty dollars will be given to the school and village libraries, owing to the large ticket sales attained for the club's production of *Macbeth*."

Thunderous applause followed Mr. Ferlinghausen's announcement, as he invited the Mayor and Mr. Lowery, the school's librarian, to the podium to receive their respective envelopes and to pose for a photograph for the newspaper.

"Now that we have given a little money away, let's enjoy this sumptuous banquet," announced Mr. Ferlinghausen, as he motioned the members of the head table to lead the way to the buffet. David watched their procession, he felt a thrill stir within him as he watched the ladies parade in their absolutely scintillating evening gowns. The men, except Mr. Gregory and Mr. Lowery, wore tuxedos. The Mayor's was of the latest style and fashion, with Mr. Ferlinghausen's similar but older, and with Mr. Pennythorpe's looking the oldest of all; Mr. Dandy's, in contrast, was the rattiest looking, as well as very tightly stretched. Mr. Gregory wore a stylish, blue, three-piece suit and Mr. Lowery wore a blue sport jacket and gray trousers and a red tie.

The gathering's great glee was reflected in the decibel level, which would have rivaled that of any school day luncheon. When everyone had finished dessert, Mr. Ferlinghausen went to the podium and instructed his wife to tap on her water glass, so as to secure everyone's attention.

"Before we get to the YARB awards, let me say, on behalf of all present, how very excellent a buffet Mr. & Mrs. Jones have provided for us tonight."

The room resounded with appreciative applause.

"Having sampled their ware here, I can assure you that my wife and I will become frequent guests at their restaurant. Thank you very much. Now that we've eaten well, we will celebrate by rewarding well. Would Bobby Perkins please come forward? Bobby is president of his ninth grade English class as well as the Learning Club. I want Bobby to present these awards as I read the citations. Bobby?"

Bobby sat like a statue in his seat, despite the proddings and pokings he was suffering from his classmates. His face was white, his eyes panicked, for he had not expected this particular turn of events. He leaned over and whispered to Zeke and Dana, and Dana stood up and approached the speaker's podium, announcing, "Mr. Ferlinghausen, our club president has appointed me to share the honor, as Secretary-Treasurer, of handing out the plaques."

"Very well," said Mr. Ferlinghausen, a smile passing his lips, "there *are* some advantages to holding higher office."

As Bobby's face turned red, laughter echoed through the auditorium.

"Before we get to the YARB Awards," the principal continued, "we have two surprise awards. The first is for Sean Potter and his rambunctious Swashbuckler Swords. Sean, please come forward."

Sean, with a grin on his face, strode toward the stage from where he had been sitting near the rear of the auditorium with Lisa, Mary, and David.

Mr. Ferlinghausen gave Dana an envelope to hold and then read the following citation, "*To the famous Swashbuckler Swords, we extend our thanks for your daring feats of sword play staged before our play* MACBETH. *We enclose sixty dollars for a pizza party for such valiant swordsmen. Fight well, but only after you eat well.*"

Sean beamed his approval as he accepted the envelope and elevated it in his right hand as he might raise his sword as he returned to his seat, mid the general applause of those assembled. Only Melvin Dandy withheld his applause, warily watching Sean's every move and gesture.

"Next," continued Mr. Ferlinghausen, "we have a gift certificate for one hundred dollars for Mrs. Prince, who was kind enough to coach and direct the play. The citation reads: *To Edith Prince, for her steadfast belief in our ability to perform a play, and for her promulgation of the theater arts in the Village of Midville, we theater creatures give her our lasting appreciation and thanks.*"

Mrs. Prince looked completely flabbergasted when her award was announced, and approached the podium with tears in her eyes. "I never ... never expected this," she began. "You all did such outstanding jobs on the play, and I am so grateful for your including me. Thank you."

"Finally, we come to the YARB awards," announced the principal. "Each recipient will be invited to say a few words after receiving his award. Mr. Mayor, would you please join me at the podium." Mr. Ferlinghausen handed Dana a plaque with a gold crest and embossed lettering.

"*The Learning Club of Midville Middle School extends its Youth Annual Recognition Benefit award to Mr. William Perry, Mayor of Midville, for his dedication to community service programs and to the creation of jobs for young people. During Mr. Perry's tenure as Mayor, the public library budget has been tripled. We recognize your support of youth and of learning,*" concluded the principal.

Dana handed the Mayor his award and shook his hand.

Applause filled the room as the Mayor spoke into the microphone, "Thank you, Mr. Ferlinghausen, and thank you members of this remarkable Learning Club. I am honored to be here and I accept this award not for myself, but on behalf of the Village of Midville and the alliance we have forged in helping the village library. Thank you."

"Mr. Melvin Dandy, please come forward. Your citation reads as follows: *In recognition of Mr. Melvin Dandy's steadfast help to insure maximum attendance of eighth graders at special school functions, the Learning Club gives this award in recognition of his persevering ability to persuade others, together with his natural qualities that qualify him for this honor.*"

Mr. Dandy accepted the award, shook hands with Dana, and then stepped to the microphone, which Mr. Ferlinghausen had to lower for him, saying, "Thank you so much for this award which will always adorn my office. The citation says that I am a natural for this award, and I agree completely with that sentiment. I notice that you are all smiling your approval, as well, and I thank you for your good wishes."

David and his cohorts could feel a subtle tension invade the room, the tension that comes from wanting to laugh but not being able to do so, from biting the tongue but not being able to cry out in pain. They looked at Bobby and his classmates, wondering if unrestrained laughter would soon erupt from their tables.

"I can almost guess why some of you are smiling," continued the counselor. "My wife pointed it out to me just before we came tonight. Some of you have noticed something about me that stands out so unmistakably that you simply can't ignore it, can't forget it."

Dana Foley suddenly burst into spasms of laughter and had to bury her head in her arms on the table in front of her so as not to embarrass herself more than she already had.

"Yes. Dana has noticed," continued the counselor. "She has sharp eyes and is very observant. Probably some others have noticed as well. To keep my remarks brief, I will share my little secret with you, especially those of you who are sitting in front of this podium. My secret is: buttons."

Those assembled sat in silence and confusion. Had the counselor gone mad? Why did he suddenly say 'buttons', instead of 'toupee', or 'wig', or 'rats' nest'? Had he finally lost it?

"I repeat: buttons," said the counselor, hoping for a reaction, any reaction from those gathered.

All sat in confused silence.

"All right, then," continued the counselor, "let me put it in a different way. On the way to this dinner tonight, my wife made an observation and a little bet about the buttons on my tuxedo. All of you, especially those sitting closest, are in mortal danger, but are oblivious to the threat now looming. The threat, you see, is from the buttons on my tuxedo. The last time I wore this tuxedo was when I received an award from a bug society for my large collection of insects. That was many,

many years ago. Since then, although I have gained no height, I have filled out in other ways. Right now there is such pressure pushing on the buttons of my tuxedo, I would be afraid to be sitting in front of it myself. Not even my cummerbund will save you. If any buttons break loose, it would be like firing a rifle shot. Doubtless, I would be tried for murder. Since no one worth murdering is sitting in the front tonight, I am forced to hold in as best I can. Those of you in front of me, be forewarned. Normally, I would never make such a silly statement in public, but now I see that I have lost my bet with my dear wife, one that I foolishly made on our way here, I might add, on the top of two double scotches. Nevertheless, a little self-ridicule is a lot cheaper than taking her on a Carribean cruise. Good Lord, talk about losing young fortunes. It would have ruined me. So there."

Several students sitting in the path of potential button fire quickly moved their chairs. The audience sat dumbfounded, for this round-about and slightly incoherent narrative was the closest Melvin Dandy had ever come to telling a joke. It was also painfully obvious to most that poor Mrs. Dandy wouldn't get her cruise, but what fun would a cruise have been anyway with her cheapskate husband grousing all the time about the expense? As the subtlety of the counselor's forced humor descended, everyone began to laugh. In truth, while many were laughing at Melvin Dandy's self-deprecating humor, all of the members of the Midville Middle School Learning Club were laughing at the Learning Club's most prized and guarded secret.

"It is, therefore, no secret that I was made for this award," the counselor concluded, "for it is natural to me. I am able to persuade others to better points of view, including eighth graders who suddenly realize that it would be in their best interest to buy play tickets. I have not convinced all of my wards. No, not all," and here the counselor gave Sean a stony glare, "but most. Thank you for this award."

"Mr. Pennythorpe," announced Mr. Ferlinghausen, as the history teacher joined him next to the podium. *"The Learning Club salutes a true learner of all things, who communicates his wisdom in all that he says and does. Thank you for being our wise soul and companion on the way."*

Mr. Pennythorpe accepted the award from Dana, paused briefly to wipe a tear from his eye before stepping up to the podium, at which point, it was clear a different arrangement was necessary, for the teacher's slight stature did not even enable him to look at his audience.

"Here, let me unhook this microphone," offered Mr. Ferlinghausen.

"Thank you," acknowledged the history teacher, wiping his brow with his handkerchief as he accepted the microphone.

"Your award touches me very deeply, and I thank you for the honor you have bestowed. Since I will soon be regaling you with some observations about learning, let me pause so that Mr. Gero, the photographer from the *Courier*, can now take a photo of award recipients."

Mr. Gero, whose luxuriant black hair was combed tightly to his head and parted down the middle, stepped forward and organized the threesome in front of one of the flower arrangements. The Mayor was placed in the middle, a place where most politicians live out their days. Mr. Dandy was placed to the Mayor's right and Mr. Pennythorpe to his left. Although the Mayor stood little more than six feet in height, the contrast provided by his fellow award winners made him look like a giant. Each man proudly displayed his award as several camera flashes recorded the event. Mr. Pennythorpe then returned to the center of the head table and lifted the microphone.

As was his custom, he studied his audience as he waited for words to flow. The members of the audience, in turn, studied their speaker. Mr. Pennythorpe could have passed for a wizened, little gnome, his gnarled hands conveying the impression of his being a person of extreme age. His bald crown had but a small fringe of white hair sprinkled around it, although what hair there was had been permitted to grow long in the back. His quiet manner still conveyed the unmistakable aura of his college professor days, his intense eyes bearing a sense of cosmic wonder and insatiable curiosity.

The Gang of Four sat at a table near the rear of the auditorium. Sean sat next to David, and was becoming a trifle impatient now that the awards had been given. He liked Mr. Pennythorpe very much, and looked forward to having him for eighth grade history during the next academic year. Having heard only good things about the teacher, Sean was eager to prove himself one of Pennythorpe's star pupils, a feat which he would undoubtedly accomplish, since both teacher and student possessed photographic memories. Tonight, however, Sean was in one of his impish moods, feeling surges of excess energy that could not be conveniently dissipated by sword fights or warrior exploits. He hovered close to David, planning to make humorous asides to whatever Mr. Pennythorpe would say. The history teacher's enthusiasm for his discipline and dramatic teaching methods, not to mention his wizened countenance, had occasioned many rumors that he was absolutely ancient, perhaps even having once walked with Lincoln.

Mr. Pennythorpe cleared his throat and wiped his brow, intoning in a moderately loud voice, "I am very honored to be invited to address the Midville Middle School's Learning Club, especially on such a festal occasion, after the notable accomplishment of a very credible production of William Shakespeare's *Macbeth*. I remember that after the war—"

"Must have been the *Civil* War," Sean whispered in David's ear.

"—that we had to forge together as a nation to meet the extraordinary demands presented to us. There was, to my recollection, an unselfish bonding among many citizens not unlike the bonding I have witnessed developing among the members of this Learning Club. I have also been pleased to attend some of your club's meetings, wherein you took courage to look into new areas of inquiry. I say courage, because I am convinced that most of our learning has become fear based and fear driven. We are afraid of getting a poor grade or perhaps of failing a course, so we grudgingly apply ourselves in a way that brings neither learning nor joy. Worse yet, we fear the ridicule of others, should we make a mistake. I have lived many, many years—"

"At least two hundred," quipped Sean.

"—and I am now convinced that the fear of failure is perhaps the greatest enemy to any kind of personal growth or significant learning that can be obtained in our society today. The sad truth is that we ourselves permit these shadows of fear and insecurity to continue to haunt our best intentions and best insights."

Here Mr. Pennythorpe winced a little and put his hand on his left forearm.

"Your club has courageously turned its attention to the topic of learning itself, not an easy topic to explore in any age, but one well worth trying on for size. Before I tell you what I believe learning is about, I will first try to eliminate some things that it is definitely not about—"

"Mr. Dandy," Sean whispered slyly, as David put his index finger up to his lip, cautioning his seventh grade companion to pay closer attention.

Mr. Pennythorpe again wiped his brow and took several sips of water.

"Learning is definitely not the age old picture of school as an assembly line, where students are empty containers lined up on a conveyer belt, waiting to be filled with the knowledge that spews into them. No one ever seems to ask why the containers aren't all full upon graduation. That is because no human being can teach another anything truly significant. Facts, yes, but facts by themselves are dead, and fail to compel our hearts and imaginations. Something more is needed. We too often try to cram facts into our young peoples' heads, without any inkling of how such information applies to life or to learning, and sadly we do this in a most repetitious way. No wonder so many students tune out, as they sit vacant-eyed in classes that offer few challenges to their imaginations."

Again the history teacher paused to catch his breath, taking in several pronounced gasps. Sean had ceased his quips, for he had become fascinated at what Mr. Pennythorpe was saying.

"He's making a lot a sense, David," whispered Sean.

David nodded, but looked worried.

"What's wrong?"

"Don't know. But something's not right," said David, puzzling out the situation as it unfolded in front of him. "Mr. Pennythorpe is different than he usually is."

"—so students become the unwitting victims of their own fear of failure," continued Pennythorpe. "They also become afraid to risk, for if they make a mistake, someone might make fun of them. If I am not mistaken, I believe many of you here actually relived some of these early fears in a guided imagery session conducted by Mr. Gregory, who, I might add, is an excellent teacher. Why? Because he will not accept second best from anyone, and schools, unfortunately, have gotten used to accepting second, third, and fourth best. Now please don't misunderstand me when I say this, for I do not blame teachers, at least, not entirely. The ultimate responsibility for learning is with every single individual, and no one else. Ultimately, the choice to learn resides with each individual. Yes, some students find certain subjects more difficult than others. But wouldn't it be a boring world if we *were* all alike?

"Mr. Gregory has masterfully acquainted you with the fascinating research findings regarding learning styles. Schools need to address themselves more to the students who do not learn best through the linear mode of teaching. We should all be sensitive to the fact that there are many ways to learn, and that there is also a great deal to learn."

Mr. Pennythorpe wiped his eyes, cleared his throat, and once again rubbed at his left forearm.

"In truth, learning is happening to all of us all the time, each minute, each day, and the formalized learning that we encounter in school is only one small aspect of the information we acquire. Some of you who are here tonight no doubt have professed to having poor memories, especially when it comes to a spelling quiz or history test. But those same individuals could recite verbatim the top thirty baseball players in the country, quoting statistic after statistic about each player and each player's team. Or the same for any other interest, for if we are interested and choose to learn something, we will. It's as simple as that. Unfortunately, schools today seem to have made an art form out of making subjects uninteresting. Although, again, I do not fault teachers. Studies have shown that teachers teach the way they were taught. The notion that a teacher needs to be responsible for the learning that takes place is misguided and injurious to real learning, for it creates a passive response in students, who often opt out of the learning loop, either from fear of failure, or laziness, or disinterest, or peer pressure. Ah, yes. Peer pressure. It is one of the great sinister engines that levels down the possibility inherent in any formal learning situation. Students are fearful of ridicule if they excel at their studies, rightly loathing to be called brains and eggheads. Some of the best students, who are compulsively driven to be like their classmates, occasionally abuse their intellectual gifts and perform far less well than they are actually able to achieve.

"I believe that one of the secrets which engenders real involvement in whatever one might be doing or learning is to allow one's self to be completely swept away by the activity. You all must have felt that special ambience of relationship and bonding in your recently shared play journey. I call your excellent play production a journey, because that is exactly what it was. You all joined together and took an extraordinary trip into the world and mind of William Shakespeare, into one of his darkest plays, which speaks to real life issues like ambition and power. You will never be the same, individually or collectively, because of that journey, a journey which has enriched and informed you more than my frail words can describe. "

Suddenly Mr. Pennythorpe began kneading his left shoulder. Looking at his wife, he paused, breathing heavily, and then drank some more water, unfastening and removing his bow tie, placing it on the head table.

"Learning, my friends, is merely making sense out of this wonderfully simple, complex, marvelous, intriguing, and fascinating world in which we live. That is all learning is. And we are all doing it constantly, whether we are aware of it or not. Our halls of formal learning are often scorned because they place straight-jackets on what is learned and how it is learned; we inflict on our students a linear and repetitive process that we call education, but one which actually educates its partakers on the fine art of tuning out. Unfortunately, we repel students' interest by holding out extrinsic rewards, which obscure the real satisfactions that can come from having worked hard to arrive at original and creative insights. It would not be wrong to say that when learning is actually occurring, that it is the learners themselves who create learning. And what a joy it is to arrive at a new insight or under-standing. Most, if not all, of you have just experienced that unique joy that is found in the delight of learning something new."

Mr. Pennythorpe paused and mopped his brow with his handkerchief. He leaned over and whispered a confidence to Mr. Ferlinghausen, whereupon the principal abruptly rose and moved rapidly to the back of the room to speak to Professor and Dr. Potter.

"I have a little more that I would like to say to you about learning," announced the history teacher, "but I'm afraid that it will have to wait until another time. I suddenly find myself unwell, and I ask your kind permission to be excused."

All present watched the unfolding drama, as Dr. Potter took out her cell phone and dialed 911. Those closest to her table heard her request that an ambulance be dispatched immediately for the middle school.

"Professor Potter will draw together my comments given thus far on the topic of learning," concluded Mr. Pennythorpe, "and so I ask that you give him your undivided attention." Mr. Ferlinghausen had returned to Mr. Pennythorpe's side and lent his arm to support the history teacher as he was escorted downstairs to the main office, accompanied by Dr. Potter and followed by Mrs. Pennythorpe.

Professor Potter had assumed the microphone, and announced, "I am very sorry for Mr. Pennythorpe's indisposition, and I pray that he will be all right. He has kindly asked me to summarize and give temporary closure to his excellent address this evening. To gain a greater appreciation for the entire concept of learning, especially as it has evolved in western culture, one must return to the rich traditions established by our Greek thinkers, luminaries of wisdom rarely equaled since that Golden Age."

"I think your dad is stalling until the ambulance gets here," David confided to Sean. "It must be pretty bad if that's what's going on."

"Yeah. Dad could talk for hours on end about anything and everything. And it actually is pretty interesting, at least most of the time. David, you look worried."

"I don't want anything to happen to Mr. Pennythorpe."

"They haven't buried him yet."

David glared daggers at Sean, "Really, Sean."

"Hey. Don't look at *me* like that. I want him to be okay, too. Let's be *positive* about it."

"And contemporary education didn't get its real beginnings until the advent of Rouseau and some of his contemporaries. Of course, so many children died before reaching maturity in those days, the necessity of schools to accommodate vast numbers of students did not arise until the advances of modern medicine considerably lengthened our average age expectancy," continued Professor Potter.

—How I hope Mr. Pennythorpe's life will not end this day, David thought in earnest prayer. He could only imagine what was happening in the office, seeing in his mind's eye a picture of Mr. Pennythorpe lying on the white leather sofa reserved for visitors in the main office, his wife sitting beside him and Dr. Potter attending to him.

David surveyed the room, and wondered if *anyone* was listening to Professor Potter. Even Melvin Dandy look worried and preocccupied. A siren could be heard in the distance. Although it was barely audible, everyone in the room tuned to its moan.

"John Dewey brought into the arena of education the concept of the ever important presence of experience as a necessity to any real and lasting mode of learning," continued Professor Potter.

The blare of the ambulance siren grew increasingly strident until it suddenly seemed to invade the auditorium itself, whereupon it abruptly ceased. Everyone now knew that the paramedics were bringing a stretcher into the building, no doubt guided by Mr. Ferlinghausen. The resumption of the siren would signal the ambulance's departure to the hospital. Seconds passed like minutes, minutes like hours, as everyone sat motionless, waiting, hoping to hear the ambulance siren.

In his preoccupied worry, a sullen chill coursed David's spine.

—If the siren doesn't resume its wail, thought David, —it can only mean that Mr. Pennythorpe has died. They wouldn't rush him to the hospital if he were dead.

The new implication of this long silence, which overwhelmed and blotted out Professor Potter's words, rose in front of the assembly, the dark specter of everyone's worst fear.

"And the well-known psychologist, Carl Rogers, brought to the fore the concept of learner centered education," continued Professor Potter, "a philosophy that empowers learners, not through extrinsic reward, but through inner and self-motivation, curiosity, wonder, and self-choice."

David began to fear the worst. Suddenly before him loomed the vision of Mrs. Pennythorpe weeping in the office, the paramedics wheeling out a stretcher with a sheet covering the corpse of the ancient history teacher. David felt his eyes moisten. Mr. Pennythorpe had been his friend and mentor, had imparted an enormous amount of wisdom to him, not so much by anything he had said, but merely by having been that rare kind of human being that he was. David wondered why people like Mr. Pennythorpe aren't fully appreciated until they are no longer around. There had always been a twinkle in his eye, a spark of enthusiasm in his bearing; he had genuinely liked his students, and they him. Although merely a dwarf when his physical height was considered, Mr. Pennythorpe had been a giant in terms of his intellect, compassion, caring, and sincerity.

When an ambulance siren suddenly intruded into his premature mourning, David started. Exhaling a relieved sigh, he looked at Sean, who was wiping his eyes.

Mr. Ferlinghausen reappeared and stepped next to Professor Potter who, in full anticipation of the principal's desire to make an announcement, quickly concluded, "And I think I shall end my remarks at this point, at least for the moment. Mr. Ferlinghausen?"

"Thank you, Professor. My dear friends, just to look at your faces I know how very worried you all are about Mr. Pennythorpe. It is Dr. Potter's opinion that he has suffered a heart attack. Just how serious that heart attack is, we have no way of measuring until tests are conducted at the hospital. As I speak, Mrs. Pennythorpe and Dr. Potter are accompanying Mr. Pennythorpe to the hospital in the rescue squad ambulance. I would ask that we all keep Mr. & Mrs. Pennythorpe in our thoughts, hearts, and prayers. Before we adjourn this meeting, please stand and join me in a moment of silence. Professor Potter will conclude our evening with his final words after our moment of silence. Please, everyone, let's stand."

The moment of silence seemed longer than a moment, but the attention of everyone in the room was focused intently on the continued health and well-being of the Pennythorpes.

Finally, Professor Potter said, "I am reminded of the words of that English mystic Dame Julian of Norwich, who said, 'All shall be well, and all manner of thing shall be well.' It was her profound spiritual insight that the forces of this universe work collectively and individually toward the highest good for each creature, for each individual entity. In that assurance, may we depart knowing that love, the final arbiter of all things, will hold Thatcher Pennythorpe in the best of care."

The Learning Club quickly adjourned.

Aunt Lillian was still sitting at the dinner table, talking to POTS, the Potter twins' nanny, when David joined them.

"David, I'm so sorry about Mr. Pennythorpe. I know he means a great deal to you," said Aunt Lillian.

POTS nodded in agreement.

"I just wish there were something I could do," said David. "Do you think we could go to the hospital?"

"I don't think there's much we can do there, at least not tonight. Perhaps tomorrow," said Aunt Lillian.

"I don't mind if I just go sit in the waiting room," said David.

"Now, David, be reasonable. Mr. Pennythorpe will probably be placed in the intensive cardiac care unit for at least a few days. If my memory serves me, they don't permit anyone in there except family members."

"But he's almost family," pleaded David.

"I know, dear, but the best we can do for Mr. Pennythorpe now is to wait and pray," said Aunt Lillian. "Mrs. Pennythorpe and the Ferlinghausens are going to stay at the hospital, probably all night. Don't forget: Mr. Ferlinghausen was a student of Mr. Pennythorpe's when he was an undergraduate."

David stood in a sullen silence. His whole world had just been turned upside down. He had seen Mr. Pennythorpe every school day since the beginning of the year. They had often visited during school. David had come to expect the history teacher to be part of his daily routine. The memory of his parents' deaths in their automobile accident was suddenly very strong and grief threatened to overwhelm him.

"I just wish there were something, *anything*, that I could do," David repeated.

"Pray, my dear. It really does help, you know," encouraged Aunt Lillian. "I daresay most of Midville will be praying for the Pennythorpes tonight."

David stood over Aunt Lillian, still scowling.

"Look, dear," promised Aunt Lillian, "I will take you to the hospital tomorrow."

"Okay," agreed David. "Let's go home."

* * * * *

Late the next afternoon, which was Saturday, Aunt Lillian and David drove to Midville Memorial Hospital.

"David, please don't get your hopes up," cautioned Aunt Lillian. "When I called early this morning to inquire about Mr. Pennythorpe's condition, the nurse told me that he was confined to the cardiac care unit, and wasn't receiving any visitors other than immediate family."

"I know," said David. "I just want to go and sit with Mrs. Pennythorpe, in case she's there."

"But she'll be next to his bed," said Aunt Lillian. "There was no answer at home, and the nurse refused to give any details about his condition when I called."

"All I know is that I've got to go, Aunt Lillian," said David stoically.

"Very well, my dear, but I don't want you to be disappointed," said Aunt Lillian.

Arriving at the hospital, which was of a yellow brick design from the early fifties, Aunt Lillian and David went to the waiting room outside the cardiac care unit. David had hoped Mrs. Pennythorpe would have need of walking into the visiting area, for then he would make his appeal to spend even a few minutes by the bedside of his fallen mentor.

After waiting for over half an hour, David whispered to Aunt Lillian, "Maybe I should go down to the visitor's information station near the entrance to see how Mr. Pennythorpe is."

"I'm not sure they would tell you, dear," said Aunt Lillian, looking up from the novel she had brought to read.

"I'm going to try, anyway," said David.

"It's too bad Bobby didn't want to come. You and he could talk while you waited," said Aunt Lillian.

"Yeah, but he's afraid of hospitals or, at least, that's what I gathered. Guess his experience of them is pretty sad," said David, as he left to go to information station near the elevators.

As he neared the visitor's information station, he was a little startled to see Mr. Ferlinghausen, who was talking to Dr. Potter. Both looked very grave, and for the briefest instant David feared the worst.

"Hello," he greeted them.

They were also surprised to see him. Mr. Ferlinghausen looked sadder than David had ever seen him.

"How's Mr. Pennythorpe?" inquired David.

"Not well," said Mr. Ferlinghausen. "In fact, he's in surgery as we speak."

"Surgery?" asked David.

"Yes, David," said Dr. Potter. "I'm afraid he suffered a second heart attack this morning. A cardiac specialist was consulted early this morning and recommended immediate surgery, without delay, which was being scheduled when the second heart attack occurred."

"What's the prognosis?" asked David.

"Not good," said Mr. Ferlinghausen.

"How long has he been in surgery?" asked David.

"Over an hour," said Dr. Potter. "He's got a very capable cardiac team, but sometimes that doesn't help if there's been a great deal of tissue damage."

"Where's Mrs. Pennythorpe?" asked David.

"Sitting in the waiting area outside the operating room. Her son and daughter flew in early this morning and they have been with her all day."

"Do you think I could go down there?" asked David.

"Yes," said Dr. Potter. "I'm going that way myself. I'll show you the way."

"Doctor, please notify me as soon as you hear anything," said Mr. Ferlinghausen.

"Agreed," said Dr. Potter. "Okay, David, please come this way."

David began to dislike this building, this hospital, where it seemed that people only came to die. His senses drank in every nuance of the sterile atmosphere, the cleaning solvents used for mopping the tile floors, the institutional colors of the walls, and the general ambience of heaviness that seemed to be invading the location.

Dr. Potter led David into a small waiting room area which lay adjacent to the operating theaters. As they entered, David saw Mrs. Pennythorpe talking with her son and daughter.

"Mrs. Pennythorpe," announced Dr. Potter, "David Andrews wanted to come to be with you and your children for a few minutes. I need to get back to the emergency room. Call me, though, if you need anything."

"David, dear," said Mrs. Pennythorpe, opening her arms to give him a hug, "Thatcher would be so pleased that you cared enough to come."

David hugged her silently for what seemed many, many seconds. The embrace said far more than any words could express.

"David, please meet Jonathan, our oldest child. He is a researcher for IBM," said Mrs. Pennythorpe.

David shook hands with Jonathan, who was, except for being much younger, a carbon copy of his father, gnome-like and all.

"I'm sorry about your dad," was all David could say,

Jonathan nodded in agreement.

"And here's Gwendolyn, our youngest child," said Mrs. Pennythorpe. "She's a medical doctor."

David shook hands with Gwendolyn, expressing the same condolences. She was a near carbon copy of her mother, bright eyed, rosy-cheeked, small in stature but ample in girth, her smile radiating an acceptance and warmth that was gratifying to receive.

"How long has he been in surgery?" asked David.

"Over an hour," said Mrs. Pennythorpe. "But don't worry. Thatcher is a fighter. He's not going to let two little heart attacks interfere with his life." It was obvious to David that Jonathan and Gwendolyn apparently shared their mother's optimism, for they also nodded, smiling in agreement.

—Maybe they're denying the inevitable, thought David, catching himself out at harboring any negativity.

"There was some damage to Dad's heart," said Gwendolyn, "but the information I have looked at would suggest that he has a good, fighting chance for a complete recovery."

"That would be so wonderful," said David.

"David is one of Thatcher's best students," announced Mrs. Pennythorpe. "They take time to talk, really talk, the way we always do at home. David has been a real blessing to Thatcher this year."

David had not realized how significant he had been in the scheme of his relationship with his mentor. Gratified that the relationship had not been overwhelmingly one-sided, he said, "Mr. Pennythorpe is, by far, the best teacher I've ever had."

"He is good, isn't he," laughed Gwendolyn. "I love to see him get so excited over history; it's his second love. Mother's his first."

"Remember when Dad got dressed up like Wellington to dramatize that decisive military victory?" Jonathan reminisced.

"I do," said Mrs. Pennythorpe. "*I* had to re-sew most of those buttons on that dingy old uniform Dad borrowed from the college theatre department's wardrobe."

"David, what characteristic of Dad do you like best?" asked Gwendolyn.

David pondered a moment, then answered, "He's a terrific listener. He also knows just the right questions to ask to help me come to a clearer insight about something."

A door suddenly swung open and a tall man dressed in surgeon's blues walked briskly to Mrs. Pennythorpe, announcing, "Please come with me quickly."

Mrs. Pennythorpe and her children followed the doctor into surgery. David sat down, worried that the doctor's haste could only mean that Mr. Pennythorpe had but a few precious minutes of life left, and that they must hurry if they wanted to say their goodbyes. Tears flooded into his eyes as he thought how he had never been able to say goodbye to either of his parents.

Laughter echoed from the surgery bay, and David looked toward the operating room door, wondering what sort of merriment could be afoot when someone lay on his deathbed.

The laughter resounded more robustly, causing David to venture to the door and look through the porthole window.

Gwendolyn could be seen returning to the waiting room.

"David, come and see Dad. He's on his way to the recovery room and he's going to be just fine; in fact, he has everyone in stitches. They've implanted a pacemaker, which is apparently what he's been needing for many months, but no one knew. When it comes to medical complaints, he's a stubborn Englishman. If I had lived nearby, I probably would have observed his chronic shortness of breath. Anyway, come and laugh a little."

David followed Gwendolyn into the recovery room which sat next to the surgery bay, and as he approached the stretcher, he was glad to hear Mr. Pennythorpe's voice. He was reciting a funny poem about a surgeon who couldn't quite remember what to cut out of his patient, so he just kept cutting and cutting. Mr. Pennythorpe's surgeon was red from laughing, as were Mrs. Pennythorpe and Jonathan.

"Is that David?" asked Mr. Pennythorpe, extending his hand.

David took hold of his teacher's hand. It was warm and firm.

"So good of you to come, to care," said Mr. Pennythorpe. "I'm sorry that I'm going to be out of school for a while."

"That's okay. As long as you come back, that's what's important," said David.

"My good surgeon here, Dr. Levine, has kept me under his judicious care until I was fully conscious. He wanted to make sure my new pacemaker was responding properly," explained Mr. Pennythorpe. "And I am most grateful to him for saving my life."

"I'm so glad you're going to be okay," said David, smiling at the little gnome.

Mr. Pennythorpe then turned to David, looking at him with great affection, saying, "I'm so glad to be back. We still have things to talk about, don't we?"

All David could do was nod and smile.

Chapter Nineteen
A Special Call is Made to Mr. Vasiloff

AUNT LILLIAN AND DAVID WERE PREPARING DINNER TOGETHER. Bobby had stayed after school with the other officers of the Learning Club to meet with Mr. Gregory. "Aunt Lillian, Mr. Pennythorpe is going to be able to come home from the hospital this coming Friday. He's still going be out of school for a couple of weeks, but at least he's coming home," said David with excitement, peeling potatoes.

"Getting out of the hospital after two heart attacks in a week's time is a credit to his resilience," said Aunt Lillian.

"Apparently his pacemaker is working just fine," said David. "Is that enough for mashed?"

"Yes. I'm so glad it all worked out the way it did," said Aunt Lillian. "One never knows, when one gets to our ages, what might happen. Of course, one never knows at any age, I suppose. Part of life's excitement is that it is very unpredictable."

"I'm sorry Mr. Pennythorpe wasn't able to finish his talk to the Learning Club," said David.

"Yes. He had a little more he wanted to say, didn't he?" said Aunt Lillian. "Here. I've finished with the roast. The garlic is in place. Let's put it in the oven to bake."

A short silence followed.

"I want to sit down for a bit. We have some time before we need to begin working on whipped potatoes," announced Aunt Lillian, sitting on a nearby stool. "What's new with you, David?"

"I think we should throw Mr. Pennythorpe a 'Welcome Home' party," said David.

Aunt Lillian considered his words, smiled, and answered, "I think Mr. Pennythorpe needs quiet and rest right now."

"After the party," insisted David.

"And where would this party be?" asked Aunt Lillian.

"At his house, of course," said David.

"David," sighed Aunt Lillian, "I know how persistent you can be over something like this, but let's just give this brainstorm a rest."

"Let me run it by Mrs. Pennythorpe," pleaded David.

"I'm sure she'll give you a polite 'No, thank you,'" said Aunt Lillian.

"If she doesn't, can we please do something special?" asked David.

"If she agrees, my checkbook is open," said Aunt Lillian confidently, adding, "Wide open."

"I'll go call her now. We have three days to plan it, if she agrees," said David.

"You will also have to wait until she checks with Mr. Pennythorpe's physicians, including his daughter. I think the welcome party should be a family decision."

"You know," confessed David, "I would never propose something like this for any regular, normal human being, but Mr. Pennythorpe is an *extraordinary* human being. If you could only have seen how he was telling those funny stories right after his surgery, and it was obvious he loved the laughter as much as anyone. Remember the funny stories he told at our Advent Party last December? I mean, isn't humor supposed to be wonderful at healing physical and emotional pains?"

"Yes. It's supposed to be, and I'm sure it is. I think I read something about that recently," said Aunt Lillian.

"You still look concerned," said David.

"Perhaps I'm just being old-fashioned, but for all the poor man has been through, he doesn't need any extra demand on his energies. I worry, too, about the additional risk of infection. How many people would be at this party? How many would have colds? How many would sneeze on him? I suspect his immune system needs several months, at least, to repair itself from the stress of two heart attacks."

"I hadn't thought of that," said David. "That's important. I bet his doctors will say 'no way.'"

"Only one way to find out," said Aunt Lillian, "and your first call should be to Mrs. Pennythorpe."

* * * * *

David returned, grinning in triumph, announcing, "Mrs. Pennythorpe thinks it's a great idea, but she also wants to consult with her daughter, just as you suggested."

"I'm glad her daughter is a medical doctor," said Aunt Lillian.

"Yes. Mrs. Pennythorpe said she'd call back later tonight," said David. "I sure hope we can do it. I think Mr. Pennythorpe would be glad to see everybody."

"You really want to hear the end of his talk, don't you," teased Aunt Lillian.

David pondered a moment, answering, "Yes. I really do."

"So do I," said Aunt Lillian. "Let's hope we can do it. If it's allowed, I have a few ideas to run by you as possible ways to give Mr. Pennythorpe a real celebration."

"Great," said David. "Who will make the corn right before we eat? Do you want to, or should I? I like boiling the corn."

"You can boil the corn and I'll make the gravy. Right now, why don't you go do your homework? Bobby won't be here for at least another hour and a half. We'll eat about half an hour after he gets home. After I've finished here, I need to make some phone calls."

Later that evening, Bobby arrived home with Zeke. They were full of news from their meeting with the Giant's son. Aunt Lillian invited Zeke to stay for dinner, an invitation he gratefully accepted.

"Let's get some soda and you can tell us about your meeting while the roast finishes cooking," suggested Aunt Lillian.

Soon the foursome sat in the music room library, and Bobby spoke first.

"The Giant's son said he was really proud of our whole Learning Club and all that we've done, and that we're all back on track for passin' *this* year," replied Bobby, glad that he had helped to save his classmates from repeating the ninth grade.

"And can you believe it?" asked Zeke. "The whole thing was a trick?"

"A trick?" asked Aunt Lillian.

"Yeah, a trick," said Zeke. "The Giant's son never intended to keep anyone from goin' on to the tenth grade. He just wanted to see what his threat would make us do."

"That's kind of mean," said David.

"No. It was one of them educational studies," said Bobby. "The real Giant was conductin' it all along, workin' through his son. I mean, we all got into it. Not our names, but descriptions of us and what we all did. And you're in it, too, David."

"Wow!" said David. "Can we ever read it?"

"Yes. He's gonna get copies to share around once it's published in some magazine," said Bobby.

"Journal," Zeke corrected Bobby.

"We're gonna be famous," exclaimed Bobby.

"Did Sean get mentioned?" asked David.

"That'll kill the whole thing, if anythin' does," said Bobby.

"What was Mr. Gregory looking for?" asked Aunt Lillian.

"Somethin' called group bondin'," said Bobby, "which means to see whether or not we could work together, and not always be at each other's throats. Ain't that a hoot and a hollar?"

"Was Mr. Gregory pleased with the results?" asked David.

"He said we exceeded everyone's expectations," said Zeke.

"Who else knew about the study?" asked David.

"Old Ferlinghausen was in on it from the beginnin'," said Bobby. "And, of course, the Giant, and the Giant's son."

"How about Mr. Dandy?" asked David.

"What?" exclaimed Bobby. "He ain't important, that measly little ne'er-do-well. It ain't got nothin' to do with him."

"But he's the school counselor," said David.

"Ya mean the school 'fool'," Bobby corrected David.

"When will you tell the others?" asked Aunt Lillian.

"The Giant's son is gonna make a big presentation tomorrow, tellin' us all about it, how we did, and what he's writin' for the report," said Bobby.

"It's going to seem pretty tame, now that all the excitement is over," Aunt Lillian observed.

"Ain't gonna be that way at all," said Bobby. "Our studies for the rest of the year are gonna be up to us to plan and to put into action."

"So Mr. Gregory thinks you've got the hang of learning?" asked David.

"Damn straight," said Bobby, nodding at Zeke, "me and the others, too. And it ain't never would've happened if it hadn't been for you, Davey boy. Thanks for helpin' us out of a jam."

"You all did most of the work," said David.

"But we didn't know what needed to be done," said Zeke.

"Them learnin' styles made me wake up and see that I'm one of them students who likes to put stuff together. I know I need to work on the other areas, but just give me anything, and in an hour, I'll have that sucker in one piece. Zeke is like that, too."

"No wonder I want to become a car mechanic," said Zeke.

"You can work on my cars, for nothin'," kidded Bobby.

"And you can be my butler for my work on your car," said Zeke.

"Call in Jiggs for that," Bobby retorted.

"Well, it seems to me that a party *is* in order," said Aunt Lillian. "David wanted us to arrange for a special welcome home party for Mr. Pennythorpe this Friday. If the entire class, or maybe the whole Learning Club, can come, we could merge this celebration with the other."

"And Mr. Pennythorpe can finish his talk," said David.

Just then the telephone rang. David sprang to answer it.

Returning from the kitchen after taking the call, David announced, "The party is on! Mrs. Pennythorpe said her daughter is coming back this weekend to supervise her dad's coming home from the hospital. It can't be a surprise, because they already asked him if he'd like a party, and he said, 'Why not? Why do you think I had these two heart attacks?' Mrs. Pennythorpe said she'd really appreciate it if we could handle all the details, including food, setup, cleanup, and entertainment."

"I would like to take care of the entertainment," volunteered Aunt Lillian. "If that would be okay with all of you."

"What did you have in mind?" asked David.

"Let me see if I can arrange it first," said Aunt Lillian. "Once it's set, I'll tell you all about it. I know you'll love it."

The timer rang in the kitchen.

"It's time for me to make gravy," announced Aunt Lillian, "and for you to do corn, David. Please excuse us, gentlemen."

The President and Vice-President of the Midville Middle School Learning Club continued to talk with excitement about the coming celebration after Aunt Lillian and David went to the kitchen.

＊＊＊＊＊

When David and Bobby arrived home the next day, Aunt Lillian was so excited to tell them her news that she met them at the front door as they were entering.

"Boys, I have wonderful news," she exclaimed, "Mr. Vasiloff will come and he will bring a small band."

"Mr. Who?" asked David.

"Oh, that's right. I never explained last night. Mr. George Vasiloff is one of the finest musicians I have ever known. After college, he had a band that toured the country and played Dixieland jazz for years."

"Were you in college together?" asked David.

"Heavens, no. He had graduated before I entered. I didn't know him until he brought his band through Midville almost forty years ago. He has come to love Upstate New York, and he chose to retire here. His band was so good that he could have retired anywhere, because they've traveled everywhere."

"So he's living here now?" asked David.

"In Ithaca, up near the university. He teaches occasionally at Ithaca College. Some of his old records have been turned into these new things—"

"Compact discs?" asked David.

"That's it. Into compact discs," said Aunt Lillian.

"You've never heard a Dixieland Band play real Dixieland music until you've heard George Vasiloff and his *Old Timers* play 'When the Saints Go Marching In.' He is just *so* good. He told me that he could get four players together to rehearse tomorrow and that they will meet us at the Pennythorpes' home on Friday."

"Sounds as if he's been doing it for a while," said David.

"More years than anyone could count. There's an agelessness to Mr. Vasiloff; he's both ancient and young at the same time."

"Sort of like Mr. Pennythorpe?" asked David.

"Yes, I suppose so," agreed Aunt Lillian.

"Although George might be older than the hills themselves, he can still wail on that clarinet," said Aunt Lillian.

David started laughing.

"What's so funny, dear?" she asked.

"I never thought I'd hear you use the word wail."

"And why not? Your generation doesn't have a monopoly on words like cool, do they?"

"No, we don't, I suppose."

"Mr. Vasiloff may appear old, but he's very young inside."

"That's just like you, then," added David.

"You may be right, David. I may appear rather elderly on the outside, but on the inside I feel quite young."

"What kind of music will they play?" asked David.

"Jazz. Mr. Vasiloff's music goes way back to the twenties and thirties, although he organized his band in the early fifties. His *Old Timers* make listeners believe they've gone to New Orleans."

"The band will be great, Aunt Lillian," said David. "Thanks so much. It's not going to be too expensive, is it?"

"Not at all. It's a bargain for what we'll be getting," said Aunt Lillian. "I know it will provide just the right mood for the festivities. By the way, I was so excited to tell you my news, I forgot to ask you about yours."

"The class loved the idea of the party, and we broke into groups and everybody will bring food. Mrs. Pennythorpe's not going to have to worry about a thing. We even got five volunteers, and I mean real volunteers, for the clean up committee."

"The class knows how to organize now," said Bobby, "I mean, 'specially after all the stuff we did for the play. Never thought I'd understand Shakespeare."

"You ended up liking Mr. William?" Aunt Lillian smiled.

"Yeah. Once I figured out what he meant, it was great. That dude was one sharp cookie. But why didn't he just say what he had to say straight out in plain English?"

"The language was different then," said David.

"Glad I was born when I was, then," concluded Bobby. "Ain't got to worry about havin' to learn all that hooey."

"But there's different hooey today, Bobby," laughed David.

"Better than that old hooey. Although, once I understood the darn hooey, it wasn't quite so bad. Better than listenin' to that measly little ne'er-do-well Dandy."

"Mr. Dandy's efforts to persuade the eighth graders to buy tickets to the play helped us to raise well over a thousand dollars," David reminded Bobby.

"Yeah. Gotta give the devil his due. But there ain't no *livin'* eighth grader who'd dare to face a full hour of old lobster breath at two paces. It's enough to curdle your soul," retorted Bobby.

"Curdle?" asked Aunt Lillian.

"Ain't that one of them there Shakespearean words?" asked Bobby.

"I'm not sure," said David. "He probably used it. Maybe you heard the word 'cur', and simply added the '-dle.'"

"Well, even if he didn't, *I* did," proclaimed Bobby.

"David, I'll need to go to the bank tomorrow and get the money you'll need to pay for all the things you have to buy for Friday's welcome party," said Aunt Lillian.

"It shouldn't be that bad, Aunt Lillian. I have agreed to provide the beverages, balloons, flowers, and entertainment."

"That means a *lot* of soda," said Bobby, smiling.

"Yes. And maybe a nice fruit punch for those who don't like soda. Aunt Lillian, could you please make arrangements for the flowers through Mr. Guenther's shop?"

"I'll call Spunk in the morning," agreed Aunt Lillian.

"Why do you call him Spunk?" asked Bobby.

"Oh, that was his nickname when he was my piano student many years ago," explained Aunt Lillian. "He was always full of energy as well as a very hard worker, so people concluded that he had a lot of spunk. I suppose he would be called an entrepreneur today."

"But you couldn't call him that, could you?" asked David.

"Not in the way I call him Spunk," said Aunt Lillian. "I'm very proud of how well he's done for himself, and his flower arrangements are absolutely gorgeous."

* * * * *

The many arrangements for Mr. Pennythorpe's welcome home party proceeded without a hitch.

"You know," David said to Bobby the night before the party, "everything has worked so smoothly, I'm afraid the other shoe will fall and something will go wrong tomorrow."

"What could go wrong?" asked Bobby.

"I don't know. Anything. Everything," said David.

"You sure that we're gonna get outa school?" asked Bobby.

"Yes. It's an official Learning Club field trip, excused and all," said David.

"Sounds good to me," said Bobby. "Amazing that the Giant's son went along with it, being tougher than nails and all."

"He's so proud of the Learning Club, he would do anything to help us with one of our projects," said David.

"So, we leave school at ten-thirty tomorrow morning by bus to go to the Pennythorpes' home?" asked Bobby.

"Yes. That will give us time to get in our places. They're planning to release Mr. Pennythorpe from the hospital about eleven. His daughter will bring him in her van. There will be a wheel chair for him to be brought into his house. We will all be waiting to cheer him when his daughter wheels him in," said David.

"But he knows about it?" asked Bobby.

"We had to see if he even wanted the party, and he does, so he'll be looking forward to it," said David.

"So, what will happen?" asked Bobby.

"His daughter Gwendolyn, who's a physician and real nice besides, will wheel him in. I will step forward and present Mr. Pennythorpe with the YARB Award that he wasn't able to take with him the night of the banquet because of his heart attack, and then I'll say, 'Ladies and Gentlemen, I give you Thatcher T. Pennythorpe.' Then everybody will cheer as Mr. Vasiloff starts his jazz band, playing 'When the Saints Go Marching In'. That will signal the beginning of the party. People will pig out on food and soda and stuff. After everyone's eaten, we'll invite Mr. Pennythorpe to finish the talk he was giving at the Learning Club banquet when he got sick. How's all that sound?"

"Fine by me," said Bobby. "That ne'er-do-well Dandy ain't gonna be there, is he?"

"Not that I know of," said David. "Only Aunt Lillian and some of the mothers who are helping with the food. Oh, yes. Sean told me today in school that his mom is coming, as well," said David.

"Will that littl' beggar be there?" asked Bobby.

"Of course, he and his friends are coming with us on the bus. So will Mary and Lisa. What's wrong with that?" asked David.

"I'll wear my boots with the steel toes," said Bobby.

"They can't still be hurting," David scolded.

"Every time I think of them, but he only got two of mine. The first one was the middle one on my right foot. When he tugged that one, I flopped around in agony like a seal out of water; then the little beggar pulled the bigger toe next to it together with the one he'd just wrenched really hard, and that's when I went frickin' *blind* with pain," said Bobby.

"You've *got* to let it go, Bobby. Forgive Sean and forget about it," said David.

"Already have," said Bobby.

"It doesn't sound as if you've forgiven him," retorted David.

"'Cause it's the pullin' of the toes I forgave, *not* the pain," explained Bobby. "I *still* owe that little magpie a really big one."

"Not tomorrow," pleaded David. "Tomorrow is Mr. Pennythorpe's day. Let's not ruin it with fisticuffs."

"Ain't nothin's been said about no fisticuffs," said Bobby. "More like some atomic sledgehammer, but the little beggar would probably laugh it off. *Indestructible*, that's what he is. It just ain't right."

* * * * *

The bus waited patiently as members of Midville's Learning Club boarded it with hushed excitement. The Giant's son was the official

434

chaperone, although Mr. Ferlinghausen stepped on the bus just before departure, after attendance had been taken.

The bus wended its way through the late winter streets. Snow had fallen the week before, but now a hint of spring stirred the air. Beneath the unmistakable aroma of early buds, a soothing spring air was carried by the clear April breeze. Spring was always hoped for at this time of year, although the last snow fall generally didn't occur until mid or late April. Whereas March teased of spring, April produced it. The wind was still brisk and chilly for so sunny a day.

The bus arrived at the Pennythorpes' home, which was built in the Tudor English cottage style, with a stone exterior on the first floor and wooden gables above. A decorative brick walk led its way from the driveway to the house's front door, although the bus parked on the street. Curious about the manner and style in which the Thatcher Pennythorpes lived, students and adults alike were delighted to get this private glimpse of so public an icon and revered a teacher.

Upon entering, members of the Learning Club noticed an oversized living room perfect for entertaining. Attractive oak beams overhead emphasized the off white walls and ceiling. One would almost expect banners to be hanging from the walls, so much did this large room remind those present of an English manor house or castle. A large stone fireplace at one end of the room blazed its warm welcome to the entering guests. On a large table at the center of the room sat a number of culinary delicacies, including a huge, three layer, white cake. Lavish arrangements of fresh flowers appeared both on the food table and throughout the room.

In the corner of the room that led into a formal dining room stood the celebrated George Vasiloff and four members of his jazz band. George held his clarinet in anticipation of the cue to begin playing 'When The Saints Go Marching In'. In the company of this jazz great stood a trumpet player, trombone player, string bass player, and a drummer.

David studied Mr. Vasiloff, wondering what had so captivated his Aunt Lillian about the man. The jazz band leader had a full head of white hair, a strong, proud face which had been steeped in the Florida sunshine of his early retirement years, betraying a few wrinkles around his eyes, kind eyes, that seemed much younger than the man himself. As Aunt Lillian had mentioned, there was a paradox about this musician that David couldn't quite articulate. Although Mr. Vasiloff was retired, there was a certain energy, an unmistakable vitality that radiated from somewhere inside of him that made him seem far younger than his years. Mr. Vasiloff was talking quietly with his band members, and they were giving him their complete attention. David also noticed that none of the musicians had music stands or music. It was obvious that they would soon play from their hearts.

A smattering of applause caused everyone to turn to the front door, in anticipation of Mr. Pennythorpe's arrival, but instead everyone was surprised and delighted to see the arrival of Dr. & Mrs. Baker. David walked over to greet them.

"David," said Dr. Baker, "I am so glad you had this wonderful idea to welcome Thatcher home in this way. And please meet my wife, Sylvia. David is one of Thatcher's best students."

"Very nice to meet you," rejoined Mrs. Baker, as she shook David's hand warmly.

"I was worried about Thatcher," admitted Dr. Baker. "When we did those guided imagery exercises at school, his journey and symbols suggested to me that some sort of medical problem could be coming, although I chose not to say anything to him at the time."

"Why not?" asked David.

"Why worry someone, especially over something that could be so prone to misinterpretation and error?"

"I guess you're right," agreed David.

"Any way, it is only a temporary setback. He's a tiger, and he will be back in fighting form and to school in a couple of weeks."

As those who were now assembled continued to wait for Mr. Pennythorpe to arrive, Sean made three trips around the food table, casing out the exact areas to which he would launch himself after the initial festivities. A murmur of anticipation echoed through the group like an evening's ocean wave.

"He's here," someone called.

A bit of clatter could be heard at the outside door well, as Gwendolyn, Mr. Pennythorpe's daughter and the attending physician for this special celebration, maneuvered the teacher's wheelchair up the outside entry. The door slowly opened, and Gwendolyn could be seen wheeling a contented and relaxed Mr. Pennythorpe through the door. At first sight, David noticed that his mentor had lost a little weight.

Advancing to where Gwendolyn had wheeled her dad into the huge living room, David handed his mentor the YARB Award, loudly proclaiming, "Ladies and Gentlemen, it is my special privilege to give to you the marvelous and magnificent Thatcher T. Pennythorpe."

Immediately, on cue, George Vasiloff's *Old Timers* jazz band began playing, in high Dixieland style, 'When The Saints Go Marching In' mid the enthusiastic cheers and applause that greeted Mr. Pennythorpe's return home. Mr. Vasiloff led the band in the familiar tune, and from the instant that David heard him play his clarinet, he knew why Aunt Lillian held him in such high regard. Mr. Vasiloff didn't merely play jazz; Mr. Vasiloff *was* jazz. It danced in his eyes, it flowed from his fingers, it filled the room. David suddenly wondered if he was hearing Dixieland jazz for the very first time, this familiar song had taken on such life and joy. Even amid the applause and cheering, the music found its cue and surrounded the celebration. David's heart soared at the festive sounds, melody weaving in and out of counter-melody, each dancing with each, creating a sonic light that seemed to lift the room. After their first number, the band continued with other selections. What they were playing didn't matter as much as what the music truly was, and what that music was doing to those who had gathered to celebrate the renewed health of one of the most revered teachers in Midville.

Mr. Vasiloff's band finally played its last tune, much to the regret of everyone present, after which the band members eagerly joined the hungry throng.

David found himself wiping a tear from his left eye, when he was suddenly being bumped from behind.

"What a spread," said Sean, exulting in all the treats which awaited tasting. His mouth was already full of cookies, and he carried a large plastic cup of root beer.

"Great party," agreed David.

"Get some food," said Sean, adding, "before it's all gone."

"There's so much—"

"Trust me," said Sean. "Remember, *I'm* in line."

"Okay, okay," agreed David, picking up a paper plate.

As he filled his own plate, David could hear Aunt Lillian as she talked with the jazz great who stood in their midst.

"Oh, Mr. *Vasiloff!*" exclaimed Aunt Lillian several times, as she and her old friend laughed together and exchanged stories. David suddenly realized that the most polite thing he could do would be to take them plates of food and to see what they wanted to drink.

The party-goers ate well, very well, indeed. Finally, the three tiered cake was cut and all present shared one of the most delicious almond-vanilla cakes they had ever sampled.

Again David stepped forward and signaled to Mr. Gregory, who tapped a crystal glass next to him, as is often done at wedding receptions before announcements are made. A hush of quiet fell over the jubilant throng.

"Mr. Pennythorpe never got to finish his speech at our last gathering, and I know he'd like to do so, and what better time than now?" announced David, with loud cheers and resounding shouts following his words.

All eyes now focused on Thatcher Pennythorpe, who sat smartly in his wheelchair. An expectant hush filled the room as the much beloved teacher considered the words he would share.

Beginning in a soft but firm voice, he said, "I ... I must confess that I am completely overwhelmed by this welcome-home party."

Loud cheers and hoots followed his words, as he wiped a tear from his cheek.

"When I was asked if I wanted this homecoming, I said 'yes', but little did I not know what that 'yes' meant. It is far more beautiful and wonderful than anything I could ever have imagined; it has been, for lack of a better metaphor, like entering into heaven *itself*."

Again cheers and hoots filled the room.

"The love that is in this room is so palpable. It's in the warmth of the fire, in the goodness of the wonderful food and beverages that so many of you have prepared, in the marvelous music—so rare and fine, and it reminds me of when I once heard and met Pops Armstrong years ago. Most especially, the love in this room is in all of your eyes ... and, therefore, in all of your hearts.

"And what I still want to say to you about learning is abundantly apparent in all that I now feel in this room, for learning is—in the last analysis, the last consideration, the last glimpse of fleeting intuition— nothing less than *love* itself. For the more we learn, the more we know; and the more we know, the more we can understand; and the more we can understand, the more we can appreciate; and the more we can appreciate, the more we are able to love, both ourselves and others, as well as this marvelous world in which we live.

"Love, my friends: never forget the enduring power of love. It is *stronger* than death itself. Love is what *we* are about, whether we have discovered it yet or not, for Love is what will bring to us the full measure and meaning of our days on this planet. And it is not the love that we have received that will be our measure, but rather the love that we have given. Let me close now, for I am getting a little tired, by saying, 'Thank you, all, for coming and I love you all very much.'"

Cheers and applause again filled the room, and not one eye in the entire room was dry. Gwendolyn patted her dad on his shoulder and kissed him on the top of his bald head. He held his right arm up to acknowledge her affection, after which Gwendolyn pushed his wheel-chair toward the bedroom, following Mrs. Pennythorpe, who led the way.

Mr. Vasiloff again signaled the band, which began to play, 'When The Saints Go Marching In.' Party revelers began to clean up the food and beverages, although several voracious students were beginning to return to the enormous food table for fourth or fifth helpings.

Sean was among the latter number, moving toward the place in the food table where cookies were being removed. Grabbing at his favorites as they vanished from his sight, he felt a gentle tap on his left shoulder.

Turning to see who had tapped him, Sean caught only the briefest glimpse of a large cream pie flying swiftly toward his face, coming too fast for him to duck or to dodge. *Splat!* His entire face, head and hair were now nothing but vanilla cream. A warrior in his deepest heart of hearts, Sean's first impulse was to repel this attack by grabbing the closest items of food and firing them back at whomever had just attacked him. But having a genuine admiration for the Pennythorpes' beautiful home, and a deep respect for the Pennythorpes themselves, and also fully mindful that his own mother was somewhere in this same room, perhaps even now watching this attack, Sean wisely determined that, instead of warfare, he would take the higher road, which is much to his enduring credit. Wiping his eyes so that he could see his attacker, and thus looking directly into Bobby Perkins' grinning face, Sean laughed as he exclaimed, "Vanilla! It's my *absolute* favorite. How did you know? Are there any other pies?"

Hedges' Casserole Recipe

1 pound of hamburger browned
    together with
1 or more large onions
1 cup of dry rice
1 can of cream of chicken soup
1 can of cream of mushroom soup
2 cans of water
    salt, pepper, or cayenne to taste

Mix all together in a covered casserole.
Bake 1 to 1 ½ hours in medium oven,
at 350 degrees. Stir occasionally.
Add more liquid if necessary.
Use earthenware casserole,
    if possible.

Companion Volumes to
Because They **THINK** *They Can*

The Canasta Capers[1]

Haunted by a recurrent dream that echoes the moments before the tragic deaths of his parents from an accident caused by a drunken driver, David Andrews must relocate to Midville to live with his Great-Aunt Lillian Biggs.

As David grieves his loss, he struggles to find a place in his new community, albeit with the intrusion of a bully and the insensitivity of several faculty at the Midville Middle School. Several new friends come to David's rescue in his determination to find a non-violent way in which to relate to the school bully.

What others have said

"Steven Swerdfeger has an eye for the details of everyday school rules and rituals that allows him to place his precocious hero and his "Gang of Four" in a convincing setting. Because he also has a feel for the fun that comes from the camaraderie of young people bucking the system, his central theme of a search for fairness and justice in life is rendered lightly. Swerdfeger remembers what it is like to be young and discovering adult hypocrisy for the first time, so he can increase the appeal of his young bunch when he creates richly comic grown-up nemeses for them to challenge. What is more, he knows how to ground the comedy in more muted and serious emotions: the smartest boy in town must confront problems for which there are no easy intellectual solutions, and in the end even the school bully has his own story to tell."

— *Paul Howe, Philadelphia, Pennsylvania*

"This is a gentle story, told with engaging warmth. Swerdfeger weaves a tale of four middle school children who deal with real life issues, from cutting in on lunch lines to tragic car accidents. Through these experiences, David Andrews learns to turn enemies into friends through compassion."

—*Joseph Downing, Syracuse, New York*

[1]Originally published in 1996 under the title *Thursday's Child*, and later accorded Finalist Honors in the 1997 SMALL PRESS BOOK AWARDS.

An Opening of Heart

The adventures continue as Aunt Lillian and David welcome Bobby Perkins into their home and decide to invite neighbors and friends to an Advent Party. Even a raging snow storm cannot prevent the planned celebration, at which Thatcher Pennythorpe recites part of Charles Dickens' *A Christmas Carol*, indicating that he at one time gave holiday readings of that story every year. David becomes determined to have Mr. Pennythorpe renew his custom of public readings, with all ticket proceeds going to the community food back.

The Potters invite Aunt Lillian, David, and Bobby to Christmas Eve services at Midville's Methodist Church, and later in the holiday the young people attend a Watch Night Service on New Year's Eve. During the vacation, Sean Potter also takes David and Bobby to the enigmatic Mr. Astor's shop of curiosities where the boys receive unexpected gifts.

On New Year's Day, Gertrude Coachman discovers that she no longer needs to continue teaching English, and embarks upon a journey that is beleaguered with unexpected frustrations and surprises.

Mr. Ferlinghausen, Midville Middle School's principal, invites David and his cohorts to host an assembly program for Dr. William Gregory, an educator and researcher who comes to speak to the school.

David becomes consumed with his science report on the megafauna, and hopes to upstage Mallory Evans, who is obsessed with the T-Rex as well as the need to be an Alpha male. David does his best to win sympathy for the megafauna during his presentation, and experiences a moment of cosmic consciousness regarding the interconnectedness of all life, which evokes in him a profound vision and transformation.

Finally, after some intentional slights, misunderstandings and mishaps throughout the story, David, Bobby and Sean discover and acknowledge a new sense of friendship and brotherhood.

STEVEN SWERDFEGER was born in Massena, New York, on July 13, 1948. He attended local public schools, later entering the State University of New York at Oswego, where he earned his Bachelor of Arts degree in American literature. He also holds a Master of Arts degree in religious education from Princeton Theological Seminary and a Doctor of Philosophy degree in creative writing from the Union Institute & University in Cincinnati, Ohio.

His various career interests have included child care work, teaching high school English, creative writing, church music, hypnosis and guided imagery, college teaching, and publishing.

He is married to Martha Grout Swerdfeger, a physician who serves as Medical Director for the CrossRoads Clinic in Phoenix, Arizona, and who practices under her maiden name Martha M. Grout.

Photo credit: Courtesy of Matthew Marchisano

LUCY SWERDFEGER was born in Syracuse, N.Y., on November 7, 1982. Having begun formal studies in painting at the age of six, she has studied art with Gale Simon Coleman and Michael White, among others.

Lucy will begin her studies for a B.F.A. degree in illustration at the Minneapolis College of Art and Design in August of 2005. Her interests include illustration and comic art.

She has kindly allowed her parents to adopt Brody, her tiger cat, while she is away at art school.

Afterword

Today it is no surprise to educators and parents alike that over one-third of our middle school and high school students are disengaged from their academic environments, that they are present in their classrooms physically, but absent emotionally and intellectually. What is it about schools or about our society that encourages such a response?

Some would suggest that our schools cannot compete with the razzle-dazzle excitement offered by computer games and other visual media, and thus bore their denizens. Others suggest that some of our teenagers feel that academic hoops are irrelevant to their chosen interests and priorities, and that time spent in school is mostly to receive a diploma. Of late, enormous pressure has been placed on the public schools, wherein some individuals with the noblest of intentions have attempted to force schools and students to measure up to prescribed standards of learning, with the sole measure of that success found in standardized test scores.

We now award grades to schools as well as to students. Most appalling has been the introduction of such tests into the early grades of primary school, where passing or failing is determined by a test score. Instead of nurturing the imaginations and wonder of seven-and-eight-year-old children, we now force their fullest attention to passing some arbitrary exam at year's end, as if that were going to afford them anything of lasting value, except a flat and condemnatory number. We unwittingly reduce them to these numbers, as if something of large importance were at stake in the process, and we rob them of the potential joy they might have found in true learning … learning unfettered by any external expectation or outcome. In the long run, it will be their imaginations that serve them best, but if we continue to place bell jars over their creativity and capacities to marvel, we will reduce them to little more than unthinking automatons. We should know better.

In his novel *Hard Times*, Charles Dickens presents an educator named Thomas Gradgrind, in a chapter entitled "Murdering the Innocents":

> A man of realities. A man of facts and calculations ... with a rule and a pair of scales, and the multiplication table always in his pocket ... ready to weigh and measure any parcel of human nature and tell you exactly what it comes to. It is a mere question of figures, a case of simple arithmetic.

Gradgrind addresses his students by number, not by name, and insists that they interpret the world through fact, and fact alone. Our children are sacred mysteries, not numbers. Their imaginations and creativity needs to be protected, not by bean-counters, but by teachers who are free to help their students explore this world and all of its wonders. Quantitative tests do have an important place in education, and offer useful information; however, they should not be accorded the emphasis that has recently been witnessed.

Because They THINK *They Can* was my attempt, through story, to show how a group of reluctant students could actually become engaged in the learning process, so much so that they would end up loving learning for learning's sake. For their time and trouble, their worlds and understandings become larger and more robust. As they take on the courage to seize the opportunities presented to them, they also manage to forget their lack of confidence as well as their aversion to school.

Whether we are in school or not, we are learning all of the time. And perhaps the most important thing that modern education can offer to its students is this: the necessary tools and training to equip them to become independent learners who think critically and clearly.

The vapid exercise of assigning quantitative scores to schools and to students will eventually recede in favor of evaluative methods that will give larger consideration to the individual, once individuals have been recognized in their utter complexity as evolving and whole human beings, fully able to manifest resilience and to discover transcendence.

Our children are and remain the greatest promise for our collective destinies. How we determine today to best serve their learning needs will be reflected in the future that they and we inherit.

STEVEN SWERDFEGER
Scottsdale, Arizona